Beautiful Dreamer

RON SHAFER

ISBN 978-1-0980-5533-2 (paperback)
ISBN 978-1-0980-5534-9 (digital)

Christian Faith Publishing, Inc.
832 Park Avenue
Meadville, PA 16335
www.christianfaithpublishing.com

This is a work of fiction. Names, characters, businesses, places, events, locales, and incidents are either the products of the author's imagination or used in a fictitious manner. Any resemblance to persons, living or dead, or actual events is purely accidental, though numerous events of the late 18th century, including actual quotations, are occasionally cited to enhance realism and heighten the historical sense of time and place.

Printed in the United States of America

Chapter 1

As Jude, Cory, Joey, Laura, and Duke walked toward their cars on Schenley Drive in Oakland, Pittsburgh, the momentous events of the afternoon hammered in their brains. For Duke Manningham, the mind-blowing revelation during the production of *Hamlet*, which they had seen a short while before in the Stephen Foster Theater, was learning that Abe Badoane had master-minded the damage to his prize '57 Chevy and, most likely, many of the other unsavory events at the Winfield Mushroom Mine over recent years.

"I've been such an idiot." Duke savagely kicked a pebble on the sidewalk. "Why can't I see the BS he pulls on people—mainly me? He's probably behind a lot of the crap at the mine!"

"Don't be too hard on yourself," Jude gently agreed. "We've all been played."

"Fret not, my boys!" Cory quickly responded. "Remember the verse Gabe used near the end of last Sunday's sermon—'God will bring every work into judgment, including every secret thing, whether good or evil' [Ecclesiastes 12:14]. Justice will eventually have its day."

Duke momentarily diverted his anger. "I remember that verse, but the one he ended with grabbed my attention even more, the one about God raining coals and brimstones on evil people. That verse made me feel the coals burning into my thick scalp!"

"Yes," Cory replied. "You're referring to a verse from Psalm 11—'Upon the wicked God will rain coals; Fire and brimstone and a burning wind shall be the portion of their cup' [vs. 6]."

3

Jude put his arm on Duke's shoulder. "You're right. That's scary stuff!"

Slowly ambling toward their car, Cory ruminated to herself about the mad improvisation scheme during the production of *Hamlet. It's good that Duke's been enlightened about Abe Badoane's evil since having his support is utterly crucial, but the price we've paid for this knowledge has been painfully exorbitant. Our present joy is wonderful, and we're grateful for it, but it definitely has a brief shelf life!* Looking at the Frick Fine Arts Building as she strolled along, she decided to voice her thought. "You realize that, despite the success of our improvisation skirmish, we've just declared war on Abe Badoane."

"I agree," Jude said, "but keep going. What are you thinking?"

Cory looked over her shoulder at the Stephen Foster Memorial Theater. "What happened on that stage was the first shot at Fort Sumter." She took Jude's hand in hers as they walked along. "My gallant soldier friends, we just launched the civil war!"

"Right you are, and we all know what a tough war it's going to be!" Jude raised her hand to his lips and kissed it. "Especially since mercy and forgiveness are our sole weapons. I'll use a poetic metaphor to frame the question of the hour."

"What's the question?" Joey asked.

"Will the fragile blossom of our love withstand the scorching sun of Abe's vitriol?"

"Nice metaphor, but let me stick with the serpent metaphor," Cory countered. "Do we have the antidote for his venomous bite? He is not one to be charmed, and a cornered cobra always strike."

"One thing is certain," Jude philosophically opined. "The battle lines are irrevocably drawn."

At Roberto Clemente Drive, Joey came to an abrupt stop. "Well, I know something that will divert our thoughts from civil war, scorching suns, and biting serpents."

"What's that?" Duke asked.

"That's where it happened twenty-eight years ago," Joey responded.

"What are you talking about?" Duke noted Joey's intent gaze at a brick wall. "What happened over there?"

"That's where Mazeroski hit the homerun in the 1960s World Series. It went over that wall." Joey pointed to the brick structure that had been part of the left field wall of Forbes Field. "Right there. That's where the Pirates beat the Yankees in that historic game."

"Are you serious? Holy hell!"

"I'm not kidding you! That's the exact place where that amazing event happened."

"Wow! The left field stands would have been right there." Duke swept his hand across the area where the left field seats used to be. "That's where Pops sat. I can't believe it!" He and Joey took a few steps toward the wall.

Seeing Joey and Duke's excitement over this signature event in Pittsburgh sports history, Jude's wheels started turning. "I have an idea," he whispered to Cory.

"Lay it on me."

"Let's go to the Heinz History Center, so we can see the memorabilia of the Pirates and the other great Pittsburgh sport teams. What better way to regain our sanity?"

Observing Duke and Joey's excitement, Cory quietly responded, "Great idea! Duke would love that, and Joey's been a sports talking-machine all summer." She took Jude by the arm. "But you realize this is a huge concession on my part."

"What are you talking about? Sometimes your enigmatic statements leave me hanging like a three-toed pygmy sloth!"

"You and your images! Do you see that building right there?" Cory pointed toward the Frick Fine Arts Building across the street.

"Yes. What about it?"

"You do realize that some artistic gems are housed right there? It's killing me that we're so close and yet so far." She looked at Joey and Duke, who, though having joined the others, nevertheless continued their animated chat about the 1960s World Series. "But I happily submit to the guys in the crowd." She paused and winked at Jude. "*This* time. We can visit the Frick later when the two of us are alone."

Of course, she'd want to see the Frick. She loves the art in that place! "This really is a compromise for you, but we can experience it vicariously right now through your eyes. Pretend we're looking at one of its gem paintings." Jude stopped and, with his index finger tapping his lip, pretended he was looking at a famous work of art. "Tell me about this one. I know this is a great painting, but I have zero understanding of its genius. Enlighten me, please!"

Cory played along. "All right, you're on. You're looking at"—she tilted her head quizzically—"a copy of Botticelli's famous painting, *The Birth of Venus.*"

Jude continued the game. "I'm glad you picked that painting since it's always been a favorite." Laura and Joey were amused, Duke mystified.

"You see that Venus," Cory continued, "is indeed very beautiful. She's alluringly naked, but not, strangely, in an erotic sense."

"What do you mean?" Duke interrupted. "How can a woman be naked and not alluring? That ain't possible in my book!"

"The Platonists of Medici's academy were interested in divine love. For them, physical beauty was a steppingstone to a higher, more exulted spiritual beauty. What you're seeing then in this particular painting is a wedding of the two: the physical—and I'll admit that the lovely woman is titillating and voluptuous—but the sensual element is married to or made one with the spiritual/divine. It's not one or the other but both in one. Make sense?"

"That's amazing," Laura said. "I appreciate art so much more just by being around you and allowing you to educate me." She looked at Duke to explain. "She's always talking this way about art. We sit by the hour looking through her art books."

"That's great!" Jude said as they ambled toward their cars. "I love it. Give us another fact out of that art encyclopedia on your shoulders."

Cory looked bewildered. "About what?"

"About the Botticelli painting."

Cory thought for a moment. "Here's one. You're picturing Venus as she stands on the enlarged scallop shell. You have the correct painting in mind, right?" She directed this to Jude, knowing that the others were most likely not familiar with the painting.

"Yes, I recall the famous masterpiece."

"Well, here's the additional fact. The Venus in this 1480s painting is a portrait of Simonetta Vespucci. The people of Florence thought Simonetta embodied the perfect ideal of feminine beauty." She turned to Laura. "You have to look at the painting. She's beautiful, and her red hair, not so common in Italy, was a mythological attribute of beauty and purity."

Duke broke in. "Wow, these freaking facts are making my day! You're as bad as the slimy serpent. The guy drives me crazy, and now here you're telling me about Botti-some-damn-thing!" *I hate that evil SOB!* "I don't care what you said back there in the chapel about forgiveness. I hate Abe Badoane and won't ever forgive him!"

I have to derail Duke's invective before his volcanic fury is ignited! Jude spoke again. "Come on, Duke. Botticelli was extremely gifted. If Cory's going to make the sacrifice and spend the afternoon with the guys at a sports museum, we can at least let her talk about art for five minutes!"

Duke backed off. "Yea, you're right. Sorry, Cory—go for it!"

"No, not now. You guys want to get to Heinz History Center so you can reflect on Pittsburgh's great athlete. Boys will be boys! And look at you, Duke. You're not making it a secret that you're bored out of your mind!"

"Duke can tune us out," Jude insisted. "One more Botticelli fact, pretty please."

"Hey, what do you expect? I wasn't prepared to give a lecture, but I do know that the original of this painting, *The Birth of Venus*, hangs in the Uffizzi in Florence and that it was most likely commissioned by the Medicis."

"I'll say it again. You're as bad as Abe Badoane." Duke pointed to the Carnegie Museum as they stood by their cars. "See those names along the top of that building?" He waited for the group to face in that direction. "The guy gave me dates and facts about every freaking one of those musicians. I kid you not. Before we went into the theater, we were standing there on Forbes Avenue, and he wouldn't stop talking. I thought I'd died and been resurrected in an insane asylum!" Duke angrily spit on the ground. "He didn't give me a chance to focus on the sweet babes." He looked up the street at the co-eds entering Hillman Library. "This place is crawling with them!"

By this time the group had strolled to the area where the cars were parked on Schenley Drive. As they neared Duke's '57 Chevy, Joey yelled, "Oh, no!"

"What!" Laura screamed.

"Look at Duke's car. The two back tires are flat!"

Duke looked at his Chevy. "You said a cornered cobra always strikes. Well, look what sneaky snake did before he slithered away!"

Chapter 2

Fortunately, the tires were merely deflated and not damaged.

"I can't believe it!" Duke angrily responded. "I freaking can't believe it! I'd bet money that sneaky SOB Abe did this!"

"We have a pump in our car," Joey rejoined. "We can use that."

Duke drew near his car. "Wait a minute!" Jude suddenly yelled. "Don't touch the valves with your bare hands. We can print them later and maybe catch Snake Eyes at his own game."

"Good idea," Duke said. "That would be sweet revenge!"

Riled by the *Hamlet* improvisation and the flat tires, Duke was fuming by the time they parked their cars on Smallman Street in the Strip District. As they walked in silence down Twelfth Street, Duke paced in front with Joey and Laura, Jude and Cory dropping back.

"I haven't seen Duke this angry since he saw his damaged car in the parking lot," Jude whispered. "His nostrils are even flared! If he starts venting now, the fiery invective would burn the enamel right off his teeth!"

"You're hilarious!" She watched Duke bang a parking meter on Smallman St. "But maybe right too! Think of something that will settle him. The meter pole's wobbling back and forth! Figure out a way to distract him."

"But how, pray tell!"

Walking more quickly to catch up to the trio, Jude timidly commented, "We're going to see exhibits of some famous historical moments in a couple minutes. Let's get in the right frame of mind by thinking of important current events in our day. I'm talking of things in the news over the last couple weeks, events of historic significance."

"You mean the stuff people will be talking about in the future?" Cory asked.

"Exactly. Cory, you go first. What's happened recently that people will speak of when they think back on June 1988?"

"Well, what can I come up with on the spot? For one thing, I thought it was fascinating that Mandela addressed the Freedomfest in Wembley Stadium, London. That was an amazing event. How about you, Joey?"

"I like the sports stuff. I think it's cool that Billy Casper won the Seniors Player Golf Championship. Dad's always been a big Billy Casper fan."

"Where was it played?" Laura asked.

"In Florida, but I don't know the course."

"Sawgrass at Ponte Vedra Beach," Duke offered, starting to calm down.

"How about you, Laura?" Cory questioned. "What June events do you think people will recall?"

"I think that Russian woman who set the long jump women's record will be remembered, but I can't recall her name. Her accomplishments were fantastic!"

"Duke, do you know the woman's name?" Jude queried.

"I can't say it. Galena something. Chimyakomsky or some damn thing [Chistyakova]."

"And you, Duke?" Cory asked.

"I'm like Joey. I'm all about sports and cars. I was stunned when Ireland beat England in that major soccer match. That Ray Houghton is dynamite, but I also thought it was cool that Marty Barrett of the Boston Red Sox stole home the other evening." Smiling by now, Duke was noticeably less agitated. "You're next, Jude."

"I think we need to keep an eye on NASA's new space vehicle. Not sure what it's called. Maybe S-213? It was just launched a couple days ago."

A short while later, the group had meandered down Mulberry Way to the Heinz History Center and were soon browsing amid various exhibits. The Steelers Super Bowl wins were especially thrilling for Duke who emoted his way through the exciting moments of Pittsburgh's sports history and then wended his way to various Pirates exhibits.

"Here's Willie Stargell's jersey—the famous number 8!" Duke nearly shouted. "And look at this—Mazeroski's glove! He used this glove when the Pirates beat the Yankees in the 1960 World Series. I've heard of that moment my whole life. Like I said, Pops was at that game and talked about it until the day he died. He said Forbes Field went crazy when that ball flew over the left field wall."

Joey called Duke over to where he and Laura stood. "Look here, Duke."

"What do you see?"

"The pitching rubber and the first base that were used in the famous game seven of the 1960 World Series."

Again, Duke nearly shouted. "You gotta be kidding. I don't believe this place!" Duke peered into another case. "This makes up for a wasted afternoon and that *Hamlet* crap!"

"Not completely wasted," Cory chimed in. "Those were pretty valuable insights you learned back there at the theater."

"I guess you're right," Duke reluctantly acquiesced. "That was really gutsy of you to pull that off. I had no idea what you were doing." Duke reflected again on *The Pittsburgh Hamlet*. "Do you believe Abe sucked me in so completely? Jude, I wanted to kill you. That's how much the smiling serpent messes with my head!" Looking abstractedly at Pirates memorabilia, Duke grew contemplative. "How can we stand up against that kind of intelligence? I'm talking about his special kind of awful evil. Sorry to be so pessimistic, but if you want my opinion, I don't think we have a chance. The guy is brilliant out the wazoo."

Neither Jude nor Cory chose to respond, so Duke spoke again. "Here's the thing about it. I'm not the smartest knife in the drawer—I readily admit that—and I'd never put myself in your league, but I'm not as dumb as Bull Chestnut either. Here's a good example. We had to write a poem in Millie Montgomery's English class, and guess whose poem she picked as a good example."

"Yours?" Cory quickly guessed.

"She really did. I know this will surprise you, but I actually got some pretty decent grades in high school. Long John McConnell and Delbert Baker said I should take school more seriously. I can still hear Mr. Baker saying, 'Now, Jim, you have real potential. You have a good head on your shoulders, and if you tried harder, you could get into college!'"

Jude commented when Duke stopped. "'Jim?' I had no idea your name is 'Jim.' I've only ever heard you called 'Duke'!"

On and on they browsed through the exhibits, welcoming the chance to calm the nerves after the tension of *The Pittsburgh Hamlet.*

"Guess what this is making me think of." The animated Duke again broke the silence after a while.

"What's that?" Cory asked.

"Pittsburgh teams have so often been the underdogs. They're the little guy who takes on the big-city teams. Look here at the great Roberto Clemente. Pops said it took him forever to get the national reputation he deserved. That's why Pops thought Pittsburgh's teams are so popular. They're the small fry against the big-money franchises."

Duke stopped talking for a moment, but as nobody picked up the conversation, he continued. "Hank was talking in the lunchroom the other day about the budget for the Pittsburgh Pirates. He follows that stuff really close. He told us that the entire Pirates team budget just about equals the mega salaries of a high-paid Yankees or Red Sox player. That's what I'm talking about—little guy versus the fat-cat giants."

The group wandered through the various exhibits. "This season's been all right too." The talkative Duke made no effort to repress his real excitement. "Goose Gossage hit his three hundredth career save." He looked at another photo of Willie Stargell. "Don't you love it that Stargell became the two hundredth player inducted into the Hall of Fame? At least he never had his athletic feats disgraced like Ben Johnson!"

"What are you talking about?" Cory asked. "That one went over my head like my mini-dissertation on Botticelli went over yours! You had no idea what I was speaking about, nor did you care!" All of them laughed good-naturedly.

"Ben Jonson won the one-hundred-meter dash at the Seoul Olympics," Duke replied, "and then had it taken back because they found out he was on some damn drug."

"Stanozol," Joey offered. "That's a steroid."

"That's it," Duke responded. "I forgot the name."

Cory watched as Duke moved from exhibit to exhibit with the excitement of a child. "You surely do know your sports."

"I live for sports. Playing high school football was my best fun ever. I loved playing football under Coach Ullom. We had some really good teams in those years. Kittanning was tough. In fact, Zane Dudek was so good he made it into Yale and broke all sorts of football records up there—in an Ivy League university no less!"

Looking at the exhibits, Jude reflected deeply. "I like these exhibits because they're so inspiring, but they're relevant to our situation too."

"In what way?" Cory asked.

"I'm thinking about what Duke said. Just as these teams faced giants and often prevailed, so we do too. Consider how many of these major victories came because the teams fought back in herculean fashion against overwhelming odds. Look at these mementoes of the Steelers Super Bowl victories in the seventies."

"I was pretty young then," the seventeen-year-old Joey interjected. "I was born in 1971, but I remember the 1978 and 1979 Super Bowls. People went crazy when the Steelers won their fourth Super Bowl. All the kids were wearing black and gold, and there were banners all over North Buffalo Elementary School. You'd have thought Kittanning was the headquarters for the Steelers!"

"I gave Pops the Steelers' highlight film for the 1979 season for his birthday gift," Duke added. "I swear he played that thing once a month until he died last year."

Cory picked up Jude's thought. "You're saying that the underdog teams are relevant to our situation in that we're pitted against our own giant. You're talking about Abe and his minions?"

"Of course."

"Yes, that's a bit like Pittsburgh taking on the Yankees in 1960 and coming out the winner." Cory reflected for a moment. "What would dear Pastor Gabe say? 'Without faith it's impossible to please God.' We must keep the faith."

"Or as Pops always said," Duke added, "'Put your trust in God but keep your powder dry.'"

"I hear that expression a lot," Cory mused, "but I honestly don't know the origin of it."

"It was something Oliver Cromwell said," Duke continued, "when his troops were invading Ireland. I've always liked Cromwell, but I never liked him going after the Irish. Pops said the original quote goes back to Cromwell."

"I think Duke's right," Jude added. "A nineteenth-century poem attributes the quotation to him. The poem popularized the quote."

"Mr. Encyclopedia," Cory laughed, "do you know the name of the poem or the poet?"

"I'm not exactly sure," Jude added, "but I think the poem is called 'Oliver's Advice' or something close to that. The poet was William Blacker, and the poem dates back to the 1830s."

Duke looked at him. "You're amazing. At least that's a bit interesting, but that crap about Chopin and Miszt, or Biszt or Liszt or some damn dude made my head spin!"

"Very good, Jude," Cory commented. "You don't disappoint. What else can you tell us about Mr. Blacker?"

"Not much. I remember that he was a British military officer living in Ireland. He attended an Irish university—maybe the University of Dublin. At any rate, the poem became pretty famous, and that quotation has resonated ever since."

While Jude, Cory, and Duke walked around and viewed the various exhibits, the preoccupied Joey, with Laura beside him, quietly withdrew to a corner. Joey had spoken only a couple times since the debacle at Stephen Foster Theater. He and Laura were currently looking at a display of western Pennsylvania athletes who had become notable NFL quarterbacks—Joey Montana, Dan Marino, Jim Kelly, Joe Namath, Gus Frerotte, George Blanda, Terry Hanratty, and the great Johnny Unitas among others.

Standing beside him, Laura clutched his arm tightly and whispered into his ear. "You'll get your chance. I just know you will."

"I don't know."

Laura cradled her head on his shoulder. "Don't let it get to you, Joey. It's going to happen!"

The subject of their conversation was Joey's experience on the football squad at Kittanning Senior High School. His frustration mounted daily as the coach continued to bypass him in favor of other less athletically-endowed players. "Life isn't always fair. Practice after practice the coach keeps me on the second-string scrimmage squad, and so he doesn't know diddly squat about my abilities. He doesn't even know that I can throw a football. I hate to say this because it sounds like I'm bragging, but all the receivers tell me I throw the ball better than any of the quarterbacks." He rubbed the bicep of his right arm. "But that doesn't matter since I still don't get my chance!"

"I understand why you feel so bad."

Joey gazed at the great Pennsylvania quarterbacks. "I wish Ullom was still coaching. He was tough but fair. Maybe the coach overlooks me on purpose. The summer practices have been awful. I didn't tell you because I was too ashamed, but I again rode the bench for most of the exhibition scrimmage up at Punxsy [Punxsutawney]."

"I'm so sorry."

"Before coming to Pittsburgh today, I actually was thinking of quitting the team." He ran his hand across a glass case that contained photographs of Western Pennsylvania National Football League quarterbacks. "I just want one chance."

Examining the heroic exploits of the legendary Pittsburgh athletes who had overcome opposition and risen to great heights, Joey's spirits began to rise. "These men made the best of their bad situations, and they all came from western Pennsylvania schools just like me." He bent closer to photographs of Joe Namath, Jim Kelly, and Dan Marino. "Do you think I'll get my break? Be honest."

"Of course, you will, Joey. If not on the Kittanning football team, you will get it someday." She put her arm around him. "A good person isn't always held down, not even by unfair circumstances."

"Thanks. Maybe I'm allowing myself to become too negative. Look at these achievements. These guys were fabulous! Jim Kelly was from up the river at East Brady. When our church visited the residents at Bradyview, we were right beside the East Brady High School."

"What's Bradyview?" Duke asked, having now joined them.

"It's an assisted-care residence for seniors," Joey responded. "Remember the last time our church went there to give the residents a party?" Laura, Jude, and Cory nodded. "Well, we were talking to Mary, Bob, and Debbie in the lobby as we parted, and the whole time we talked, I kept looking down at the high school and thinking, Jim Kelly was once a high school kid just like me. He sat in those very classrooms, possibly in those very chairs!"

"I remember it well," Cory said. "Remember how much you talked to Dad about seeing the school the great Jim Kelly attended?"

"Yea. He always told me not to be discouraged. Funny he'd say that. Who's more discouraged than Dad these days?" Looking at the exhibits, Joey returned to his main point. "Maybe I should think twice about quitting the team. Laura keeps saying I'll get my chance." Joey took hold of her hand. "I hope you're right!"

By the time the group of five walked out of the museum late that afternoon, they were animated in spirits and braced for the next chapter. "It's a good thing these exhibits inspired us because we're going into a den of vipers!" Cory sighed.

"But at least we've got Duke on our side," Jude said with a smile as he looked at Duke. "And what a difference that makes!" Cory gave Duke a big hug.

Duke brushed a tear from his eye. "How true that is!" he said. "'If the truth sets you free, you will really be free.' The verse in Heinz Chapel says something close to that, right?"

"Yes, that's close," Cory responded.

"It's like the weight of the world has been lifted off my shoulders. I'm so glad I came to Picksburgh. I feel free and clean for the first time ever. I never felt this way before. I never knew what it was like to be without shame or guilt or feel rotten inside." Clenching his hand, he pounded his right fist into his left palm. "But sorry, I still hate that bastardly Abe Badoane!"

Chapter 3

At the mushroom mind lounge on Monday morning of the next week, Cory and Jude were bombarded with a barrage of questions as they chatted with co-workers about the production of *Hamlet*.

"Is it really true?"

"Did it happen the way the paper describes?"

"Did animal Duke truly tear into that poor actor on stage?"

"Bet that kid was scared to death!"

"Cory, were you the center of the whole deal as people are telling me?"

Jude and Cory desired to make the incident a thing of the past as quickly as possible. "The improvised scene," Jude explained as they walked toward the personnel carriers, "exposed Abe and enlightened Duke. That's what we wanted, so in that regard our little scene succeeded."

"But the thing was as crazy as Salvador Dali's painting, *The Lugubrious Game*!" Cory added. "That's one of Dali's controversial paintings, but our improvised *Hamlet* scene, crazy as it was, served its purpose. From our point of view, it's now time to mend the wall and move on. As Jude said last evening after church, 'the map of the future, though frayed at the edges, stretches boldly and beautifully to the faraway horizon.' That's how we want it to be."

"By the way," Jude concluded, walking toward the driver's seat, "this may surprise you, but what we want is total reconciliation with Abe. We seek his reformation, not destruction."

"Good luck!" one of the women yelled, taking her seat on the carrier.

During lunch that day, Jude and Cory, seated near Morley Spencer, happened on a most interesting finding. Having learned of the integral part his film clip had played in the Pittsburgh production of *Hamlet*, Morley had sought them out to talk about it. "That's really something to think that the film I pieced together played such an important role in Pittsburgh. I thought it was for your eyes only. How naive!"

"Well, our eyes," Jude quipped, "and because of wide media coverage the entire tri-state area too!"

"What did you think of the sequence with Cory? I found that more intriguing—I guess I could say mysterious—than the sequence of you and Abe at the back of Duke's car."

Dumbfounded, Cory and Jude looked at each other. "What are you talking about?" Cory was the first to speak. "I'm not in the film because I wasn't even near Duke's car!"

"I'm talking about the videotape of you," Morley replied. "The one that begins with the back of your head and cuts to your direct address to the camera."

"Whatever are you talking about?" Cory incredulously asked, looking at Jude to see if he was also clueless. "We saw the clip of the men at Duke's car, and then the screen goes black. That's it, and I'm certainly not in it. I was standing over by the entryway to the mine—out of my mind like Ophelia, I might add!"

"That's only part of the film. There's another whole sequence involving you, which commences as the incident at Duke's car was winding down." The stupefied Cory peered at Morley as he continued. "You don't remember walking toward the car, turning around, and then speaking directly to the camera?"

"No, I don't remember it, nor can I imagine doing something so strange."

"You apparently stopped watching after the first film clip."

"We did," Jude hastily replied.

"Well, there's a short delay, just a couple seconds—and yes, the screen goes black for that very brief period—but then the second clip begins. It's a pretty strange clip since you end up talking directly to the security camera. You can tell me later what that was all about."

Morley paused for a moment. "That is if you can figure it out! You can either come to my office to see the second clip or look at the copy I gave you. Either way's fine with me."

Jude and Cory were taken aback by the revelation. "You've spent enough of your precious office time," Jude said. "We'll watch it by ourselves, but we thank you for the offer!"

"One more thing," Morley said. "I just remembered. You recall, Jude, how I told you I had experimented a lot with my handheld tape recorder after I first bought it. I got a big kick out of recording people and watching the surprised look on their faces when they heard their own voices for the first time."

"I know. That often amuses people."

"Well, in a quite a few cases I recorded some things that you might find interesting, especially the conversations when Abe Badoane was present. That stuff is pretty fascinating and now suddenly relevant too." He handed Jude a cassette tape. "This is for your ears only of course. I'm giving this to you in case you want to listen to it someday."

"Thanks, Morley. I'll definitely do that, but first, we'll watch the second mystery clip. We'll give you our reaction as soon as we view it. Stay tuned!"

"Back to Morley's earlier point," Cory said, exiting the lunchroom with Jude. "I'm referring to the second film sequence. I don't remember a thing about it. The pain pills made me out-of-my-mind delusional, so the whole day is a blur, but how crazy if I spoke directly into the security camera the way Morley says!" Cory thought for a moment. "You didn't see any part of this, right?"

"None."

"You think it happened the way he said?"

"I have no idea what he's talking about, but I don't question its accuracy. When I was at Duke's car that day, you'll recall I was a tad busy dealing with loose cannons, a coiled serpent, and a lynch mob thrown in for good measure!"

That evening at Cory's house, with Zoe by their side, they played the second clip, which picks up shortly after the first one at Duke's car ends. Based on what Morley had said during lunch, they paid particular attention to the round object in the center fore-ground. "See it?" Jude asked.

"Yes, what is it?"

"That's the back of your head!"

"I don't believe it!"

"Throughout the entire clip, the round object in the fore-ground—your head!—doesn't move." In the film, Cory stands rock still directly in front of the camera but starts to move when the scene at the car is finished. "Watch this. You take a couple steps toward the car, turn, and then you frontally face the camera. Look at it again."

"I can't believe this!" Cory interjected. "I'm talking directly at the security camera as though it was a person! Look at my mouth! Why am I speaking with that ridiculously exaggerated lip and mouth movement? It's as though I was emphasizing enunciation to make the words more readily understandable."

"Let's replay that again. You can see your mouth and lip move-ment really well since Morley blew this up so much. Let's see if we can figure out what you're saying."

"Good idea. This will be my first crack at lip-reading!"

"That makes two of us!"

Though they replayed the clip repeatedly, they could not deter-mine what Cory had said that day or why she faced the camera to say it. "I just can't make out my own words. It's as though I'm not speaking English. Maybe that's it. Maybe in my incoherence, I lapsed into gobbledygook!"

"Cory Mohney speaking gibberish? I don't buy it!"

"Seriously, all I can remember is that when Old Mary and I talked about the rose vision in her hospital room, she gave me some new details about it."

"Yes, you said."

"But because I was so sick that day, I just couldn't absorb it all. It was like I was talking to someone on the phone and had a bad connection, the way phones cut in and out. I caught part of what she was saying, but then my brain tuned out and I missed whole stretches of words."

"Go over it again in your mind," Jude pleaded.

"I just know that I was so shocked at her new revelation that I nearly jumped out of the chair. I had a splitting headache and wasn't rational when she said those scary things. I only remember that they were about you and me and some impending danger."

"That's really amazing."

Cory continued to ponder the video clip. "Two facts stand out. This was a new revelation in Old Mary's ongoing dream, which she never had before, and second, it jolted me terribly."

"Maybe Old Mary was trying to warn us that we were facing something really dangerous?"

Cory paused for a moment. "Maybe even worse trouble than the madness concerning Duke's sabotaged car!"

Jude watched as she squirmed in her chair. *Maybe it's coming back to her.* After a moment, during which neither spoke, he said, "As I see it, the only solution is to talk to Old Mary and ask her to repeat what she told you that day."

"You're forgetting that she's still in the hospital, possibly suffering from a stroke, so we can't ask her what she said—at least not now."

"You're right."

Cory stopped to watch her moving lips on the film clip again. "When Old Mary told me about this dreadful thing that was going to happen, I remember that her face contorted into terror. It scares me to say this, Jude, but it's coming back to me a little."

"Good!"

"Old Mary was so shaken by what she was saying that it seemed to affect her physically." Stricken, Cory looked at Jude. "I wonder if she was so worried about our coming danger that it put her in the hospital!"

"How could that be?"

"Maybe the dream, the dream of *us*, caused her so much anxiety that it brought on her sickness. How awful if it did!"

"If you could just remember that revelation!"

"Why can't I recall it?" Cory slammed her fist on the arm of the sofa. "Somehow we have to find out!"

A moment later, an idea came to Jude. "Guess what. Perhaps you're talking in French! Maybe that's why we can't figure out what you're saying."

"I never thought of that! Maybe so."

"I thought your different-looking mouth movements were caused by exaggerated enunciation. Maybe I was wrong. Speaking French requires somewhat different mouth formations. Vous comprenez? Watch my mouth when I speak French. The mouth movements are decidedly different. Take note." Jude uttered a statement from his very basic knowledge of French. "Pourriez-vous me traduire ca? [Can you translate this for me?] What about this one? Watch my mouth movement. Qu' est-ce que ca..." He stopped, not able to complete the sentence. "My French isn't good enough to finish the sentence. I was trying to say 'what does this mean?' I know I need the word 'veut' in there."

Cory finished his sentence. "Qu' est-ce que ca veut dire. [What does this mean?]. Is that what you were trying to say?"

"Yes, that's it. I never did as well in French as I did Latin because I always messed up the grammar!" He stopped speaking and watched Cory's mouth as she spoke. "My point is that a person's mouth moves differently when speaking French. Maybe that explains your different mouth shapes!"

"Je suis d'accord [I agree]. Maybe you're right. Remember I told you that I had been boning up on my French back in the winter. I should remember something after four years of high school French!" Cory rubbed the fur on Zoe's back. "But why would I lapse into another language? That's as crazy as talking to a camera!"

Jude thought for a moment and ventured a thought. "Possibly you felt the need to hide. You knew the danger I was in as I faced an angry mob. Maybe you slipped into a coded language to protect the secret revelation intended solely for our ears." He looked at Cory to get her reaction. "I'm not a psychologist. Besides, La plupart des gens pensent que je suis fou [Most people think I'm crazy]!" They both laughed, especially at Jude's poor French.

"Your pronunciation is totally ridiculous!"

"Hey, give me a break. I told you I only had two years of high school French."

"But what you're saying makes perfect sense. The problem is, I can't lip-read English, let alone French!"

"Isn't there anything you can remember?" Jude asked, turning helplessly to Cory. "I know we've been down this road before, so don't get mad at me for bringing it up again, but I was hoping this clip might help you remember."

Cory wrinkled her brow. "I recall nothing. My brain's as empty as a bear's tummy after a long winter's hibernation!"

"You're such a visual person. Think of the details. Try painting this new thing Old Mary told you about. What would you put on the canvas? What would be the focus? Pretend you're going to paint her vision. Prepare your paintbrush, Yvonne Jacquette."

"Yvonne Jacquette! That's impressive. How did you know about this Pittsburgh-born painter?"

"Sorry, I don't know anything except that I read an article the other day on famous Pittsburghers. It spoke of some award she won. Let's see." Jude cupped his chin in his hand. "Wasn't she the one elected to the National Academy of...something this year. Am I right?"

"Very good! She was elected to the National Academy of Design."

"Okay, Yvonne. Your brush is ready, and you're going to paint Old Mary's vision."

The idea, as it turned out, actually worked. At first Cory blankly stared into space and patted Zoe's head. "Still nothing! Yvonne has a fried brain today!" She again pretended to pick up a paintbrush, lifted her hand in the air as if to paint, and after a moment blurted out, "Yes, I do remember something!" Her eyes gleamed wildly. "The image of an inverted cross tattoo on the arm! I recall that Old Mary said, 'Beware of the man with the cross.' That's one thing she said. What a great thought, Jude!"

"Let's go back and watch the first clip again," Jude said. They rewound the clip to the place where Abe extends his arm and places his hand on Jude's. "I can't believe it," Jude screamed. "Look at Abe's arm. There's the inverted cross on his forearm! Why didn't we see this before. It's so obvious."

They stared in amazement.

"Because we were focused on the fingerprints. Now if I could just remember what Old Mary told me about the man and the cross tattoo!"

"Back to your painting," Jude said. "Think of the scene you imagined as Old Mary described the dream. The arm is in the foreground of your painting, right? What's in the background? Think, Yvonne, think!"

"Cory closed her eyes and waved her hand back and forth as if painting on the canvas. Back and forth, but nothing came to her mind. "I can't think of anything. I'm seeing nothing!"

"What about color? Did any stand out when she spoke? What color will dominate your canvas?"

The idea instantly triggered Cory's recollection. She jumped back from the canvas. "I've got it! Orange! I remember orange and red. That's it! There was a horrible explosion and an awful noise. Old Mary said that the explosion of the nightmare sat her up in bed screaming!"

"Think of what she said. What did she see?"

"She said the cross was in the foreground." Cory buried in head in her hands trying desperately to recall. "Then there was a terrible explosion."

"What of us? Where were we?"

"I remember now!" Cory shrieked, grabbing Jude's shoulders. "We were huddled in fear, and then there was this awful blast!"

Chapter 4

The Pittsburgh Hamlet, that bizarre but revelatory interlude, had a major impact on several characters in the Jude and Cory saga. One of the most telling of these involved Professor Charles Claypoole. The cardiac symptoms of recent months, endured but concealed, came to a head during the *Hamlet* interlude, which markedly intensified his chest discomfort. After the dress rehearsal at Stephen Foster Memorial Theater, he drove himself directly to the emergency room at Allegheny General Hospital on the Northside. Over the next week, he learned that all tests—EKGs, treadmill exam, and echocardiogram—yielded negative results, that he had no heart ailments like his deceased brothers, and that he was "essentially asymptomatic."

"Most of your problem," the electro-physiologist, Dr. Chenarides, explained during a post-test exam, "appears to be in your head." He paused and looked directly at the perplexed Charles. Because they were good friends from way back, the doctor spoke frankly. "Charles, you see the results of these tests. You might find a cardiologist who would order a catheterization, but to me that is an invasive and unnecessary measure." The doctor sat down in his chair and looked at Charles. "Might it be that your brothers' deaths are making you worry excessively about your cardiac health?"

"Possibly so. I dwell on their passing very often."

"Based on what I'm seeing in these tests, I'd say a real part of this is psychosomatic."

"I see what you mean."

"You might want to consult another doctor for a second opinion, and I won't be at all offended if you do, but from my vantage

25

point, your fear stems from excessive concern over family history rather than current cardiac function." He gestured again at the negative tests. *How frank should I be?* "The readings across the board actually indicate a strong heart."

"I see why you say that."

"Do you think the discomfort you were experiencing during *Hamlet* was stress-induced?"

The comment resonated with Charles. *Did the pressure of the theater debacle induce my chronic indigestion, which is often proportionate to the tension I face?* "I wonder, Doctor, I wonder."

Even more than Charles, Abe Badoane was also profoundly affected by *The Pittsburgh Hamlet*. Shaken to the core by the incident in Pittsburgh, Abe was thrown into despair. The morning after the play he sat scrunched in his chair at his library desk with a murderous look on his face. *Before Jude Hepler came on the scene in May, I was on top of the world, respected by the workers and community, and perceived as kind and smart. "Very smart," they would say, occasioning me to flippantly observe in my journal, "I call the shots, connect the dots, control the tots." The workers are essential, useful idiots—yes, tots—whom I manipulate to do my bidding. When I talk, they listen; and I give them light, but if they anger The Snake, then I give 'em the bite!*

That's how it used to be, but that sweet era for Abe Badoane had passed. "Gone with the wind," he wrote in his journal. Almost overnight, his respect had dwindled, the illusion of his having a son, his dear Martin, discovered, his sordid past unearthed, and his insidious machinations exposed—"all because of Jude Hepler." *He has ruined everything, especially my reputation and my manipulative strategies.* It wasn't his inability to control people like figures on a game board that bothered Abe so much as the fact that people were on to him. *They know my game, they respect me less, and my credibility has plummeted to zero! They're on to me!*

As his reputation was jettisoned, his desire for revenge escalated. *Sweet vengeance consumes me!* On the morning after the production of *Hamlet*, he sat at his library desk, the Ray Charles's song, "Born to Lose," playing in the background.

Born to lose I've lived my life in vain
Every dream has only brought me pain
All my life I've always been so blue
Born to lose and now I'm losing you

Reading in the book of Job, he underscored several passages: "May the day perish on which I was born… May that day be darkness. Because it did not shut up the doors of my mother's womb, nor hide sorrow from my eyes. Why did I not die at birth? Why did I not perish when I came from the womb?"

Job, you speak such truth here. No truer words were ever spoken. Why died I not from the womb? "Every dream has only brought me pain." Sing it, Ray!

Several articles on bomb-making lay scattered on the desk, as the accounts of various terrorists fascinated him. "Surely Jefferson was right," he wrote in his journal: "'What signify a few lives lost in a century or two? The tree of liberty must be refreshed from time to time with the blood of patriots and tyrants. It is its natural manure.' If the blood of patriots and tyrants makes for adequate manure, surely the same is true for preppy profs!"

Abe mused to himself. *What was that quote about guns that Huddy recently shared with the men at the North Buffalo Rifle Range? Something about peace being that glorious moment in history when everybody stands around reloading. Huddy said it was ascribed to Jefferson, but I'm not so sure. I never checked it. Maybe I should see what Mr. Jefferson said on that controversial subject.*

He went over to one of his library books and perused several books. He finally selected a biography on Thomas Jefferson and started leafing through the pages. *Well, this is interesting!*

Laws that forbid the carrying of arms…only disarm those who are neither inclined nor determined to commit crimes. Such laws make things worse for the assaulted and better for the assailants; they serve rather to encourage than to prevent homicides, for an unarmed man may be attacked with greater confidence than an armed man.

How very true! Laws that ban the carrying of arms only make things worse for those assaulted, and make it easier for the assailants to wreak havoc on innocent people. You were a bright man, Mr. Jefferson, but how does this relate to explosives? There's a philosophic question you can ponder, Professor Jude!

The Ray Charles song continued to play in the background, as Abe sat and scanned the books.

There's no use to dream of happiness
All I see is only loneliness
All my life I've always been so blue
Born to lose and now I'm losing you

Cory and Jude, you drew the first blood—I'll give you that—but it won't be the last! You won the first battle, but you won't win the war. Sherman was right: 'War is hell,' and you have just arrived at Gettysburg. The problem is, you're in the Slaughter Pen adjacent to Little Roundtop. You'll recall why it's named that because you know your Civil War history!

The effects of the momentous production of the *Hamlet* dress rehearsal rippled out beyond Charles and Abe. The employees in the mine had also been greatly affected by news of the improvised scene, already referred to by the employees as *The Pittsburgh Hamlet*. In nearly every locale in the mine—lunchrooms, compost yard, parts room, mechanics' shop, mine corridors, packhouse, management offices, pasteurization rooms, even the lavatories—everywhere the talk was the same: Abe Badoane had been exposed as a fraud in Pittsburgh and in a single day went from beloved icon to rejected villain. He was openly snubbed by some of the employees and even ridiculed by a few.

"So the high and mighty one has fallen."

"Who'd have known that he was such a slimy serpent?"

"Right along, I took that smiling ass for a decent man. He sure sucked us in!"

Talk in the underground world, however, centered in the main on Duke and Jude, who had gone from sworn enemies to allies. Cory had also become a friend of Duke, at least of sorts, and not number one on his future-conquest list. The women couldn't believe the change.

"Duke only looked at her as a broad to make in the past."

"I didn't think animal man was capable of anything else!"

Talk of the sabotage of Duke's car, which filled the lunchrooms, picking rooms, and corridors, was the biggest topic of all. "If Jude didn't smash Duke's car, then who did?"

"What idiot did Abe use to accomplish his scheme?"

"It shouldn't be that hard to find out!"

Though this discussion for the most part went on behind Duke's back, the men and women sensed the change in him. Over the next weeks, a serene look slowly replaced his perpetual scowl. Even Duke's speech was modified, as his enraged cursing and angry outbursts were less frequent. One of the pickers on his crew spoke for many. "I'm telling you the guy's changed. He hardly even swears. It's as though his mouth was washed out with nitric acid!" Nevertheless, his friends shied away from the topic of his Chevy. "His blood boils every time someone speaks of his prized baby!"

When Duke and Jude met at the packhouse together one morning shortly after the Pittsburgh event, they warmly shook hands and, like long lost brothers, greeted each other with huge smiles. Duke often spoke to Cory as if she were a princess.

But through it all, Bull Chestnut slinked from dark corner to dark corner. *Am I safe? Will Abe tell people our secret as a way of deflecting the stream of catty barbs aimed at him? Holy hell, I'm scared! What if the slimy snake squeals on me! As my old man always said to me, my arse won't be able to hold the kicks. But it won't just be my arse that's in trouble this time!*

Under the influence of Jude, Cory, and to some extent even Joey and Laura, Duke's metamorphosis continued, but would he not tear into Bull for demolishing his car if he learned the truth? Bull worried about this incessantly. *Where can I hide? How can I get through this?*

As much as the employees in the mine, the worshippers in the Center Hill church were also deeply affected by *The Pittsburgh Hamlet*. Consistent with his promise, Duke had started to attend Bible study. The people were blessed by his awakened spirituality, but they also enjoyed being around a principal player in *The Pittsburgh Hamlet*. Because the media gave him extensive coverage, he was even pictured in a large photo in a *Pittsburgh Tribune Review* feature story. While they enjoyed the company of the man who had played such an important role in Pittsburgh, they reveled much more in Duke's dramatic change. In their book, he was a man who stepped back from the brink of disaster in the nick of time.

Pastor Gabriel especially had welcomed him warmly. "Sinners often feel at home here. They find their place in our church family because that's what we all are, sinners saved by unmerited, undeserved grace. As I often tell our people, this is not a social club. It's a hospital where people find the cure for the horrible disease of sin."

At the conclusion of the Esther Bible study on the following Wednesday, a number of the churchgoers spoke at length of the theatrical interlude which Cory and Jude had orchestrated. Joey had brought a dubbed film copy of the inner play for pastor to see and, after Bible study, showed highlights to the pastor who wanted to see it. A handful of others, also wanting to view the clip which featured the improvised scene, proceeded to the adult Sunday school classroom for the screening.

"Cory, you were some actress!" Trisha said as the tape finished. "You were as brave as Esther!"

"Were you influenced by Esther's courage?" Barry queried. "I'm guessing you were since Pastor Gabe has given that topic so much emphasis recently."

"You created your own mousetrap," Zane laughed. "Just like you talked about on pastor's porch!"

Cory and Jude were the subject of a lengthy discussion, but after they spoke of the interlude—what it was like, what happened, and how they settled on the mousetrap approach—they deftly turned the discussion to more important matters. Cory spoke first. "A really big thing that's come out of this is Abe Badoane's need for prayer. His heart is completely consumed with hate."

Jude continued the thought. "If he doesn't defuse it, he'll likely resort to something desperate since that's always been his tragic pattern."

Jude and Cory did not divulge the detail of the explosion in Old Mary's vision to the group at this time, though it was clearly on their minds. Little could be done at this point, but they made the matter the number one concern on their prayer list. "We'd just ask you good folks to lift him up in prayer," Cory concluded.

"Maybe he'll be another prodigal son who turns his life around," Gail exclaimed.

The swelling in Cory's face had gone down completely by now, and only the slightest discoloration was present. Nevertheless, the clip on the film indicated the severity of the blow to her face. Despite Jude and Cory's efforts to divert attention to Abe's recalcitrant heart, the interest in Cory continued.

"You must have taken a savage blow!"

"It's a wonder your neck wasn't broken."

"Or your face smashed in."

These latter comments were made by folks who did not realize that Duke and Tina had slipped in late and sat at the back of the Sunday school room. Duke slunk in his seat.

"Not to worry!" Cory laughed. "It wasn't as bad as the medicine-induced hallucination!"

Clarence spoke for many. "I think you're being modest, for in my book you were as brave as Esther."

To appease Duke's anguish during these comments, Jude interrupted to say that the group welcomed him, noting that Duke had confessed and repented of his dissolute behavior. Drawing the attention of the group to the couple, Jude apologized for not formally introducing Duke and Tina. "Duke and Tina, we welcome you to this church, especially to the screening of this clip." The folks, embarrassed that they had spoken so forthrightly about Duke, now applauded him.

"I'm so sorry," one of the women stated. "When I commented on Cory's face, I didn't say that to make you feel bad. Please forgive me for saying this in your presence!"

"We didn't know you folks came in," another kindly declared.

Duke was amazed at their largeness of heart and forgiving nature. *People don't behave this way in my world!* "I was an animal, and I can't believe what I did. I'm grateful that Cory forgives me." He looked around at the group. "You guys amaze me. You should be treating me like a monster because that's what I was." A tear came to Duke's eye as he looked down at the floor. "That's what I am, but here you are loving me. I've never seen nothing like this because this kind of love doesn't exist in my world. I don't deserve it." He wiped a tear on his sleeve. "But I thank you for it."

Pastor Gabe smoothly covered. "There is rejoicing in heaven over one sinner who repents. If you listen carefully, you can hear the hallelujah chorus on high, and there's much of that in this church for you and Tina too! We warmly welcome you to our—and your—church family."

Chapter 5

Cory's speech into the security camera at the mine parking lot was the other topic of conversation after the Bible study. "I have no idea what I said," Cory explained, "though I spoke of an urgent matter which Old Mary told me about at the hospital. I maybe spoke in French."

"I have an update on her condition by the way," Pastor Gabe asserted. "Old Mary appears to be gaining ground. Just today, Dr. Buck told me that she'll probably return to her apartment fairly soon, though of course it's too soon to make that call yet."

"Praise the Lord!" Rose rejoiced.

"She comprehended every word I said this afternoon but is still too weak to speak much." Frail and gaunt as though carrying the weight of the world, Pastor Gabriel looked at the group and spoke again in a soft voice. "Keep up the prayer, please. She may rally yet again."

After the Bible study, Charles volunteered to show the clip to his colleagues in the French department at Grove City College. "Maybe one of them lip-reads French or knows someone who could. Lip-reading appears to be the key to this very real mystery." Folks expressed gratitude to him and after a few further comments about *The Pittsburgh Hamlet* parted for the evening.

The breakthrough came a few days later when Renee, one of Charles's colleagues in the French Department, offered him a translation of Cory's strange speech into the security camera. The professor friend obtained the assistance of her friend, a deaf-mute specialist in Pittsburgh, who had successfully translated the speech.

Charles invited Jude and Cory to his house, and seated in his study, the three of them puzzled over the enigmatic translation. "Before I show it to you, I'll forewarn you. What you said is the strangest thing in the world! You not only spoke in French, but you did so in riddle form, and in rhyme no less!"

"You're kidding! I did all that in my stupor?"

"Talk about a coded text!" Jude chimed in.

"All right, here goes." Charles read the translation.

> Angelos, the bright eagle,
> And Zoe are the same.
> Explosion has no equal.
> To roses large wing came
> To save as in Ezekiel.
> Tattoo cross explodes game,
> Destroying every sequel.

"Renee also presented me with this English translation of the French original which, as I've just shown, consists of a seven-line verse paragraph with an abababa rhyme scheme."

Trying to tease out the meaning, Charles, Jude, and Cory were completely nonplussed. Eventually Jude broke the silence. "I can't believe it! In your madness, you spoke a riddle in perfect rhyme!" He lightly tapped Cory's thigh with his fist. "That's impressive, Chaucer!"

"What did you expect from the poet laureate of Armstrong County?" She laughed heartily.

"Who does something like this?" Jude scratched his head and thought. "We're often told that you artists are strange birds, but this is ridiculous!" All of them laughed. "Seriously, the thing is so complicated I have no idea where to begin, but how about with Angelos? Just who is Angelos, and how can our favorite dog in the world be him?"

Cory voiced her consternation. "Can we be certain that the Zoe of the poem is our pet?"

"The link between the roses and the large wing adds another layer of complexity," Charles reflected. "The whole thing is impossible to figure out."

"The one deduction I feel comfortable with," Jude remarked, "is linking Abe, the tattoo man, to the explosion. We can be reasonably sure about that, yet how does a giant wing save the roses?"

"For me," Charles added, "the most baffling thing of all is the abstruse reference to Ezekiel."

"One thing is sure," Cory offered.

"What's that?" Jude asked.

"We need to talk to Pastor Gabe to see if he can ferret out the Ezekiel allusion. The guy's a genius when it comes to the Bible. Maybe he can make sense of that part."

Charles called Pastor Gabriel who, free at the moment, walked across Freeport Road and joined the group in Charles's study a short while later. The evening was important enough to the pastor that he described it in his journal.

Pastor Gabriel's journal:

All of us knew that we were, in some measure, holding the key to Jude and Cory's future in our hands, since the vision bears a mysterious, one-to-one correspondence to their lives. We spoke for a while and puzzled over the content. We didn't get very far and eventually broke up for the evening.

In my study later, I paid attention again to Abe Badoane's name. Run together, the name becomes Abebadoane. Playing around with it a little, I saw its similarity to Abbadoane, and dropping the final "e" produces Abbadoan, possibly homophonous with Abaddon. That, I recognized in a second, is one of Satan's names as it appears in the Book of Revelation. The word, which appears only that one time in the entire Bible, means in both Greek and Hebrew "the destroyer."

I was pleased with this progress, namely, that Abe Badoane, referred to in the riddle as "tattoo cross," may well be the destroyer of the riddle; but if he is the destroyer, does that mean that he is connected to the explosion or the cause of it? Is the

explosion, in other words, the means by which he destroys? That was as far as I got before going to bed, but I did take time to ring Charles with the little breakthrough. He says he'll pass along my hunch to Jude and Cory tomorrow.
End of Pastor Gabriel's journal

Early the next evening, Charles drove to the home of Rosetta Wakefield to see Jude. Learning that he was over at Cory's house, Charles then motored to the adjoining Mohney farm.

"They're up on the ridge, Chuck," Pete said, shaking his friend's hand. "I swear that's their second home! Actually, they're working this evening—mowing hay, I think Cory said. It's quite a hike to the top. You better take Joey's horse, Bullet. He's very tame, so he won't give you any trouble. You won't even need to throw a saddle on him."

"It's been a long time since I rode bareback."

"It won't be a problem."

After Charles happily agreed, the men walked to the barn and Pete watched Charles mount Bullet. Soon the professor clip-clopped out the barn and up the hill.

Cresting the ridge of Vinlindeer, Charles could see the tractor in the distance. *The smell of the freshly mown hay fills the air. Jude and Cory sit tightly against each other in the wide tractor seat. Even at this distance I can see her leaning into him, her head resting on his shoulder. I've never seen two people so much in love! What a perfect match! Zoe walks briskly by the side of the tractor. Van Gogh, you need to be here to paint this scene of unspeakable joy! It reminds me of your* Laborer Plowing a Field.

Charles tied Bullet to a fencepost and walked toward the couple, kicking the hay. Clumps of hay shot upward and fell on his shoes or to the side. *This reminds me of Donald Hall's poem, "Kicking the Leaves." Wonder if I can remember any of the lines?* He stopped, turned toward the valley, and thought for a moment. *I have it! "This year the poems came back, when the leaves fell. Kicking the leaves, I heard the leaves tell stories." So good, Donald Hall. Yes, if we listen closely, we can hear the leaves tell stories. These clumps of kicked hay tell stories too. I must learn their language so they can tell me their wonderful tales. Talk, hay, talk!* He swept his eyes across the panorama below. *Talk, leaves. Talk, trees. Talk, fields and stones!*

By this time, Jude had driven alongside him. Turning off the tractor, he and Cory dismounted, and soon the three of them congregated by a fence post at the top of Vinlindeer.

"Good evening, Professor," Cory began. "What brings you to our beloved Vinlindeer?"

"Good evening! Pastor Gabe has been thinking about your French riddle and has made a bit of progress."

"Fascinating!" Jude said, draping his arm around Cory. "Lay on, Macduff!"

"That I shall. Gabe says it's a modest, little thing, but I think it's important. He wonders if Abe Badoane is homophonous with 'Abaddon,' which you Bible scholars will recognize as one of Satan's names. I think he said that's recorded in Revelation."

"It is," Cory agreed.

"And that it means 'the destroyer.' In that interpretation, Abe Badoane is the destroyer who's probably linked with the explosion." He gazed across the valley. "As I say, it isn't as much as we want, but we have to start somewhere."

"It's a good beginning," Jude opined. "As tattoo man, Abe explodes the game, so he may well be the destroyer."

As Charles spoke, Zoe sat and listened with a look of comprehension on his face. He perked up at the name—"Abaddon."

"I see Gabe's point." Jude was the first to respond. "That definitely has possibilities, but what does the riddle mean that Zoe and Angelos are one and the same? We still don't even know who Angelos is!"

"That's one of many questions," Cory responded.

"Let me give it a shot," Jude said, scratching his head. "Do you think Angelos is another name for Zoe?"

"Possibly," Cory replied. She turned to Charles. "According to Old Mary, Jude and I are the roses, but how in the world are we saved by the eagle? What a riddle! And to think I said this when I was hallucinating off the chart? Can you imagine my genius when sane?" Charles and Jude laughed.

"My new name for her is Chaucer, and in the presence of such a masterful poet, I consciously try to speak in iambic pentameter!"

"Will you shut up!" Cory pecked Jude on the cheek.

Charles heartily laughed again. "And what of Ezekiel? The arcane reference to the Old Testament prophet remains extremely elusive. If Gabe doesn't come through on that one, we're dead in the water!"

Leaning against the fence post, Cory said, "We have to hope and pray that Old Mary gets better and that we can talk with her. She might have the answers to every single one of these esoteric symbols." When Cory said that, Zoe came forward, licked her face excitedly, and reclined in her lap.

"What a dog!" Charles said. "What was that all about?"

"Oh, nothing," Cory joked. "Zoe follows our conversations like a human!"

The group sat in silence and scanned the scenery below—the wide-open fields, the sprawling woods beyond, the farm houses which dotted the landscape, and the cows meandering in the pasture.

"Everything is so lush and green this summer," Charles said. "We've had the perfect mix of sun and rain." He bade goodbye and trotted Bullet across the ridge. *I'd like to canter, but that would be risky without a saddle!*

Their mowing job finished a while later; Jude and Cory sat against a tree and cuddled in their favorite position. Jude was the first to break the silence. "Angelos, shining eagle, explosion…"

"Ezekiel, tattoo cross. It would take a genius to figure out this riddle."

"Oedipus, where are you when we need you?"

Jude noted in his journal that evening. "In the balmy summer dusk, we continued to puzzle over the riddle. The questions are endless, the answers frustratingly few."

Chapter 6

The next day at the mine was uneventful. Abe had called off sick—everybody knew that, humiliated, he was lying low—and the other pickers and mine employees delighted in the end of the feud. Now that Jude and Duke were reconciled, Duke made a passing comment to some friends that he ought to "show more interest in Tina." Many were pleased about that, especially her co-pickers, since before Duke's fling with Cory, he and Tina were together much of the time. Back in the early spring, there had been speculation among her friends, in fact, that he would be settling down with Tina permanently. While that was far from definite, the women in the mine had often heard Tina wittily lament, "I need a dad for my kid and a stud for my bed. Right *now!*"

Would Duke and Tina end up together after all? Was Duke harboring guilt that he was possibly the never-acknowledged father? He was heard to say, "I think her kid is my son. If I am, it ain't right that I don't help raise him. Even a jackass like me sees that!"

Despite Bull's vociferous denial of damaging Duke's car, there was, at another front, a growing sentiment among the men that he was guilty, simply because Bull's ability to mask away his guilt was woefully inadequate. When Cory passed along this sentiment to Jude, he commented, "So full of artless jealousy is guilt…"

Cory joined him in finishing the famous couplet, "It spills itself in fearing to be spilt." "Ah, *Hamlet,* that amazing play. And guess what," Cory added. "I have an artful thing that I need to spill to you."

"What?"

"About an unbelievable vision I had last night."

"I know you like surprises, but don't keep me waiting too long."

"I'll tell you this evening."

"I want to know now, you sneak!" Jude pecked her on the cheek as they went their separate ways.

That evening, Jude and Cory returned to the mine after work hours to spend time in Little Gidding. Cory put her painting on hold and began sketching an angel about which she dreamed the previous night. "It was so clear to me. The angel was magnificent and reminded me of what the angel Gabriel or Michael might look like. I couldn't help but think of a verse in Psalm 91. 'He shall cover you with His feathers, and under His wings you shall take refuge?' [verse 4]."

"Is this the surprise, the sketch of the angel? Have I been a good enough little boy that you'll let me in on your secret?"

"No, that isn't the surprise. Well, not exactly."

"You've kept me waiting long enough. What is it?"

"The angel has a name. Are you ready?"

"More than ready."

"This is a little breakthrough in our riddle, which we've been dying to have. The angel's name is Angelos! That's the name I heard in the vision. Gabe told me that it's a Greek word that means 'messenger.'"

"That's really strange that in your vision you both saw and heard something, but how great if this cracks part of the riddle!" Jude continued his rumination. "Then this is the question. If the eagle and the angel are the same, does that mean that Zoe is the angel/messenger?"

"If so, that's a major piece of the puzzle."

"But how is Zoe the angel/eagle? Yes, he's one strange dog, but an angel or an eagle? I don't think so!"

"I know. Let me recite the first two lines of the riddle." Pulling the riddle from her pocket, Cory again examined it. "'Angelos, the bright eagle And Zoe are the same.' Even if that solves part of the riddle, it doesn't answer all the questions." Cory continued to peer at the riddle. "Messengers carry messages, obviously, but what's the eagle's message, and what's its relevance?"

"The idea of taking refuge under God's wing was a recurring theme for David. One place he says that is Psalm 17, I think, though I forget the exact verse."

"Good recall."

"The verse was cited in a daily devotional pastor gave me." Jude turned in his Gideon pocket Bible, which Cory had given him, found the verse, and said, "Here it is, verse 8: 'Keep me as the apple of Your eye; Hide me under the shadow of Your wings.' That's the phrase I was after—'the shadow of your wings.'"

Cory showed Jude the sketch she had been drawing. "What do you think? The angel in my dream was huge and imposing like this. How would you like to take refuge under that?"

"It's beautiful. You drew that after you had the dream?"

"I was on a roll!"

"That's as good as your sketch of Penn Bar in Wells, England." He looked closely at the detail of the angel's wings. "Let's hope this angel shows up in one of your dreams and solves the riddle!"

Cory and Jude spent a couple relaxing hours in Little Gidding that evening, during which time Jude again read the famous passage from Eliot's *Burnt Norton*:

Footfalls echo in the memory
Down the passage which we did not take
Towards the door we never opened
Into the rose garden.

"Isn't this the poetic excerpt under Old Mary's picture of the rose?" Jude asked.

"Yes. It's actually in a frame along with the picture of the manor house, Burnt Norton. If I remember right, the house is in the center, the rose garden is at the left, and a large red English rose is at the right. At the bottom center is that poetic excerpt from Eliot's poem. It's a lovely work of art which her Sunday school class had framed professionally at Transue's Custom Framing. It was a gift to Old Mary from her class when she turned eighty. It hangs above her chair in the living room."

"What a work of art it must be!"

"It really is beautiful."

Jude then turned to two books which he had brought with him. "I've been reading Kenneth Paul Kramer's *Redeeming Time: T.S. Eliot's Four Quartets*." Jude opened the book to a marked passage. "Kramer says that the 'rose garden is filled with echoes—both earthly and mythic, personal and universal, from the present situation and from the inner recesses of his memory' [p. 36]. Isn't that good? I agree since the rose garden is filled with echoes. In one sense, Old Mary's echo takes the form of the recurring vision, because the vision is her echo."

"That's great," Cory responded. "Read that last phrase again."

"The echoes are 'from the inner recesses of his memory.'"

"That truly is good, and that's how it is with Old Mary because the vision comes from her inner recesses, clear from the bottom of her unconscious!" Cory had placed her sketch of the angel on her easel and added a few deft strokes. "Is anything else you've been reading relevant to Old Mary's vision?"

"Maybe. I came across this line from Thomas Howard's *Dove Descending: A Journey into T.S. Eliot's* Four Quartets." Jude picked up a second volume and read from a dog-eared page. "Howard says the poem invites the reader 'into a vision where memory seems to be operative, summoning things that one would have thought were gone forever'" [p. 40].

"There's another fine insight since memory is very operative in Old Mary's vision. Her memory summons the old vision again and again and keeps it from being 'gone forever.'"

"You're right, because here it is all these years later being replayed so dramatically on the stage of the present moment."

"Exactly."

Stepping back from the sketch, Cory scratched her head. *I'm ransacking my brain for some of the postulates about art which I once read in one of my art books.* "I enjoy reading what famous artists say about their art. Michelangelo's sonnets about his art are amazing."

"I've never read a single one."

"Few people know that Michelangelo wrote about one hundred more sonnets than Shakespeare. Did you know that, Mr. Literary Dude?"

"I had no idea. Okay, I'll bite. Can you remember a line from a Michelangelo sonnet?"

Cory thought for a moment. "I need to think about that, but I do remember that he wrote a sonnet to his protégé, Tommaso Cavalieri, and said something like this in the poem: 'nor can there be achieved / eternal form in time, since flesh decays.' That's all I remember, that one phrase. But think about it because what Michelangelo says is so true. Temporal forms—things of this world—can never capture eternality. At least that's my take on Michelangelo's line. What's yours?"

"I should read the whole sonnet before I comment, but your analysis is surely accurate. The temporal can't embody the eternal, just as the finite mind can't grasp infinity. Michelangelo is definitely on to a profound truth here."

"I don't remember much about his sonnets, but that line has always been engrained in my head. Michelangelo—now there was another genius!"

"He died in 1564, the year Shakespeare was born. Maybe Michelangelo's genius passed to Shakespeare, transmigration at its finest—ha!"

"Interesting theory, encyclopedia man! Here's something just as interesting. How does Michelangelo's line from the sonnet relate to Howard's theory that a vision helps us recollect realities that we thought were lost forever?"

"I haven't thought this hard since my PhD comps! Well, I'll take a shot. Howard says visions connect us with enduring realities outside the present moment, whereas Michelangelo says art tries to do the very same thing. In the end, both fail simply because the eternal world can never be fully grasped on the earthly plane. How'd I do?"

"Excellent, my star pupil! Art yearns for expression of the eternal, as does a vision. We're haunted by Old Mary's vision, because it's been with her so much of her life." Cory paused and looked again at her sketch of the angel. "Speaking of Old Mary, I just can't get her out of my mind."

"In what way?"

"Pastor Gabe says that she has nicely progressed over the last few days."

"We certainly don't want to rush it, but wouldn't it be something if she'd be well enough to talk to us? If we could rummage through the files in her brain, she'd crack the mystery of the riddle in seconds!"

"This might be more of a possibility than you realize. Pastor said that he spoke with her just this afternoon."

"What did he say?"

"That she's progressing well and will come home in a couple days. He said her mind was as sharp as ever and that she's experiencing absolutely no effect from her mini-stroke."

"What great news!"

"She's just a little weak from this last little episode, so they're keeping her in the hospital to monitor her."

"Then it's Old Mary or bust!"

Chapter 7

During the rest of the evening, Cory returned to her painting, *New Every Morning*, while Jude resumed his reading on Shakespeare's *Hamlet*. After perusing the play for a short while, Jude rested his eyes. "Cory, it's hard to believe how Claudius-like Abe really is. The calculated subterfuge, the sly and controlling manipulation of everyone around him, his evil motives—well, Abe is like Shakespeare's villain in so many ways."

"Interesting parallel. What gave you this idea?"

"I'm reading Harold Goddard on *Hamlet*. He says"—Jude turned to the page—"that it's 'plain that he,' meaning Claudius, 'becomes a criminal not through viciousness but through weakness, and that his nature contains the seeds of repentance.'"

"Talk about a scintillating insight! And here I thought that Shakespeare's villain was just pure evil."

"Goddard says that Hamlet, by extension, is as much to blame as Claudius, since Claudius manifests real guilt and contrition. He could have been led upward to repentance instead of downward to further evil. That is one amazing thought."

"Truly profound."

Jude sat on the edge of the couch and clutched the book tightly with both hands. "Listen to this. Goddard says Claudius is a 'man conscious of his sin and longing to be rid of it—a fit subject for the redemptive power of art.' Think about that, Cory. Goddard sees Claudius as having a redeeming, noble side. He goes on to say that 'Rarely have a man and an opportunity been more made for each other than Hamlet and the chance to save his uncle.' This is so astute. Goddard thinks Hamlet should have tried to save his uncle!"

"I've never read the play in that light."

Jude read several more sentences. "Listen to this. 'The highest duty of any man is to be true to the divinity within him, to remain faithful to his creative gift.'"

"That is totally unbelievable. Being 'true to the divinity within'—I love that! And what was the other part, the statement about creativity? You know I picked up on that!"

"That the highest duty of man is to remain faithful to his creative gift."

"Pure genius, Jude. What a brilliant thought!"

"I agree." Jude looked again at the passage in Goddard. "Hamlet chooses to 'make his art an instrument for finding out whether the King is guilty, an instrument not of revenge, but of revelation.' Revelation and not revenge. That runs completely against the grain of those many critics who think it was Hamlet's obligation to seek vengeance and that his delay speaks to a psychic abnormality."

Jude continued to read Goddard's luminous commentary as Cory painted. Eventually he put his book down and rubbed his eyes. "Taken all around, this critic is pretty hard on the famous prince of Denmark. Listen to his take on *The Murder of Gonzago* playlet. 'But in so far as he [Hamlet] regards it as a trap, an engine for torturing a victim, for catching not the King's conscience but the King himself, the play is nothing but a contrivance for murder on the mental plane.'"

"'A contrivance for murder on the mental plane.' That is one profound phrase. What a superb critic!"

"Yes. Goddard makes it seem as if Hamlet's as much to blame as Claudius, since Claudius longed for 'open penitence and confession'—Goddard's words—and asks, 'who was better fitted to perform that miracle than a man with the spiritual endowment of Hamlet?' He maintains that Hamlet should have rescued Claudius and been an instrument of his salvation rather than the agent seeking his death. Oh, how smart a lash this speech doth give my conscience!"

"Mine too!"

Jude got up, walked over to Cory, and put his arms around her. "Darling, surely you know what I'm thinking!"

"Possibly, but tell me."

"Look at how this applies to Abe."

Cory stepped away from her easel and dropped her brush to her side. "I think I know where you're headed but continue."

"We have the chance to save and reach out to mystery man Abe as surely as Hamlet had the chance to save and reach out to Claudius. Yet here we are—us fine, noble Christians—blowing our opportunity as surely as Hamlet blew his. Instead of seeing Abe as a man to reform and a lost soul to save, we've been seeing him as the enemy to defeat in a sordid drama of death. Talk about rank hypocrisy!"

"So true, Jude, as we talk of love but act with hate. Christ called such people Pharisees!"

"That He did. And snakes too!" Jude looked over at his volume of Shakespeare on the couch. "That's kind of a theme in Shakespeare."

"What's a theme?"

Jude thought for a moment. "The consequences of not loving. When we cease to love, bad things happen."

"I've heard you refer to a couple passages along that line. Can you cite one?"

"*Othello* comes to mind. I know I've shared this line before."

"Lay it on me. I'm always ready for some Bard brilliance."

"'And when I love thee not, Chaos is come again.' Think of that. It's when we stop loving that chaos comes into our lives."

"As when we fight with our spouses and kids."

"And neighbors and work associates."

Cory thought on this. "Give me another William witticism. I give that one a ten."

"How about Angelo's line in *Measure for Measure*? It's another text I frequently quote."

"I'm all ears."

"'When once our grace we have forgot, Nothing goes right.'"

"Shakespeare's saying that once you stop extending grace to others, nothing goes right in your life? Or as philosopher Duke would say, your wheels fall off!"

"Exactly!" Jude laughed. "All right, let's track back to Hamlet. The brilliant young prince had learned and practiced Christ's commandments of love, mercy, and grace in Wittenberg. That's a safe assumption, given the spiritually rarefied air of that sacrosanct city." He looked at Cory. "You're with me so far?"

"Yes, but once Hamlet returns to Denmark, he replaces the commandment of love with the Ghost's commandment of vengeance and retaliation. Is that your point?"

"Yes, but it's worse than that. Once Hamlet stops loving and extending grace to others, as he does with Claudius, he begins his slide into chaos. I could say his slide into hell."

"That's pretty pessimistic!"

"But pretty true. Why doesn't Hamlet kill Claudius when he sees him at prayer? Because Claudius, in his mind, is 'fit and seasoned for his passage,' meaning he's in a penitent state of saving forgiveness and ready, according to the ethos of that day, to pass directly to heaven. In short, Hamlet won't kill Claudius because that would put him in heaven, and he'd rather see Claudius burn eternally in hell!"

"That is truly malicious. You're making me see Hamlet in a new light."

"I'm summarizing Goddard's point. Hamlet originally sees the play—the play that he selects for Claudius and Gertrude to view at court—as an instrument of revelation. Anyone would agree that is a noble intent, but later that playlet within the play, *The Murder of Gonzago*, becomes an instrument of revenge, a mere contrivance for murder according to Goddard."

"Tell me again why he finds that so appalling."

"Because deep in his lost and tortured soul, Claudius wants to confess and repent. He's crying for salvation and is filled with remorse. He desires what the old Puritans called 'the gift of tears.'"

"I think I know what the 'the gift of tears' means, but give me the Puritan understanding of the phrase.'"

"A person can't repent by himself since his carnal indulgence and happy hedonism take him in the exact opposite direction. The urge to confess and repent can only be prompted by the Holy Spirit. If Claudius wants to repent and get right with God, then that is proof that God is stirring him. That nudging of the soul to get right with God is surely a beautiful gift because, without it, a person is hell-bound and awash in his own carnal impulses. You see why the Puritans saw penitential tears as a much-needed gift."

"Got it! That really is profound. Now back to Goddard's point."

"He says nobody is more spiritually endowed and suited for this high calling of saving the king—Goddard actually calls it a miracle—than Hamlet, but instead of saving Claudius's soul, Hamlet chooses to damn it to hell!"

Deep in thought, Cory walked from the easel and sat down by Jude and held his hand. "I never saw the play that way before, but Hamlet surely blew a golden opportunity."

"Remember how Goddard says it." Jude picked up the book and read again. "'Rarely have a man and an opportunity been more made for each other than Hamlet and the chance to save his uncle.' Hamlet, in short, was shaped by God for the important work of reaching and redeeming his uncle."

"I love the critic's point that God, at least indirectly, created Hamlet for this role."

"Which the prince rejected. That God sovereignly controls all is a major theme of the play."

"Beautifully rendered in the old axiom that God tempers the wind to the shorn lamb."

"That, Cory, is beautifully stated, but Hamlet completely blew this golden opportunity by reverting to retaliation, bloodshed, and war. How very tragic!"

"It really is since the Wittenberg-schooled prince should have acted with love, love that 'covers a multitude of sins,' 1 Peter 4:8. Your turn."

"Turn for what? What are you talking about?"

"Your turn to quote a Bible verse on love."

"Talk about catching me off guard!" Jude thought for a moment. "How about 1 Corinthians 13? Those verses on love are the very best."

"Love that…"

"That does not insist on its own way, isn't irritable or resentful, and never rejoices in wrongdoing. That's a paraphrase."

"A very good paraphrase of 1 Corinthians 13:5–6. Well done."

"All right, chairwoman of games and activities, your turn!"

Cory thought for a moment. "Romans 12:10 has always been a favorite—'Love one another with brotherly affection. Outdo one another in showing honor.'"

"Doesn't the Apostle Paul expand that point in the next chapter?"

"Yes, in Romans 13."

"The one about owing no one anything except to love them because we're called to love our neighbors as ourselves."

"Very good! Paul says that we must 'cast off the works of darkness and put on the armor of light.'"

"But alas, our shorn prince casts off the light and puts on the armor of darkness!"

Exiting Little Gidding a short while later, Jude and Cory took a detour to the new section where the bolting crew had been working.

Riding down the darkened corridor, Cory reflected on their discussion in Little Gidding. "As those Bible verses make very clear, we should treat Abe kindly like a friend, brother or even a father despite his evil intent."

"But our objective up to this point has been to expose him in our Hamlet-like game of cat and mouse."

"In an effort to bring him down! Tsk, tsk! According to your famous critic, Hamlet should have shown love. Consider this point: Goddard suggests it, but Jesus commands it!"

"Hey, look!" Jude exclaimed, arriving at the worksite. "The men have made substantial progress. I bet in another week or so this new section will be open."

"It will be good to see this place in action."

"We've waited a long time to initiate this area."

Up to this evening, Jude and Cory had viewed Abe as the destroyer, the Claudius-like rival, who must be disposed of, the cancer in the mine's body. On occasion, the thought of illuminating the cavernous darkness of his soul and of praying for him crossed their minds, but they had never taken the initiative to follow through, nor had they, in Jude's words, "made a sincere effort to rescue him from his own self-made madness."

After this evening in Little Gidding, Jude and Cory began to reframe their attitude toward Abe Badoane. "Our higher calling," Jude said as they rode through the dark corridors of the mine, "is first to forgive him and then to save and rescue him."

They arrived at this altered perception, ironically, at the very moment Abe Badoane plotted to destroy them forever. Who would win the battle—Abe's vengeful hate or their forgiving love?

Chapter 8

Upon arriving at Cory's house, Jude and Cory learned during a telephone call from Pastor Gabe that Old Mary would be coming home the next day from Armstrong County Memorial Hospital and was looking forward to talking to them. Cory called Old Mary on the phone to wish her a good recovery.

During that conversation, Old Mary told them to stop over in the near future. "Please do visit me soon, child. I need to know that *you* are all right! My goodness, girl, but you were plum out of your mind in the hospital! Give me a day or two to get on my feet, and then we'll talk."

Jude and Cory were pleased that Old Mary was returning to good health but were frustrated that the occasion when they could broach the subject of the vision wouldn't occur for another few days. Jude voiced their frustration. "The waiting game continues, the missing links still buried."

But the arrangement of another momentous meeting was not delayed. Duke telephoned Pastor Gabriel at the same time Jude and Cory were in Little Gidding, during which conversation Duke made passing reference to Abe Badoane. "I know my heart ain't right toward the man. Cory says I have to forgive him, but that's the last thing I want to do. I'm just being honest with you, sir. In my book he's a SOB. Sorry." A pause. "I need to watch my language and respect a man of the cloth, but this forgiveness thing doesn't come very easy for a red neck like me!"

"We can talk about this in my office, Mr. Manningham. For right now, I'd simply counsel you to soften your attitude toward Mr.

Badoane. We must realize that he too is an unhappy man struggling in a very difficult world."

The comment nudged Duke to start thinking about his treatment of Abe, who was, as the pastor suggested, too big a player to keep at arm's length. *The pastor believes we need to show him love, for that's the godly way. If adequately riled, the old man could cause serious trouble. I've found that out the hard way!*

Like other people at the mine, Duke and Tina began to sporadically interact with Abe Badoane again. On the surface, the situation appeared to be smoothing over, but inwardly Abe remained a raging caldron, slyly planning his next move against Jude and Cory.

"He appears friendly enough," Duke said to Tina one day coming out of the lunchroom, "but you never know what's going on behind those beady eyes. Just what's he really thinking? Know what I mean?"

"You're right. You can never tell about that guy."

"One thing I've learned over the years is that he can smile and be happy and tell jokes till the cows come home, and yet be planning, at that very moment, to carve out your heart!"

"This morning in the locker room, Cory quoted a proverb about that—something about a person disguising his hate with lying lips" [Proverbs 26:24].

In one of his journal entries, Abe himself said it best: "All of them—Jude and Cory, and even Duke and Tina—have passed the point of no return. There's no hope for any of them. Forgiveness? I'd never even consider it!"

A few evenings later at Old Mary's apartment, one of the most defining and exciting events of the entire summer occurred for Cory and Jude. As they got out of Jude's car, Zoe by their side, and sauntered up the grade to Old Mary's apartment, Jude asked, "Why is she called Old Mary? Isn't that name a bit offensive?"

"Not at all," Cory replied. "Center Hill people don't see it that way. We use that term to differentiate this dear soul from the two other Marys in our congregation, both of whom are much younger. Believe me, the name is used with utmost respect. It is so much a part of her name that we don't even think of her age when we say it."

"You mean it's more like a suffix or even a title."

"Right. To be honest—and I know this will sound strange—it's actually a term of endearment. That's how much we love her."

As Jude and Cory approached her apartment, they were surprised to see her sitting on her porch swing, rocking back and forth and watching the hummingbirds. Conversation commenced slowly and gently, since Jude and Cory were concerned about Old Mary's well-being and did not want her to overdo. "I thought the drought might affect the crops," Jude said to ease into conversation, "but the corn and hay look very good. The field corn is very high in fact."

"Yes," Old Mary responded. "Even the lawns don't look so dry as they sometimes do. I guess we had just enough rain to keep everything green."

"Another blessing is Mark and Lisa's baby." Cory brought the discussion around to a praise item of the sort Old Mary frequently spoke about at Bible studies. "She's going to be fine. Little Rebecca's lungs are completely clear."

"That is such an answer to prayer," Old Mary immediately responded. "I worried so about that dear baby." With that, Old Mary broke into the subject of the rose vision. "I know you want to talk about my dream of the roses." She watched a hummingbird drink from the feeder. "I told you most everything I know in the last conversation." A pause. "But not everything."

"You probably realize," Cory responded when Old Mary paused, "that I was highly medicated when you were talking about the rose vision at the hospital. I hardly remember anything except that at one point I was shocked at something you said. Even in my stupor, I can remember thinking that we were in serious danger, but for the life of me, I can't recall the frightening details or even the gist of what you were saying. My mind is still a jumble about all of it."

"I knew you weren't feeling well that day. Your mind was wondering all over the place." Old Mary leaned forward and looked directly at Cory. "Missy, I was worried about you." She laughed and lovingly wagged a bony finger at Cory. "Truth is, you had me downright scared!"

"You're absolutely right. I was not myself." Cory shook her head as she recalled that afternoon in the hospital. Old Mary remained quiet as if she wanted Cory to continue. "Before you tell us about the rose vision, do you want me to tell you what happened to me?"

Old Mary enthusiastically nodded. "Please do."

"Well, can you believe that I've had my own vision?"

"Really?"

"The other night, I saw this magnificent being in my dream, which made such an impression on me that I made a sketch of it. I've been getting back into my art again lately, so it was fun to draw. May I show it to you?"

"Yes, of course, please do. Maybe that will make it easier to talk again about my dream."

Cory reached into her handbag and pulled out a sketch of the angel but showed only half of it, thereby revealing just the one wing. "Here it is."

Old Mary responded with excitement. "That looks very much like the eagle's wing I've always pictured in my mind! Remember the sketch I told you about?" Old Mary thought for a moment. "Maybe you saw my sketch in your dream and unconsciously drew it?"

"Impossible. I never saw your sketch."

"Maybe you had a dream about my picture?" She picked up the fragile sketch that she had laid on her swing and held it beside Cory's.

Cory again looked at Old Mary's fingers as she held the pictures. *I didn't know fingers could be that shiny and smooth. I don't think you could even get fingerprints from those tips because they're so worn smooth with age. They actually have a patina to them!*

"I'll compare the two pictures." Old Mary silently studied the two drawings that she held side by side in front of her. "They're practically the same."

Cory looked back and forth between the two pictures and Old Mary's gnarled hands. *Her hands remind me of a story I once heard that Albrecht Durer allegedly memorialized his brother Albert's disfigured hands in his famous fifteenth-century drawing, the praying hands. Wonder if that's true.* "I don't think they're exactly the same," Cory finally replied, wresting her eyes from the crooked joints. "I saw more than just a wing." Cory unfolded the paper to reveal the entire angel.

"My goodness!" Old Mary exclaimed. "You've drawn a complete angel, but look at the two wings, yours from yesterday and mine from years ago. They're nearly identical!"

"They really are."

"I've always surmised that the shadowy wing of the original vision was that of an eagle, but maybe I was seeing an angel's wing instead!" Old Mary peered at them in amazement. "Look how similar they are!" She laid the pictures in her lap. "Do you really think I saw an angel?"

"I wonder."

"If I did, that changes everything, since it means the roses were rescued by an angel and not an eagle." She drew the pictures close to her, squinted her eyes, and looked more closely. "I do declare! Maybe I've been having a vision of an angel all those years and didn't know it! Goodness!"

"This gives new meaning to the idea that many have entertained angels unknowingly," Cory replied. "You've interacted with an angel by way of your vision for decades!"

Old Mary gave a hearty laugh. "Sakes alive, girl, I guess you're right, but I didn't know it!"

"That still leaves lots of questions unanswered," Cory resumed. "You link us with the rose story because we're the characters in your vision. That's the one thing I remember for certain, but my memory is faulty about the other details you shared with me in the hospital." Out of concern for Old Mary, Cory paused, noting her tired look. *Is she strong enough to continue this conversation?* A prayer on her lips, Cory forged ahead. "We've have had a major breakthrough since I saw you in the hospital."

"Whatever do you mean, child?"

"Did you hear about the incident of Duke Manningham's car being vandalized in the mine parking lot?"

"I did."

"That's the day I came from the hospital." *She studied Old Mary. Should I be recounting this to her? Why would she possibly want to hear this? The dear woman is so frail-looking!* "Believe it or not, I saw the whole incident."

"Please tell me about it."

"All right, but I'll share the condensed version. As the incident at Duke's car wound down and I saw that Jude was in the center of the melee, I turned and faced the security camera and spoke into it."

"Why did you do that?"

"I have no idea, but I nevertheless did. Well, when I spoke to the camera, I uttered a very puzzling riddle. That's strange in and of itself, but two things make it even stranger."

"Don't stop now!"

"I spoke in French, and—get ready for this—framed my thoughts into a perfectly rhymed riddle."

"Well, I declare."

"I told you it's strange!"

"Why did you do that?"

"It was all unconscious, and I didn't know that I was doing it. In fact, I don't remember a thing."

"You say this happened shortly after I saw you in the hospital that day?"

"Yes, very shortly afterward." Cory pulled the riddle out of her bag. "Here it is." She handed it to Old Mary. "One of Charles's colleagues in the French department at Grove City College found a friend in Mount Lebanon who lip-reads French. She translated my enigmatic riddle."

Old Mary said nothing as she carefully read the poeticized riddle, though she viscerally reacted when she came to the line about the explosion. "Oh, dear. 'Tattoo cross explodes the game.' That's awful!" Old Mary continued to read. "'To roses large wing came.' Isn't it interesting that your riddle refers to just a wing instead of an angel? That's how my vision was too. I always saw a majestic wing but never a complete angel."

Cory steered the discussion to the main point. *We've stalled long enough!* "Let's get to the reason why you wanted us to come. You had stopped at the point when you said we were the roses."

"Yes, that's exactly what I said. You and Jude, together, are the roses of my dream."

"That's hard to believe, but let's assume that we understand that. What about the upside-down tattoo and the explosion? Did you tell me that we were in danger? Is that why you reacted the way you just did when you read the line, 'Tattoo cross explodes the game?'"

"Yes, that's exactly right."

"This is the question that's been haunting Jude and me." *I dislike being so blunt, but I know of no other way to ask the question.* "Is the explosion the danger you told me about in the hospital?" *Jude, in our zeal to get to the bottom of this, are we taking advantage of this dear but frail woman? Lord, I would never want to do that!* "My head was pounding so much, and I was apparently so medicated that I can't dredge up any of the pertinent details you shared in the hospital."

The paper shook as Old Mary held the riddle. "You need to be asking these questions, for if the vision's right, I mean if it's about you as it seems to be, then you're in real danger. That's the part that keeps me from sleeping, and that's why I needed to talk to you."

The paper in her hand is shaking fiercely. Is that normal for Old Mary, or are we really unnerving our dear friend? Jude, I wish I knew what you were thinking! "We're so sorry that your dream of us upsets you so much."

At last Jude broke his silence. "I'm sure we're not worth that."

"I have to be honest," Old Mary resumed. "The word 'explodes' shakes me severely."

Noting Old Mary's agitation, Jude felt it best to divert her to a different subject. "As Pastor Gabe never tires of saying, we just have to keep the faith that God will protect us."

"Of course, young man. We hope that's the case. I had always hoped this part of the vision was wrong or wouldn't come true, but my goodness, the riddle confirms it! If the rose vision corresponds to your life, and we know it does, then we have to be aware of all possibilities!" She laid the riddle on her lap and rubbed her shiny fingers together. *There's no way to say this gently.* "I, too, believe that you're in danger!"

Chapter 9

Intently watching as Old Mary and Cory continued to speak, Jude grew more and more concerned about the effect of their conversation on Old Mary. *We're talking to a sickly woman well on in years.* When she and Cory paused, he decided to bring the discussion around to a more positive viewpoint. "Could the rescue of the roses relate to the explosion? The riddle says the roses are saved, so maybe the danger is miraculously averted?" *However, intellectual honesty demands that I ask one important question.* "But we don't know sequence here."

"What do you mean?" Cory interjected.

"Are they—are we—saved before or after the explosion?" *This topic is still too hot for Old Mary to handle. Look at her shaking, so we have to get to safer ground!* "My hope is that you might have said something about Zoe when you spoke to Cory in the hospital."

Old Mary gazed in wonderment at Jude. "What do you mean?"

"What I mean is that her 'camera poem'—that's what I call the riddle—makes the point that Zoe and Angelos are one and the same." Zoe perked to attention at the sound of his name. Jude looked at Cory as if that was her prompt to continue. *Sweetheart, that's your cue!*

Very smooth, Jude. I see what you're doing, you clever chap! "We're trying to see how all the crazy pieces of the poem fit together. Why did I turn and face the camera, why talk in French, and why couch this riddle in rhyme?"

"On the spot, no less!" Jude added.

"That's a lot of questions," Old Mary, overwhelmed, feebly replied.

Cory again noted Old Mary's physical condition. *The paper is shaking more uncontrollably, and Old Mary appears to be more slouched on the swing. Has she been that weak right along, and have I been so preoccupied with the rose vision that I didn't notice her exhaustion? We can't be insensitive to her plight!* Cory compassionately reduced all of her anxieties to one overarching question. "We don't want you to be concerned about our problem. After all, the only part of this which touches you is the danger you told me about." *Here goes!* "Do you really think we're in danger?"

"That's why we desperately need your help," Jude interrupted.

She's not responding! "I heartily apologize for bringing the discussion back to the part that is so unnerving to all of us." Cory looked warmly at Old Mary. "We're sorry to hit you with this when you're just getting out of the hospital."

Jude reached across and gently touched Old Mary's arm. "We better continue this some other time."

"Don't worry about me. I'm feeling fine." Fidgeting with the paper in her lap, Old Mary sat more erectly. "I'm just trying to figure out how to connect all the pieces." *It's going to be a beautiful sunset this evening.* "But I can tell you two things. First, remember how I told you that the rose is symbolic? In the vision, I saw the picture of the most beautiful little girl in the center of the rose." Old Mary stopped speaking and fingered the pillow fringe. "I need to back up so you understand this better."

"If you're sure this is the right time," Jude commented.

Old Mary looked across the valley as though trying to figure out how to begin her tale. Now that she wasn't speaking about the explosion, she spoke with more energy. "Once many decades ago, I saw the memorial stained-glass windows of Stephen Foster in the library museum at the Stephen Foster Theater in Pittsburgh. The one that really stuck in my mind was the 'Beautiful Dreamer' window. Shortly after my visit, I had the dream for the first time. In some ways, I tried to put it out of my mind simply because I didn't know what to do with it. Why did I have the dream, and what did it mean? Those and similar questions were in my mind constantly in those days. Thankfully, Pastor Gabe came to my rescue. He never hesitated and turned immediately to a passage in Job. How that man does know his Bible! I marked the passage because it dealt so directly with my vision."

"This is fascinating." Jude filled the silence, as Old Mary reached for her Bible beside her on the swing.

Old Mary found the passage in Job. "Here it is—Job 33:15. It says, 'In a dream, in a vision of the night, when deep sleep falls upon men, while slumbering on their beds, then He [God] opens the ears of men, and seals their instruction.' Gabe says this verse shows the importance of our dreams, since it says God opens our ears at night to give the dreamer instruction."

"What a verse!" Jude exclaimed.

"Gabe said I should pay serious attention to the vision and see what it means or what it leads to, because God speaks to me specifically—and vividly, I might add—through it."

"But in our day," Jude expanded the thought, "we've lost our ability to understand dreams or take them seriously, so we usually miss these subtly coded messages wherein God 'seals their instruction.'"

Old Mary held her Bible more closely and tried to read a notation she had written in the margin. "I can't read this." Old Mary gave her Bible to Jude. "Tell me what this note in the margin says. I asked Pastor Gabe to write down what he said, but I can't read his writing!" Old Mary laughed vigorously. "Don't tell him I said that!"

Jude examined the marginal notation. "He quotes Matthew Henry, the famous Puritan nonconformist minister in England. I think Henry lived in the late 1600s and into the 1700s. One thing is certain—his commentary on the Bible is brilliant. Gabe wrote in your margin an excerpt from Henry about this very verse." Jude held the Bible up to his eyes. "This really is small writing. It says the phrase that God 'seals their instruction' means God 'makes their souls receive the deep and lasting impression...of the instruction that is designed for them and suited to them.' And then Gabe put in parentheses 'From Matthew Henry's Commentary on Job 33:15.' He underlined the phrase 'designed for them and suited for them.'"

The reading of the citation jogged Old Mary's memory. "Now I remember! Gabe said that this vision was specifically suited for me—

mind you, designed just for me—so he told me to take the message with utmost seriousness. Can you imagine how humbling this is? To think that God designed a specific vision for little ole me!"

"It really is amazing," Cory agreed. When Old Mary paused to try to fit together the pieces of the vision, Cory filled the silence. "Your recollecting this vision reminds me of something Henry Ward Beecher once said. I memorized it. 'Every artist dips his brush in his own soul, and paints his own nature into his pictures.'"

"I really like that!" Jude exclaimed.

"For me that's what you're doing here," Cory said, looking at Old Mary. "You've dipped into your soul, found the beautiful rose vision, and now paint it! Voila!"

"That's a great quotation," Jude said. "You never shared that one with me. Well, I find it to be very true. The vision is Old Mary's painted canvas." Jude turned again to Old Mary. "So how did Gabe know what Matthew Henry said about that verse?"

"He had looked that up in Henry's commentary and then scribbled it into the margin." Old Mary took her Bible from Jude and laid it on the swing. "Now let me see if I can recollect the event more clearly. I had the first vision the night I saw the window. I think it happened that way. The first vision was sketchy—roses falling into the river, floating downstream, being rescued, and so on. Many years later, Ruby and Pete Mohney started going to church up here." She motioned over her shoulder toward the church behind her. "A certain beautiful teenage girl with long blond hair and the most angelic face I had ever seen was with them, along with her cute little brother."

Cory looked down in embarrassment.

"My, but your face is red! That girl's name was Corinna Adelena Mohney. She must have been about fifteen or sixteen years old." Old Mary smiled at Cory as though remembering the event like yesterday. "When I first saw you, I nearly died of shock, because you looked just like the woman in my vision and a bit like the woman in the Beautiful Dreamer window too. You see, in my mind they were the same. I was so struck by the similarity that I even asked your Mom and Dad for a picture of you! I bet you didn't know that. I told your Mom not to tell!"

"They didn't, and I never knew!"

"When I started seeing you at church about ten years ago, the vision began to reoccur, and I started getting more details in my dreams. When the bits and pieces slowly came together, the dream made more sense." Old Mary began fumbling through a stack of papers on the swing. "Do you want to see something that amazes me? Look at this picture your Mom and Dad gave me a decade go." Old Mary gave Cory the picture. "You match almost completely the girl in the vision, and you're also similar to the girl in the Beautiful Dreamer window. Don't you agree?"

Cory compared her photo with that of the head of the woman in the Beautiful Dreamer window in Pittsburgh. "I've never seen this picture of me. At least I don't remember it." She gave it to Jude who looked at it and then kissed it.

"You don't need to kiss the picture. I'm right here!"

Jude smooched her on the cheek and laughed.

Old Mary resumed her story. "I started seeing a man in the vision. Mind you, this was a couple years before Jude started coming here to live with Rosetta for the summers during his high school years. The young man in the vision had a full head of auburn brown hair. Imagine how I reacted the first time I saw you and Jude together. It was at church one Sunday morning when I sat behind Roberta at the piano. You two came in the side door at the front, you in your blond hair and Jude with his reddish-brown hair! I had a good look at you when you stopped to say hello to Roberta."

"That's quite the coincidence," Cory said. "Please continue!"

"Sometime later, you showed me a picture of the two of you standing by the Allegheny River. You were in Kittanning's Riverfront Park on your way to the prom at Kittanning High School. You had stopped for pictures in the park. Remember the photo, the one with the bridge in the background?" Cory nodded. "You've never seen the photo of the Beautiful Dreamer window at the Stephen Foster library museum, right?"

"No, I just saw the photo of the woman's head."

Old Mary picked up another picture from her stack of papers. "Hold these side by side, the photo of the stained-glass window and the one of you two on prom evening."

Jude and Cory saw in a moment that the similarity was pronounced. In the prom photo, Cory wore a long and flowing light blue gown, her head shyly tilted sideways, her hand positioned at her throat. Jude wore a tannish, rust-colored suit with a blue shirt. His head is also bowed slightly and his hand outstretched toward Cory. The lovers in the Beautiful Dreamer stained-glass window, dressed much the same, hold similar positions.

"To this day, I'm still amazed at the similarity." Old Mary held the pictures side by side. "Maybe it's not the similarity as much as the coincidence. Or maybe"—she winked in her Old Mary way—"I just marvel at the beauty of this young couple."

Jude and Cory grew red in the face.

Old Mary turned toward Cory. "Originally, you were the sole subject of the rose vision. It was always about you, but then Mr. Jude came along." She gave a wink at Jude as she petted Zoe.

When it looked as though Old Mary was forgetting the second thing she meant to say about the vision, Jude prodded her memory. "If you're getting too tired, we can leave now and pick this up later. But you did say there were two new things to tell us about the rose vision." Jude looked at Old Mary to see if her energies were flagging. *She appears as strong as when we first started speaking, so I don't think our conversation is wearing her down.* "The first thing was that the roses symbolized Cory and me. What's the second thing you wanted to tell us?"

"I didn't forget to say the second thing, though this old brain is getting more forgetful these days. My goodness, I burned the eggs I was boiling when I came home from the hospital the other day. The pan was plum dry, and the bottom of the eggs were charred black. The smell was awful!" She laughed as she recalled her mental slip.

Old Mary grew silent and rolled her eyes to the side as she thought. Zoe, at this point, jumped up on the swing and snuggled contentedly against her thigh. As usual, Zoe seemed to be following their discussion, especially Old Mary's next comment. "The angel,

Angelos, was truly a messenger sent by God." Zoe barked loudly. "Well, I'll be. What do you make of that?" Old Mary put her hand under Zoe's chin then lifted his snout to her face and bent down to talk directly to the dog. "It's as though you understand every- thing, almost as though you desired to look into the affairs of us little humans." She vigorously rubbed Zoe's head. "What's going on inside that noggin of yours?"

They all laughed amid the flowers and hummingbirds of sum- mer. Old Mary knew that she had to bring herself back to the topic at hand, but just how much should she say about it? When she grew silent, Jude and Cory felt that she had finally arrived at the main point, but how to broach it? *Is that her dilemma?* Cory wondered to herself.

Old Mary picked up the Beautiful Window photo again. "Look at the photo of the Foster Beautiful Dreamer window." As Cory held the photo in her hand, Jude and Cory leaned together and studied the picture carefully. "What do we know about the beautiful dreamer?" Old Mary took a small hanky from her apron pocket and dabbed a tear in her eye. "Is she tilting her head in shyness or..." Old Mary paused and looked up at her hummingbird feeder. *I have to say this.* "Or is she dead?"

"Why do you think she's dead?" Cory asked, unable to hide her surprise. "That's a pretty shocking statement!"

"The window itself doesn't contain the clue, but the song does. Do you know it? Do you remember the words? You young folks don't know the lovely songs of yesteryear. That was real music back then. Tarnation, I can't make heads or tails of today's music. I don't even call it music! I hear the young people talking about Roses and Guns and Aeroplane or Aero-something and Bon Joey or some such thing. We didn't have such music in the old days." Jude and Cory laughed as Old Mary botched the names of the late eighties pop rock groups.

"This is real music though this old voice can't sing a note any- more." With that Old Mary commenced to sing the opening lines of "Beautiful Dreamer" in a raspy voice Jude and Cory never forgot.

Beautiful dreamer, wake unto me.
Starlight and dewdrops are waiting for thee.

Mary stopped singing after the initial couplet and spoke. "Why would the lover ask his beloved to awake when the evening stars and dewdrops appear? She should be awake at that hour of the day and not sleeping. That's very strange, wouldn't you say? I won't inflict my awful singing on you. I'll just recite the words." Old Mary shut her eyes to recollect the lyrics and, eyes shut, slowly recited them.

Sounds of the rude world, heard in the day,
Lull'd by the moonlight have all pass'd away.
Beautiful dreamer, queen of my song,
List while I woo thee with soft melody:
Gone are the cares of life's busy throng.
Beautiful dreamer, awake unto me!
Beautiful dreamer, awake unto me!

When Old Mary paused from her recitation, Jude and Cory commended her voice. Though raspy with age, it was still rich and full—"hauntingly tremulous and gorgeously gravelly," Jude noted in his journal.

Jude was not certain what direction Old Mary was moving, but if she was on the verge of hinting that the beautiful dreamer was dead—and thus Cory, by poetic extension, dead as well—he felt the need to protect Cory who remained emotionally fragile from all the recent upheavals. *Playing devil's advocate is probably my best way to go, but how to do so with a frail, old woman who is obviously still getting back on her feet from her recent hospitalization?* Jude began slowly. "I see your point. The beautiful dreamer may no longer be in the land of the living, but there's nothing definitive in the poem's imagery to suggest that. Am I right?" *I'll let it go at that.*

"You don't know the lyrics of the song, do you?" Old Mary's question, without being unkind, was characteristically blunt. "Probably not, so I'll recite part of the second verse."

Beautiful dreamer, beam on my heart,
E'en as the morn on the streamlet and sea;
Then will all clouds of sorrow depart.

Old Mary allowed a moment to slip and then frontally faced Jude and Cory. "If she's merely sleeping, there would be no clouds of sorrow. What would be so sad about that?" Old Mary was cautious of Cory's condition but decided to push her point home. *I must tell them. They have to know the truth and must be forewarned!* "Perhaps the lover is sorrowful because, though he wants her to awake, she is dead and can't. If the beautiful dreamer is dead, and if Cory is the beautiful dreamer, then…"

Unable to complete her point, Mary bowed her head and wiped another tear from her eye. A moment later, she looked wearily in the direction of the sunset and sighed, "'Tattoo cross explodes the game.'" Another pause, another tear. "Explosions bring death." She stopped and looked at Jude. "And clouds of sorrow to lovers." Tears filled her eyes and freely ran down her cheeks. "There's such a thing as being honest enough to speak the truth in love. I love you too much not to tell you how I really feel. I mean, to tell you about this danger." She reached out and firmly grasped Cory's arm. "I think the danger you face is very real!"

Chapter 10

The next day in the mine, Abe Badoane—"in full Machiavellian form," Jude whispered to Cory in the lunchroom—hit on the perfect plan for "toppling the terrible twosome," as Abe noted in his journal.

After waiting all morning for a chance to get Bull Chestnut by himself, Abe finally bumped into him outside one of the picking rooms. "Bull, we need to talk. And soon."

"How about the lunchroom?"

"No, not there. Too many nosey ears and gawking eyes. Meet me outside in the parking lot at lunchtime." Abe's eyes bore into his soul. "Don't forget because your job depends on this."

What does that mean? Abe is no one to mess with. Man, I need to play my cards right! Bull also knew, too, that because he was the one who had wrecked Duke's car, the atmosphere could turn nasty in short order if he was found out. *Just what the hell did I get myself into?*

Abe and Duke met near Bull's car in the parking lot during lunch. "What do you have for me there, old man?" Bull put on a cheerful demeanor, naively attempting to cushion the coming blow. "Want to go with me to see the new *Friday the 13th* movie? I've been waiting for this part 7 for a long time. I love these scary-ass movies!"

Abe smirked at him. "You idiot. No, I'm not going to some freak-show movie! Listen to what I'm about to say, and you'll know why you're smack-dab in the middle of your own *Friday the 13th* movie." Glancing at his watch, he said, "I only have a minute" and then looked at the pitiful wreck of a man groveling in front of him. "Remember how I said the security camera wouldn't pick you up when you made your little trip out of the woods to punch out Duke's taillight and dent his beautiful mag wheel?"

Bull's response was barely audible—a grunt as much as a word. "Yea."

"Well, seems as though I made a slight miscalculation. The security camera picked up your escapade clear as day. You look like a prowler with your helmet pulled over your head." Bull cringed as though slammed with a Mohammed Ali knockout punch. "I've seen the close-ups, and there's no question it's *you*."

"Holy shit!"

"Stand there like a man and quit grabbing yourself." Abe peered at him in disgust. "In the security film, you look like a criminal. Here's the part that will not elevate your joy quota."

"What the hell does that mean?"

"It means this, genius. The managers have asked for the footage because word got back to them that the security tape shows the incident when Duke's Chevy was damaged, and they want to take fast action. Are you listening, you moron? They vow to find the guilty party and bring him to justice. Do you understand the hot water you're in? Your tiny hiney is history if this gets out."

"I'm in damn hot water!"

"Hotter than you realize. I'm talking about the stiff fines, I'm talking about Duke's wrath, I'm talking about character assassination, and I'm talking about the blackballing you'll take from Smitty, Hank, Blassie, Skeeter, Al, and one Hudson Graham Weaver!"

"You're scaring the living daylights out of me, man!"

"Huddy will rip out your spleen and dice it into crochet for the barn swallows—a field day for the birdies!"

"Shut the hell up!"

"The guys will destroy you if they find out. You'll have more than that dirty slicked hair running in your beady eyes."

Abe looked at the shaking man in front of him. *Look at him— hunched forward, shoulders rounded, mouth open in fear. Part of me actually pities him, but to advance the plan, I have to deploy this idiot.* Abe looked across the lot to the open area under the trees where the children congregated and waited for their parents and caregivers at

69

the end of their work day. *Yet I hate being the arch-villain, always destroying, further damning my lost soul, but how to extricate myself from a trap I created?* "It comes down to one question."

"What?"

"Are you going to cooperate with me? If you do, I just might be able to save your ugly arse from swinging on the gallows."

"What do I have to do?"

"I know the guy who's head of security. He's carefully examined the footage of you attacking Duke's car and, in fact, produced blow-ups. The close-ups of your face look like mug shots."

"I've never been so scared!"

"I know this is true because Morley showed me the photos. You look more like Ted Bundy than anyone I've ever seen. I'll start calling you Bull Bundy!"

"Don't say that. I hate that creepy bastard."

"I do too. I've followed him in the news a lot and can't get the names of his victims out of my mind. Joni Lenzi, Lynda Ann Healy, Donna Gail Manson, Susan Elaine Rancourt—she was the brilliant nineteen-year-old if I remember correctly—Brenda Baker."

"Abe, shut up! You're driving me crazy. *I don't want to hear about all the girls he killed. On the other hand, talking about the Bundy murders, sick as they are, sidetracks Abe from dwelling on the freaking mess I'm in.* "How can you remember all those names?" *Go ahead. Keep talking about them instead of me!*

"You haven't heard about photographic minds? I make no effort to remember stuff. It just sticks, but I do agree with you about one thing. Bundy's a sicko. The rat even decapitated ten or twelve of his victims. No wonder the Eleventh Circuit Court has recently ruled against him, so his execution date's been set for January of next year. I heard on the news recently that he's incarcerated in the Raiford Prison in Starke, Florida."

"I know. That's the big thing in the news these days."

Stopping his rant long enough to think about Bundy's victims, Abe looked again at the open area near the woods where he often performed magic tricks for the waiting children and told stories. "I feel so bad for those girls, and I can't imagine the pain their dear parents have endured. What a tragic thing to lose a child, to be separated from the thing you love the most!" Abe bit his lip and looked away. "We'll see how this turns out for nutcase. The SOB deserves to die!"

Like I do!

"I'd murder him myself for killing all those innocent people! I've seen the pictures of his victims, many of them beautiful women."

"That's enough! Don't talk about that disgusting loser. They say he's killed a ton of unlucky women like the ones you mention. I heard on the news that he bit Lisa Levy on the ass so hard that they could actually trace his teeth marks. That helped them convict the sick bastard. And if that wasn't enough, he almost bit her nipple off!"

By now, distracted from his invective against Bull, Abe thought for a moment before responding. "Isn't it sad? Bundy was a man of such potential. It's tragic when a person with something on the ball becomes such an underachiever and derails completely." The contemplative Abe struck his familiar stance—fingers across his chin, index finger on his lips, eyes faraway. "A person interviewed on TV said Bundy was 'kind, solicitous, and empathetic.' How awful that this bright man came to such a tragic end!"

"I don't know what those words mean. Solic-something and empa-whatever."

"They mean he was a nice guy, well liked, and popular. He's bright too, with an IQ of 124, and had even been admitted to law school. Do you realize how many points higher that is than your IQ, you living, breathing, walking dumbass?"

"Don't make fun of me, Abe. I'm feeling bad enough as it is." *I'm getting sick to the stomach and need this bullshit to cease right now!* "Tell me where things stand with me."

Abe returned to the topic at hand. "Here are the unpleasant facts. The security head will turn the footage over to the personnel manager and the vice-president of operations. The circuit court in this joint will definitely rule against you and take stiff action. That's where things stand!"

"Holy hell, I'm a goner!"

"They want the footage immediately. Here's your only ray of light, you Ted Bundy of the mushroom mine!" *You're as worthless as the weeds growing in the asphalt cracks under your feet.* "You disgust me, but if you do what I say, I'll arrange to get rid of the film completely. I think I can buy off Morley Spencer and his boss and, in the process, save your unforgivably, ridiculously, unalterably sorry behind. Do you understand, you butt plug? Quit playing with yourself!"

"What do I have to do?"

Abe put his arm on Bull's shoulder and strolled toward the mine entrance, whispering the whole time into his ear. Moments later, he patted him on the back and said, "Do exactly as I've told you." Abe, by now in the presence of others, bade him goodbye with that hearty if fake smile.

"I can't thank you enough, Abe, but what if this plan mucks up too?" On his way back into the mine, Bull whispered to himself, *What in the hell did I get myself into? I hate doing this, but it's the only way I can save my sorry behind!*

Chapter 11

Pastor Gabriel perfectly summarized Bull Chestnut's situation at the Bible study that week during his examination of Esther. At one point, he keyed on the disturbing reality that sinful people like Haman, "whom the god of this world has blinded," eventually reach the point where they feel no shame, guilt, and remorse.

The pastor cited two texts. "In Ephesians 4:19, the Apostle Paul describes people who, because of the blindness of their evil hearts, arrive at a place of being 'past feeling.'"

Thinking of a few of the students in his classes who have seemingly little moral compunction about anything, Jude whispered to Cory, "They're essentially aimless, lost souls, adrift on an ocean of postmodern turbulence." When Pastor Gabe paused for a moment to check his notes, Jude quietly continued his aside: "It seems as though their highest goal in life is to wallow in an anesthetized state which numbs their psychic pain."

"I think you just described a certain Bull Chestnut to a tee," Cory whispered, "since the guys are laying for him. Talk about a tormented soul!"

"Yes, the god of this world has blinded him. I'd say that's a perfect description."

Finding his place in his notes, Pastor Gabriel described such lost souls with another Pauline verse. "Paul says in chapter 4 of 1 Timothy that some people have 'their own conscience seared as with a hot iron.'"

Like the Ephesians phrase, this one also grabbed Jude who saw in the verse another perfect assessment of Bull Chestnut. Reflecting on Pastor Gabriel's point, Jude again whispered to Cory, "How sad to go through life with a seared conscience like Bull…and some of my students too! They're powerless to follow their soul's inner promptings and track back to the light. Can you imagine such horror?"

What Jude, Cory, and Pastor Gabriel did not realize was the extent to which the biblical verses accurately described Abe Badoane as well. Abe's journal entry, prompted by his Ted Bundy allusions earlier in the day, addressed the intriguing parallel.

Abe's Journal Entry:

I've been thinking all evening of what I said to Bull today about the sadness of Ted Bundy, a man of real talent and ability who nevertheless settled for such appalling underachievement. Half brain-dead, Bull Chestnut would not have had the slightest inkling that I was talking about myself. Surely not since the intelligence of this man, not "the most gifted mind on the planet" in Duke's sarcastic words, processes so ineptly the incoming sense stimuli that rattles in his peon brain like an mini-asteroid in a vast universe.

Ted Bundy, on the other hand, was capable of so much. As was I. Ted Bundy totally wasted his life. As have I. Instead of helping others and edifying those whose paths he crossed, he destroyed them. As have I. Why did Ted Bundy give his pearls to the swine? As have I. Why did he kill Caryn Campbell, Julie Cunningham, Denise Lynn Oliverson, Melanie Cooley, Shelley Robertson, and Melissa Smith? Why am I killing Bull Chestnut and Duke Manningham? Why did I destroy my beloved wife? And why do I now have Cory Mohney and Jude Hepler in my crosshairs?

Like Ted Bundy, I killed off—in Lincoln's memorable phrase—the better angel of my nature. What a wretched human being you are, Ted Bundy! Poor Ted Bundy. What will happen to him come January? I wish I could have reached you, Mr. Bundy, and touched your sick soul. And I wish I could have touched your sick soul, Abe Badoane. What a sick psycho you are too! Poor Abe Badoane! Malcolm says in *Macbeth*, "Angels are bright still, though the brightest fell." Well, in my opinion, angels are not very bright on this forsaken earth. At least not in my sick world!

Because I can't stop, the destruction, alas, will continue. If I have killed off the better angel of my nature, then, tragically, I'm forever lost and helpless to change. A villain I am, and a villain I'll stay. As Hamlet says, "I set it down That one may smile, and smile, and be a villain." Or in my case, a sneaky snake! Yet like Claudius, I cry for the light of grace and love and forgiveness and peace—yes, sweet but ever elusive peace!

End of Abe's journal

When Abe Badoane returned to the mine after his talk with Bull, he went directly to the bolting crew and, feigning a random pass through that area, stopped for a fast hello. His reception was markedly cool from these men who, before the debacle in Pittsburgh, hailed him as the wise father figure of the mines. He flashed his smile as in times past, but it brought little response. *The men are on to me. No doubt about it!* "I just stopped by to see how the bolting's coming along. Do you know the slated opening date for this new section?"

The foreman, Bert Ishman, updated him on their progress. "This whole section is done, and we're satisfied that it's completely safe. In fact, they're installing the trays in a couple days. We're just securing the roof in those two back rooms." Bert gestured behind him. "The one room has been a bit of a problem because that's where the previous cave-in occurred. Surely you with your memory remember that disaster? It was the worst one we ever had. I forget how many were killed."

"It was awful."

"We're getting close now." He started walking away as it was time to return to work. "But this time, we're making sure it's absolutely safe!"

"Thanks for the information. Much appreciated!" Abe mounted his shop mule and drove off in the dark.

That evening, while Cory was busy with housework, Jude went to his grandpa's study and read through his journal. Digging into his grandpa's mind—"touching his soul," Jude called it—was a favorite pastime. He was particularly drawn to the entries near the end of his life when Jeremiah Wakefield had completed the manuscript of his novel which awaited publication. Jude leaned back in Grandpa's seat and ran his fingers across the cracked leather of his ancient desk chair. *The hand of the great one rested right here!* Perusing the desk and its treasured contents, he reverently opened the journal to read.

Jeremiah Wakefield's journal:

It's been a long struggle, decades in fact, but at last it's done. A writer never knows if what he's written is any good, and that's especially the case this time. I just don't know if I've said what I wanted to, but I'll have to be satisfied. I say with David, "My tongue is the pen of a ready writer" [Psalm 45:1], and with Solomon "Of making many books there is no end" [Ecclesiastes 12:12]. May my pen have captured the thoughts of my mind, and may this old and weary world bear this one more book I thrust upon it. World, I give it to you. Are you ready for it? Can you handle it? I know what I face, for "the poor man's wisdom is despised, and his words are not heard" [Ecclesiastes 9:16]. World, you will see George Washington in this novel as you've never seen him before!

When I mentioned these points to Pastor Gabriel, he quoted Amos 7:10 on the spot: "The land is not able to bear all the words." How that describes my feeling! How will the world bear the words of this humble country man? When I made this point to Clarence Bowser, he said, "A man is not a prophet in his own country. You will get your message to the world. Fear not, Jeremiah. He who began a good work in you will complete it." How good that made me feel!

To you, little Jude, I mantle your shoulders with the blessings of God. I see in your bright eyes the hope of the future. How my heart thrills when you are near to me! Your face lights up when I tell you stories or read the Bible to you. It's as though you transport yourself completely to the distant places described in the writing, as though you're totally immersed in it, as though your ingesting life at every wide-open pore of your little body. My Little Jedidiah, you are the bud of childhood, which I know will blossom one glorious day in the garden of the future. You remind me of an epitaph I once saw on the grave of a young child in New Orleans. I don't remember the dear girl's name, but I do recall the epitaph:

This lovely bud so young and fair,
Called home by early doom,
Just came to show how sweet a flower
In paradise would bloom.

That is a perfect description of you, Little Jude, but our prayer is that we may see the bloom here and not in heaven. My hope rests on you.

But, oh, Abe, you poor man. You poor, poor man.

A later passage from Jeremiah Wakefield's journal puzzled Jude even more than the enigmatic reference to Abe Badoane:

Job says in his lugubrious book that "the thing I greatly feared has come upon me, and what I dreaded has happened to me" [3:25]. No truer words have ever been spoken. The novel I started decades ago at Malibu II cabin near Clear Creek State Park at Sigel, PA, is now complete, and yet I live in constant fear that it will disappear and that something will happen to the manuscript before it's published. What should I do? Should I hide it? Why am I feeling this way?

Is it merely "anticipatory anxiety"—I think that's Frankl's phrase in *Man's Search for Meaning*; I never went back to check—or is it something more? Am I suffering from dementia? Or the early stages of Alzheimer's? I have become forgetful of late, and my once sharp mind—always remembering dates, and Bible verses, and phone numbers—now lets me down too often. Why the horrible fear of late? Am I fighting demonic oppression? I definitely war against evil of some sort!

Whatever it is, I can't get past the feeling that someone or some force is trying to steal this manuscript. I had a vivid dream of it recently, and in my dream evil people were trying to destroy it! Lord, help me, please! I realize that whatever is not of faith is sin and that the just shall live by faith, and I know too that we believers must trust that You reward those who call upon You. But why then do I fear, and doubt, and tremble exceedingly?

I have obsessed over David's words in Psalm 6: "I am weary with my groaning; All night I make my bed to swim; I drench my couch with my tears, my eye wastes away because of grief" [vs. 6]. My cry is that of the distraught man in Mark 9:24: "Lord, I believe; help thou mine unbelief." My unbelief! Oh, how that verse turns my eyes into my very soul. Lord, where can I hide this poor book so I can protect it, this slight little effort? Should I hide It, or is that the response of fear? Lord, you know this novel is for Your glory, a work that, I trust, will honor You. Lord, help me please!

End of Jeremiah's Journal

As Jude withdrew from Jeremiah's study, three thoughts obsessed him. *Why did Grandpa experience such a morbid fear? What was the basis of it, and why did he feel led to bury the novel? The second more fleeting but still haunting concern is my name. Why Jedidiah instead of Judah? Was this a simple mistake by an aging, forgetful man? After all, there are similarities between the two names, but what if the use of my middle name was intentional? If so, why? Third, what do I make of Grandpa's reference to Abe as this "poor, poor man"? Whatever does that mean? Did Grandpa know Abe's circumstances so well that he could refer to him in such a familiar way? What mysteries!*

Chapter 12

After a period of rumination, Jude could stand the frustration no longer and picked up the phone to call Pastor Gabriel. *Maybe Gabe will have some insight on these matters.*

"You just caught me, Jude," Gabriel said moments later. "Martha and some of the women are knitting this evening, and I was just headed for a ride down Johnston Road. Want to ride along? It's been a while since we've had a good tete a tete!"

"I'd love to. I haven't been down that road for ages."

"Excellent!"

"The scenery along the creek is beautiful."

When Pastor Gabriel mentioned Grandpa's death a short while later as they walked by the stream, Jude reflexively hid, his natural and engrained response, which he learned in childhood and which he resorted to as frequently as Cory. "I wish I could remember what Grandpa said when he died," Jude lamely commented and then deftly changed the subject. "Did you know that the Pirates' first baseman, Sid Bream, was born in Carlyle, PA? He's having a pretty good year, but it was his '86 season that I remember best. He had 166 assists at first base that year to set an MLB record."

"Very interesting, Jude. Thanks for enlightening me about one of the Pirates' exciting players, but it's obvious to me that you're deflecting the topic at hand. Cory agrees with me that this is one of your seasoned strategies." Pastor Gabriel picked up a pebble and threw it into the stream, pursuing the subject as quickly as the pebble stabbed the water. "Possibly there's a way for you to remember Jeremiah's dying words. To this point you think you've tried, but have you really? I ask that kindly, Jude, because the world really needs to see that man's excellent novel; and you're the only one entrusted with the clue to find it."

"I agree with everything you're saying. No argument there."

Sensing the difficulty of the subject, Pastor Gabriel proceeded gently. "Have you ever made this a matter of focused prayer? This topic is obviously worthy of heartfelt prayer and fasting too. In my book, it's time we did so together. You know the promise of Scripture. God answers the prayers where two or three are gathered together in His name—Matthew 18:20."

"I've heard Cory cite that verse on occasion."

Pastor stopped walking to watch the swimming minnows, and then the two men meandered along the stream a short distance. "Let's covenant right now to stop running and start rummaging through that computer brain of yours. Yes, I know there's lots of data up there—oceans of it including details about the Pittsburgh Pirates— but we need to locate one little fact: the few frantic utterances of a dying man in a barn. Are you up to this formidable challenge?"

Jude took in the pastor's comforting words, those words fitly spoken, "like apples of gold in settings of silver" [Prov. 25:11], as he later wrote in his journal. *I know that the key to the lock lies secretly buried in my very deep subconscious.* "Yes, I'm game. To be honest, I'd like nothing better."

The walk along the valley floor was refreshing for both of them. The steep hills rose sharply upward from the stream which meandered along the bottom of the ravine. At the top of this cleft, which had been cut out eons ago when the water slashed down this ravine in torrents, the fields, "like surging ocean swells," glided along to the distant rolling hills. Vividly picturing them, Jude remembered that, as a little boy, Grandpa had often brought him and Cory to the farm at the top of this gulley. *Cory and I rode horses out across these very fields in those bygone days, the happy days that are so more.*

A tear came to Jude's eye. *Tennyson, you said it so well in "Tears, Idle Tears":*

Tears, idle tears, I know not what they mean,
Tears from the depth of some divine despair
Rise in the heart, and gather to the eyes,
In looking on the happy autumn fields,
And thinking of the days that are no more.

Tears of divine despair rise in my heart and gather to my eyes as I think on these happy fields and that glorious past and that wonderful father figure who, to this day, glistens in my mind like the amber gleams of a glorious sunset. Grandpa, Grandpa!

Although these were the late sixties, reruns of the 1950s westerns—Hopalong Cassidy, Gene Autry, the Cisco Kid, Ponderosa, Gabby Hays, Bonanza, Have Gun—Will Travel, and many others—often played in the Wakefield home when Jude was a little boy. Grandpa and he watched them by the hour. As a young lad Jude felt, while riding Grandpa's horse, that he was galloping across the plains of the Old West, the wind blowing his cowboy hat and flopping the Roy Rogers gun in his holster. As the young boy sped along, he imagined the white smoke from the shooting cowboy guns, the mining towns, the stampeding herds of buffalos, El Paso in its heyday, the streets of Tombstone, Wyatt Earp and the shootout at the OK Corral, and the westward-bound wagon trains. *Yes, the happy autumn fields and the days that are no more!*

He even remembered the name of the horse on which he rode—Bullet. As a little boy, Joey Mohney also rode Jeremiah's horse and enjoyed the experience so much that when he later obtained his own horse, he named him Bullet. How Jude had loved that horse, loved those simple days of yesteryear! Looking up the ravine, he again thought of Grandpa. He could see him standing by the barn and the two horses, Bullet and Bonnet. "You can ride him, little Jude. Bullet's safe and gentle. Don't give in to your fear but beat it. These are the experiences you'll remember for a lifetime. You'll recall this very moment forever."

Grandpa—now there's something I really loved! Jude flashed forward to that fateful day a year or so later when he fell from the high barn loft—flailing, thrashing, tumbling through midair. He veered quickly from the stream, his lips pursed in anger, his face white.

Later that evening, Gabriel called Charles on the phone to inquire about the progress he had recently made on "the Jude matter," as the two of them had come to call it. Gabriel informed Charles of the walk he had taken with Jude along the stream by Johnston Road. "He has a desire to confront the subject in a way I've never seen before," Gabriel began. "At least that's a healthy step in the right direction. He doesn't appear to be running from it as he always did, at least not as much."

"That's a notable beginning."

Gabriel slid his finger along a silver cross he had picked up in Jerusalem. "I'm convinced that Jude wants to beat his fear as completely as Cory has defeated hers. Here's my opinion. I think that Cory's confronting her fear during the production of *Hamlet* has given him impetus to do the same."

"Absolutely fascinating, Gabe. Surely you're on to something here."

"He knows the fate of Jeremiah's novel is in his hands, and that's become a very heavy burden for him to carry. Based on the extended portions I read earlier, I'd say the novel is very fine indeed."

"We both need time to reflect on the Jude matter and plan our strategy. For now, that's where things stand," Charles said, winding up their conversation. "Since I have nothing else to add, except that we have to come up with a plan to help Jude ferret furiously through those fertile frontal lobes."

"You're not a professor of poetry by any chance?" Gabriel said with that twinkle in the eye his congregation loved so much. "You and your alliteration! Good night, Chuck. Rest well."

The matter on the surface was simple, but its resolution was not. The facts as Charles reflected on them over an evening cup of chamomile tea were simple. *My good friend Jeremiah Wakefield fell to his death in a barn in front of the helpless and traumatized little Jude. Cory witnessed this terrible tragedy but chose to run and hide from it, commencing the pattern of running from any and all circumstances that reminded her of that terrible betrayal of little Jude. On a stage in*

Pittsburgh, Cory had recreated the scene of Jeremiah's death during our Hamlet *dress rehearsal, thereby frontally facing and obtaining closure in her own mind at last. In a manner of speaking, she came out of hiding that day, learned to "put on Christ instead of fear," as she said to Gabe and me later, and acted with an Esther-like boldness.*

Unlike Cory, Jude has not faced the trauma of his past. Granted, the tragedy was much worse for him for three reasons: in his mind he and only he was culpable, he was the only one present in the barn with Jeremiah, and he was the only one who attempted to save his grandfather with his desperate grasp at thin air. I agree with Gabe that Jude wants to face his fear and end once and for all his hide-and-seek game with the past.

As Charles continued to massage his brow in deep contemplation, he knew he was face-to-face with the question to end all questions. *How to make Jude root through the trillions of synapses and the tens of thousands of words stored in his capacious mind and locate the precious and hidden handful—Jeremiah Wakefield's dying utterance— the discovery of which could lead to finding the lost manuscript. Jude, this matter has tied you to the stake. You cannot fly, but like Shakespeare's pitiful Macbeth, you are the bear lashed to the stake which the dogs of the past will devour. It is imperative that you cut yourself free while there is time. Remember the verse which you said Duke was stirred by in Heinz Chapel, "If the truth sets you free, you will be free indeed." You too need to be set free from this weighty burden.*

A number of searches were going on at this time in the Jude and Cory saga in that many of the principals in the drama were caught up with a variety of quests. Cory and Jude wanted to know about the fearsome explosion, the eagle/angel connection, and the mysterious details of the rose legend, especially as revealed in Cory's French-worded, rhymed riddle. Jude's search for a buried novel and extrication from the current morass was as complicated as the intermeshed corridors in a limestone quarry in western Pennsylvania.

Duke's search, on the other hand, was for a new beginning, a way to free himself from his self-sabotaging tendencies, which had botched his life so completely. Tina searched for a way to reunite with Duke and eventually marry him, since the shame of not having a father for her son grew in her mind like the blight on the elm trees of main streets in neighboring towns.

Charles's quest was in the main psychological. Might there be some way in which he could help Jude locate the buried novel? *I think this novel is an undoubted masterpiece.* Gabriel's quest, predictably, took the shape of a caring and loving shepherd. What was the best way he could teach his flock pertinent lessons about the events of that crazy summer, and, more to the point, what were those lessons?

Abe's search—how to deal with his abiding enmity toward Jude and Cory—was of tragic dimension, since his growing desire for lethal vengeance, if acted upon, could completely destroy their lives and his too.

Bull's search, in some ways the most pathetic of all, was for a way out of his claustrophobic, Abe-smothering, nightmare life. Even Duke comprehended this, as he shared with Huddy one evening after work. "Dumbass Bull is pitiful. The guy's become a total disgrace. Even I see that!"

Which of these searches would dominate this quiet western-Pennsylvania community, and which of them, if any, would end successfully?

Chapter 13

The next day, Duke, walking out of the lunch room toward his shop mule, bumped into Bull Chestnut. What neither realized was that mystery man himself, Abe Badoane, out of view around the corner, squeezed himself into the wall to eavesdrop. The tension between Duke and Bull was instant. Before he knew what he was doing, Duke reverted to his old nature and squared off to fight Bull on the spot. "Huddy, Blassie, and the others tell me you're the one who demolished my car. I ought to smash in your ugly face right here, you freaking dumb bastard!"

His face white and his hands trembling, Bull backed away. "I didn't do anything, Duke! Honest!"

Duke started for him and was ready to take a swing when Pastor Gabriel's words from Wednesday's Bible study suddenly leaped into his mind. *Gabe said something about a man slow to wrath having great understanding. Pastor has spoken to me at length about the way a soft answer turns away wrath* [Proverbs 15:1]. *Those words seep into my brain like scalding lava! And that other verse Pastor told me to memorize and Teenzie beat on me till I did: "Whoever guards his mouth and tongue keeps his soul from trouble"* [Proverbs 21:23]. *Keeps his soul from trouble. Keeps his soul from trouble!* Drawing closer to Bull, Duke was inches from his face. "You did it, didn't you? Tell me!" Fearful of being crushed by one of those massive fists, Bull lifted his arm to shield his head. "I can tell by your guilt that you did!"

"I didn't do it! It wasn't me!"

Duke vice-locked his fist on Bull's shoulder and violently pulled him around so that Bull faced him squarely. Then squeezing his jaws between his thumb and fingers, Duke contorted Bull's lips into a freakish shape. "Answer me! Why did you do it?" *"The heart of the righteous studies how to answer"* [Proverbs 15:28]. *Man, I have to think about what I'm doing here!* "If I weren't turning over a new leaf, I'd punch your lights out right here!"

"Please don't hurt me!"

Duke paused for a moment and bit his lip. *I ought to tear him limb from limb, yet Pastor and Cory's gentle words of love swirl in my mind like that Southeast Asia typhoon I saw on TV. "The forcing of wrath produces strife." I've allowed that to happen across my entire life— always responding in anger, flying off the handle, firing like a loose cannon at anything in my path. Pastor Wyant says I can choose to stop that pattern and that it's a choice I simply have to make.*

Around the corner, Abe squeezed himself into the wall and breathlessly listened. *What's Duke going to do? Smash Bull's face into the wall? My heart's pounding in my chest like a Pileated Woodpecker whacking away at a dead tree!*

Then an astonishing thing occurred. Duke unclenched his hands, took a deep breath, and slowly backed away. "You're one lucky SOB." He gave Bull a slight push and took another step back. "I'm going to let you live." *I've always been quick-tempered—"emotion-dominated," Jude called it—and Pastor's goodbye words when we parted at the church door whirl in my messed-up head. "Love is the better way, Mr. Manningham, which you can choose. Believers opt for a better way, the path of Christ-like love. Here's another verse I didn't give you before: "The discretion of a man makes him slow to anger, and his glory is to overlook a transgression"* [Proverbs 19:11]. "Yea, you can walk."

A faint smile came to Duke's lips as he marveled at his own transformation. *Damn it, I really am making progress at last!* He paused for a moment beside the quivering Bull and said, "I'm going to let you live. *"When a man's ways please the Lord, He makes even his enemies to be at peace with him"* [Proverbs 16:7]. I'll even do you one better than that." He put his arm around Bull's shoulder. "I forgive you, even though you don't deserve it." *Pastor said whoever has no rule over his own spirit is like a broken-down city without walls. Control your spirit, Duke, starting with this worthless rat!* "You are such a disgusting human being."

"I know I am."

"But just tell me so I know for sure. You did it, right?" Bull nodded his head. Duke paused momentarily, looked him in the eye, and then shook his hand. "You know what?"

"What?"

"You too can change. You don't have to be such a miserable wretch." Patting the top of Bull's helmet, Duke walked away.

Bull gasped for air. "Well, I'll be damned!" Bull turned and high-fived the wall. "Ape man allowed me to walk! I'm going to live!"

He spoke loudly enough that Abe, hearing every syllable, put his head against the wall and shut his eyes. *Duke's vengeance was the centerpiece of my ploy. Now what?* His mind aflame, Abe aborted his errand to the shop and drove off into the darkness.

That plan's down the rotten tube, Spoiled by Bull the dumbass rube. Love you say's the better way? Guess I'll try that another day!

That evening, Abe sat in his study and wrote in his journal of the event. That done, he flipped to a worn passage in volume one of his journal, written when a little boy.

Abe's journal (composed when he was a young boy):

> We sat on the kouch in his cabbin. We come to look at pick-ures of his hunting trips, and they was taken out West. I think Wyeoming. That's why I went with him. To see the large rackes too. He said if I was good I could handel his Civil War riffle. His great great grandpap was a soulder in the Sivil War. He served in a Pennsvania regment. I think the 103rd. I'm not sure. He told me his grandpappy left Armstrong County in 1862. I remember the year cuz I'm gud on dates. He served under a kernel and I dont remember the name. Maybe Kernal Lehman.
>
> He showed me his rifel. I got to hold it. He sed this rifel had ben in many batles. It had niks on it and things like that. He sat real close to me as I tuched it. He said his grandpappy fought at Bull Run, Fare Oakes, Malvern something and other places. I

cant remember all the names. I liked his storeys. He sed we can be good frends. He slid closser.

He pikked up a large photo alblum. He sed one of the photos was the big boy up on the wall. He pointed to a mule dere. What a big anmal. It was great hanging above the door. I liked it. He shoed me an elk he shotted up in Canda. He called it his monster. It was real big. Monster was a giante. He sed it was big like this and pointed to hisself. I looked away. I dont know why he did that. He sed I could kepe looking at picktures. But only if he put his arm arund me.

He sed he was hot. He kickt off his shoes. Then he took off his jeans. My face got red. I looked away. He told me I dint look comfterbel. It was hot. There was a big fire. He lifted waits. His mussles was very big. He rubbed himself a lot. I dint like that. But I liked the animal piksures cuz they were nice. His hand brushed my thigh. He said scuse me it was an acident. It kept happning. He turned the pages of the photo alblum. I tried to leave. I really liked the mountted anmals.

From a later journal entry:

The whole birth experience was horrific. Even though Freda was sickly, we were not getting along during her pregnancy—not "the quintessence of harmony and blissful joy," as I joked, especially the last couple months of it. Several things had happened in those days, one serendipitous eventuality after another, I guess I could call them: her deteriorating health, that bastard Claypoole taking my teaching job out from under my nose at Grove City, which I fully deserved and he didn't, and my chronic knee problem, which flared up and gave me severe wound flashbacks of my childhood trauma. It all came to a head and made me revert to the old rage-and-fury cycle, but like a caged monster, I was blinded to my evil. Or to be honest, I did know it, but could not stop my transgressive behavior, sealing myself off completely from the terrible truth of what I had become and what I was doing to myself and especially Freda.

I loved Freda with all my heart. I'd have done anything for that woman, and she loved me too. We were perfect for each other. She was smart and caring, and the sex was good too. Why then did I treat her so terribly? After JJ died, I took all my fury out on her. The painful truth is obvious and I won't hide from it: she died of a broken heart, the ravages of cruel hate which I unleashed on her, more than the ravages of the cancer that relentlessly spread through her little frail body—cell by cell, icy stare by icy stare, unkind word by unkind word, cruel act by cruel act.

How I miss her and little JJ! He was the cutest baby. I remember the obstetrics nurse saying that he had the most perfect features of any baby she had ever helped birth. Quoting Exodus, she referred to the infant Moses: "He was a beautiful baby" [2:2]. When she lifted JJ out of the crib, she said, "Moses must have been a perfect baby like this!" and she gave him to me. How I loved that little boy. My son, my son!

End of Abe Badoane's Journal Entry

Chapter 14

The next day at work, two unprecedented events happened in the life of Abe Badoane. He had been drinking the night before, heavily in fact, and the smell of whiskey was evident.

"So I guess Abe's embarrassment in Pittsburgh has pushed him to drink," one of the pickers whispered to a small group.

"I know. I could smell it on him as soon as he came in the lounge this morning."

"I'd say the fiasco in Pittsburgh made Abe a little too cozy with the bottle."

The other phenomenon was also without precedent. Some of the women openly began to taunt Abe. The emotions of most of the women toward him oscillated frequently in those turbulent days. Most of the time they paid him the respect normally shown an older person, especially a man of his kind demeanor and extraordinary intelligence, but across the years that deference had often been laced with fear and apprehension. Abe was a powerful man to whom they usually cowered, since it was a given that he controlled the underground world of the mine and was never to be crossed. More than one person had learned the hard way that he was, in the language of the mine employees, "not to be messed with."

Thus, the recent ridicule was without precedent but steeled by his recent humiliation and the instantaneous leveling it caused, a handful of brash and heartless employees began to vent years of pent-up frustration.

"Bested by Hepler the college prof, eh, Abe? Who'd have thunk it!"

"Hey, Abe, they said your line in the *Hamlet* play about the light—what was it? 'Give me some light!'—was great."

"With the condition you're in, you could use some light!"

Digging his fingernails into the palms of his hands, Abe glared at the women, but still the barbs continued. *I hate you worthless women!*

"I don't know which vapor is worse—the fume of anger from your eyes or the booze from your mouth!" another intelligent woman jabbed.

The women laughed uproariously as Abe slammed the baskets of freshly picked mushrooms into the bin. He recklessly drove off to the packhouse screaming over his shoulder, "I'll be revenged on all of you!"

At lunch a day or so later, Jude and Cory sat beside one of the workers on the bolting crew. "When is the new section scheduled for completion?" Jude inquired.

"In another day or two," he explained. "It's all done but the two back rooms. It took us a while to shore up that rear room where the cave-in occurred, but we're nearly finished now. You want to take a ride back there with your little sweetie, huh? I know about you young hot lovers." He gave Cory and Jude a wink. "I've heard what goes on in some of those back rooms."

"That's another place we can explore soon," Jude whispered to Cory after he departed, "but just to see and not use as a place for extra-curricular activities as Mr. Mind-in-Gutter suggests!"

"Talk about a guy with a one-track mind!"

Seated nearby, Bull Chestnut, like others in the vicinity, was close enough to hear this conversation. Unlike the other diners, however, he carefully listened to the exchange though he feigned interest in the banal chatter around him. "The Pirates' current winning streak has been really good," Blassie said, "and it's really being helped by Van Slyke's .290 batting average."

"Yep, you're right," Smitty added. "I follow the stats too." He spoke about the Pirates more often than any of the other employees and held the record for the highest number of games attended by any mine employee three years in a row.

At the end of the table, a couple of the more informed women spoke of politics. "I heard in the news that Reagan's Attorney General, Ed Meese, ordered Joseph Doherty deported to the UK."

"That's a pretty strange deal!"

Of all this chatter, Bull knew that Abe would be interested in only one piece of news: Jude and Cory were planning to visit the soon-to-be-completed new room. Immediately from the lunchroom, Bull hurtled his way through the mine to Abe's crew. *I think Abe will destroy the security footage of the day I wrecked Duke's car. After all, that SOB was the master-mind behind it, but you can't ever be sure about sneaky snake, so I just don't know what he'll do!*

It was just like Abe to keep him in a perpetual state of emotional bondage, since that had become one of Abe's successful weapons in his arsenal of control strategies. As Abe ruminated to himself, *It can be used opportunistically to accomplish a variety of purposes.*

"Hey, boss," Bull said moments later to Abe. "I just overheard something you might find useful. Jude and Cory are planning to visit the new section of the mine when it opens. I don't know why I thought you'd find that useful, but I'm telling you anyway."

"I do find that useful, and you do too."

"I could freaking care less what they visit, when they do it, and even if they get it together when they do—ha!"

"No, you care a lot. You care very much indeed. You want me to show you how much you care?"

"What are you talking about? I won't be near the damn place."

"Listen to me, genius. It seems as though the security camera videotape was already passed on to management by the time I got back to Morley Spencer. You know the footage I mean, the footage that shows you beating the crap out of one Duke Manningham's prized '57 Chevy, that marvel of Detroit engineering, that heralded icon of classic automobiles."

"Holy shit!"

"Dedicated employee that he is, Morley has already given the footage to Felix Lockard in the personnel office. No doubt Felix your fearsome foe is probably watching it right now. All things shall be brought to their destined end, and yours, my friend, is not going to be happy."

"Holy mother!"

"It's worse than that as you'll soon be flipping burgers at McDonald's in another day or two."

"My dad will kill me. He says I'm the biggest loser he's ever seen." *That's all that sorry louse has ever called me.*

Wonder why he'd say such an unkind thing. Now there's a mystery! "You have one ray of light, you moron. I know Felix, and if I can get him to destroy the tape before he passes it to the brass, I might be able to save your pitiful arse, but that will take a lot of jawing on my part—Abe Badoane at the height of his loquacious lucidity." Abe paused, drew close to Bull, and looked him in the eye. "Jawing like that comes with a price."

"What do I have to do, and why don't you speak English?"

"When the time's right, I'll give you an easy job."

"I hope so!"

"You know the new room where the bolting crew's working?"

"Yepper."

"The warning light outside is on red because they're still working in that area. Are you following me, you mental midget, you who hold the world's record for the most infinitesimally small cranium, you cognitively-challenged dwarf?

"Why don't you speak English?"

"Because you don't understand that language either. I want you to change the sign to green and take down the "No trespassing" signs, so people, including Jude and Cory, will think the coast is clear for spelunking.

"What the hell is 'spell lungcat'? I can never understand your freaking words."

"Spe-lunk-ing is cave exploration, you ignominious, ignoble ignoramus. You know the temporary support poles that are bracing the unbolted ceiling sections in that room? I'm talking about the first one you see when you enter the room."

"Yea."

"Quit playing with yourself and listen to what I'm saying. Knock that center one loose, so it's slanted and not giving solid support, but don't make it obvious that it's tilted."

"I know what you're up to. You're trying to suck Jude and Cory into a cave-in, aren't you? You're as bad as a-hole Ted Bundy."

"I'd never do that. But a few little chunks of flaking limestone will give them the scare they more than deserve. I want to get Jude Hepler out of this place once and for all." Abe extended his arm and held Bull's chin in his hand. "By the way, who are you, piss ant, to question me?"

"Ouch! Don't do that. Earlier Duke corkscrewed my face like a lump of clay. It still hurts! But what if we start a real cave-in? What if more than a few pieces of limestone fall?" *Holy hell, here I am questioning Abe! I know I crossed the line!* He nervously swayed on his feet as he spoke.

"We won't, not even close."

"Isn't that the room where the bad cave-in happened? I think that's the room where my old man's best friend, Melvin Grafton, was killed. He lived in West Winfield."

"Look. You do as I say. That roof's like solid limestone. I checked it out myself, and I've talked to the bolting crew. They tell me the room is completely safe, and there are just a few places where a couple small chips might let loose if given some assistance."

"Are we sure?"

"There will be no 'cave-in.' You're just going to encourage a couple small falling rocks to scare the dickens out of them!"

"I don't know, Abe. I don't like the smell of this."

"Who cares what you like and don't like. Are you a man? Just do as you're told. I sure wouldn't want the brass to see the footage of this little episode." Abe took out a couple of photos from his shirt pocket and unfolded them. "Let me see what we have here. Oh, yes, it happens to be pictures of you at Duke's car." Abe dangled two five-by-seven photos of Bull's smashing Duke's car in front of his face.

"Holy hell!" Bull screamed hysterically.

"What a tragic development if these ended up in the hands of our ever-astute administrators. What we have here are incriminating mug shots." Abe carefully returned the pictures to his pants pocket. "When I give you the go-ahead, just tell Jude and Cory that you've noticed that the no-trespassing signs have been take down and the room's finished. That's it. They'll take it from there."

"Do you think he'll take her there? Get it? *Take* her?"

"Get out of here, pea brain. Stupidity like yours is scandalous. It's criminal. In fact, the Pennsylvania legislature ought to pass a law against it when they're in session this fall. Maybe I'll have my good friend, PA congressman Henry Livengood, introduce such legislation. He's a powerful man in the Harrisburg legislature and chairs the Legislative Budget and Finance Committee. If unconscionable lunacy like yours was outlawed, then I wouldn't have to contaminate my brain with such colossal idiocy." Abe screamed at the top of his lungs, "Get out of here!"

Chapter 15

Abe Badoane and Bull were not the only people currently looking at photos. Shortly after Abe had spoken to Bull, Pastor Wyant noted in his visitation log that he had stopped by Old Mary's apartment. An entry in his journal indicated that as he approached her porch to see her, she was looking at a photo album while sitting on her swing. When he walked toward her, he observed that the familiar church directory lay open beside the photo album.

Pastor Gabriel described the occasion in his journal.

Pastor Gabriel Wyant's Journal:

When she went into the house to get a glass of apple juice and some of her legendary snickerdoodle cookies, I was alone for a couple minutes on the porch, seated in the chair beside the swing. The photo album was open to some pictures of people that were taken a couple decades before. Two of them, I could not help but notice, were of the young Abe Badoane. I did not pick up the album to take a close look since it was not my place to snoop, but I clearly recognized the youthful, handsome Abe. When I had walked up the steps, Old Mary, after deliberately turning one page, lay the church directory on the swing beside the album. Somehow that page-turning gesture seemed calculated on Old Mary's part, though I'm not sure why I feel this way.

While she was in her apartment, a breeze blew a single page of the directory so that the one she had been looking at before I arrived was again face up. There were the pictures of the families beginning with "H" in our congregation—Hartmans, Hankinsons, Hendersons, Hilemans, Holbens, Hooks, and so on. I can't be certain why Old Mary had positioned the photo album and the directory side by side when I approached her, but possibly she had been comparing the album and directory photos. This is such a little matter, but I find myself thinking about it quite often, since it somehow doesn't seem to be as irrelevant as it appears at first blush.

End of Pastor Gabriel Wyant's Journal

That's all Pastor Gabriel wrote at the time, but the event subsequently roused his curiosity to the point that he mentioned it to Charles. Both men wondered about the photo connection and, of more importance, if the amazing revelation that later unfolded within the community—and in the Cory/Jude narrative—was somehow evident in the photos which Old Mary examined that July day. Was it possible that the clue to a mystery in Jude and Cory's lives could be so demonstrably evident?

At Gabriel's suggestion, Charles reluctantly acquiesced to pursue the matter with Old Mary "if and when the right occasion presents itself. I'm not sure I see what good might come of it. Gabe, it was probably just a coincidence."

"Maybe so."

"Nevertheless, I'll give it a shot."

When he entered her apartment a short while later, Charles was again struck by its coziness: pumpkin candle burning on the kitchen stove, "neat-as-a-pin" living room with the hanging grapevine light suspended in the corner, the large sixties-era consul stereo record player, the plum-colored recliner, pictures of her seven children in their oval frames on the wall, and more framed pictures of grandchildren and great grandchildren on the tabletops and stands. Old Mary invited Charles to sit.

"My coming here will possibly seem strange to you," Charles began, "since it deals with an event a while back when Pastor Gabe had visited you. At the time of his visit, you had the church photo directory and a photo album lying side by side on the swing."

Old Mary looked at him a bit quizzically. *What's he driving at?* "I remember the occasion."

"Pastor Gabe wondered if you had been comparing photos." Charles paused for a moment, not exactly certain how to proceed. "If this is a wild goose chase, then we don't need to pursue this at all, but the two of us wonder if the photos contain a clue."

"I see your point, but I have a question for you before I answer yours."

"Shoot."

"Why are you pursuing this instead of Pastor Gabe?"

Just how to answer the query of this wise woman? I was afraid she might say something like that! "Well, he thought this might be a sensitive topic. Perhaps he thought that I, with a fresh perspective, might broach it more effectively, or maybe I should say 'tactfully.'" Charles crossed his leg and sat back in his chair. "I honestly don't know."

"He's such a dear man." Charles wrinkled his brow at Old Mary's evasive reply. "Perhaps you're right."

"When the two of us talked about this, we decided to look for any and all clues that might shed light on the narrative of Jude and Cory's lives. Our idea is simple, so I'll be direct."

"Go ahead."

"Is there a clue in the photographs at which you were looking when Gabe visited you?"

As it turned out, the whole visit to Old Mary's house was a little unnerving for Charles. *I would never ever accuse her of deceit, but yet it seems to me that she's somehow withholding information—*"inexplicably nonplussed," as he later explained to Gabe. *Based on the flipped-page detail, Gabe had the feeling that Old Mary did not want him to know that she had been comparing the photos,* and now *she's being conspicuously slow in formulating her responses to me about the incident. Yet this isn't the slowness of speech of an older person trying to corral a maverick word or pin down an elusive thought. Rather, she purposely sits there in silence for a long time without the least indication of nervousness or social awkwardness. How the woman formulates her calculated responses! Guess I'll try to ease out of the situation.* "It's all right if you don't want to show me the pictures or talk about this."

"No, you can see them. I remember exactly what I was looking at the day he was here. Can you hand me the album on the bottom shelf of that curio?"

Charles breathed a sigh of relief that Old Mary didn't seem put off by his probing a sensitive subject. *She's worked her way past tentativeness and is on board with the idea of comparing photos. What a relief!* Charles gestured toward the bottom shelf. "This blue one?"

"Yes, that one. Thank you very much. The church directory is in this stack somewhere." She shuffled through a small pile of books on the end table beside her recliner. "I'll show you the photos I was looking at back in the summer." After leafing through the pages of the directory and the album for a moment, she handed them to Charles. "Anything interest you?"

The photo album page had several pictures, most of them of the young Abe Badoane. Charles, therefore, assumed he was to focus on him. *What a handsome man Abe was—head of thick, wavy brown hair, winning smile, bright and intelligent eyes, square jaw, and a look as self-assured as Alexander the Great!* Charles studied the picture for a moment and again felt the old twinge of guilt that he had been chosen for the teaching job at Grove City College. *Abe was the better candidate for that professor post. I truly believe that!*

Then he looked at the church directory. His eyes eventually settled on the picture of Jude Hepler, included in the directory with a handful of other fringe people because of his occasional attendance. *I think Old Mary wants me to note the facial similarities between Jude and Abe—same brow, similar head-shape, intelligent, knowing eyes, full shock of brown hair, and that undeniable confidence. What am I to make of this? Old Mary, just what are you thinking?*

Completely awestruck, he lifted his eyes quickly from the album and the directory. Old Mary had tilted her head upward and rolled it back and forth against the top of her recliner. *Her eyes are closed, and I can tell she's deep in thought. Is she contemplating something perturbing, maybe even painful? She's obviously bothered.* Out of embarrassment he looked down at the book and around at her apartment, not wanting to stare at her. *But that's essentially what I'm doing!*

He coughed a bit and looked at her, but still she kept her head tilted back, her eyes closed. Charles noted the awkwardness in his journal.

I gathered that she did not care if I saw her ruminating so intently. She even began talking while holding that posture. She even dabbed her eye with a tissue while speaking! "Your conclusion?" she simply said, her head still tilted backward and her eyes closed. Completely poised, she waited for me to speak. I think I now see why Gabe wanted me to have this assignment. The whole experience was indefinably unnerving!

Charles at last broke the silence. "I don't know what to say. I see a similarity between Jude and Abe's pictures. That's the one thing that stands out the most. Am I supposed to note anything else?"

"Maybe that's it. I was just curious."

With that, Old Mary went silent on the subject of the photos. Charles sat on the couch and, in disbelief, looked at her. Her head was still resting on top of her recliner, her eyes closed. She toyed with the crumpled tissue in her hand, while Charles nervously tapped his foot.

Chapter 16

Old Mary had apparently made up her mind that she would offer this single comment about the directory and album and nothing further. After a moment's silence and again looking at Charles, she spoke. "Maybe you'd be interested in a couple other pictures of Abe, since he's always seemed to interest you. If you want my opinion, he's the one guy who's as intelligent as you." She replaced the church directory on the end table. "Except Cory's suitor, Jude. That young gentleman's another brain!"

"I agree."

Old Mary glanced over at the curio in the corner. "You'll have to be a contortionist again. Can you get another album on that bottom shelf? It's at the bottom of the stack."

"This one?"

"Yes, the purple one. Thank you."

The prospect of seeing more pictures excites me since they might motivate Old Mary to move beyond her willful silence. What else am I supposed to see? Something else about the photos? Did I say the wrong thing, and did her silence owe to that? "You're welcome."

Old Mary eventually broke the silence after turning several pages of the album. "Yes, this is it. Look here."

As she held the album on her lap, Charles slowly got down on one knee beside her for a better look. There were numerous pictures of the youthful Abe Badoane, always smiling and full of life, in a variety of settings: relaxing at a church picnic at Bingo, standing by a tractor along with Nancy and Shelby on the McKelvey farm, posing by the Bonner Cemetery with Paul and Ernest. An attractive woman stood beside him in many of the photos.

"Do you see this woman?" Old Mary began. "You'll recognize her as the young Freda Gehman, Abe's future wife. I know you remember her, since you're native to this area. In these pictures, they're not yet married."

"I remember her well."

Old Mary stopped speaking to concentrate on the photos. She ran an old and shaky finger across the photo of Abe's face.

Her knuckles are enlarged and the fingers arthritically-crooked. Talk about the ravages of age!

A tear fell from Old Mary's eye onto the laminated page, which she hurriedly blotted with her balled-up tissue. "You see how happy they were, even though Freda was a woman with a rough past."

"Yes."

"You probably remember that better than I since you were nearly the same age as Abe. You were around him a lot back then, weren't you?"

"Yes, we spent a lot of time together."

"Abe had been no angel as far as that goes, yet we all somehow felt that he and Freda would be good for each other."

"I felt that too."

"At least we thought that for a while. They did get along very well for a while, didn't they?"

"Very well indeed. I think he loved her very much."

She turned to another page in the photo album. "Now look at this picture." She removed it from its plastic holder and held it side by side with the earlier, smiling picture of Freda. "See the difference? Mind you, Freda knew her picture was being taken and yet she still didn't smile for the camera."

"You're right."

"Look at Abe. His hand is on her tummy and he is so proud and excited that they were going to have a baby. She must have been five or six months along by then."

"He's surely the picture of joy!"

"I never saw a guy like children the way he does." Old Mary again paused and rubbed her eyes.

Why these indefinable hesitations?

"That was the happiest I ever saw Abe."

Charles nervously adjusted his glasses. *I remember so vividly how Abe's life fell apart that summer, but to my way of thinking, it owed as much to his being passed over for a plum job as to losing a son.* He bit his lip in anguish but said nothing. Talking to Old Mary was what Charles wanted more than anything, but he began to sense an increasing apprehensiveness in her comments. *She's turned the pages of her photo album to other pictures, but she's not saying anything. Apparently, she changed her mind? Because she's distracted and preoccupied, or maybe just tired?* "Maybe I should offer to go now?"

"Well, I guess we can take a gander at photo albums again some other day."

Your statement, you cagey Old Mary, was so very subtle! "Thanks for showing me the albums. I've really enjoyed this, but I think I should leave now. It's been a full day for both of us."

They bade goodbye, and then she started to rise, though Charles told her to remain seated. When it was obvious that she was going to stand anyway, he helped ease her up from her recliner and then took a step backward. Old Mary held the side of the chair to keep her balance and then motioned for him to come near. Then, a gesture Charles never forgot, she put an arm around him to give him a hug and a peck on the cheek.

Normally restrained and formally dignified, she rarely indulges in such demonstrative gestures. I'm astounded!

She looked Charles in the eye. "What you and Pastor Gabe are doing is a good work, and I'm happy you're doing it." She slid her glasses up her nose. "But your search isn't finished yet."

"It's very important to several people."

"Which is why you need to keep searching."

The conversation ended with that comment, but when Charles looked at her, he saw a moist eye. He started walking from Old Mary's living room toward the kitchen. Approaching the archway, he heard Old Mary call to him in a weak and strained voice.

"I thought of some other pictures you might want to see."

Is she feeling guilty for cutting the session short? Has she changed her mind? In the archway, Charles turned around and watched Old Mary sit down again. *I don't know what to say!* "But there's always another day."

"I was going to show you these some other time." Again, Old Mary paused and reclined her head on the top of her recliner.

Has she had made up her mind to divulge some important information at last? Am I on the verge of a revelation—maybe THE revelation? Why has Old Mary called me back? He walked to her chair.

"If you have a minute, I'll show you some more pictures. We can do this even though I'm not so perky today, but it's better to do this while it's on my mind. You never can tell because I may not be long for this world!" Old Mary looked blankly into space. "The photos relate to a big secret I've carried my whole life."

"Really!" *You don't say! Is this the moment?*

"I was going to tell Pastor Gabe this secret." Old Mary spoke at last. "That's why I paused there a minute ago, but that man of God is not in the best of health and doesn't need to be burdened with another thing. Not one more blessed thing."

"He definitely works too hard."

"How I worry about that godly man!" Old Mary straightened the buttons on her dress. "I've made up my mind to tell you instead." She chuckled softly. "You can be the burden-bearer!"

She showed Charles a picture of an older nurse who wore a starched, white cap, that staple of a nurse's outfit in bygone years. In the second photo, Charles saw the same nurse some twenty-five years earlier in the OB unit of Armstrong County Memorial Hospital working amid a number of infants in their cribs. "Here, I'll show you one more picture of the scores in my albums." She took a photo out of the sleeve. "This is a picture of Abe and Freda in this same OB unit on the day of the birth."

Charles bent over to look more closely. "Yes, Abe standing beside Freda. Look how he has his hand on her bulging stomach."

"Abe is smiling from ear to ear, but Freda looks scared to death. You men folk don't know what we women endure at birth!"

I somehow feel that this is a kind of test and that I haven't given the proper response. "What else am I supposed to see?"

"You didn't comment on the attending nurse. See the nurse there in the background?"

"Yes, I see her now. I was concentrating on Abe and Freda front and center. Am I supposed to know her?"

"There's a chance you might. Look again." The nurse neared retirement, but her hair was only partially gray, she wore no glasses, and she was well preserved for a woman her age.

"I haven't a clue."

"Sometimes you professors aren't so bright."

How pregnant sometimes her replies are! Shakespeare would be pleased with that response since I quoted Hamlet *and simultaneously punned on the OB-delivery ward connection through use of the word "pregnant." Good job, professor!* "Don't I get a clue?"

"None. Just the answer. The nurse is me a couple decades ago!"

"That's you?" Charles said incredulously.

"Of course, it is. Look again. Surely I haven't withered into an old prune that much!"

The hair on the woman in the photo is dark brown and streaked with wisps of gray, but now Old Mary's hair is full and white like Barbara Bush's. Old Mary wears no glasses in the photo; now she does. In the photo she wears a cap on her head; now she doesn't. She was much thinner then but now sports a few medication-induced pounds.

"Don't be embarrassed. I wouldn't know it was me either!" She laughed in a way that put Charles at ease for the first time.

Charles again chuckled at her humor. "You were there the day Freda birthed her baby?"

"Yes, I was there when the baby was born." Old Mary stopped smiling and turned sullen. "And during the awful events that followed." She motioned toward the chair. "Sit down, please."

He had been seated on the edge in the posture of someone who was on the verge of leaving. *What does "awful events" mean? I hope we've worked our way to revelation time!* "Thank you."

A moment later she resumed speaking. "I saw it all, I was party to the whole mad business, and I've never gotten over it." Old Mary wiped two large tears from her eyes. "You think that was a tough day for Abe. Well, you have no idea what it was like for me."

"Sorry but I'm completely clueless."

Old Mary nervously twirled the edge of the coffee table doily. "You never get over some of life's tough moments." She nervously fidgeted with the doily. "You just dance around the hole in your life."

Again silent, Old Mary rested her head on the chair back.

What a marvelous line—"You just dance around the hole in your life"! How that reminds me of Emily Dickinson's poem, "There is a pain—so utter."

> *There is a pain—so utter—*
> *It swallows substance up—*
> *Then covers the Abyss with Trance—*
> *So Memory can step*
> *Around—across—upon it*
> *As one within a Swoon—*
> *Goes safely—where an open eye—*
> *Would drop Him—Bone by Bone.*

Since he's so enamored of Emily Dickinson, Jude would like my connection!

Waiting for Old Mary to speak, Charles reflected on the Dickinson poem. *She's again silent and lining up words in their proper order at the entryway of her mouth. But, Emily Dickinson, you were right. Some memories are so intense that they obliterate all other realities—swallow them up, to use her metaphor.*

As Old Mary rested her head on the back of her chair, Charles continued his reverie. *To cope with these past harsh events, people allow themselves to go into a trance-like state that substitutes contemplation of pleasant realities for harsh ones. Why? Because a head-on contemplation of those awful events would destroy a person bone by bone. What an image!*

Well, because Old Mary hasn't yet escaped the dark, she too remains in a kind of trance as a coping mechanism. Charles lowered his eyes from the painting over her head and again quickly peeked at her.

Woman, what secrets are you holding in that head of yours? Are you near to swooning, and are these secrets nearly dropping you bone by bone?

When Charles took his eyes off the photos and looked at Old Mary, her eyes were wet with tears. *She continues to sit in stoic silence while another big tear rolls down her cheek. Right to the corner of her mouth!*

"Abe, Abe!" she softly uttered. She suddenly shut the album—decisively, firmly. "I'm suddenly feeling quite tired."

"It's been a long day."

"Yes. Maybe I best give these old bones a rest, but I've so enjoyed this time together, professor."

"Thank you, Old Mary. It's been delightful for me too."

The conversation ended that abruptly, since Old Mary had clearly chosen silence over revelation.

Damn! She was so close to saying it! What was she about to divulge? I know one thing: I'm the one being dropped bone by bone!

Chapter 17

One day in the mine the next week Jude and Cory joined Duke and Tina for lunch. By then, Duke's reformation had become quite the topic of lunchroom and watercooler conversations. He had apparently stopped drinking—at least he refused a couple offers by the guys to stop on the way home from work for a beer—he cursed less frequently, and there were indications that he was slowly getting back with Tina. Most shocking of all, he had shown up for services at the Center Hill church. The sentiment of the mine employees was embodied in a comment by one of the women on Duke's crew. "I can't believe it! Sex fiend was in church last weekend. My aunt thought the flipping roof would fall in!"

Two related topics of discussion were in the air of the mine corridors. The first was the picture Tina produced of her son Tony. Duke did not know for certain that Tony was his son though, nagged by guilt, he strongly considered the possibility, nor did he recognize the pronounced facial similarities. Jude, Cory, and many others, on the other hand, did. "I surmised in a second he was Duke's boy," Jude wrote in his journal.

Tina herself was not completely sure that Tony had been fathered by Duke, though she always suspected so. The proof, the DNA test, was not utilized until years later.

Besides the current change in Duke and Tina, the other focus of conversation in the mine was Abe—his hatred, profound unhappiness, and his growing isolation. Jude and Cory pitied him, Duke studied him, and Tina feared him.

Possibly more than the others, Duke knew that Abe's savage evil should not be underestimated. "I wouldn't put anything past him, not a thing, because he's really been humiliated. Did you know the women are actually poking jabs at him? A couple of them ridicule him to his face. How dangerous!"

"I know," Tina rejoined. "I couldn't believe my ears in the lunchroom today."

"I've never seen anything like it. Like Jude says, that man is a walking volcano, and when it blows, it ain't gonna be pretty."

"A lot of people will be scalded by the spewing lava," Cory stated, extending the metaphor. "But Pastor Gabe believes that love melts the hardest hearts."

"Are you kidding?" Duke responded. "His heart would make a good ad for Portland cement: 'always tough, always durable, never cracks. Ever!' Have you taken a good look at his stone face lately?"

"Duke's right," Tina quickly assented. "He's aged ten years in the last weeks!"

"'A wicked man hardens his face,'" Cory shot back. "That's Proverbs 21:29. Or maybe I should quote the verse Gabe shared with me, Proverbs 28:14—'He who hardens his heart will fall into calamity.' Pretty accurate descriptions, wouldn't you say?"

"Very accurate. A man that unhappy," Jude postulated, "is seeking release from his pain. Look at the change in you in a matter of weeks. Abe wants that too. Our challenge is to pierce through the protective walls he's built around his heart and inject a massive dose of mercy and grace."

"Yes," Cory quipped, "before he dies of a massive underdose of love."

"There's a real difference between Abe and me," Duke continued. "I have Tina. We're going to make it, aren't we, baby?" He gave her a smooch on the cheek and put his arm around her. "And in time I might have Tony as my son. That boy is the greatest, and I just I love him. You ought to see us play pitch and catch."

"He's right!" Tina smiled.

"He's a dynamite pitcher. My point is that I have something to look forward to." He looked admiringly at Tina. "I'm excited that I'm finally getting my life straightened out."

"You've come a long way, Duke," Jude commented.

"I'm even considering taking some classes at IUP Northpointe, but what does Abe have? Remember that early seventies song—something about the only stars we could reach were just starfish on the beach?" Duke swallowed another bite of his sandwich. "Pops used to play that song all the time. It describes Abe perfectly."

"I know the song," Jude said. "That was Terry Jacks's 'Seasons in the Sun.' Yes, I remember it well. I recall another line from that song, 'Goodbye, papa, it's hard to die.'"

"Why do you remember that line so well, Jude?" Tina asked, stabbing an olive in her pasta salad.

"Because it reminds me of my grandpa. Every time I hear that song, I think of Eddie Fisher's 'Oh, My Papa.' You won't know it, but Grandpa said it was a smash hit back in the mid-fifties. Eddie Fisher was one of Elizabeth Taylor's first husbands."

"The very first," Cory interrupted. "What about the song?"

"Back in 1969, when Grandma learned that Grandpa had fallen in the barn, that oldies song was playing in the kitchen. Now every time Grandma hears that song, she of course flashes back to his death. She said it was the saddest song in the world and just couldn't listen to it. By the way Grandma continues to play the golden oldies of the fifties and sixties a lot, doesn't she, Cory?"

"Constantly!"

On and on the group talked, bonding with each other, getting past the rift of earlier weeks, and growing to trust each other. They talked trivia ("Did you know that *The Price is Right* model Janice Pennington was knocked out by a TV camera recently?") and important subjects too ("Becoming a new creation in Christ is the greatest game-changer in the world").

"Don't forget Wednesday evening Bible study," Cory said as they departed the lunchroom. "I'm sure Pastor Gabe has a good session planned. He always does."

"Church just doesn't do anything for me," Tina replied, loudly smacking her gum as she walked toward her personnel carrier. "I think the church is hypocritical. There may be lots of good men in the church, but what about all the young children who have been molested by priests? That's awful."

"Don't be so harsh, hon!"

"When I get near a priest, I want to grab Tony and run. You might think that's a terrible thing to say, but I don't care. I'm calling it like I see it. When I used to put money in the offering plate, I saw it going to pay off all those huge lawsuits against the church. I felt that way for years. Sorry, but this church business doesn't sit well with me."

"The church," Jude opined, "has its flaws, I'm sure, but look at the much good it's done too. Don't judge Christianity by the flawed institutions and men who have poorly represented it through the ages. I don't think we should misjudge the beautiful teachings of Christ by fallible clergyman, since they're not one and the same."

"Jude's right," Cory chipped in. "As we Christians frequently say, Christianity isn't about 'religion.' It's about a beautiful relationship with Jesus; but over the centuries, the institution of the church has grossly distorted the Man from Galilee's Gospel message."

On Wednesday, the four of them, as planned, attended the evening Bible study which Pastor Gabriel centered on the subject of love and truth. Tina and Duke had never heard anything so profound as the pastor's teaching that evening. Whereas Jude and Cory were accustomed to Bible-based exegesis and expository preaching, Tina and Duke were not. They were riveted to the pastor's words the whole time he spoke.

"Love and truth are inseparable in Christianity," Pastor Gabriel explained. "This is how Dr. John MacArthur says it: 'Truth must always guide…love.' That's a direct quote. I think he means that love goes hand and hand with truth and must be its leader."

"This stuff is great," Tina whispered to Cory. "But lots of church leaders don't practice the kind of love he's talking about!"

"Don't let their bad example ruin your idea of what real love is," Cory whispered in reply. "Gabe's talking about the love Jesus intended, not the marred love people exemplify today."

"You're always so wise!"

After people departed the church at the conclusion of the Bible study, Charles, Jude, and Cory met briefly with the pastor in the church library. "Aren't you thrilled that Tina and Duke joined us for Bible study?" Cory began. "Tina said she hadn't been in a church for years."

"Yes," Pastor Gabriel commented. "It's been a long time since I've seen someone under such heavy conviction. Tears streamed down her face almost the whole time I spoke. You say her name was 'Tina?'"

"Yes."

"When I spoke about the old tapes playing in your head—'You'll always be a loser; you'll never get out of this mess. No one will ever like you. It's no use trying to start over again. When you've messed up this much, there's no hope for you. God doesn't love *you*'—she almost started sobbing."

"Yes, I know," Cory said. "She leaned over and whispered in my ear that you were describing her perfectly. She added, 'My mind's a dirty mat and he's walking on it right now!' Then she laughed, 'Hope he doesn't get his feet dirty as...,' and then she used the 'H' word!"

"She's been living in an emotional trap for many years," Jude added. "She was without hope until you spoke tonight."

"I kindly suggest that you and Jude do some follow-up work with her," Gabriel said. "And Duke too. They obviously need guidance, and a dose of wisdom will be a balm for their hurting souls. You were there for our brief exchange in the vestibule before they departed the church. Tina said that facing the tough characters at the mine would be her most difficult challenge because they would make fun of her for trying to reform her life."

"Yes, I know she feels that way," Cory agreed.

Pastor Gabriel continued. "Tina went on to say, 'They think I'm a tramp, and the men see me as an expendable object to briefly enjoy—you can imagine in what way I mean—and then toss me aside.' Those were her exact words. She ended by saying, 'People would laugh their heads off if they found out I was going to church.'"

"I heard her say that," Cory assented.

"I appreciated Duke's response to Tina," Pastor Gabriel replied. "Maybe you heard him. He said, 'Who cares what people say? They made fun of me for a few days and then stopped. Truth is, they want what I have.' Then he turned to me and said, 'How'd you say that, pastor? Something about sin taking you further than you want to go and making you pay more than you meant to pay.' Then he said the 'H' word and apologized for cursing in the church! Honestly, I chuckled when he said that."

"That's Duke!" Cory laughed. "The guy is the poster child for rednecks!"

The pastor continued. "Well, I see Mr. Manningham as a rough, very rough man, I admit, but with a heart of gold and a brain in his head. Duke ended by saying, 'You described those losers to a tee. And me too until I started seeing the light!' He used the 'H' word again. He said, 'H———, I didn't even know there was a light before I started coming to church!'"

"Yes, I heard it too," Jude responded and then added, "After you walked away from us to talk to someone else, I said to Duke, 'Your face virtually shines these days.'"

"That was a nice thing to say," Gabriel offered.

"I then walked Tina and Duke to the door and stood on the church porch as they departed. When they started down the steps, he turned to me and said, 'I love living in the light. You know, darkness isn't what it's cracked up to be. Remember when the pastor quoted the guy—I forget dude's name—about the light coming in the middle of darkness?' I told Duke that he was referring to Cardinal Newman's famous line from the hymn, 'Lead, Kindly Light, amid the encircling gloom, for the night is dark, and I am far from home.' Well, at any rate Duke said, 'Yep, that was me. I was one messed up SOB living in darkness and far from the light.' He swore again and said, 'Oops, I shouldn't say that at church! Pops says that inconsiderate.'"

"That's Duke for you," Cory laughed. "Redneck to the bone!"

Chapter 18

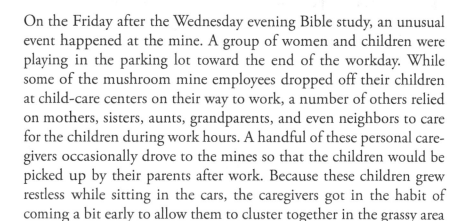

On the Friday after the Wednesday evening Bible study, an unusual event happened at the mine. A group of women and children were playing in the parking lot toward the end of the workday. While some of the mushroom mine employees dropped off their children at child-care centers on their way to work, a number of others relied on mothers, sisters, aunts, grandparents, and even neighbors to care for the children during work hours. A handful of these personal care-givers occasionally drove to the mines so that the children would be picked up by their parents after work. Because these children grew restless while sitting in the cars, the caregivers got in the habit of coming a bit early to allow them to cluster together in the grassy area at the edge of the parking lot for much anticipated "playtime."

On this particular Friday afternoon, Jude and Cory watched the following event transpire. "What we're seeing here sheds considerable light on mystery man Abe Badoane." Jude laughed as they observed the proceedings from their car.

"It also corroborates Gabe's post Bible-study comment that 'Abe needs release from his pain.' Remember when Gabe said that?"

"Yes, I do. He said that Abe is an 'essentially good man' who struggles to be free of 'the venomous hate which consumes him.' I think those were his words."

Some five or six children were romping and playing in the grass at the edge of the woods. Abe Badoane, parked nearby, had been irresistibly drawn toward them as he walked toward his car. When he joined the children on the grassy knoll, they came to him like a magnet, as they had on previous occasions; and in a moment's time, he was performing magic tricks. The amazed children laughed and giggled.

In one of the tricks, Abe placed a single, puffy nerf ball with his left hand in the hand of Rex, one of the little boys. Abe showed the children that he held two other miniature nerf balls in his right hand and then gave one of the balls to Gracie. "All right, kiddos, I have one ball. How many does Gracie have?"

"She has one!" Rex shouted.

"No, Rex. Gracie is a magician and turned the one ball into two! Now she has two, and I have none."

"She did not!" Rex screamed. "You have one, and she has one!"

"I don't have two," Gracie screamed. "You gave me one. I was watching. I saw you!"

"No, you did a hocus-pocus trick and turned the one ball into two."

"I did not!" Gracie was adamant. "I have one!" She jumped up and down with excitement. "Only one!"

"Well, we'll see," Abe said. "Come on, Gracie, open up your hand. We know you do magic tricks."

Sure enough! There were the two balls in her hand instead of the one Abe placed there. The children squealed with laughter. "How did you do that?" one of the children said to Gracie.

"Are you really a magician?" another asked.

"Do another trick for us!" a third squealed.

Watching as Abe performed this magic trick, Jude and Cory decided to check out the fun. "There he is at the center of the kids," Cory observed, "one of the younger ones sitting on his knee."

"He looks like Jesus with the little children, doesn't he?" Jude quietly whispered.

"Yes," Cory agreed. "'Suffer the little children to come unto me.' What a contradiction he is—lover of children, hater of men."

"He inflicts venomous poison on us and irresistible magic on them! This is the perfect opportunity to break the ice with Abe. His easy, fun demeanor astounds me!"

"Away from the mine and in the presence of these adorable little ones, he is a completely changed man. Can you believe this smiling, carefree man is Abe?"

"The guy is a walking contradiction, no doubt about it!"

"It would be great if we could join in the fun."

"Do you think we should?" Jude whispered.

"Why not? It wouldn't hurt."

They watched the group for a few moments, and then the most remarkable thing happened. Abe saw Jude and Cory and motioned for them to approach. "Come over here and join us!"

Jude and Cory, clearly astonished, were soon part of the circle surrounding Abe who performed another trick, this time on Jude. Seeing the laughing children, Jude decided to take advantage of the moment by trying a magic trick himself. He surprised Abe that he could do a complicated illusion that involved a watch, in this case Abe's. While many illusionists have this trick in their repertoire, it takes a long time to perfect.

Jude had done magic in bygone years, and while he had not tried this particular trick for some time, he thought it was worth it. *It won't matter if it fails since I'm in the presence of these innocent, fun-loving kids. The important thing is that being near Abe might thaw the frigid temp between us.*

Jude asked Abe, "What time is it?"

"Three forty," Abe responded, looking at his watch.

"Good. That's what time I have too. Now hold your arms in the air. Yes, like that."

While Jude distracted the children with the cards, he deftly removed Abe's watch from his wrist and placed it in his own shirt pocket. Jude correctly identified the mystery card as though that were the trick and walked away. As an afterthought, he turned to Abe and asked, "Oh, by the way, Mr. Badoane, what time is it?"

The children looked at Abe's arm. "There's no watch!" one of them screamed.

Then Jude said, "Here it is!" He pulled Abe's watch out of his pocket, quipping, "I see Abe has lost the time."

Before Jude returned the watch to Abe, amid the peals of laughter from the children, he glanced at the back of the watch and noted that his name, Abraham Badoane, was inscribed there. "I see," Jude said, "that this man has lost both his time and his name. See?" he said, showing the children the name on the back of the watch. "He lost his name. See it here? I found it and now return it to him."

When Jude handed over the watch, Abe smiled and said, "Thank you for giving me back my name. You're as kind as the son I wish I had."

"Yes, and this time we shouldn't allow"—he made certain he was looking directly at Abe—"all the history to get in the way."

Abe said nothing but looked with his characteristically penetrating gaze. *That had to mean something, but what?*

Cory turned to the men and spoke. "It's great seeing the two of you reconciled. You remind me of the relationship between King Saul and David in the Bible. They were at each other's throats constantly. The way of love is much better."

"Right you are!" Abe concurred.

As Jude and Cory walked to their car, Abe continued to play with the children but simultaneously cast an admiring glance at the couple as they ambled across the lot. *I once enjoyed a love like that!*

That ended the strange incident at the edge of the woods, an event that was "layered with symbolism," as Jude noted in his journal. "In losing his watch," Jude wrote, "Abe had lost his time and identity, but by returning it, I restored both."

In his strawberry patch that evening, Abe also reflected on the incident. *Did Jude make these comments to underscore their symbolic underpinnings? When he commented that I lost my watch, he said I "lost the time." Was he hinting that I had wasted time and, by extension, my life too? The same is true of his crack about my lost name. Did he mean, through indirection of course, that I had lost my real identity, thereby disguising his real intent as I often do? I can't stop thinking about this!*

Cory, on the other hand, fixated on Abe's warm behavior. "The warmth and humanity which Abe demonstrated toward us today was so unusual," she remarked as they strolled on Vinlindeer that evening.

"I agree. That was such a contrast to his normal, cool treatment."

Ironically, Jude nevertheless suspected that Abe was hatching a scheme at this very time. *If I'm right, then I have a question. How could a man who was planning our destruction simultaneously extend such warm love in the parking lot? This knotty enigma reminds me of tales of the American Civil War.* "During the Civil War," Jude remarked as they meandered along the field, "men from the Union and the Confederacy would occasionally meet in the evenings, converse like gentlemen, and then go back to warring against each other the next day."

"Talk about crazy!"

"One such event allegedly happened at Spangler's Spring in Gettysburg when men from both sides congregated at the spring at the south base of Culp's Hill to fill their canteens. Wonder if that could possibly be true."

"I have no idea. I've watched a lot of Civil War specials and read lots of books but never came across that. Ask dad. He might know."

The discussion resumed a short while later in the kitchen of the Mohney homestead. "Far as I can tell, many historians debate that point to this day," Pete began. "I just finished reading that new book by, what's his name? McPherson, that's it. James McPherson. What's it called?" Pete thought for a moment. "*Battle Cry of Freedom.* That's it, but I don't recall if he comments on the incident."

"Did you know that book won the Pulitzer Prize?" Jude asked.

"No, I didn't."

"He's a Princeton University professor. What a treat to sit under a man of such profound depth!"

"I'd go crazy if he were my teacher. Or Shelby Foote. There's another brain!"

"I heard some of the history profs at IUP say that a filmmaker is doing an in-depth documentary on the Civil War and that Shelby Foote is one of the featured interviewees."

"Who's directing it?" Cory asked.

"Ken Burns? I think that's the name, but I'm not sure, nor do I know his work."

"Well, I sure hope that series materializes," Pete opined. "I'll be glued to the TV if it does!"

That evening in his study, Abe continued to maul over the event that took place at the side of the parking lot with the children. *How can I nurture such hate toward Jude and Cory and turn around and treat them as warmly as I did today? I wasn't being a hypocrite, because I felt genuine warmth and love for them during those few moments.*

With his journal in front of him and strains of Johann Stauss II's *divine Wiener Blut [Viennese Spirit] Op. 354* filling the air, Abe mused on Cory's comment about King Saul and David. Turning to the passage in 1 Kings in the Bible, Abe read of Saul's oscillating love/hate relationship with David and reflected on Saul's conflict.

Abe's Journal:

Saul tried to love David, but his jealousy and envy threatened that love. After one incident when David was particularly magnanimous toward the neurotic king, whose life he had just saved, Saul said to David, "You are more righteous than I, for you have rewarded me with good, whereas I have rewarded you with evil." What Saul said of David, I say of Jude. You have been the nobler person. You are David, I am Saul. Saul tried to overcome his hate and love David, but he could not because hate had overtaken his soul. Oh, woe is me. I do not want to be a Saul but cannot stop myself.

Why am I unmaking myself? Jude was right—I have lost my name and wasted my life. But why am I so hell-bent on destroying myself and Jude and Cory in the process? Why do we humans deliberately and willingly self-destruct? Do I have more of Ted Bundy in me than I'm willing to admit? One thing is sure: we need a Savior. At least I do!"

Abe lifted his eyes from his journal to a couple of pictures that were framed and sitting on his desk. One was a photo of Abe standing beside the smiling Freda, his wife-to-be. Beside it stood another picture of Freda, "the best picture I have of her," Abe had once noted in his journal. *She was carefree and innocent in those days, eyes aglow with light and love, but there I sit at the far right. It was not the intention of the photographer to have me in the photo at all, but the wide-an-*

gle lens caught me nevertheless. Unaware that I was being photographed, I sport my normal face—that fiercely unhappy, scowling, angry mug! I always meant to cut away the damn embarrassing picture of me at the periphery, that ugly visage, which contaminates this beautiful photo... just as I contaminated Freda's life.

He remembered a line from a Whittier poem: "Of all sad words of tongue or pen, The saddest are these: it might have been." *How true! How very true! How hard it is to live through the death of a perfect love, to be the agent of her destruction. It might have been so perfect. It might have been. If I hadn't ruined it.*

But that's my life's credo: I've mangled everything I've ever touched.

Chapter 19

A day or so after the incident of Abe with the children, Jude, upon bumping into Bull, learned that the new section of mine was due to open soon.

Bull's uneasy today and even looks guilty. More than usual. Wonder why? Maybe he realizes that I along with the others think he sabotaged Duke's car. Or maybe he's uneasy because of his generally dissolute behavior or his terrible treatment of women. Something's rotten in Denmark! Come to think of it, Bull has been ill at ease around me, but he's that way around others too. But to be honest, some of the other mine employees are uncomfortable around me as well!

The latter assessment was definitely true. Because Jude's learning intimidated them, some of the employees found it occasionally difficult to talk with him. He found the topics that dominated their discussion boring—TV programs, pop culture, mine gossip, economic woes, and sexual exploits—and thus the only real subjects at which they could comfortably intersect were the Pittsburgh sports teams.

I'm glad I keep up with the Steelers and Pirates to hold my own among these men. Some of them have the history and stats of the sports teams down pat. I wasn't showing off but today just happened to spout off Bobby Bonilla, R. J. Reynolds and Barry Bonds's batting averages—.274, .248, and .283 respectively—and that scored big points with the guys. Tomorrow, I'll push the stats even further since they seem to like that. They'd probably be interested in pitcher Doug Drabek's earned-run average and Bob Walk's strike-outs to date.

That evening, Jude dashed over to Cory's farm on his motorcycle. His heart light, he belted out Nat King Cole's "That Sunday, That Summer," one of the songs of bygone years, which he occasionally heard at his Grandma's house:

> If I had to choose one moment
> To last my whole life through,
> It would surely be that moment
> The day that I met you

As he drove down Cory's lane, he looked at the barn, the house, and the grounds and was struck by the good progress made to date on Cory's farm. *The house is freshly painted, and the bright Williamsburg blue around the windows and on the shutters contrasts beautifully with the white exterior of the farmhouse. Good choice of paint, Cory! The flower beds are blooming vibrantly, and the lawn is neatly mowed in razor-sharp diagonal rows. Nice job, Joey! Even the small details make a big difference—the new bird bath in the center of the front flower bed, the American flag standing proudly on the pole by the corner of the house, a couple pieces of statuary along the front walk, and the neatly manicured edges. We've come a long way!* As he bound up the sidewalk, he shared the Mohneys' gratification. *The house was in near shambles a couple months ago, but now it's pristine and fully restored—a lovely ante-bellum Pennsylvania farmhouse. Come to think of it, my life was also in shambles a couple short months earlier. Cory and I had been separated by what Frost calls 'a panic moment,' and though our panic moment stretched into five agonizing years, we managed to fight against the stiff current and happily reunite. Some things do work out. O happy day!* Stepping onto the porch he saw a penny lying on a stand near the front door. He thought of his recent discussion with Pete about his renovation of the fireplace in the den prior to his illness and depression. Pete had explained to Jude that when he was repointing the bricks several years back, a penny fell out. Upon examining it, he saw the date—1860.

"To think that this farm house was built in the year Abraham Lincoln became president!" Pete explained. "It was the custom in the nineteenth century to date the time of a building's construction by inserting a coin from that year in the brickwork of the fireplace. If that's what happened here—and I'm guessing it did—then this farmhouse dates from the year Lincoln took office. That's getting back there!"

Jude picked up the coin and examined Lincoln's face on the coin. *He's one of my favorite presidents too, but, Mr. Lincoln, how did you manage to carry such a heavy load on those war-wearied shoulders? How could one human being bear the egregious burden of well over a half-million deaths?*

The ponderous thought, coincidentally, was mirrored by the emotional atmosphere in the Mohney house, to which Cory alerted Jude as soon as he stepped onto the porch. "Dad's fallen into the throes of depression again and won't get off the couch. Even Zoe can't rouse him this time!"

"How bad is it?"

"He's barely eating, hasn't shaved for days, has one suspender hanging to the side of his bony shoulder, and the other dangles clear down to his thigh."

"How pitiful!"

"If that isn't bad enough, his shirt's unbuttoned, and his fly's half unzipped!"

"I didn't know he was this bad. You minimized his condition when we talked on the phone."

"I was afraid he'd hear me talking."

"What sent him into this tailspin?"

"He was looking at pictures of Mom all afternoon, and that does him in every time."

Jude and Cory slipped quietly into the kitchen and softly closed the door behind them. They could hear Pete talking between stifled sobs. "Why did she have to die? Will my grief never end?"

As Jude stuck his head into the doorway of the den, Pete whispered, "I want to be strong for Joey and Cory." Pete lay slouched in his couch, arms listlessly folded across his chest. Not wanting Cory to hear, he spoke quietly. "Is Cory there in the kitchen?"

"No, she went upstairs."

"Jude, how can I be strong for them?" Pete sat more upright on the couch. "I can't even face the day myself because I'm such a wreck!" He picked up a photograph of Ruby and him standing in front of the barn. "Look at this picture. See those arms? I used to be very strong." Pete buried his head in his hands. "Now I'm a disgusting wimp!"

"Clouds gather around the highest peaks."

"What's that supposed to mean?"

"That the grief you carry puts you head and shoulders above many other folks."

"When he gets this despondent," Cory said a short while later in the kitchen, "I can't reason with him or barely talk to him. All I get out of him is guttural monosyllables, grunts really. Those sentences he spoke to you are the most he's said in days."

"I'm so sorry to hear that."

Cory opened the oven to check her shepherd's pie. "Maybe I should get him to listen to Pastor Gabe's sermon from last Sunday. Remember how uplifting Gabe's comments were about dealing with adversity?"

"It was a powerful message."

"If there's any topic Dad needs to hear about, that's it!" She rinsed her hands at the sink and dried them off. "Sit tight and say a prayer. I'll be right back."

Cory put the cassette player on the coffee table by the den couch and inserted Pastor's sermon from Sunday. "Dad, I know you probably don't want to hear this, but it will do you good." Pete turned his head away. "Please listen to it. Pastor spoke on Romans 12:1–2. Those verses are about renewing your mind in Christ. We both know that's something you could use." She gave him a hug and a peck on the cheek. "I love you, Dad. You will get through this!"

"Thank you, darling Cory. What would I do...without you and Joey?"

"Here's his message on that Romans text. It's what you need."

"I know that verse. Your mother used to quote it." Pete grew quiet and thought again of his wife. "Knowing the verse in your head isn't the same…the same as having it here." He flopped his dangling hand on his chest. "I know the idea"—a pause—"but I can't live it. Don't know how." He shrugged his shoulders in despair.

"You're not alone, Dad. Pastor Gabe helped us see how we can make these ideas the basis of true joy and not just useless thoughts." Cory looked at her Dad. *What a pitiful man—my dear father!* "Well, some new thinking won't hurt! Please listen to it."

"All right, turn it on. I have nothing to lose, but if he uses lots of big words…like Jude does, I won't learn much." He chuckled at his own comment.

"That's the first half-smile I've seen on his face in days!" Cory, back out in the kitchen, whispered to Jude.

Just then Joey and Laura walked in from the porch. Joey made no attempt to suppress his frustration.

"Hey! What's going on?" Jude asked. "You look like you're a Yankee soldier headed up Marie's Heights in Fredericksburg." Laura walked over and joined Cory by the sink while Jude and Joey talked at the kitchen door.

Jude put him guard. "Your dad's in pretty bad shape. Keep your voice low so he doesn't hear you."

"Thanks. I'm having the same problem as before with football." Joey muffled his voice even more. "The coach only plays his pets, and I never get a chance. I can't even get a shot at playing." Joey threw down his book bag and dirty practice gear in disgust. "I just want one chance!"

"I feel for you."

"They simply use me as bait on the scrimmage squad to play against the first string. Imagine how much action I'll see in our season-opener Friday night against Freeport!"

"No wonder you're upset."

Joey walked to the refrigerator to pour a glass of milk. "I've never quit at anything in my life." In his frustration, he raised his voice. "But I'm giving serious thought to throwing in the towel."

Hearing this comment, Pete put his head back against his chair and covered his face with his hands. *God, how much more must we endure? Is Joey being punished for my backsliding?* Pete laid his arms weakly at his sides. Wiping a tear from his eye, he looked across the room to a picture of the Good Shepherd on the wall. *He's innocent, oh, God. Please punish me and hold my lambs in Your loving arms...like You hold that lamb. Watch over them, I beg You! I'm the one who should suffer—not Joey, not Cory!*

Chapter 20

Motioning for the group to go out on the porch, Cory spoke to her father as she passed the entryway to the den. "That sermon will do you good, Dad." She walked over to him and wiped a tear from his eye. "Please keep listening." She gave him a peck on the cheek and joined the others on the porch.

Once outside Jude and Cory sat on the swing while Joey and Laura perched beside each other on the top step. The four of them lifted eyes toward the meadow to watch the grazing cows. Laura put her hand on Joey's.

"Are you sure you don't want to eat first?" Cory asked Joey. "You must be starved."

"Yes, I want to eat, but I need to blow off some steam first. Sorry to vent, but it all got to me today at practice." Joey and Laura continued to talk.

Several feet away from the high school sweethearts, Cory cupped her hands around Jude's ear and softly whispered, "What can you say to help him?"

Jude put his hand to Cory's ear to respond. "Because Joey's frustration has such deep roots, he isn't about to be placated with glib maxims. No talk of scars-to-stars and pain-for-gain platitudes for this guy. He's too smart!"

"'He who gets wisdom loves his own soul,' Proverbs 19:8."

"You know the Bible as well as Pastor Gabe! Now we need to apply that biblical wisdom to Joey's problem."

"For a young man, he carries quite a load."

Jude and Cory realized that Joey was a mature thinker for whom the daily injustice of life was growing harder and harder to endure. His losses had been substantial. In the wake of his mother's death and his father's incapacitation, he had been forced into adult maturation in his midteens. For him, partying teammates who were lackadaisical about reaching their physical prime bothered him as much as their general immaturity.

"Why do these young and healthy guys abuse their bodies?" Joey continued to vent. "Here's what really ticks me off. The coaches insist on playing them when they're not a bit better than me. I know that for a fact!" When he paused briefly, Laura slid tighter to Joey and placed her head on his shoulder. "I hate the hypocrisy of some of the key players. I'm talking about their two-facedness. They suck up to the coaches during practice and yet shamelessly ridicule them, even knife them in the back, when they're not looking. The coaches are so dumb they don't even know these guys are doing it!"

Joey knew he was a decent athlete and in excellent shape, largely because he had been training steadily since winter. By now his weightlifting and running regimen had yielded impressive results, and he was a marvel of muscular agility. *But what good has all that hard work done? It hasn't paid off a bit!*

Joey drained his glass of milk and stood on the step. "I guess I better eat. I'm starved." As he and Laura walked toward the door, Joey turned and asked Jude a question. "Do you think Jack Lambert and the other great Steelers dealt with this kind of crap?"

"I have no idea."

"What about the western Pennsylvania quarterbacks that were star performers all over the NFL? If they'd have been coached by guys like these, they probably wouldn't have had a chance." He massaged his calf where he had been kicked in practice. "Wish I'd bump into Lambert sometime. I bet he'd give me an encouraging word. They say he's awesome."

"You know he helped coach the girls' basketball team at Kittanning. Or at least he used to," Cory said. "The players loved him as a coach."

"Yea, I know, but I've only ever said hi to him in passing. I'd never get up the nerve to stop and talk to him. Can you imagine being one on one with the great middle linebacker? I'd shake in my shoes!"

After talking on the porch for another few minutes and enjoying the pleasant evening, Cory and Laura went into the kitchen to finish preparations for dinner, and Joey continued his conversation with Jude. "The other thing that gets me is Dad."

"Cory says he just sits in that room day after day."

"But I won't deny it. The thing that's working on me the most is football. The one coach told me to be patient. He said I'd get my turn, especially in these early exhibition games and the season opener. Well, the start of the season is here. Can you imagine if I did get in Friday night and Dad misses it because he's lying on the couch down and out as usual?"

"What if Laura's right? Maybe this is your year."

"Dad wants me to play football more than anything in the world." Joey drained the bottom drops of milk from his glass. "People tell me he was a good player in his day. They say he had great hands and was a ferocious tackler, but now he just mopes around like a dying dog. How can a person just give up so completely?"

Cory came out on the porch to call the men to dinner. "The shepherd's pie is done. Time to eat! At least our tummies will be cheerful amid all this heavy gloom." She laughed and gave Joey a big hug. "It will get better. All things work together for good!"

By the time they went into the kitchen, they were surprised to see that Pete had gotten off the couch and was standing in the den, Zoe by his side. His suspenders were strapped properly, his shirt buttoned, and his fly zipped. "He's standing more erect than I've seen him in days," Joey whispered to Cory. "He's only a bent-over slouch anymore. I don't believe it!"

"Could Pastor Gabe's sermon be the reason?" Cory whispered. "He couldn't have listened to more than the first half."

While Cory and Laura began to lift the dishes, Joey and Jude went into the den to join Pete. "Cory gave me this sermon to listen to," Pete began. "It's the one Pastor Gabriel preached last Sunday. No wonder people like him so much. He's a preacher of the Word if there ever was one. Did you hear this sermon on suffering?"

"Yes," Jude and Joey answered simultaneously.

Joey carefully watched his father. *Dad's speaking in full sentences, and he has a glint in his eye that hasn't been there for weeks!*

"I'm looking forward to finishing it."

"We were there when he preached it," Joey replied.

Jude jumped at the chance to keep Pete talking. "What's one of the main points you've picked up so far?"

Pete thought for a second. "The pastor says people must consider their thoughts. What they think about. What the voices in their head are saying. He called it their self-talk." Pete struggled to summarize Pastor Gabriel's main point. "People need to examine what they silently say to themselves. I think that's true."

"Yes, Pastor Gabe gave that a lot of emphasis," Joey commented when Pete paused.

Pete reflected deeply as he spoke. "We keep playing the same tired messages in our heads. I know I do. My thoughts are weary—just like me, or I'm weary like my thoughts. I'm not sure which comes first!" Leading the way, Pete smiled and took a few steps toward the kitchen. "The reverend says that the negative words in our heads are real destructive." He paused to develop his thought. "That's also true because we look too much at negative things, the things that tie us to our pasts. All the bad stuff that happened years ago." Pete stopped speaking and walked back to the coffee table where he picked up a tablet.

Joey continued to watch him closely. *His steps are firm and intentional.* Standing by Jude in the kitchen, Joey turned and whispered, "Can you believe it? He hasn't talked like this for ages!"

"If you'd give him a pen, he'd write an epistle!"

Pete continued speaking as he strolled toward the kitchen. "Here are a couple lines I wrote down. They hit me so hard I played them several times to get the words right. Pete squinted as he looked at his pad. "My writing's awful any more. Pastor said, 'We shouldn't allow our emotional state to be determined by external phenomena.' I struggled with that a long time to know what he meant. Then he went on to say this." He again read from his pad. "'The stuff happening in our lives—the day-to-day events and circumstances—should not determine our emotional state, because external realities should not govern inner thoughts and emotions.' I think that's true, but that's what I've been doing—allowing my emotions to be controlled by the junk in my life." He looked at Cory and Joey in dead earnest. "I have to stop that."

Once seated at the kitchen table, Pete continued to ruminate on the words he had written. "Pastor says it's crazy to allow your emotions to be influenced by circumstances that lie beyond your control." Pete blotted a speck of sauce that had splashed on his notepad. "Here's one more thing. 'Doing so is not advantageous to, or the basis of, successful living.' I copied that word for word. That's exactly what I've been doing—letting all the bad stuff of recent years control my emotions."

"You're not alone, Dad," Cory said, swallowing another bite of shepherd's pie.

Pete laid down his notepad by his plate. "We're lucky to have that man of God in our Center Hill church."

"I remember the sermon well," Joey said. "Laura and I, and half the congregation, were on the edge of our seats the entire time he spoke."

"He was on a roll last Sunday," Laura agreed. "But as far as that goes, he usually is!"

"I haven't listened to the second half of the sermon," Pete said as he spooned a generous portion of shepherd's pie on to his plate. "What does he go on to say? How we can keep our emotions from being controlled by stuff around us?" Pete wiped his mouth with his napkin. "I'll tell you one thing. In this sermon, he's talking directly to ole Pete Mohney!"

"Keep listening," Jude said. "He quotes one of Paul's famous passages to the church at Philippi. I can only paraphrase it. He says that people should look at things that are true, honest, just, and pure, and a couple other things that I don't remember." Brain will know since she's our Bible scholar!" He looked at Cory and patted her on the arm.

"That are lovely and of good report," Cory said with a twinkle in her eye, "Philippians 4:8. Joey, tell Dad more about the sermon. You're the one who said after church how extra good it was."

"Tell him how the people responded," Jude added.

"If you insist." Joey spoke between giant bites of food. "Gabe said we're supposed to actively focus on those good sorts of things and not let Satan rivet our attention to the bad. The devil wants us to keep looking at the filth in our past since that makes us feel worthless and guilty and kills our self-esteem and makes us feel useless to God." Joey took a drink of water between bites. *Like it's killing mine!* "That, in turn, makes us think we're completely rejected by God."

When Joey coughed, the result of eating and talking at the same time, Cory continued the thought. "When we feel rejected by God, we choose to put ourselves on the shelf—isolated, useless, pitiful."

Joey threw Zoe a bite of food. "Sis is right. Well, that sermon ends on a really upbeat note. Keep listening!"

Zoe listened attentively while Joey spoke, licked his lips, and waited for another bite. "Dad, you ought to listen to the second part right away."

Cory watched Pete eat as Joey spoke. *Instead of picking at his food, eating a couple half bites, and covering his plate with his napkin—his custom in recent weeks—he's eating a large helping. Bravo, Dad!*

"This is really good, Cory." Pete talked between bites. "Nice work. You cook just like your mama."

"Thanks, Dad, but it was a team effort all the way."

Cory looked across the table to where Laura was seated. *She's sitting in Mom's chair!* Cory reflected on the Tennyson line of poetry from "Tears, Idle Tears," which Jude had referred to earlier in the day: *"So sad, so strange, the days that are no more." Mama, these are indeed strange days, but at least Dad is coming around. He's been pretty much himself here at the dinner table, and that is one incredible blessing. Step by step, we work our way out of the pit of despair. Thank You, Jesus, for always being there!*

Chapter 21

That evening, Cory and Jude had some free time and decided, after tossing a coin, to saddle the horses and trot up to Vinlindeer instead of lounge in Little Gidding, even though "the latter," in Jude's phrase, "beckons like the siren's song."

"You know I'm nearly done with my painting. That's why I too would like to go back to Little Gidding, just to put on the finishing touches."

"It will be good to take the evening off since you can do that tomorrow."

"You're right. Relaxing this evening and enjoying the panorama will be wonderful."

"Let's go for it!"

On Vinlindeer a short time later, the two were seated in their customary position—Jude leaning against a fence post, Cory sitting between his spread-eagle legs. Jude began the conversation. "Where do you think we'll be a year from now? Time to get out your crystal ball!"

Cory spoke with absolutely no hesitation. "I see myself married, happy, and worshipping the ground you walk on every moment of every day." She craned her head sideways and kissed him on the cheek. "Any other questions, ever inquisitive one?"

"You're too much."

"Your turn to tell me. What do you want? And by the way, I'm serious. That's what I wish for, though maybe I should add that I might want to be pregnant too. We're both twenty-six, you know."

Jude put his arm around Cory and drew her tightly to him. "Yes, I want to be married. The dark days are done, beautiful dreamer, and we are for the light."

"I know what you did there. You inverted Cleopatra's line in Shakespeare's *Antony and Cleopatra* when Cleopatra says, 'The bright day is done, and we are for the dark.' We're destined for the light and will enjoy it like no other!"

"Why wouldn't I reverse Shakespeare's famous line? It's the opposite for us, and the dark years are behind us, the years the locusts destroyed."

"So true!"

He stroked her hair, kissed her, and then gazed across the vale. "The glorious years of our rapturous bliss stretch before us—I need a good image here—stretch before us like the sprawling, spangled mesas of the coppered Canyon Grand."

"You poet—you marvelous wordsmith!"

"You artist! You want some more poetry? How about Stephen Foster's lines? If you beam on my heart, beautiful dreamer, e'en as the moon on the streamlet and sea, Then will all clouds of sorrow depart.' I couldn't say it better. When you beam on my heart, all sorrows depart. Forever!"

"That is so beautiful, Jude."

"Stephen Foster gets the credit. He was quite the gifted poet, one of Pittsburgh's real gems." Jude straightened the part in her hair. "That's how I view our future, but I know we need an action plan, so let's get a detailed plan in place. What does it consist of, and what specific steps do we take to realize our dream?" He leaned forward and kissed her head. "That's the male brain kicking in—thinking, organizing, calculating!"

"All right, here goes. Applying to IUP and taking classes there, either part-time or full-time. Then getting married and helping you write your dissertation and land a teaching job." She thought for a moment as she looked across the vale. "Maybe you could get hired at one of the fine nearby schools here in Pennsylvania—Thiel, Westminster, Allegheny, Chatham in Pittsburgh, maybe Grove

City, or Geneva. There are tons of fine institutions here in western Pennsylvania, and I'm sure they'd hire someone of your caliber."

"What a great idea!"

"This would keep us near Dad and your grandma, so there's one good way of putting a foundation under our dream."

"You remind me of Thoreau's famous dictum about foundations."

"I'm waiting."

"'If you have built castles in the air, your work need not be lost; that is where they should be. Now put the foundations under them.' That's from *Walden*."

"What an excellent quotation!" She looked into his eyes. "Give me your version of our future master plan. I suppose you want me to become another Sandra Day O'Conner, the Supreme Court's first female judge!"

"Not even close, but getting you enrolled in classes and starting your degree means every bit as much as finishing my dissertation. I'm completely serious. Sometimes I think about not finishing my PhD so I can spend more time with you. I want to have kids and raise a family."

"Thank you for saying that."

He buried his head in her hair. "I could never separate from you. I don't want to be out of your sight for a minute. I don't care about me. I care about us, since the pronoun 'I' died a long-delayed death. Good riddance! So speaks the happy twosome!"

"Right you are, wise professor!"

When they entered Jude's house a short while later, Jude's Grandma told them that Old Mary had called and that they should try to see her as soon as possible.

"What's it about?" Jude asked.

"She didn't say, but it's something important. She sounded concerned—I'd say even distressed. I'd go right away if I were you. I tried to get her to talk, but you know Old Mary."

"So very well!"

"When she makes up her mind about something, it's settled, so she wouldn't tell me. But I do think you should go as soon as you can."

"Let's call first," Jude said.

They learned by phone a short time later that Old Mary was free and that the present was a good time for them to see her. Moments later Cory and Jude were riding his motorbike over to Center Hill.

"You see why I like my bike," Jude said as they drove through the quaint village.

"Yes, I love it too."

"Hey, I have a favor to ask as we breeze along."

"Lay on, Macduff."

"Sing that song you were humming on the way home from the mine yesterday. What was it?"

"Clarence 'Frogman' Henry's 'I Don't Know Why I Love You.'"

"I really like that song! Sing it, please."

Cory began to sing the catchy tune.

> I Don't know why I love you but I do
> I don't know why I cry so but I do
> I only know I'm lonely and that I want you only
> I don't know why I love you but I do

"Good job, hon. Any song is great when you sing it."

Soon the couple pulled into Old Mary's place and ambled up the lawn to her apartment. Even though it was nearing dusk, Old Mary, as usual, sat on her porch.

"Hi, Old Mary," Jude said. *Is it my imagination, or does she look a bit grim this evening?* "Grandma said you wanted to see us. Well, here we are."

"What did you want to talk about?" Cory asked.

Jude later wrote in his journal: "This conversation proved to be the single-most important bit of information I have ever learned across my entire life. At first blush, that looks like exaggeration, but it isn't—not at all!"

They sat on Old Mary's porch, Jude and Cory, out of excitement, leaning forward in their chairs as she spoke. Old Mary started slowly as if warming to her subject and then broke into full gallop. Jude shook violently as he received the information, each syllable hitting him with the force of a Mohammed Ali upper cut. He clenched the side of Old Mary's porch chairs so firmly that his knuckles turned white. He tapped his foot nervously, a mannerism so obvious that Cory whispered. "Jude, you're tapping your foot so hard that Old Mary's flower box is shaking!"

"I can't help it!" Jude could not restrain himself and started to weep as Old Mary continued her narrative. He looked at Cory in disbelief. "Can you believe this!"

"I knew it would be a shock to you," Old Mary resumed, "a very terrible shock."

"Sorry, ladies. I just can't help myself." When Jude's words caught in his throat, Old Mary and Cory stopped talking, sensing that he was trying to continue. Soon he gained his composure. "Have you always known this?"

"Always. It's been the tragedy of my life, the awful thing I've carried all these years."

"You've known this through the decades and yet told no one, not even one of the godly Center Hill preachers—Pastors Gauntz, Gehman, Smith, Norris, Berkebile, or Peters? Not a single one of them?"

"No one. I just never knew how to tell you, Jude, or maybe I should say get up the courage to tell you." Old Mary tapped the arm of her swing with her pointy index finger. "This revelation affects many but none like you. That's why I was afraid to tell you. Afraid how you'd take it. Afraid to see you react exactly as you are at this very moment. I did not want to see this. I swear I did not want to!" Old Mary's hands were shaking, and her head bobbed back and forth.

"I just can't believe it!" Jude said again. "That poor, poor man! So what do I do? Does anyone know beside you?"

"As I said, not a single person."

"You say not even Chuck or Pastor Gabe?"

"Not a soul. Pastor Gabe came years after the fact. Charles was here of course, but he was kept in the dark at the time of the event like everybody else. You see, this was information I felt I had to carry myself, because it was my cross in life. Nobody else can carry the cross meant specifically for you."

"That is so true," Cory agreed.

"Pastor Wes used to say that all the time, and now Pastor Gabe says it a lot too." Old Mary placed her hand on Cory's thigh and looked up the hill toward the lilac bushes at the top of her lawn. "Oh, dear," she said softly. "Telling you this is even harder than I thought it would be. I just didn't know how to inform you! Please forgive me if I've done so poorly."

"You've said it gently," Cory replied.

I don't want the conversation to end on this sad note, so I'll change the subject. Old Mary showed Jude and Cory a book she had been reading on Armstrong County and leafed through some old photos of the county in the late 1800s and early 1900s. "I think it's time to change that heavy subject since I've pretty well exhausted it." She leafed through the pages of the book. "Here's one of the things I recently learned. Did you know that John Gilpin's large mansion down on Market Street had been built over Chief Jacob's ammo supply?" and "I knew that Chief Jacob was the commanding chief of the Delaware Indians at the time of Col. John Armstrong's attack on the village in September 1756," Jude responded, "and I know that decisive battle started the French and Indian War."

"That was the center of the Delaware Indian village," Old Mary resumed. "Right there on Market Street."

Jude did his best to remain attentive and even enjoyed the bowl of tapioca pudding Old Mary served before they departed, but his mind was racing wildly. *I can't believe it. I simply can't believe it!* In a short while, he stood up to leave and thanked Old Mary for sharing her long-held secret. "I have no words to express how I feel, Old Mary. This is the biggest game-changer I've ever heard."

"I knew it would be." Old Mary rubbed her hands and folded them. "I'm sorry I waited so long to tell you, but I simply lacked the words and the courage." She drew close to Jude, embraced him tightly, and for a brief moment, uncharacteristically, lay her head on his shoulder. Backing away from him, she looked Jude in the eye. "I'm so sorry that I was weak and acted poorly. Very poorly." She kissed him on the cheek. "Well, goodbye then."

Walking down the grade to his motorcycle a short while later, Jude's mind was still reeling. "I just can't believe it. Do you realize how this changes everything?"

"Yes, it really does. You'll never hear a more profound revelation your entire life!"

Chapter 22

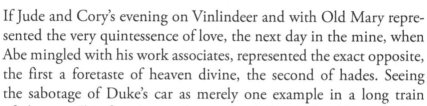

If Jude and Cory's evening on Vinlindeer and with Old Mary represented the very quintessence of love, the next day in the mine, when Abe mingled with his work associates, represented the exact opposite, the first a foretaste of heaven divine, the second of hades. Seeing the sabotage of Duke's car as merely one example in a long train of abuses—"his favorite modus operandi," as Jude glibly noted in his journal—the mine employees finally admitted that, underneath Abe's winning smiles and oily rhetoric, lurked the scheming manipulator who deftly, and routinely, exploited others. The frustration, especially in those not endeared to Abe, led to varying degrees of alienation.

As Abe's world crumbled, a small fringe group felt empowered in a strangely exciting way. Elated by his comeuppance in Pittsburgh, they even had the effrontery to ridicule him to his face, a savagery that intensified incrementally. The majority of employees, on the other hand, remembered Abe's former status and, kinder by nature, settled for a period of aloofness. Two camps, thus, developed in the mine—those who, after a brief flirtation with the newly-constituted relationship with Abe, resumed their deferential treatment of the older, intelligent gentleman; and those who, seeing the once "high and mighty" man marginalized, chose to keep him down, the sentiment of the latter group embodied in an older woman's assertion: "It's high time we give that bastard the dirt he deserves!"

At lunch on the day after Jude and Cory had spent much of the evening on the ridge, Abe spoke with a few of the people about the Omnibus Foreign Trade and Competiveness Act, which had passed in the House on July 13 and the Senate on August 3. "We can't have these countries dumping surpluses on the USA," Abe complained. "In time that will kill our manufacturing sector, which has always been one of the great strengths of our nation. We especially need to keep an eye on China." *Talk of politics always settles my nerves and redirects focus away from unpleasant topics. Today I definitely need it!* "But here's one good thing. The Soviet Union's pulling out of Afghanistan is a blessing for world-peace advocates. The damage they've inflicted in Afghanistan is incalculable."

"Can we talk about something a bit lighter?" Midge yelled from the adjacent table. "Like movies. No offense, Abe, but you're over my head today. Who's seen a good movie recently?" A peacemaker at heart, Midge noted the hostile reaction to Abe's discourse on politics and thought it wise to divert attention.

"Great idea since I dislike talk of politics," Connie enthusiastically agreed. "Well, I really liked *Rain Man*. Tom Cruise and Dustin Hoffman are excellent in that movie. Somebody else pick a favorite."

"I'd go with *Crocodile Dundee II*," Al chipped in. "Dundee is a cool dude, and that Linda Kozlowski is one gorgeous woman."

"*Die Hard* is my pick," Blassie stated while others thought of recent movies.

"He was bending our ears about that movie up at the packhouse," Al chuckled. "Ain't that right, guys? Go ahead, Blass. Might as well spoil it for them too!"

"I'm happy to comply! *Die Hard* is about an NYPD detective named John McClane. Well, when he visits his wife at a party in LA, he runs into a bunch of German terrorists. You think Dundee's cool? You ain't seen nothing till you see Bruce Willis in this movie! I don't say this for many movies, but I give this one a thumbs-up!"

The favorite-movies discussion momentarily lightened the atmosphere, but during a lull a couple of the women, who had been waiting anxiously to worm their way into the discussion, ganged up on Abe.

Barb, a woman with a notoriously savage mouth, took the lead. "Hey, Abe. I hear that Jude Hepler made an ass out of you in Pittsburgh. Bet you didn't look like Bruce Willis or Crocodile

Dundee down there!" She looked at the women to drum up support for the character assassination she had launched. "Maybe instead of Claudius we should call you Clod for short!"

Lilly, sitting beside her, joined in. "I don't know who the hell Claudius is, but I dig the name Clod. Girls, don't you think the name, Clod Badoane, has a certain ring?"

There was a chorus of affirmative responses from several of the nearby women who were poised to unleash their conspiratorial vitriol.

Savage mouth resumed the attack. "From here on in, it's Clod!"

Abe tossed his uneaten sandwich into a nearby garbage can, wiped his mouth with a napkin, and crashed the lid down on his lunch box. He stood to depart, but Huddy Weaver, entering the room and walking behind Abe's table at that very moment, smashed a massive hand on Abe's shoulder so forcefully that it pushed him back down into his seat. Knowing that Abe did not like anyone to touch his body, several folks gasped at this. People reflexively gave Abe space to make sure they never brushed against him even in tight quarters. One of the intelligent pickers, Robin Peate, described the prevailing sentiment one day in the women's locker room: "His is the royal body no crusty plebian hand ever touches!"

Huddy lowered his face and spoke within inches of the back of Abe's head. "Maybe it's time you took your medicine. Because of what you did to Duke's car, you can take a little heat from the women." Huddy looked in the direction of the cavorting females. "Ladies, proceed since the floor is now open for comments. The jury can decide the verdict, but keep it fair and just. I won't allow mud-slinging, for we just want simple facts!" Abe fiercely glared at his lunch box and dug his nails into it.

Several of the women proceeded with merciless cruelty, whereas others, harboring no innate ill will toward Abe, merely played along in a minor key, amused at the novelty of seeing Abe on the receiving end of the biting sarcasm. For them, it was an enjoyable change of scenery. Still other pickers, intimidated by the powerful personalities in the group, symbiotically indulged in the hurtful frivolity, as weak people do, because they feared being on the receiving end of the lacerating invective. Hard experience had taught them that staying on offense kept them out of range of the serpent tongues' deadly venom.

As for Abe, he was dying inside. *Only three other times have I been psychically devastated like this. Once by the monster at the cabin, that SOB I'll never forgive! Another by the death of my dear little JJ, and a third which no one—far as I can tell, thankfully—knows about. But now again, I experience this intense mortification, searing tongue-lashing, utter helplessness, and a feeling of nauseous abandonment. All of it constitutes a savage machete gash to my dying soul, and my precious spirit slowly bleeds away. You bitches remind me of Job's lament: "Leave me alone, that I may take a little comfort, before I go to the place from which I shall not return, to the land of darkness and the shadow of death... where even the light is like darkness" [Job 10:20–22]. May I go to this undiscovered country soon, that consummation devoutly to be wished!*

When the women finally stopped their jeering, Abe looked at them through ferocious animal eyes. "I hate all of you and loathe the very sight of you." He pulled a handkerchief from his pocket and dabbed a tear. "Look what you've made me become! I'm better than all of you, and my IQ's higher than all of yours put together." He glared at the women, saliva shooting from his mouth as he shouted. "I was born to better things than to spend my life around a bevy of dumbass, bawling beavers!"

"Oh, come on, Abe, we were just joshing," one woman timidly laughed.

Since Huddy had backed away, Abe was able to rise from his seat and shakily stand by the table. Leaning on it for support—his knee had again given way—Abe continued his diatribe. "I was a mere twelve years old when I first read and memorized extensive passages from Milton's *Paradise Regained*. I've never forgotten the lines because they perfectly describe the innocent boy I was in those happy, carefree days:

> When I was yet a child, no childish play
> To me was pleasing, all my mind was set
> Serious to learn and know...

143

"'To learn and know.' Can you imagine such a noble quest for a wide-eyed, aspiring, little boy?" He wiped another tear from his eye. "What a crime to waste this brain"—he gestured to his head—"this continent of learning and ennobling scholarship on you wretched, wicked swine! How sad, how very sad, to cast my pearls to the swine as I so very often do!" He surveyed the blank looks of the women who hung their heads in shame. "You've never heard of *Paradise Regained*, have you? Tell the truth!" he screamed. "You've never heard of the poet John Milton either. I knew it! He was only the greatest poet of the western hemisphere, you mindless morons!" He slammed his fist into his lunch bucket. "I was definitely born for better things than this!"

"Abe, we're sorry," one of the women said when Abe tucked his lunch bucket under his arm and started to leave. "We was just having fun!"

"Come on, Abe. You know we dint mean anything by it," said another.

"We know you'le Einstein compaled to us." Bonnie's speech lessons had had no visible effect to this point.

"We ain't mad, Mr. Abe—we just bad! And, sir, we're sorry as hell that we crossed the line!"

Realizing that they had made Abe genuinely suffer, the women were shocked to see his reaction. Though they tried to remedy the damage, Abe rebuffed their efforts, turned his back on them, and limped to the door. At the entryway, he glowered at them through blood-engorged corneas. The women watched with baited breath, sensing that he had saved his final hurricane of invective for his grand exit.

Abe did not disappoint them. "I'd die if my eyes were backed by pea-sized brains like yours!" With his hands shaking uncontrollably, Abe stomped out of the lunchroom and slammed the door so hard it cracked the glass.

Chapter 23

More than any other event, the incident in the lunchroom pushed Abe Badoane over the edge. Up to this point, he had handled the losses, suffering, and defeats which life had dealt him with the poise of a battle-toughened warrior. Through the pain of setbacks and reversals, he had always plodded on, managing to do his daily work competently and even brilliantly at times, and through it all, garnered admiration and respect from his colleagues. As a young man, he felt destined for high places: a prestigious professor's chair, a deanship, a college presidency, a judge's bench, or a successful businessman. While the list was endless, he had settled for this obscure life in a darkened labyrinth of corridors and, over the years, learned to make the best of it.

He had recently written of the phenomenon in his journal:

Abe Badoane's Journal:

Truth is, I've come to enjoy my life in the mine and experience the gratification that results from watching the mushrooms reach fruition in their darkened caverns far underground. That's the life impulse which, no matter what, cannot be stopped! Growing anywhere, anytime, anyplace, the mushrooms remind me of Carl Sandburg's poem, "The Grass": "I am the grass; I cover all. I am the grass. Let me work." And how those mushrooms work in the dark—grow, grow, grow, you little buggers! I hear your irrepressible cry, "Let me work!"

Watching the mushrooms work their way to maturation gives me a sense of accomplishment and joy too. It's a little world I inhabit, an insignificant, faraway world, but in an inex-plicable manner it makes me feel close to God. If people were to ever read that, they would think I was crazy in even referring to our heavenly Father, but it's true. My relation to the Deity is most unorthodox—that I freely admit—and it's obvious that I wreck it daily. But the good Lord knows my heart, knows the good life I wanted and purposed in my soul, and not this pitiful life I daily eke out like a cursed slug on a blighted branch. What I am appalls me, but I still keep sliming my way up that little, dead branch.

Abe Badoane's journal entries, which index his precipitous demise from the fateful lunchroom day, became pitifully heart-wrenching and reveal much about a giant of a man who became in these days utterly cynical and misanthropic. In the parlance of Jude's college students, from this day onward he "lost it." The entry for the lunch-room day is especially revelatory:

Abe Badoane's Journal:

In my tirade at work today, I cursed the people at my lunch-room table and cited a line from Milton's *Paradise Regained*. I quoted the part when Jesus says that as a young boy "no childish play To me was pleasing." I told them how the lines described me as a little boy—always at the books, always reading, always desiring to know. Truth is, through the early years of my life I felt like the boy Jesus in so many ways, wanting to accomplish, in Milton's words, "What might be public good." Like the Jesus of Milton's *Paradise Regained*, "victorious deeds Flamed in my heart" during those halcyon days of beautiful innocence and childlike wonder.

But what have all those lofty ambitions of green youth brought me? All those dreams of doing public good, all those vaulting deeds I wanted to achieve—what have they come to? They've merely brought me to this pitiful state where I am hated, called The Serpent behind my back, willfully misunder-stood, rejected, scorned, ridiculed, and trampled into the dirt!

That's the thanks I get for all the years I have poured wisdom into their little craniums, broadened their horizons by telling them of foreign cultures and other peoples, enlightened them about the great personages of history and the visions that fired souls, and sought to lift their sights beyond the darkened corridors in which they daily grind out their pitiful existences! That's the thanks they give me! "Clod it is!" Indeed! "I hear that Jude Hepler made an ass out of you in Pittsburgh!" Indeed!

When I was leaving work today, I said to jackass Bull, "If brains are mountains, I'm Mt. Everest, and those people are piss-ant mounds! If brains are measured in RPMs, I'm five hundred compared to their five! If brains are trains, I'm the long Shawmut line from Kittanning to East Brady, and you, Bull Chestnut, are a miniature Mattel locomotive spinning in meaningless circles on my basement ping pong table!"

I'm done playing Mr. Nice Guy! Ted Bundy, I understand the hate in your heart. I reject what you've done to innocent lives, but I definitely comprehend the hate! Since these folks around here want to play with fire, it's conflagration time!

End of Abe's Journal

Chapter 24

Morley Spencer, the main security technician, typically ate his lunch in the manager's lunchroom at the administration building, but fascinated as he was by both people and gadgetry, he occasionally joined the employees for lunch in the various mine lunchrooms to demonstrate some new electronic device which he had recently purchased.

On a day prior to Jude's arrival in the mine, Morley showed them his handheld cassette player, new to the late-eighties market. After turning it on and recording a few moments of conversation in one of the lunchrooms, he pushed "play." The group was amazed that a device so small could record so clearly. Those who had never heard their recorded voices were especially intrigued.

"I didn't know I sounded like that!"

"I can tell you one thing—that's not how I sound in real life!"

"Oh, yes, it is!"

After demonstrating his latest novelty, Morley put the recorder on his lap to guard against food and drink spills but—*just for the fun of it*—kept the device on "record." Because the ensuing conversation keyed on Abe Badoane's spontaneous interaction with his work associates, Morley passed it on to Jude. "You'll like this conversation since it captures so perfectly what you call a 'true slice of reality' and since it reveals so well the nature of Abe's interactions with his mine peers. That's a topic that seems to fascinate you a great deal these days."

"Thanks, Morley. I'll enjoy this glimpse of Abe's world. You're right, the guy really interests me."

"By the way, there are a lot more where this came from, since I've been doing random recordings ever since March. Just let me

148

know if you want to hear some others! By the way, I have no dark underlying motive in doing this. You know it's for fun, right?"

"Of course, I do."

"It's given me and a bunch of others a ton of good laughs."

"Same with me, Morley. I have no clandestine intent either. I merely want to learn about Abe and get an accurate glimpse of what his world was like before I appeared on the scene and, to my lasting regret, somehow hopelessly reconfigured it."

"I understand. That's why you'll enjoy hearing this particular conversation. By the way, the trivia business you'll hear in the tape is typical and, to me, downright fascinating. That guy is always spouting tidbits of history and trivia. It annoys some people, but Abe's knowledge is legendary and his recall amazing."

"Encyclopedic in my book."

"Let me know what you think of this authentic 'slice of reality,' as you call it. I have lots of these recordings, so give a shout if you want more!"

"Stay near your phone!"

But it isn't just Abe, though admittedly he's front-and-center in my mind much of the time. I'm also intrigued by mine life generally and the people who work here, their daily lives, what makes them tick, and, most of all, their interactions with mystery man. These details are never too mundane, especially for the way they touch Abe's life.

From Jude's perspective, historical novels and artists' creative renderings of past life are occasionally worthwhile. *But on the whole, they are, in my judgment, woefully inadequate imitations. Why? Because their contrived interpretations of the glorious past are simplified and sometimes factually inaccurate, and while that might placate authorial whim, it doesn't do justice to those rich and teeming ages.*

He spoke of this one evening to Cory. "I'm like many others in wanting to have as accurate an understanding of the past as it's humanly possible to create. No more wildly errant renderings and crazy distortions that result from a writer's half-baked views of what he thinks the past was or what she wishes it had been."

"The really bad thing is that some of this revisionism serves clandestine, political agendas."

"Orwell warned us about the coming thought police!"

"So true."

"I'm searching for truth in the best way it can be understood, honestly recreated, and graphically presented. I know that's a quixotic quest which is impossible to accomplish, but that doesn't mean I shouldn't try to do my best."

To Jude, this life in the mine was the real thing, a perfect example of how ordinary people live their day-to-day lives. *I can't get enough of it, so I'm thrilled that Morley gave me this cassette tape, because it will afford me an unedited glimpse of Abe's world prior to my arrival. What amazes me the most is the contrast in Abe: the humane man he had been for years versus the enraged and hate-filled being he's become in recent weeks, especially after the awful lunchroom attack.*

Morley Spencer's taped lunchroom conversation in late March (prior to Jude's arrival in early May):

Abe: It's about time you guys get your minds out of the gutter and talk about something of value.

Huddy: Like what, Einstein?

Abe: Like current events. Did you hear that an attempted assassination was made on our Secretary of State Shultz? This happened recently in Bolivia.

Brat: Who cares? Doesn't interest me.

Abe: Then let's try something closer home. What about Denny Daugherty?

Clark: Who, pray tell, is he?

Abe: He lived in Kittanning and was the gentlemen who created the Daugherty Visible Typewriter. That's why "Typewriter Hill" near the Edgewood Intersection bears that name. That's where the typewriter factory was, and that's where the nation's first typewriters were produced.

Duke: Frankly, I'm not interested. [A pause as Duke swallowed his food] Nor is 34-C at the end of the table. *Woman, you are gorgeous!*

Abe: You ought to be.

Blassy: Why's it matter?

Abe: History's important. It matters, for instance, that the Duchess of York gave birth to a six-pound, twelve-ounce baby girl on August 8. [A fumbling noise as Abe apparently reached in his pocket to pull out a picture] And this is important too. [Abe holding up his photo.] Look at this photograph of my typewriter keyboard.

Brat: What about it?

Abe: Note the keys above the left-hand home keys. Read them off, Brat.

Brat: "q, w, e, r, t, y." What's so special about that? Big deal!

Abe: The "e, r, t, y" is the end of Denny Daugherty's last name, the last two syllables. It's a coded configuration that he secretly embedded into the keyboard. Maybe he did it so he'd be remembered as the inventor of the modern visible typewriter. People who knew him said he did it for that reason. Here's the point: the arrangement of those letters is not accidental.

Hank: That's amazing to think that the first typewriters were made in Kittanning. But I have a question. [Apparently speaking to Brat.] What kind of a name is Harrelson Stetson Brattleboro? Where were your parents' heads when they named you? What's wrong with Bob or Jim or Ed? Why freaking Harrelson, and what kind of a middle name is Stetson?

Brat: Lay off my name.

Smitty: [apparently to Abe] You say the typewriters were made on Typewriter Hill?

Abe: Yes, that's where Mr. Daugherty located his typewriter plant, and that's where the world's first typewriters were manufactured. The building is still there though it now houses another business.

Al: Hank's right. That's amazing. I gotta admit, Abe, most of what you say is bullcrap and nonsense, but sometimes you do say some interesting things. Daugherty must have been as bright as MacGyver! Did you guys see last night's program? It was called "The Secret of Parker House." I never thought he'd get out of that one, but he did. That guy could escape from anything."

Huddy: He couldn't escape Bonnie's web.

Bonnie: Scwew you, Weavel.

Abe: Shush, boys and girls. We need to know our history. If we don't
know it, we're doomed to repeat its mistakes—an idea usually
ascribed to George Santayana of Harvard, though I'm not certain that he was the first to say it.

Huddy: I can handle this kind of trivia but lay off the musicians. You
were driving me nuts yesterday when you were talking about
classical composers and all the famous violinists. Who gives a
rat's behind about Mantovani's version of *Charmain*?

Al: And that BS about Tchaikovsky's violin concerto gave me a
migraine. Who cares if he died at fifty-something or wrote the
1812 Overture in six weeks, or came to America and performed
at Carnegie Music Hall in New York in some damn year?

Abe: 1891. Ah, yes, Tchaikovsky's *Violin Concerto in D major, Opus
35*—music fit for the gods! But I see, Hudson and Al, you prefer
less cerebral, less cultured trivia. Then how about this one? You
have both elbows on the table as you're eating. That's considered
poor etiquette in today's etiquette manuals. Here's a trivia question for all of you. Centuries ago, were arms and hands on the
table during meals considered good or bad manners?

Blassy: I say poor.

Al: Yea, I agree. My wife's always on me about keeping my left arm
down on my lap when I'm eating. And more and more, I find
myself doing what the voices in her head tell me. [Lots of laugh-
ter] But I like to rest my arm on the table, since it feels comfortable. Know what I'm saying? When I see people with their
hands under the table, I think they're probably... Well, I won't
say it, but you know where I'm going! [Hearty laughter.]

Abe: Do most of you feel that way? [A brief pause and indistinguish-
able sounds] Actually, that's the wrong answer. Hands on laps
or below the table constituted poor manners and was a sign of
disrespect in bygone ages.

Al: Why?

Abe: Because the chief or sultan or sheikh or king wanted to see all
hands and arms on the table as a sign of safety and loyalty. You
see, hands under tables can engage in nefarious activities like

passing weapons and conspiratorial notes. All that to make this point to Alfred: your table manners suit the eleventh century well but not the twentieth.

Bull: [After a brief delay] Abe, you should talk to Jude Hepler. Now there's another walking encyclopedia. I was talking to him the other day about motorcycles, and the first thing I know he was bending my ear about Play Dough and Soccer tees or some damn idiot. Yunz suckels listen to this. What the hell does Play Dough have to do with Soccer-face?

Duke: That's Plato and Socrates, you dumbass. Bull, look at me. I said look at me! [A pause] I have something I want to say to you. You are one stupid SOB. I bet you never even heard of the brilliant Socrates and Plato.

Bull: Really? As if I care. Plato Pluto. It's all freaking worthless. Al's right. This stuff is bullcrap and nonsense, and that's a fact, Plato Duko.

Duke: Is that so, Bull-O Dick-O? Here's how it went down, ladies and gentlemen. May I have your attention for a moment. At the time Bull was born, his mom and pops were in the hospital nursery looking through the window at their new-born son. Taking his eyes from the new little baby, Bull's dad turned to his wife and said, "Princess, my favorite 36-D in the world, you and I have screwed up a hell of a bunch of times in our lives. We done bad when we tried to be Bonnie and Clyde and robbed those banks. I admit it. We messed up when we stole that string of cars. I confess. We blew it when we tried to burn down the train station or when we campaigned for lowering the drinking age to 12. I admit it. And we really botched it when we tried to create the Free Sex League for Minors in Armstrong County. No denying any of that. But this in front of us is the master-piece of all our screw-ups. Just look at what we've gone and done now. I mean you see lying in that bed the most disgusting loser of all losers, and we made him!"

Bull: Shut up, losel. [Bull must have given Duke the finger here.]

[An unidentified female voice]: "Way to give him the bird. Bull, bet your parents never said [singing], 'You must have been a beautiful baby!'"

[Scraping sound of a chair: possibly Bull rising to his feet.]

Bull: Screw you, Bonnie. You can play dough with this for a while. [Peals of laughter] If you'd sit back and get your 40-Ds off the table, the space for our lunches would be doubled. [More laughter] Ain't that right, Duke-O Dick-O? There'd even be enough room for my samich!

Duke: While we're doing math, I'll say this. If your brain was half the size of another of your body parts, your intelligence would be tripled. [More boisterous laughter]

Abe: We'll pick up with Plato and Socrates tomorrow, lads and lasses, and maybe Aristotle too; but for now, it's time to deflower some little darling mushrooms. Keep your knives sharp and ready.

Duke: My knife's always sharp and ready!

Huddy: One more thing before we go. Why didn't George Washington's old man punish him for chopping down the cherry tree? [A chorus of "I-don't-knows."] Because Georgie boy still had the ax in his hand!" [A din of laughter.]

Blanche: Huddy, that made me laugh so hard I can feel the tears running down my leg. [more laughter]

Alice: Blanche, I swear you're the funniest woman in the mine!

Chapter 25

Morley's transcription offered Jude valuable insight into the nature of Abe's association with his mine associates. *He used to get along with the workers very well—that's obvious—even if there had been some serious ups and downs along the way. Why, then, did the day when the women ganged up on him in the lunchroom reconfigure the dynamic so completely? What made it so drastically different from other bad days?*

Jude pondered the question extensively over the next days. *I can conceive of only one answer. The lunchroom trauma brought his past failed life into polychromatic, 3D clarity. All the hurts of the past compacted into one dense ball that piteously dangled in front of Abe's eyes; and that relentless pendulum, always front-and-center in his mind, eventually hypnotized him to evil. Up to this point, Abe's method of suppressing life's past hurts and injustices had been more or less successful. He coped with day-to-day living simply by doing what most of us do: he compartmentalized the ugly stuff in his mind and marked it "Life's rejected unpleasantries. Don't ever touch!"*

Jude's ruminations were precisely correct. As a result of this strategy, Abe Badoane across the years had essentially been able to forget the trauma in the cabin, deeply sealed in his unconscious mind. The boss on the job forgot the dead baby in the OB unit. Sealed! The strawberry horticulturalist conveniently failed to remember his irresponsible outbursts of rage toward his battered wife. Tightly sealed!

Forget, deny, suppress, and move on, simple really, simple until this day when the mega-pain of the lunchroom debacle crashed down on him with the force of Damocles's soul-lacerating sword. Out of that wound in Abe's heart spewed forth the deadly vitriol of decades.

Abe described his state succinctly in a journal entry. "I say with David, 'For I am poor and needy, and my heart is wounded within me. I am gone like a shadow when it lengthens' [Psalm 109:22–23]. My poor, wounded soul!"

The journal entry for that day begins with King Lear's anguished cry from Shakespeare's famous play, "I am a man more sinned against than sinning." A few other excerpts from literary masterpieces function as a superscription for this particular day's journal entry.

Abe's journal:

"None of us can help the things life has done to us. They're done before you realize it." [Eugene O'Neill's *Long Day's Journey into Night*]

A person "can't help being what the past has made him." "How do we get back to all the great times?" [Willy Loman in Arthur Miller's *Death of a Salesman*]

"The thought of our past years in me doth breed Perpetual benediction." [Wordsworth's "Ode: Intimations of Immortality"]

One can keep the past at bay for so long but not indefinitely. The experiences of one's past are huge ruts in the mind, like those on The Oregon Trail which, once the wheels slide down into them, are rarely escaped. Thus, the weary traveler is locked in them for the duration of the long, torturous ride. Are we condemned to stay on these "metaled ways," as T. S. Eliot calls them in *Burnt Norton*? Can we never muster the needed strength to hoist the enormous bulk of our lives onto a smoother track, a less tortured rail? Apparently, we cannot. At least I cannot.

Because that's the sad truth, I have no choice but to pursue this thing through to its destined end, for there is no other way. How very far I've come from those youthful days when I felt like Tennyson's Sir Galahad and, with him, could say, "My strength is as the strength of ten Because my heart is pure." That was I in the early years of my life—strong, pure, noble. What a beautiful, aspiring heart I once had! With Galahad I could speak of "Pure lilies of eternal peace Whose odours haunt my dreams."

And they did haunt my dreams. All the aromatic beauty of those lustrous childhood dreams was as sweet in my mind as the bouquet of Freda's fresh-cut summer flowers on the kitchen table. In those days, only I aspired to have visions of the Holy Grail, the cup Jesus Christ used at His Last Supper, and only I actually experienced those visions. How blessed was I, in visions, to see the awe-inspiring Holy Grail! No wonder I say with Wordsworth in his "Lines Composed a Few Miles above Tintern Abbey," "I cannot paint What then I was." That is so true, for words fail me when I try to describe the pulsating heart that throbbed within me in those early years, when I strove with all my heart to be the best person I could be, to be as pure and good and holy as Jesus. I wish I could paint the kind of boy I was in those pristine days, but I can't, since it would take a Shakespeare to describe what then I was!

I used to say with David the Psalmist, "For You [God] will light my lamp; The LORD my God will enlighten my darkness... You enlarged my path under me, So my feet did not slip" [Psalm 36:28, 36]. But I say that no more. Never again. The people in the mine used to say, "Abe, you're as smart as a prophet." No more. Never again. I say with the prophet Micah, "The sun shall go down on the prophets, and the day shall be dark for them" [Micah 3:6]. Well, it surely is dark for this one-time prophet! The Old Testament writer Isaiah puts it even better: "If they do not speak according to this word, it is because there is no light in them" [Isaiah 8:20]. Well, God, I don't speak according to Your word, because my light, sadly, has been extinguished. The psalmist says, "Unto the upright there arises light in the darkness" [Ps 112:4]. There may be light in the darkness for the righteous, but in my soul, there is only damnable darkness. No more to add on there.

Yes, the old days! My imagination romped and raced like a Kentucky race horse—Secretariat, Seabiscuit, Omaha, War Admiral, any of them. Imagination was so beautiful to me and every bit as important as knowledge. No wonder I've always appreciated what Einstein said about this: "Imagination is more important than knowledge. For knowledge is limited to all we now know and understand, while imagination embraces the entire world, and all there will ever be to know and understand." Einstein, you brilliant man, thank you for saying that!

But the time when I felt that way is completely gone. How well I understand what Wordsworth says in "Lines": "That time is past, And all its aching joys are now no more, And all its dizzy raptures." So true, so true! The aching joys of youth are gone, the hilarity and ecstasy of life, and the dizzy raptures of my childhood have evaporated, as surely as every trace of warmth and humanity have evaporated from my arctic heart.

Robert Frost you had it right when you said in "Desert Places," "I have it in me so much nearer home To scare myself with my own desert places." The desert places of this lonely heart, which beat right here, right here in my breast, frighten me to death. This is the coldest place on planet earth. No need to visit the tundra of Siberia. Merely look on the heart of Abraham Badoane!

Goodbye, Cory and Jude. I hate being this way, loathe doing what I'm about to do. But it's too late to change, and I cannot stop.

Farewell, Jude and Cory. Jude, you're so like me that you could have been my son!

Chapter 26

During those moments when Abe was enduring the lunchroom mortification, Old Mary was looking at her picture of the Stephen Foster *Beautiful Dreamer* stained-glass window for the thousandth time. Up to this moment, she could never be certain whether the beautiful dreamer was sleeping or dead. However, in recent days two details—the unnatural position of the beautiful dreamer's head and the use of the word "sorrow" in the lyrics—made her lean more toward the view that beautiful dreamer was deceased. *I hate to admit it, but the poet insinuates that the lovely lass is not of this world. Still, I can't be certain.*

While stewing over this quandary, Old Mary fell into a nap on her bed and dreamed yet again of the beautiful dreamer, but this time a new interpretation, during sleep, crashed into her mind with the force of the Ceres Asteroid. The thought was so horrible that it woke Old Mary. Rousing herself from her stupor, she hurriedly picked up the picture to confirm the accuracy of this new dream-delivered idea.

In my dream, beautiful dreamer was truly dead. How could I be so certain after such a long time of wondering? Because it came to me in my dream that the beautiful dreamer lies on the other side of the river! The river in the stained-glass window, like crossing the Jordan into the afterlife, represents the separation between life and death! Beautiful dreamer is on the other side of the river because she's already dead!

The African American spirituals of yesteryear, often sung when she was a little child, flashed in her mind. *I wonder if I can dredge up the words:*

159

I'll meet you in the morning
When you reach the promised land
On the other side of the Jordan
For I'm bound for the promised land

Old Mary continued her feverish ruminations. *That's it! The river is the river of death, and Beautiful dreamer has crossed over it! The African American spiritual, "Deep River," uses the same image. "Deep river, my home is over Jordan, deep river." Another one! The stained-glass window pictures a lover who mourns because his beloved has already crossed the Jordan into the afterlife! Beautiful dreamer is not sleeping. She's dead!*

Old Mary's brain worked furiously. *If the beautiful dreamer is truly dead, then Cory, her real-life counterpart, also crosses Jordan even though she's so young. The cause of death? No doubt the explosion caused by the man with the tattoo on his arm. My dear Cory is in terrible trouble! No wonder the song refers to clouds of sorrow! No wonder the head of beautiful dreamer is tilted so awkwardly—she's dead! Cory, I must warn you immediately! Oh, Cory, oh, Cory! You're in horrible danger!*

Old Mary hurriedly arose from her bed. Normally, she rested on the side of the bed before standing on her feet to avoid the light-headedness which accompanies rapid movement and, in turn, leads to falling in older folks. In her frantic haste, she stood up quickly and, her head spinning, grasped the various chairs as she stumbled through the living room to the kitchen phone.

Cory, I must warn you! Old feet, you've got to do your job. Body, you cannot fall. You cannot. I must warn Cory! I must tell beautiful dreamer! By her recliner, she again started to fall but caught herself on the chair. *Old feet, you must do your work. My beautiful dreamer's in danger! Lord, help me! I can't faint. Later, all right, but not just yet! Help me, Lord!*

She made it to the kitchen, though she again nearly lost her balance as she stood in the archway. Once at the phone she fumbled in her haste and dropped the receiver. When she hastily bent over to pick it up, she again, rising quickly, had a fierce attack of light-headedness and swooned as she rummaged through some papers for

Cory's phone number. Holding on to the wall, she managed, despite the wildly swirling digits in front of her, to locate the number.

You can do this, crooked old finger. You can dial this number. Stop shaking, finger! Why is everything spinning in front of me? Her finger violently shook as she tried to push the correct numbers. Clearly in a state of panic, she breathed hard, her pulse racing. *Cory, you're in danger! Please, Lord, don't let me have a heart attack. Not today, and I mustn't faint. I can faint later. A nap will do this old body good even here on the hard linoleum floor; but, Lord, not now, not yet, for I have to warn beautiful dreamer!"*

Again, she tried to dial the right numbers. Again, she swooned and braced herself against the archway. Finally, she managed the miraculous. *Thank you, Lord, I think I did it. I hear it ringing! I hope I dialed the right number! Lord, let it be. Pick up, beautiful dreamer, pick up! Beam on my heart, beautiful dreamer!*

In her nervousness, she babbled incessantly. *Don't faint, Old Mary. Thank You, Jesus. Cory, please don't die. Cross the Jordan some other day!* The phone in Cory's kitchen continued to ring. *You're too young to cross over now. Pick up, beautiful dreamer!* Old Mary's heart pounded, and her face was flushed. *Please, please answer the phone! You're in danger!"*

Cory picked up the phone. "Hello, this is the Mohney residence."

Old Mary started to speak, "Hel…," but she fell to the floor in a heap, dropping the receiver, which banged to the floor beside her head.

"What was that?" Cory shrieked, jerking the phone away from the racket crashing in her ear. "I just heard an awful banging sound on the phone, but no one was there."

"Who do you think it was?" Jude asked.

She listened intently again. "I don't know. No one's there, but wait." Cory pressed the receiver to her ear. "I hear someone breathing!"

"Why won't the person talk?"

"I don't know." Cory again talked into the receiver. "Hello! Hello!" Nobody answered. "Must be a wrong number."

"That happens too often."

"I'm dying to get to Little Gidding, so I can finish a certain painting. And you, love of my life, must finish that wonderful poem."

"We can visit the newly-opened room too."

Cory stole a quick glance at the telephone. "That was strange. Must have dialed a wrong number."

"I have no idea, but let's go, my love!"

They hugged and kissed and walked out the door.

Chapter 27

Abe Badoane was aware of Jude and Cory's plan to return to the mine in the evening. While he did not know of Little Gidding, he suspected that they had located an underground cubicle which they utilized for their secret meeting place. He continued to reflect on his revenge plot.

> *Cat and the mouse—*
> *I like this game.*
> *Wanna play house?*
> *Serpent's my name,*
> *And on you I'll douse*
> *Some rocks and flame!*
> *Yes, I like this game and will sniff them out! Here*
> *mousie, come get your cheese!*

Jude and Cory pulled into the mine parking lot and walked toward the main entrance. In his backpack, Jude carried a couple of books for his hideaway "library" in Little Gidding and additional art supplies for Cory. "You have a regular atelier in there, my beautiful dreamer! Yes, a real art studio. I can't imagine you'll need any more art supplies beside these."

"You're right, so no further excuses now. I have everything." She looked at her watch. "Let's finish our discussion about art as we drive back into the mine."

"Great idea." They continued their walk across the parking lot.

"I loved our discussion of those famous quotations." Cory thought for a moment. "Give me the Leonardo da Vinci one again. You only gave me the first part."

"Leonardo said, 'The artist sees what others only catch a glimpse of.'"

"That's so good, and I completely agree. That's because we artists look with a sanctified imagination."

"I agree, but you're the one who rattles off the art quotations. I'm open for more."

"How about the Emerson one I shared with you last week? 'Every artist was first an amateur.'"

"I like that one, since it gives us would-be writers hope."

"Another of my favorites is by Robert Henri. This might not be the exact quotation but it's close. 'The object isn't to make art; it's to be in that wonderful state which makes art inevitable.' For me that is so true, since it's the artist's task to stay, much as possible, in the right frame of mind to produce art."

"That means clearing the mind of the junk and clutter which obstructs the artist's vision. Is that his point?"

"Exactly."

"No wonder you like that one. By the way, how do you know so many quotes? You were spouting them off non-stop on our way here."

"You really want me to answer that?"

"I wouldn't have asked if I didn't."

"I read about art constantly in the dark years." Cory traced the grain in the door frame of the lounge. "The five long years when we were separated. I have a whole journal full of famous quotations about art. I'll show you some day."

"I'd like to see it."

"There are some winners there which helped me decide to stick with my art. You know I almost abandoned it altogether during the long winter of my discontent. Those quotations inspired me and gave me hope."

"Sorry to bring it up."

"You can apologize by giving another quotation out of your encyclopedic brain. You know more than just literature."

"I tend to know what literary folks say about art. Like Kurt Vonnegut who said something like this. 'To practice any art, no matter how well or badly, is a way to make your soul grow. So do it.' That's close. I agree with that one too because the soul grows and deepens and matures as it expresses its art."

"Kurt Vonnegut's not my favorite writer, but I do like that."

"Your turn."

"How about Van Gogh? 'I dream my painting and then I paint my dream.'"

"I've heard that before but didn't know Vincent said it."

"I'm pretty sure it is. Your turn."

"I'm at the end of my list, beautiful dreamer. I don't know art as you do." Jude put his fingers to his mouth in thought. "Wait a minute. I remember something Picasso once said. Help me say it. The one about art washing away something. Remember that one?"

"Yes, I wrote that one in my journal. 'Art washes away from the soul the dust of everyday life.'"

"That's it!"

Cory watched as Jude donned his backpack. "You realize that people think your backpack is part of your body. You're never without it."

"I know. I got in the habit of carrying it on campus. I guess I picked up the habit from the students. One sees fewer briefcases these days." He patted his backpack. "There are some things in here which I'm never without." He smiled at Cory and touched her art satchel. "Speaking of addenda to the body, what about your satchel? You're joined at the hip with it!"

"You got me there!" An effervescent smile came to her lips as she put her arm in Jude's. "But let's talk about your backpack." She patted the top of it. "You keep the rope in there, right? But you avoid talking about it."

"There's nothing to say except it was Grandpa's, and it was the rope he was using the day he died—the rope that killed him, I could morbidly add! I also keep Grandpa's Pirates ball cap in there too. He was a big Danny Murtaugh and Bucs fan." Jude clutched the backpack. "Those are my only tangible links to him."

"That's so sweet that you keep these palpable connections with you." She looked at her watch. "All right, it's a plan. We'll go see the new section about eight o'clock."

"That will give us a good hour and a half to work in Little Gidding."

"This might be the day when I finish my painting."

"This lovely time when we can immerse ourselves in our glorious art!"

At this point, Zoe's head dropped and the fur came up on his back. "Hey, what's going on with Zoe? Look how rattled he is. You'd think he saw a grizzly!"

"Or a king cobra! My goodness, his ears are even laid back! Take it down a notch, Zoe. You like Little Gidding. Remember?"

Jude and Cory were not aware that mystery man Abe had been departing the building when they pulled in the parking lot, exited their car, and started toward the mine entrance. When Abe saw them walking toward the entryway, he came back into the building, quickly ducked out of sight behind the vending machines, and waited for them to pass. *It's not my intent to eavesdrop on their conversation, so I'll just hide over here behind the vending machines until they pass and then continue on my merry way to the parking lot. Lay low and hide from the enemy—my well-honed strategy!*

The news Abe gleaned from listening to them as they entered the mine, however, was the last remaining piece of information he needed to launch his plan. *I loved what they were saying about art and actually had a few quotations in mind which I could have contributed to the discussion—like Joshua Reynolds's famous pronouncements in his* Discourses on Art. *But I now have a different task at hand, so the quotations will have to wait, especially since I've learned something important. Jude and Cory plan to explore the newly-opened section this very evening! How very fortunate. For me, that is, but not for them! They'll romp to room eight! Be prompt and not late!*

Abe continued thinking to himself. *Very interesting! They probably don't know that the bolters hit a major snag. Those back rooms won't be open for a couple weeks. Ignorance is bliss, but sometimes it spells disaster, and I'm, alas, the tragedy master.*

Abe had learned from the plant geologist that when bolting this section of the roof, the roofing crew had discovered a most unusual phenomenon, prompted by a few pieces of loose coal which had slipped through a seam in the limestone roof. Though seams in the ceiling were always a source of worry to the bolting crew, since one could never know when chunks of loose limestone would sprinkle through them onto the floor or bodies, they were actually quite common. In the mushroom mine, thus, cave-ins were the real and constant threat, but fortunately newly-enhanced bolting procedures had all but eliminated the threat in recent years.

The sighting of bits of coal, on the other hand, was unheard of. The mine geologist spoke with a fellow scientist about "the rogue seam of coal which runs above and parallel to the limestone seam." Abe had learned from the geologist that the normal band of separation between the limestone and coal seams was atypically thin in this particular region of the county and that, as a result, chunks of coal filtered down through the limestone crevasses into this particular mine room. The geologist had reported to the administrators that the coal deposit of the Kittanning seam, which lay directly overhead, was separated from the limestone by "an unusually thin stratum of earth." This thin stratum, he explained, "resembles a mere encrustation, known to us geologists as an exudation, more than a typical seam."

Speaking "in English" to some of the employees, the geologist explained that the coal mine above had been a major industry at one time but was completely abandoned once it was mined out years ago. Even the thriving mining town which had grown up overnight had vanished, not a sign remaining of its former glory days. The geologist concluded his report by noting that "the coal miners in that distant past could never have dreamed that, as they extracted coal, a huge limestone quarry lay directly beneath the huge mining operation. To put it bluntly, those miners were in real danger as they extracted the coal!"

"It's the same for us," he continued. "Until this finding, we had no idea that we are only feet away from the coal mining operation overhead. I'll say this in 'plain English.' Because an unusually thin band of earth separates the coal and limestone seams in this particular area, it's one hell of a dangerous place. While those guys were mining coal in this region, they were in constant danger that the coal mine floor they stood on might collapse into the limestone cavern below. Given the thinness of the band of earth that separates the coal and limestone seams, it's amazing that never happened." He paused to shuffle his papers together. "It's just as amazing that the coal mine above, with all its heavy equipment, never crashed into our mushroom farm!"

Abe had originally planned his attack against Jude and Cory in the near future, but learning that they would be in Little Gidding this very evening, he decided to act immediately. *I had counted on brainless Bull to take down the do-not-enter signs and no-trespassing cones at the worksite so that I, meanwhile, could retrieve and plant the explosives. Even more advantageously, that would have given me a stooge to share the blame. But Brainless Bull is not around, so in his absence I am forced to act alone. No problem for the sneaky snake, For Jude and Cory's lives I'll take! With much unmitigated joy, I'll deftly work my lethal ploy!*

Chapter 28

After Jude and Cory proceeded to Little Gidding, Abe slipped from his hiding place and went directly to the room under construction which was cordoned off by a variety of safety ropes, cones, and warning signs. Alone in the dark, he removed and stashed them around the corner. With his miner's lamp, he inspected the front and center support beam overhead, which secured enormous chunks of limestone, not yet plated and bolted. Normally, several beams would be in place to brace such a weakened area, but in this case a single metal post held up an entire section of compromised slate.

Abe carefully examined the crevasse overhead. *Someone's goose would be cooked if that carelessness were reported to the authorities! There should be multiple plates and posts supporting this highly dangerous area, but in my case this faulty placement of the support posts works to my distinct advantage. Small chunks of coal and dust cover the floor here. Dark streaks of coal dust have striated the sides of the roof crevasse overhead, indicating that the coal seam has to be a mere few feet above these limestone rocks! As the plant geologist says, "That is an extraordinarily rare phenomenon!"*

Abe quickly completed his two-fold task. After removing the signs, cones, and safety rope, he then slammed the top of the support post with a sledge so that, leaning even more perilously, the post secured the huge chunks of limestone overhead with only the slightest edge of the metal plate. As he hit the support beam, a large chunk of limestone dislodged from the roof and fell. Abe saw it coming, dodged in the nick of time, and sustained only a graze to the side of his helmet. Immediately overhead, he could hear the rocks as they grinded and grated against each other.

He noted in his diary, "I haven't moved that fast since my getaway that day at the cabin! A mere sliver of steel plate keeps the entire roof from caving in. I hid all tools and the chunks of limestone that fell, including the one that nearly hit me on the head, and walked back and forth several times in this area to give the appearance of heavy traffic. The place looks as though it had been cleared for use days ago!"

His draconian task complete, Abe Badoane sped through the mine in his electric cart. He saw a couple people outside the pasteurization rooms and made a point to tell them he was leaving for the day. As he bade them goodbye, he asked Curley what time it was. "Thanks. Darn watch! It just doesn't keep accurate time." Curley gave him the time. "Okay, seven fifteen." Abe pretended to reset his watch. "Take care, boss. I'm clearing out." He started to leave. "Oh, you're the baseball enthusiast. Did you catch in the sports news that the Minnesota Twins had their second triple play of the year the other day?"

"No, I hadn't heard."

"Can you imagine having two triple plays in one season? It was the August 8 game, I think."

"Thanks for telling me, Abe."

"Take care. My strawberry patch is beckoning to me!"

Abe exited the mine, strolled slowly to his car, and then, pretending he forgot something, returned and paused in clear view of the security camera, making certain that he was fully visible. He went back inside the lounge and picked up a magazine and departed a second time. There could be no mistaking his departure from the mine at 7:23 p.m. Abe went to his car, slowly drove, and waved warmly at the security guard on his way out. *A calm appearance is absolutely crucial. That way, the idiot will not suspect what I'm up to!*

Thinking on the spot of another way of verifying departure time, he backed up to talk to Sam the guard. "Hey, Sam, I know you like a good joke. Here's one for you."

"Lay it on me."

"It was two o'clock in the morning and a husband and wife are in bed when the phone rings. Let's say the woman was Beavers to make the more joke relevant. After all, we know of *her* reputation. When the phone rings, her husband picks up the receiver and sleepily says hello, pauses while a man speaks on the other end, and then says, 'How the heck do I know. What am I—the weatherman?' Beavers rolls over and mumbles through half-opened eyes, 'Who was that?' The husband says, 'Some jerk who asked if the coast was clear.'" Sam laughed uproariously.

Abe held his watch to his ear to see if it was ticking. "By the way, what time is it?"

"I have seven twenty-seven."

Abe looked at his watch. "Guess it's working after all—thank you. You have a good evening, sir. I'm on my way to do some weeding in the strawberry patch."

Once out of sight, Abe drove like a madman to Yellow Dog, and after hiding his car in the brush, he retrieved his fishing rod and gear which he strapped to his back. He walked through the brush and checked several spots along the stream as if looking for trout. After pausing a few times, he slowly wound his way up the hill to the back entrance to the mine. *I will walk slowly in case any fishermen in the brushy areas along the stream might see me.* At the mine entrance, he ditched his fishing rod in the brush and entered the hillside opening to the mine. Once inside, he hurriedly raced toward the new section. *Though I have quite a distance to traverse, I think my timing, based on Jude and Cory's reference to eight o'clock, is good. Well done, Abe!*

Within fifteen minutes of brisk walking, he had serpentined his way through the mine labyrinth to the new section. Once in that area, he gently took a small pouch of home-brewed dynamite which consisted of nitroglycerine mixed with sawdust.

Because it's moist, the compound is highly explosive. I'll carefully position the home-made dynamite in the crevasse above the metal plate at the support post. Yes, right there. Easy does it, and don't move a millimeter, baby—not yet! The falling rocks ought to ignite the dynamite upon impact and cause a nasty cave-in.

This final detail complete, he took his place in a secluded niche immediately around the corner where he waited in the pitch black.

My timing is absolutely perfect. All I have to do is wait for the hot lovers to make their grand appearance.

> *Now to the mine at last they come*
> *On this good and lovely night.*
> *For it's a fe, fi, fo, and a fum,*
> *When explosives blast so bright!*

In his dark and lonely cell, Abe Badoane reflected on past events in his life, and soon his infant, little JJ, came to mind. *How I loved that baby who in his few hours of life looked up at me with those bright, blue eyes!* At Abe's request, he was allowed to hold the infant for a few precious minutes. *I held my darling baby, and how very beautiful you were! I remember every single detail of your face. That was the pinnacle of joy in my life!*

Huddled against the cold wall of his dark cell, Abe remembered those happy moments when his large hands cradled the little infant. *As I looked into the baby's bright eyes, which glistened like sun-blanched diamonds, my big fingers stroked his delicate features. The pastor used to quote a verse from Peter, something about the light shining in a dark place and the morning star rising in your hearts. Well, that babe was my shining light, my morning star; and he breathed new life into my pathetic heart! Thank You, Lord! For those few hours, life was good, but out, out, brief candle! As Robert Frost says, nothing gold can stay, and that golden moment was as fleeting as the duration of Macbeth's brief candle.*

Abe Badoane was in those days a man on the rise—joyful, hopeful, and extremely bright. Today, he was a man whose star had descended. *Far below the horizon! Instead of a beloved baby, I cradle a box of dynamite in my hands! How very sick!*

Having taken off his miner's hat, he rocked his head back and forth on the hard limestone wall and felt the scalding tears stream down his face. As he waited, he felt a trickle of cold water from the side of the limestone wall run down the back of his neck. *That reminds me of another time when I felt the same drip-drip trickle of water run down my neck. I was a twelve-year-old boy and was at one of the ponds in the Center Hill area. I had just been baptized by Pastor William B. Gauntz and was standing in the pond beside this loving man, water up to our chests. He had always been like a father to me.* The tradition of that church was trine immersion, and consequently Abe had just been completely submerged three consecutive times—in the name of the Father, the Son, and the Holy Spirit.

After the immersion, the pastor laid his large hand on my head. As he prayed in the blazing afternoon sun, I felt the warm life-giving water from his hand and sleeve drip down the back of my neck. It made such an impression on me that, though a kid of twelve, I wrote about it in my journal.

Abe's Journal (written when twelve):

I never felt so loved and accepted and appreciated as I did in the pond after baptism. I float these days on a dreamy cloud of warm and loving forgiveness. For the first time since the rape, I feel clean again, and I feel happy all over. I'm now even going to forget the monster in the cabin. Well, I'll try real hard. I forgive you, horrible man. I won't even call you a bastard anymore. I have enough love in me that I can even forgive you. Even the shame that's always with me is now gone.

Pastor says the love of God is shed abroad in our hearts. I dint know what that means so I asked him. He said we can choose to tap into God's love anytime we want. We can use His love, instead of our own, to forgive anyone of anything. He said something like this. "Human love can't love at that transcendent level." I told him I didn't know what that means. He said, "We humans don't naturally love the way God does, but we can learn to use His love. It's called "agape" love. Use it, Abie! Activate it, especially at difficult times like the one you had after the cabin trauma. When your love runs out, tap into God's love."

If Jesus said, "Father, forgive them for they know not what they do," I can do that too and learn to love that way, so starting right now, I forgive you, monster. I don't wish you well. Not yet. But I'm praying about that too, and I'm going to do what pastor said Christians ought to do, and that's "give up their right to retaliate." He told me that meant to get back at someone, or I think he said to seek revenge. I won't do that. Maybe I'll learn to love you, monster man.

In his mind that trickle of warm baptism water down his neck had conjured up images of rebirth, regeneration, and transformation during that lovely age of innocence.

As a twelve-year-old boy, he had written a number of entries in his journal. A week after the baptism, he wrote the following.

Abe's Journal (Written when twelve):

The seventeenth-century poet Thomas Traherne describes my feeling more than anybody: "How bright are all things here." That's how I feel since I was baptized last week. How bright the world is, and that includes everything in it! "And all the works of God, so bright and pure, So rich and great did seem." Mr. Traherne, I feel the exact same way. I really do. Traherne says, "I within did flow With seas of life, like wine." Yes, seas of wine now flow through my being too. I can't suppress the ocean of love and goodness in my heart these days.

I really like this Traherne poem. I'd do anything to be able to write like that. To express things so good. Here's what he says in this poem:

Rich diamond and pearl and gold In ev'ry place was seen. Great wonders cloth'd with glory did appear, Amazement was my bliss.

That's exactly how I feel—alive and surrounded with rapture and everything dressed up nice and good with glory. I wish I could meet monster man just so I could tell him I love him and forgive him. Everything amazes me, and everything shines like gold and diamonds! Thank You, Jesus, that I live in this magnificent, beautiful world, and life really is wonderful. I've just now decided that I like Traherne as much as I like Milton and Shakespeare.

But today the water—trickling in the dark instead of dazzling sunlight, ice-cold, not sun-warmed—embodies Abe's mission of death, the pain of past loss, and the heinousness of evil. *What happened? I had been joyous at times in the early days of my youth but only at times, since the rape had obliterated all chances for true happiness and lasting joy. Still, I felt true ecstasy in the months after the baptism, but it didn't last. How could it? Still, many people commented in those days on my bright eyes, loving nature, good heart, and "gregarious personality."*

My teachers said: "He is such a fine boy and a whiz at the books." "What a bright young man, and what a great future awaits him!" How did I, from that promising if troubled youth, arrive at this prison house of pain and endless sorrow?

Abe took a flask from his pocket and, in the pitch dark, took a large swig of whiskey. *Since there's no way out of this pain, my only option is to escape it briefly and keep myself happily anesthetized. After all, that's the world's temporary cure.* He took another swig, but as he did so, his mind returned again to his boyhood baptism. *On that evening, the initiates participated in communion. As Pastor Gauntz held up the chalice, he contextualized the rite of communion within ancient Jewish wedding tradition. I was so moved by the experience that to this day I can paraphrase that loving man's statements.*

"When you candidates agree to drink from this cup, you are doing exactly what the Jewish bride of yesteryear did in the presence of her groom. You are saying, as she said to the groom, 'I am committed to you, husband, and you only for my entire life. I reserve myself for you and am betrothed to only you. There will never be another rival in my life. My drinking this cup is symbolic proof of my desire to love exclusively you, to be with only you.'"

Abe rolled his head back and forth against the cold, jagged limestone and clenched his fists in anguish. *"In drinking this cup, candidates, you are, similarly, making Christ first in your life. You are promising to honor and love Him as surely as a bride pledged herself solely to her betrothed. New believers in Jesus, when you drink this cup, understand that you are making a life-long commitment to our Lord. That is a commitment and a pledge which one makes with the utmost seriousness since it is a pledge never to be broken under any circumstances. Do you under-*

stand? *It is important that you comprehend the gravity of this moment. That means its seriousness. The cup is never taken lightly, flippantly, or half-heartedly!*"

As Abe fingered the flask in the dark and held it to his lips, he recalled the pastor's words about drinking this cup. *What a falling off is there! I hold a flask instead of a communion cup. I cradle a box of dynamite instead of a baby. I feel the water of death on my neck instead of the water of life. I crouch in the dark instead of leap in the sun. Instead of Traherne's pearls, and diamonds, and gold, I see only evil, snakes, and scorpions! What a wretch I am!*

Almost in an attempt to get away from himself, he crawled further into the darkened niche where he slouched against the wall. *Damn this place. Once I rapturously danced in the light.* Abe again escaped to the beauty of a Thomas Traherne poem, "The Rapture," which he had memorized as a twelve-year-old: *"From God above Being sent, the Heavens me inflame." Yes, I used to feel inflamed by heaven and on fire with spirit. I actually experienced that. Now Satan coils about my heart and fills it with cold death. What a wretched man I've become! Frailty, thy name is Abe!*

I recall the passage I read in Isaiah the other day. "We look for light, but there is darkness! For brightness, but we walk in blackness! We grope for the wall like the blind, And we grope as if we had no eyes" [Isaiah 59:9–10]. How very true that is! There is only darkness and blackness in me…like this dark corridor. I wish I could see you in heaven, Isaiah, just so we could discuss our similar feelings, but I know that will never happen because I'm doomed for the other place. Yet I thank you for writing something that describes my feeling so perfectly.

In the dark, he sobbed and sobbed. *JJ, my poor JJ! And my pitiful life. I say it again and again, say it many times every day: serpent man, you've mangled everything you've ever touched!*

Chapter 29

Back in Little Gidding Jude and Cory commenced talking after a period of silent work. "What do you think?" Jude asked. He had just added five more books to his hideaway study. "I'm getting quite a collection here. Pretty soon I'll be able to start a lending library." Both laughed. "Did you know that Benjamin Franklin started the world's first lending library?"

"I didn't know that."

"Yes, indeed. In Philadelphia, Pennsylvania. Okay, this is the big moment. Show me your masterpiece."

Cory had spent the last couple days working on her portrait of Jude, and while she hadn't finished all the final touches, she had made good progress and was generally pleased. She always called herself an amateur painter—"Amateur, preppy, very amateur!"—but in this case, she had captured Jude's likeness amazingly well.

Even Jude was astounded. "Cory, it looks just like me! I dislike most photos of me and always figured I'd hate my portrait even more, if there ever was one, but this really captures my likeness. It has similarities to my college graduation photo. You keep calling yourself an amateur, but this is pretty darn good."

"What was the famous quotation about artists starting as amateurs?"

"That was Emerson. He once said that every artist was first an amateur."

"You can see that I added a few features to show how boyish cuteness has hardened into handsome ruggedness." She enjoyed watching him blush. "That's a nice shade of scarlet on your face by the way! I could use that exact shade for this section here on the jaw." She made a brush mark at the bottom of his right cheek.

"What can I say but that I'm embarrassed? You did a good job, Cory. You really did."

"I took a couple of my favorite pics of you and blended them all together." Backing away, she studied her own work. "So it's actually a composite of several photos." Cory detached a couple photos that had been clipped to the top of her easel. "The squared jaw from this one, the curls down across your forehead on this one, and that smirky smile from this one!" She lay the photos on the table. "I'll modestly opine that the picture is all right in a pinch, but the guy is definitely great!"

"Well, you flatter me because I don't look that good, but one thing is certain."

"I'm waiting."

"It shows how your talent has progressed—really impressive. And here I thought you were putting the final touches on *New Every Morning*."

"I was going to touch up the right forehead but decided to leave well enough alone. Sometimes the artist has to move on. Mirlarna Armstrong wrote that in an essay once."

Jude continued to look at the portrait. "Do you think he'll like it?" Jude faced Cory and took her hand. "What do you think he'll say when we tell him the news?"

"I'm guessing he won't believe it at first and will probably deny it."

"But he'll have to since we have incontestable proof. Cory, I just can't get over it. And to think Old Mary knew all those years. I think it's amazing that she kept that secret to herself that whole time." Jude drew Cory to himself. "Well, that explains a lot of things, including the way he is."

"When are we going to tell him?"

"The next chance we get, for there's no need to wait. I want him to know now so the healing can begin."

Jude hugged her and kissed her passionately. "My love, my love, I wish we could stay right here forever, just like this! I'm crazy over you. I love you so much my heart hurts. I mean that. My heart aches with love."

"Mine too."

"I've read endless accounts of people loving so much that their hearts ached, but I always thought that was hyperbolic language and the stuff of poetry. This isn't. I say it again. My heart aches for love of you, Corinna Adelena!"

A tear came to Cory's eye. "Yes, my love. I know how you feel. I want so much to be able to show you how much I love you. This is so difficult. Why don't we get married right away?"

"You know I want to!"

"We could make it work!"

"Of course, we could." He hugged her firmly and slid his hand down her lower back and further. She noted Jude's frustration as he pulled away and tossed a book on the couch. Though feeling a torrent of emotions within, he chose to remain silent. There was nothing to say, as he was not about to sublimate through verbiage yet again. Slamming himself onto the couch, he thought of Eliot's line from "Burnt Norton." *"Words, after speech, reach Into the silence." They may reach into the silence, but they don't reach where I'd like to reach!*

When Jude departed Little Gidding, Cory picked up a couple things to take home. Although he was outside in the corridor, he came back into the hideaway and kissed her again. Jude's gesture of returning for a second kiss was, for Cory, unusual and caused her to reflect to herself as they rode in silence to the new section.

I loved it that Jude came back into Little Gidding to kiss me again. That was so tender of him, but that's my Jude! I knew he was aroused, really aroused in our hideaway, but this repeat kiss was not hormonally-induced like the earlier ones. The kissing in Little Gidding had really turned him on, but this second kiss was not about continuing the passion that had stirred us moments before. This was about something else. Maybe a desire to preserve the moment for its rare and sacred beauty. I guess that's it: it communicated farewell instead of passion. But why a farewell kiss that lies somewhere between a deep kiss and a goodbye kiss? It was strange and very different, but why feel that way about a simple kiss?

As Cory held his arm while they drove through the labyrinth of darkened corridors, a strange kind of foreboding came upon her. She again reflected in silence. *I know it was the second kiss that's making me feel this way.* Holding him very tight as they sped toward the new room, she continued her rumination. *I'd die if anything happened to my Jude!*

Seated in the back of the cart, Zoe drew near and licked Cory on the back of the neck at the moment when Cory's fear came upon her and then rested his snout on her shoulder. *What's going on here! First I get this inexplicable kiss from Jude, which of course I loved, and then Zoe for no good reason snuggles up to me like a long, lost friend. Both were lovely but very different gestures.*

As they sped down the corridors, Jude asked Cory to keep the map in front of her. "You be our navigator and tell me the turns. I'll do the driving!"

On and on they sped, turn after turn, corridor after corridor, deeper and deeper into the mine. "It's just ahead," Jude said as they approached the worksite. "They were right. The rooms are ready for use, and the warning light is now green. What are we waiting for?"

"Let's go for it. I've never been so excited!"

As Jude parked the cart, Cory jumped off, started running, and yelled, "Catch me if you can!" She sped toward the new room. A moment later, Jude parked the cart and started running after Cory who was some fifty feet in front of him.

As she ran into the room, an idea came to her. *I'll cup my hand around the front support pillar and, clutching it tightly, spin in a circle. The full spin complete, I'll continue my mad sprint into the new room ahead of Jude, yelling a second time over my shoulder, "Catch me if you can, slowpoke!" Even with the second it will take me to loop the pole, I'll still be ahead of Jude and arrive in the new room first.* "Last one in is a rotten egg!"

She sprinted into the front section of the room and arrived at the pole. As she twirled around it, the slight centripetal pressure, which she exerted on the support pole, kicked it violently to the side.

With a deafening, grating sound, huge chunks of limestone, supported by a mere sliver of the metal plate, came crashing down!

Chapter 30

The following is a compilation of Jude's random thoughts and impressions, which he distractedly scrawled during moments of intermittent sanity after the disastrous cave-in.

Jude's journal:

I had never seen her smile more radiantly—that full, ear-to-ear smile which I had been observing more frequently in recent weeks. She didn't smile that way in the first days after our reconciliation, since it took a while for the heat of our love to thaw her arctic soul. Far as that goes, it wasn't until later in the summer, when I was able to compare her former and present states that I realized how emotionally dead she had been back in May. When I speak of psychic deadness, I ought to know, for I'm the pro!

As she pirouetted around the pole, her hair flowed behind her head, jiggling and bouncing and cascading downward, unfolding waves of luxuriance airily floating along. Neither of us had worn our mine helmets, that dreadful error for which I'll never forgive myself! But the absence of head protection allowed her beautiful tresses to blissfully bob in the breeze.

Because it was a scene that etched itself into my brain so vividly, I often replay her pole spin in slow motion. Even as it unfolded in front of me, I knew it was one of those experiences which was so defining that it would always be with me, would replay endlessly on the screen of my mind. First, I see her run toward the pole in slow motion. Her left arm slowly extends to grab the pole for her counter-clockwise spin. She starts into her twirl, her right arm perpendicularly bent at the elbow and gracefully extending upward, Spanish-ballerina style, with the index finger arching overhead. She merely needed a rose in her mouth to complete the iconic image!

Her swing around the pole continues in very slow motion until she frontally faces me. I stop the tape instantly for my favorite freeze shot, the one that is always before me. Cory is looking directly at me, her free hand reaching skyward, her outer leg kicking upward—a fluid, graceful, dancing glide. Time has completely stopped during this moment when I can never gain the prize, kiss her, or win her love. I have, alas, become the lover in Keats's "Ode on a Grecian Urn":

> Bold lover, never, never canst thou kiss,
> Though winning near the goal—yet do not grieve;
> She cannot fade, though thou hast not thy bliss,
> Forever wilt thou love, and she be fair!

How very true: she will never age, nor will her goddess beauty ever fade. Frozen in time, she is forever beautiful, immortally youthful.

As all people of all ages have desired, my beautiful dreamer has defeated time and, in doing so, has become Shakespeare's Cleopatra: "Age cannot wither her, nor custom stale Her infinite variety." Like Cleopatra on her Nile-gliding silver barge, like the lovers on Keats's urn, my Cory will never wither, never age, never lose her statuesque beauty, for she has crossed the Jordan— oblivious to time, angelically beautiful, serenely ensconced in that eternal paradise of glorious perfection.

Why do I describe this moment in such detail? The answer is simple: I'm looking at a photo on my desk—the one of her in this precise position! Because the new section of the mine was under constant surveillance, it was easy for Morley Spencer and his assistant Barry Kepple to produce the footage of the disaster, from which he extracted and enhanced this priceless photo. He framed it and gave it to me as a gift a few months later.

This photo of the radiant Cory, which I call "My Pirouetting Princess," has always been my favorite, for it depicts Cory at the very pinnacle of earthly beauty. How she starkly contrasts to the dark surroundings—this beautiful woman, my pulsating, shining angel, who is moments away from being swallowed into the black womb of eternal night, beautiful dreamer goddess, entering the afterlife moments later!

In one of his many monumental works on the Civil War, noted historian Shelby Foote describes the scene at Gettysburg on the third day of the decisive battle. He asks the reader to imagine the moment right before Pickett's Charge at Gettysburg on July 3, 1863. It is a hot July day in the lush fields of southern Pennsylvania. In the opinion of many, certainly Robert E. Lee, the South is a single battle away from winning the Civil War. As a result, the Confederate troops, whiling away the nervous hours on Seminary Ridge, brim with hope in this time-stopped moment before they charge the Yankee troops garrisoned on Cemetery Ridge.

The Confederates had more or less won these first two days of the awful fighting at Gettysburg and merely have to see the thing through to the end. The battle will be tough—they readily admit that they're in for the fight of their lives in the torturous heat and will face heavy casualties—but they already savor the sweet taste of victory. According to Shelby Foote, the Confederate sympathizers must have luxuriated in that pre-battle confidence when they couldn't refrain from feverishly scripting themselves as the inevitable victors. If only time would have stopped during those moments of ecstasy when they were so close to winning, so close to ultimate triumph! If only a different set of circumstances had eventuated that fateful day! If only.

That idea of relishing the moment prior to the disaster, that intense backward look before the course of history was forever changed, is exactly what I have been doing for many long months. In Eliot's memorable phrase, I have been trying to ring the bell backward, but that is not possible. The bell doesn't ring backward; it only rings forward. Time progresses, never regresses.

Yet how close, how very close to being different! Why did Cory and I go to the new rooms that evening? Why didn't we wear helmets? That simple detail by itself would have prevented the tragedy. Why had Abe Badoane become such an evil man that he plotted the deaths of two totally innocent people? What happens to a person that he or she becomes the very incarnation of evil? What would life have been like had my beloved Cory lived? Where would we be living now? How many kids would we have? What are their names? Did we name the one daughter Cordelia as Cory wanted to? ("You have to admit, 'Cordelia' is a bit like 'Cory!' We could call her Cordy which rhymes with your Aunt Dordy!"). Do the kids favor Cory or me?

I have to stop this monologue! I say with King Lear, "O, that way madness lies." I'll drive myself insane if I keep thinking of how it might have been. John Greenleaf Whittier, you were so right: "For of all sad words of tongue or pen, The saddest are these: 'It might have been!'" It might have been! If Cory had lived, it might have been! But it wasn't!

I'm at the sad epicenter of describing the fateful day of the mine tragedy, the day that ended the life of the beautiful Corinna Adelena Mohney. Someday I'll rework the following notes into prose and continue what I've started here, but I can't do so now. However, since my publisher has repeatedly asked—let me be honest, prodded me across weeks—for this material, I at least make a beginning by jotting down some skeletal reflections which I'll one day flesh out when this mind is sane. "When this mind is sane!" There's a laugh! As if I really expect that to happen! As if this distracted globe will ever know normality again!

But right now, I'm doing this lecture tour through Egypt and Jordan. My hope is that my revisitation to those places I frequented so often during my lecture-abroad months will reignite the creative flame and help me slough off the inertia that has plagued me for months. "Out of Egypt I called my Son" [Hosea

11:1], and out of Egypt may I call this story. The Hosea story is about God's love for mankind which culminated in the birth of the Christ. The second is the story of Cory's and my love for each other. May I summon the strength to relate the details of our love, including her tragic end which occurred the awful day the music died.

Life stopped, Keats-style, at that moment when Cory circled around the upright support beam. Tension on the pole wasn't exerted until she completed the spin and, to maintain her balance as she faced me, tugged on the pole—that slight pull at the end of the ballerina twirl which sent the pole flying.

As I hurtled toward her, I spotted the huge slab of limestone which perilously hung above her. *It's ready to drop at any second!* Just as I screamed for Cory to jump backward, a huge chunk of limestone came down and hit me on the head. I fell to the ground, dazed, incoherent, and fighting to stay conscious. Events swirled in my mind as I floated in a twilight zone between consciousness and unconsciousness.

I saw myself stagger to my feet, nearly falling twice as I did so. When I flicked the hair from my face, I felt a hot stream of blood oozing from a deep gash on the side of my head. *Blood has already drenched my shoulder and puddled around my collar!* Though in and out of a comatose-like state, I guess I had presence of mind enough to take off my outer shirt and tie a tourniquet around my head to stop the bleeding. I tried my best to think sanely and stay calm. As I did so, one thought kept pummeling my brain: *Why didn't we put on our helmets?* I cursed myself for that stupid error!

I can honestly say that during those awful moments after the accident I wasn't concerned about myself. Assessing my own physical state was a self-indulgent luxury for which I did not have time and shunned completely, because only Cory mattered. Amid the thick dust from the cave-in, I knew I had to find my bearings. In those first minutes after the cave-in, I was so disoriented that I didn't even know for sure where I was, what was happening, or if I was alive. Was it the dust in my eyes or the dust in the air that kept me from seeing properly? Eventually, after my eyes started to focus, I shined my miner's light in Cory's direction. The shock hit me as hard as the limestone boulder to my head.

Through the heavy dust, I could see Cory's inert form, sprawled lifelessly amid the rocks!

Chapter 31

Jude's Journal (Continued):

I could imagine how she had been slammed to the ground and pinned by a large rock, possibly the huge slab of limestone that had been suspended above the support brace. While I couldn't tell at that distance through the thick dust, her leg appeared to be unnaturally twisted under the slab. Completely motionless, she had sustained deep abrasions to her upper torso and head which awkwardly tilted to the side.

Precisely like the beautiful dreamer in the Stephen Foster stained-glass window—same exact position! How sick of me to make that awful comparison at this dread moment, but I've never been able to stop this mind from making endless associations and connections! Looking again at the position of her head, I feared a broken neck. Zoe lay beside her with his head on her stomach, the faithful dog loyal to the end.

Imagery of Vietnam soldiers crawling in the swampy mud and trying valiantly to get one knee ahead of the other filled my head as I struggled to crawl toward her amid the rubble of fallen limestone. Eventually, I dragged myself to her side and lay my head on her chest to see if she was breathing. Though dealing with my own racing heart and tears which blinded my eyes and impeded my vision, I listened carefully. I couldn't stop screaming, "Please beat heart. Don't stop. Beat heart! Be strong!" I picked up a very weak pulse. "Cory!" I screamed, "Don't die! You can make it, honey. Please don't die! I'll get an ambulance here soon. Hang on, beautiful dreamer, just hang on!"

It was then that I looked at her face and saw the blood issuing from her mouth. The ghastly bright red contrasted with the gray of her blouse, the blackness of the room, and the sick whiteness of her skin. Life-giving blood, lying in a small pool in her Adam's apple, had already drenched her sweatshirt. *No doubt about it, that quantity of blood indicates massive internal injuries! That is death's harbinger. Hello, Grim Reaper, you most unwelcome of visitors!*

I hated the thought that came to my mind, but the reality in front of me was so awful that for one second, I deflected the pain by thinking of something Keats once wrote to his beloved Fanny: "I almost wish we were butterflies and liv'd but three summer days—three such days with you I could fill with more delight than fifty common years could ever contain."

How true, how agonizingly true! Oh, that Cory and I were butterflies and could fly out of this death trap right now. Fly and romp in cerulean blue skies where stars glisten like diamonds. Far away from this unimaginable hell on earth where my beautiful dreamer lies drenched in her life-giving blood.

Though battling my own disorientation and fighting to think rationally, I struggled to face the stark truth. While I couldn't articulate it, the thought finally slammed into my mind. *My beloved Cory is fighting for her life!* When all is said and done, humankind can bear only so much reality, and so we develop clever ways of dodging unpleasant truths. Nevertheless, even in that ghastly moment, I knew that my beloved Cory was dying. "Please, my darling, don't die. Please, Cory, live!"

I struggled to my feet and tried to walk but stumbled over rocks and fell twice. Eventually, I was clear of the cave-in and limped out into the corridor to the emergency phone. I dialed 911, sounded the alarm bell, and reported the accident to mine security. The ambulance from Worthington sped toward the mine in minutes. I did my best to stay calm, but my head throbbed, my mind whirled like a child's top, and my eyes focused poorly.

I staggered, then fell, and crawled back to Cory, to my beautiful dreamer. *She remains totally unconscious and oblivious to any stimuli, verbal or physical. Is it my imagination, or is she lapsing deeper and deeper into unconsciousness? I can barely get a pulse.* That was one thing I was absolutely sure about. *I'm sure she's slipping away!*

Right after the accident, the small pool of blood that lay in the indentation below her Adam's apple—my doctor later informed me that it was the "suprasternal notch" or "jugular notch"—was one of the clear signs of life, since I could actually see in it the slight, rippling vibrations of moving blood when she breathed. But as time went on this pool of blood stopped quivering. *There is less and less movement! Quiver, blood, like before! Beautiful, dreamer, wake unto me!*

Without moving her body, I placed the side of my head on her chest. *Her pulse is definitely weaker!* I put my face against hers, spoke softly to her, and gently caressed her head. I padded the blood from her seeping wounds. Strands of her beautiful hair, now blood-streaked, lay across her face. *Those are supposed to be bronze-lit, flying strands of hair atop a jouncing summer hay wagon, not blood-soaked in a cave of death! Oh, God, please don't let her die.*

The minutes while I waited for the ambulance to arrive seemed to take hours, but the speeding ambulance arrived in a mere sixteen minutes. The activity from the moment when it slammed to a stop was chaotic. As I watched the ambulance pull up outside our room, I remember being grateful for the wide corridors that allowed large vehicles to navigate the mine tunnels. *At least that's one slight blessing since they won't have to carry her a long distance on a gurney!*

By this time, the safety engineer and the head of human resources had also arrived. Like me, they stood helplessly by, since we could do nothing but wish the paramedics success as they tended to Cory. I remember a comment the safety engineer made to Mr. Guthrie, the human resources head. "Where are all the no-trespassing signs and cones? This area should be completely cordoned off."

"There's something fishy about this."

Writing this is even more difficult than I thought it would be. I may be thinking rationally now as I sit at my desk here in the All Saints' Cathedral Guest House in Zamalek, Cairo, but the night of the tragedy I definitely was not. More than that, how can I sit here and narrate the saddest event of my life? How does one write about the loss of his love, his soul mate? But for my own future good, I have to try to record that hideous sequence of events.

What was especially crazy was that I vividly heard Cory yell, "Jude, Jude!" the whole time the paramedics tended to her. I guess that shows how desperately I wanted for her to speak my name. Frantic through it all, poor Zoe stayed by Cory the entire time, uttering guttural sounds that were a cross between a groan and a stifled bark.

The ambulance medics tended to Cory immediately. First, they lifted the huge slab from her leg, which I had been unable to lift myself. They surmised that her foot was badly sprained and possibly fractured. Her neck, fortunately, was not broken, though her head had been awkwardly jammed sideways when she fell. Fearing a possible spinal injury, the medics took appropriate precautions. They placed her on a gurney and hastily gave her oxygen and units of blood, monitoring her vitals the whole time.

I heard one of the paramedics comment, "When she was knocked backward and pinned, one of these large limestone rocks must have come down and hit her squarely in the chest." He paused, looked at me, and then said, "I fear massive internal injuries." The paramedic—I heard his friend call him Feeney—pointed toward her bloody shirt. "A lot of blood has come out of her mouth. It's the internal injuries, not the foot, that worry me."

Mr. Feeney looked at me intently for a moment but didn't speak, as though he wanted to say something but declined at the last moment. Though I knew what he was deliberating, he settled for a minimalist observation. "I'm sure you know how serious this is."

I know you're preparing me for the worst!

Chapter 32

Jude's Journal (Continued):

When one of the two paramedics taped the wound on my head, I said, "Don't worry about me. I just want Cory to live. Nothing else matters. Nothing!"

I remember him looking at me gravely. "Yes, we're taking care of her, Mr. Hepler, but we need to tend to you as well. You took a vicious hit to the head. Your shirt is soaked in blood across the shoulder and down the front. You've lost more blood than you realize." He peered at me with that how-much-do-I-tell-him look. "Truth is, we're every bit as concerned about you as we are your girlfriend. What did you say her name was?"

"Cory."

I looked again at my beautiful dreamer. After taking her pulse, Mike, the paramedic in charge, spoke again. "Her pulse is weakening, and her blood pressure is very low." He hesitated as people do when saying something they don't like. "Dangerously so. We've already contacted the ER at the hospital." As they carefully placed her on the gurney and wheeled her toward the ambulance, Mike slowly began to open up. "Life can't be sustained for long when the pressure's that low."

Don't say that!

"They're prepared to give her immediate treatment before life-flighting her to Pittsburgh." Again, he hesitated, but finally the dreaded words came, "Be prepared for the worst."

Weeks after the accident, Morley Spencer located the security footage which showed the mine cave-in and the activity surrounding the rescue operation: the ambulance's screeching stop, the scurrying medics, the fast but smooth placement of Cory on the gurney, and the quick departure. Combing through this footage, he came across a clip from the security camera which was positioned at the mine entrance. From this angle, the ambulance is readily visible as it speeds down the main corridor; but the detail that caught Morley's attention, and mine too, was the camera clip of the rear of the departing vehicle.

The ambulance interior was clearly visible during those torturously long moments while the vehicle was completely stopped to allow the large exit door to rise. Through the back window of the ambulance, the film shows me lowering my head to Cory's face. This is the second photo which Morley gave me, and while it has been too painful for me to display, I keep it in a treasured place in my library. Someday I'll have the courage to look at it and maybe even keep it on my desk, but not just yet!

Months later, I called Morley to thank him for the pictures, and during that phone conversation he told me that he had something else that might interest me.

"You know the second photo I blew up of you and Cory through the rear ambulance window?"

"Yes, I like having it, but I can't look at it. Don't be offended, but it's just too painful for me to look at as I do the picture of her circling the pole. 'My pirouetting princess'—that's what I call it! I love that photo because it shows Cory so vibrantly alive and happy."

"It's a beautiful photo."

"I gaze at it daily for the longest time, but the one of her lying and dying in the ambulance is just too painful to look at. I'm sure you understand."

"That's why I hesitate to bring this up, but I thought it best to anyway." Morley hesitated for a moment." Do with this information as you please."

He's hesitating. "Say it, Morley. I can handle it!"

"You know that this second photo is taken from the footage when the ambulance paused while the door rose."

"I never thought about it, but of course you'd have the entire sequence. How else could you have obtained this photo?"

"Exactly." Morley again paused.

It's very difficult for him to talk about this!

"Here's the thing. Cory is readily visible not just for that instant, which I captured in the photo, but for the entire time when the ambulance was parked at the door. It's—well—I don't know how to say this, Jude."

He paused apparently hoping I'd say it for him. I didn't. *He'll have to say it because I can't!*

"It's the last video footage of her alive—her precious, final moments of life. The entire sequence when you were stopped at the door is on that clip, every second of it; and it's surprisingly high-quality film, since the ambulance had apparently been recently washed. The clean rear window accounts for the excellent resolution."

He again paused, probably wanting me to say something to make this easier, but I again chose silence. *You say it, Morley, because I don't like where this is headed!*

"Here's the thing. She must have come to in the ambulance before lapsing back into her coma. Remember that moment when she tried to lift herself on the gurney and reached her hand toward your face?"

I can't talk about this!

"Remember when she did that? Well, that entire sequence was caught on film. As I say, it's surprisingly clear footage even though taken through a rear window."

I knew he was stammering, but because I remained silent, he had no alternative but to keep rambling. Far as that goes, I wasn't giving him any choice, because speech had eluded me, and I just couldn't talk about it. At last he broke his own silence. "I didn't give this to you before since I figured you wouldn't be able to handle it, but that's not my decision to make. At least you need to know this footage exists. That's why I called you."

"Thanks."

"It's up to you what you do with it."

Finally, when I gathered strength to respond, the words burst from me. "I can't believe it! You're saying you have the entire sequence when the ambulance was stopped at the door?"

"Yes, the whole thing. Here's what I really have trouble saying. If you look carefully at the enhanced photos, you can even see her lips moving. She had lifted her head off the pillow, and so her lips, in the enlargement, are distinctly visible. I had missed that before, and that's what gave me the idea to contact you. She was trying to say something." He paused. "Do you know what this means, Jude?"

Coward that I was, I remained silent, though at one point I honestly tried to speak but couldn't since the words choked in my throat.

"I'll say it for you, Jude. These are Cory's last words before she died. You said she didn't speak either at the cave-in site or in the ER, right?"

"Correct."

"Then these are her final words. There, I said it, and I apologize for being way too blunt."

The words crashed into my brain like a thunderbolt. *I don't believe it!*

Out of sheer nervousness, Morley continued. "Well, as I say, do with this information what you want. I know it's painful to reopen a slow-healing wound, but I wanted you to know that I made a copy of the entire ambulance ride out of the mine. I even blew up the scene at the door and put it in slow mo. The resolution is amazingly good."

"That's very kind, Morley."

"I have a copy if you want it. Just let me know."

"I can't thank you enough. Yes, please send the copy as soon as you conveniently can. By the way, I apologize for not being very talkative. I don't mean to make this so tough for you."

"It's all right. I fully understand."

I broke down and wept at this point. "It's just that I don't have the strength to talk about it. That makes me feel like such a weakling, but it's the absolute truth. I just can't speak about her death."

"I understand, and you're more than welcome, Jude. But one more thing before we hang up." I could hear Morley's heavy breathing. He probably was waiting for me to stop crying so I could receive his final words. "Based on what you just said there, I probably shouldn't even bring this up, but I promised myself I would, so here goes. Do you remember her final words?"

I coughed. *Why'd you bring that up?* "I'm not exactly sure."

"I studied her lips but can't make out what she's saying. I've done a bit with lip-reading over the years because that's how I communicate with my nearly-deaf uncle. Well, you were traumatized at the time and probably not thinking clearly, so I can see why you wouldn't remember. Still, I imagine that this is probably an important detail to you."

"It is." *Surely that's a lie!*

"That's why I mention this whole thing. These are probably the last words Cory ever spoke." He paused for a moment to allow that profound thought to sink into my overwrought brain. "That's heavy stuff when you think about it."

As I cogitated for that fast moment, I was relatively certain I knew what her last words were, but I wouldn't let myself say them. I certainly wasn't ready for that just yet. Not even close. "I'm not sure. I'll have to look at the clip to see if it jogs my memory." I knew there was an element of deceit in my response. *Why am I lying? Why hide from it?*

Why am I writing about Morley's phone call? I know the answer to that. I'm delaying the painful truth as long as possible. How can I write about the final moments of Cory's life? How does one summon the strength to do that? But I promised myself that I would do it. In fact, I came on this lecture trip to Egypt and Jordan for the sole person of mustering the strength to work my way through the tortured memories of that terrible day when my life ended. This lecture trip isn't about sharing my love of Shakespeare, Milton, and other brilliant writers, nor is it about squeezing in occasional visits to exotic places of intense historical interest. It's about summoning courage to address the huge tragedy in my life, the day the music died. No offense, Buddy Holly, but that's why I'm on this trip—to write. Time to do it, Jude!

All right, here goes. The rest of what happened after the ambulance sped out of the mine is a blur in my mind, a montage of fleetingly surreal images, from which I can never escape, never fully comprehend, never describe satisfactorily. But I do recall the ambulance ride very clearly. Because Mike was driving at breakneck speed, I felt the ambulance careen from side to side. *If you're out there, state troopers, please understand that her perilous condition justifies this reckless speed!*

We hurtled up to the ER of the Armstrong County Memorial Hospital, where the ambulance screeched to a halt. Mike and his helper hurriedly wheeled Cory into a bay. The doctors and nurses—they had been notified ahead of time—descended on us and administered immediate care. I've only ever said good things about them, and that won't change even though Cory passed right there in the emergency room. Though she died, it wasn't because of their failings.

It was because a mountain of limestone came down upon the most beautiful woman that ever walked the earth. Because fallen people do fallen things in a fallen world. Because lovely roses sometimes attract cunning serpents. Because beautiful dreamers cross over the Jordan River.

Since it's so painful for me to write of the next events, I'll settle for impressionistic descriptions, a montage of random, fleeting images, because writing this account, besides handling her death, is the most difficult thing I've ever faced. Seeing the King Tut exhibit in the Cairo Museum pumped me up a bit today and enabled me to temporarily circumnavigate my pain for that welcome hour. Possibly that experience helped me resolve to write this evening instead of walk the streets of Zamalek and people-watch at the Gezira Club and along the Nile River as I've done for several evenings.

For now, minimalist descriptions are the name of the game. Details can be added to these impressions later as I acquire sufficient stamina. I start with one particularly vivid memory of my standing by her side as she lay on the ER bed. The doctor and nurses had gone out of the room to give me a few minutes alone with Cory. The whole time her words screamed in my head, "Jude! Jude!" I couldn't get the sound to stop no matter what I did.

While sobbing by her bed, I buried my head in her breasts and squeezed her body next to mine. I was so close those breasts but in such a different way from what I had fantasized by the hour. *Not this way, Lord, but rather in our honeymoon hotel room when I can unshackle these hands and let them blissfully fondle and rove, touch and wildly caress!*

As I held her tightly, I brushed the tears from my cheeks and lifted my eyes to the horizon. *I can't believe what I was seeing!* From this window in the Armstrong County Memorial Hospital, I could clearly see the middle hill of the Center Hill community—that domed knoll for which we thought the community was named.

Then to my left, I panned slowly across the rolling fields, on the back side of which was the ridge, our beloved Vinlindeer—the ridge where we walked and dreamed and loved by the hour! I looked at Cory and kissed her. *Cory, my love! There's our beloved Vinlindeer where we spent hour after blissful hour!* She looked asleep. I peered again out the window and shifted my eyes along the horizon.

There lay Route 28. Under those undulating hills was an underground labyrinth of tunnels that extended for miles and miles, one-hundred-fifty miles of corridors and caverns. In one of them, somewhere out there, a few large slabs of limestone let loose and killed my beloved Cory.

"Jude, Jude!"

Chapter 33

Jude's journal (Continued):

The next minutes went by so quickly and were so awful that even now I can't fully recollect them. I remember that I called Pete first, then Grandma, and then Pastor Gabe and left word for them to spread the news. Pete, Joey, and Pastor Gabe arrived at the hospital in a very short time.

We met in the small meditation room by the third-floor hospital elevator. I could not stop crying. The only thing that kept me from breaking down completely was Pete who could not stop wailing. I feared he'd die of a heart attack on the spot, so I knew that, somehow, I had to be strong for him. I've never in my life seen a man cry like that.

Seeing Pete's body shake violently with sobbing, I couldn't help but think of Kent's line as he viewed the dead king in Shakespeare's *King Lear*. Of course, I thought of Shakespeare in that damnable moment because I always run from things I hate. Kent, reflecting on King Lear, had hoped that the rack of this tough world would not stretch Lear out any longer, since the king had been racked and tortured enough. *As has Pete Mohney! God, please hear our prayers and give us strength. Please bestow on Pete the strength and grace he needs to endure this hellish hour!*

Here I offer a jumble of vignettes. They won't be chronological, since I'm just jotting them down as they flit through my mind and, to be honest, as I acquire strength to write about them. The decently-composed narrative will come later if—that big word "if" again—*if* I develop the heart for such a herculean task. But what, if in the process, I lose my mind? Given the daunting nature of the task before me, that is a distinct possibility which puts me in the same boat with Van Gogh. I can approximate what Cory said when she quoted him on our way out of church Wednesday evening. She said Van Gogh once lamented, "I put my heart and soul into my work, and have lost my mind in the process." Brilliant artist Van Gogh, I truly understand that delicate balance, for I too wonder how long memory will hold a seat in my distracted globe. Mind, hang on. Soul, fight on!

But why write about the memories of the past? Why record and remember them, since, plainly and simply, life has lost its meaning? There was a song back in the late sixties, Petula Clark's "This is my Song." Here I go again—deflecting when in pain, dodging things I don't want to talk about or, in this case, write about. At any rate, I remember two lines from that song: "The world cannot be wrong if in this world there's you." Well, Cory's gone, and the world now *is* wrong. Period. No more to add on there, as Frost would say.

Nevertheless, I scratch out these few impressionistic vignettes as I recollect them.

In the morgue:

At the hospital, the attendant departed the morgue so I could be alone with Cory for a few moments before I made the phone calls. When I entered the room, I had to look around to find her, since I was in a surprisingly large space. When I first saw her laid out in the corner, I could not believe my eyes. They didn't have my beloved Cory in a body bag, and the attendant had kindly pulled down the sheet so I could see her face. She was so serene and exquisitely beautiful that she looked asleep, as if napping, as she occasionally did in Little Gidding.

The line from Shakespeare's *Romeo and Juliet*, when Juliet's father sees his dead daughter for the first time, leaped into my head as I stumbled toward her: "Death lies on her like an untimely frost Upon the sweetest flower of all the field." I ran the last couple steps, tightly clasped her to me, and sobbed. *My sweetest flower of the field, my Cory! My rose, how beautiful you are in death! How this untimely frost has destroyed your beautiful dreamer life!*

As I looked at her face, the *Romeo and Juliet* thoughts persisted, that play Cory and I talked about by the hour. Romeo's lines when he sees the dead Juliet in the vault were hauntingly relevant as I held my dead Juliet: "Ah, dear Juliet, Why art thou yet so fair?" *Say it, Cory, say it. You're supposed to shout, "I know that one. You're quoting* Romeo and Juliet." *Please yell it out, Cory! Wake up; nap time's over! You always guess my Shakespeare quotations, for only you know them. Say it! I beg you, my love!*

I wrapped my arms around her, but there was only silence and stony stillness, except for the voice in my head, "Jude, Jude!" If I heard that voice in my head there in the Kittanning hospital, and if I even hear it vividly here in faraway Cairo, why can't I hear it in reality? Wake up, Cory! How I understand Romeo's line at Juliet's tomb: "I will stay with thee And never from this palace of dim night Depart again!"

That's what I wanted with all my heart—to stay here in that dim night forever with my beautiful Cory, never to leave our last meeting place. The two of us together in an exquisite dream of lovely death where Cory is forever beautiful, and we are forever young. *People in death are supposed to be ugly, but here you are, my love, more beautiful than the legendary Venus herself!*

Then, for whatever reason, the image of Sleeping Beauty came to me, and I started hearing, as I held Cory in my arms, the enchanting music from the old Walt Disney movie, *Sleeping Beauty.* Maybe it was adapted from Tchaikovsky's *Sleeping Beauty Ballet*? The whole time I held her, I kept hearing the lyrics—quiet, far away, thin and fluty.

Later I listened to the song and even wrote down the words, since singing them or even humming the tune recreated those intensely sacred moments in the morgue when I was alone with her for the last time. To hear those lyrics now is to hold her warm cheek to mine, to feel her breath on me again.

> I know you
> I walked with you once upon a dream
> I know you
> That gleam in your eye is so familiar a gleam
> Yet I know it's true
> That visions are seldom all they seem

In the church:

These days, some people opt for cremation or delayed memorial services, but at Center Hill the memorial service occurred shortly after death, the body placed in the open casket front and center in the church.

I looked around the sanctuary during the funeral service—that awful time. Horrible, horrible! There were no happy faces and no sprinkling of flower petals on the center aisle, soon to be trod by the radiant bride as she gracefully makes her grand, here-comes-the-bride entrance. Our joyous church wedding was supposed to be the happy reason for our being assembled here. Instead of Mendelssohn's glorious *Wedding March*, Chopin's *Funeral March* played in my mind. I covered my ears to shut out the dreadful sounds.

I thought seeing Cory dead in the ER and the morgue was difficult, but somehow seeing her laid out in the front of the church was much worse. And little wonder since the Center Hill Church of the Brethren had been the scene of so much of our joy, since there we were reconciled, since there we spent hours together in various activities; and there, more and more, we envisioned our joyous wedding day. I couldn't stand to be in this building without her at my side, hand in mine, poking me in the ribs. *"This point of Gabe's sermon is about you! Sit up and take your medicine, professor!"* Then she'd smile joyfully and squeeze my hand three times—I love you!

The church was packed out for the funeral service, because so many of Cory's friends from work and so many of my professor friends and students unexpectedly showed up by the carload. I must remember to thank them, for they were such a help to me. Many of the Center Hill church family were also present, creating a crowd, according to the ushers, of some three hundred people.

"We never had a funeral that filled the church like this one."

"The ushers had to put folding chairs in the aisles."

"A state trooper oversaw the parking of cars in the cemetery and along the highway!"

I especially remember the open casket. Though painful, I feasted my eyes on Cory the entire time except for when, albeit with guilt, I stole glances at the photo montage on the screen. There was one moment during the service when I completely broke. Here's what happened. I think it was Roberta and Joanne's idea to play the recording of the time Cory sang "Whispering Hope" at her Mom's funeral. While the song played, a montage of pictures of Cory flashed on the large screen. I learned later that Joey and Laura's idea was an uncommon thing in country churches in 1988.

Seated in the front row by Pete, Joey and Laura, I sobbed the entire time the photo montage flashed on the screen: pictures of the two of us or Cory alone at Crooked Creek, on the rocks at Buttermilk Falls, on "Jude and Cory's Trail"—as we came to call the path on the ridge above the Allegheny River at Reesedale—on the couch in Little Gidding, or atop the horses on Vinlindeer. So many photos, each one a masterpiece. What a beautiful woman you were, my rose, my beautiful dreamer, my Corinna Adelena!

Through tear-filled eyes, I drank in every detail of these pictures, yet because this was the last time that I would see my beautiful dreamer, I often looked at her in the casket too. Back and forth from the screen to the casket. *This is goodbye, Cory. I'll always remember you, always have this image in my brain. Yes, even this image of you lying in the casket. People in death are ugly, but you, my princess, my beautiful dreamer, are stunning even in death. Beautiful dreamer, wake unto me. Starlight and dewdrops are waiting for thee.*

Please, Cory, wake to me, to starlight, to dewdrops, to these aching, waiting arms. Sounds of the rude world heard in the day, lulled by the moonlight, have all passed away. So true, Cory: you no longer need to hear the songs of this rough, rugged, ugly world since they have all passed away; but why did you pass away with them? Beautiful dreamer, queen of my song, list' while I woo thee with soft melody. My Cory, you will always be the queen of my song, my life, my every waking moment, my everything.

Pastor Gabriel's sermon:

Gabe's sermon was a moving eulogy though I heard little of it on the day of the service. It was later, when I got up the nerve to play the cassette tape of the service, that I realized how poignant and excellent his eulogy was.

In his sermon, Gabe brilliantly contrasted the two ends of the spiritual spectrum—first, the hopelessness of those without faith, embodied both in Macbeth's dark lines, "She should have died hereafter," and Job's probing metaphysical question," If a man dies, shall he live again" [Job 14:14]? Gabe then contrasted this despair with the hope which people of faith have, embodied in another of Job's assertions: "For I know that my Redeemer lives, and He shall stand at last on the earth" [Job 19:25].

Despair and hope, darkness and light, it was a brilliant sermon. I've often wondered how Pastor Gabe summoned sufficient strength to deliver that eulogy when he was so ripped apart. On top of that, he was unwell in those days. Surely it was God alone who empowered him for that difficult challenge.

What else stands out about the memorial service? I have to mention the spray of roses on the casket, since my Cory loved roses so much. But not these, not here, not hers, not roses—our special flower, the Crimson Glory—like those we dropped from the bridge in Kittanning and watched float down the river.

Goody-goody, mine's winning!
Mine's the cruiser, and your's the loser!
Go, baby, go, and get with the flow!
Beat Jude's rose and give him some woes!

Then her child-like, lilting laughter.

The roses made me flash back to Old Mary's rose vision. I looked across the church where she used to sit under the side clock. In her seat sat Nannie, crying as she had when she received word that her son had died of a massive heart attack while pushing a man out of a ditch in a North Carolina snow storm.

I looked again at the spray of roses on the casket and then at Cory. *Darling, you look so beautiful lying there. Why can't you wake up? Beautiful dreamer, beam on my heart, E'en as the morn on the streamlet and sea.* Please, Cory, beam with those big beautiful eyes on this sad, sad heart. Beam, eyes, beam!

And Duke, sitting over there and weeping like a baby the whole time. Tina Reynolds held him and comforted him as a mother would her terrified child. Even though Cory had forgiven him, I wonder how much guilt he felt. I was certain she had forgiven him, but one doesn't easily forget the hurt he inflicts on another. Did her death make him relive his attempted rape and awful treatment? Sobbing myself, I felt sorry for Duke. From sex-crazed animal to this godly, upstanding gentleman—what a transformation! Yet people say the Gospel isn't real and doesn't radically change lives. Skeptics, consider Duke!

I refer to Pete last. I have no idea how he made it through the service. I heard him whisper to Joey, "First my wife. Now my daughter. I can't take it!" He sobbed as hard in the church pew as he had in the hospital ER and meditation room. *One cannot sustain this level of grief,* I thought to myself. *The man will die of a broken heart!*

That's enough for now. I can't take it, and thinking of Pete is the final straw. I'm going to go for a walk around Zamalek, this lovely island in the Nile River. I'll stroll down Sheikh El Marsafy

Street, then walk the track at Cairo's famous Gezira Club, and maybe go stand by the Nile River for a while and look for reflections of Cory in the water.

Maybe I'll get a cup of tea at my favorite café along the Nile as I did last evening: "Earl Grey tea with two sugar cubes, please." That snapped me out of my daze at least momentarily. Maybe I'll watch the water lap the base of the piers of the Kasr El Nil Bridge and the night-time fishermen in their dancing feluccas.

Writing these remembrances is the hardest thing I've ever done besides losing Cory, since each word is a stab to my heart. How right you were, Macbeth: "She should have died hereafter!"

Chapter 34

Jude's Journal (Continued):

I sit here in my room at All Saint's Cathedral Guest House in Zamalek, Cairo, sipping my tea. Cory, you would have loved this excellent blend—"full-bodied, rich, exquisitely tasty," as you said of the teas you liked. The constant din of the traffic from over in the city, especially the infernal honking of car horns, filters into my third-floor room. No wonder that I prefer the old-world clip-clop of the donkeys passing through the quaint tree-lined streets below. Enchanting Arabic music from a nearby apartment wafts upward from a lower room. Fluttering the window curtains like a flag on a pole, the breeze is especially welcome this evening after an especially sultry afternoon.

I return to my desk in a better frame of mind. The stop at my favorite café along the Nile has refreshed me considerably, and I will once again try to face this overwhelming task: offering the impressionistic vignettes of the hours and days after my beloved died. A couple more came to my mind as I sat sipping tea and looking across at the bustling city of Cairo and the historic Shepherds' Hotel.

On the way to the cemetery:

The pallbearers had carried the casket down the porch steps, but in my dreams, I often see myself walking beside the casket and reaching out my hand to grasp the metal handle. My hand is at the same position as it would have been had I been doing what I had dreamed of doing for months—namely, holding the embroidered finery of her wedding gown as she slowly descended the steps so she didn't trip. I knew it was a simple thing, but I had actually imagined, and looked forward to performing, this simple task during the wedding recessional.

In my dream last evening, I held the cold handles of a metal casket instead of her gown. Instead of a wedding bouquet, which should have bounced in her hands as she excitedly descended the steps, there were only wilting rose petals inside the dark casket. I could imagine the petals, jiggled by the movement of the casket on the steps, falling from her face and breast to their eternal rest in the fleecy folds of her dress.

Instead of flower petals and handfuls of rice joyfully cascading over her as we descend the stairs, in the Center Hill tradition where smiling people cheer the bride and groom, there is silence and death and hysterical weeping. Instead of tossing rice and petals, people's arms dangle lifelessly and awkwardly by their sides. Heads bow, eyes weep, and hands nervously clutch damp tissues.

I discreetly whisper to Cory as we descend the church steps at the conclusion of the wedding service, "Cory, only a few more hours and the wedding reception will be done, and we'll be in a hotel bed!" *A hotel bed where I'll blissfully romp and sport with this utterly naked body! How we have waited for this delectable moment!*

> Gather ye rosebuds while ye may,
> Old Time is still a-flying;
> And this same flower that smiles today,
> Tomorrow will be dying.

Cory, why were you the rosebud that was untimely snatched in youth and cruelly taken in her prime?

> Tomorrow, and tomorrow, and tomorrow
> Creeps in this petty pace from day to day
> To the last syllable of recorded time.

She should have died hereafter. Ah, Macbeth! How well I understand your lamentation after Lady Macbeth dies. Cory, too, should have died hereafter. Yes, later. Even three score years and ten. The youthful age of seventy would be fine, but not this—not this hellish, mid-twenties end!

I can't stop the hemorrhage of poetic lines in my brain. "O dark, dark, dark, amid the blaze of noon!" That one from John Milton's play on strong Samson. Ah, Samson, I feel your darkness—yours brought on by blindness, mine by the tragic death of my beautiful dreamer.

In my mind, I see her head jostling on the casket pillow as the pallbearers carry the cold vault up the cemetery lane to the grave. That same lane we had trod so often, especially that glorious evening of our reconciliation back in that emerald month, when May had spawned sweet growth on rolling knoll and along the meandering meadows green.

As I walked up through the cemetery on the day of the funeral and imagined that impending horror—her vault entering that jagged, shale-lined hole in the ground—I tried to make my mind escape to something pleasant but, not willing to be corralled at that moment, it dredged up instead a line from T. S. Eliot's *East Coker* which described a corpse entering the tomb: "O dark dark dark. They all go into the dark."

Yes, the dark of the tomb! Into her dark bed in the ground she will soon descend—down, down, down. Instead of our hot and sporting bed of wild marital ecstasy, her inert body will repose on a cold bed which descends into the dark, stony abyss. Now I too inhabit a world of decay and darkness, for life without Cory is black and silent death. O, dark, dark, dark!

"Jude, Jude!"

At the graveside:

Finally, the funeral procession arrived at the grave. When the body was being positioned atop her grave for the brief committal service, I could stand it no longer, and my soul took flight and indulged the perfect mental escape. She was not here in

209

this cold casket, and we were not about to begin this lugubrious graveside service. Cory and I, instead, were standing over there by that large tombstone dating from 1795, that hallowed place where we stood on the night of our joyful reconciliation.

"Can you beat that?" I had said. "This David Bowser was born in 1795. Can you believe it? That's the year John Keats was born. Can you imagine that? This man first saw the light of day the exact year as the great English poet." "Your mind is a concordance, encyclopedia, and unabridged dictionary all rolled into one!" Cory, please say such things again, even silly ones like that, beautiful dreamer!

As I stood by her grave I switched to another perfect escape, a place of contentment where life made sense. We were swinging together on the Tarzan rope at Reesedale and falling into the Allegheny River—lunging outward, madly hugging, laughing hysterically, and dropping entwined, as I sneak a delightful peek at her orbed fullness.

"Tsk, tsk, Jude Hepler! Naughty boy, I saw you gawking! Again!"

"Am I every inch a man?"

"I'd kill you if you weren't!"

I switch the scene again and this time we stroll the fields and lanes together. As we amble along, Cory sings the famous Connie Francis song "Together":

> We strolled the lane together,
> Laughed at the rain together,
> Sang loves refrain together,
> And we won't pretend it would never end.

But we did pretend it would never end, and why wouldn't we? Most people live more normal lives and average lifespans. In fact, Armstrong County has a very high percentage of senior citizens, as people live long lives amid these rural vales of rolling verdure green. But not Cory. The good die young. Is that the cliché? Why did it have to be true in our case?

But one day we cried together,
Cast love aside together;
You're gone from me,
But in my memory
We always will be together.

Now that part of the song is true! We will always be together… in death if not life. I see us walking the paths together, meandering amid the meadows of my mind—tree-tunneled lanes, rugged trail passes, and Elk County's sweeping mountain grandeur, holy as the pining pilgrim's prayer.

"Look at the red-tailed hawk! I know you see it. I swear you never miss a thing."

"That's because we artists have an eye for detail. I've told you that a thousand times! Yes, I see the red-tailed hawk, and don't you just love that large weeping willow beneath it there by Buffalo Creek? I could paint a picture of that in a heart-beat—the hawk, the willow, and the stream. That's my picture ready-made!"

"I caught your allusion there to Browning's 'Andrea del Sarto'—the 'picture ready-made.'"

I imagined us laughing in Little Gidding, working, pausing and kissing madly. Hundreds of pictures of Cory in a variety of places flashed on the screen of my mind as I stood by her grave. All beautiful places. All lovely because she was there, the epicenter of every single sight, but now that world is gutted. Only a massive sink hole in my heart remains. Standing at her grave, I pounded my chest.

Our life together had been rapturous because we had always been together, but not now, not in this bad place, not in a cemetery, not by Corinna Adelena Mohney's grave. We were somewhere else—together, laughing and smiling, so very much alive.

During the graveside committal service, I again thought of John Donne's "Elegy XX":

License my roving hands, and let them go
Before, behind, between, above, below.

O, my America, my Newfoundland,
My kingdom…

Instead of caressing that gorgeous body with roving hands—behind, between, above, below—I caressed flower petals and fingered soil as I stood by her grave. I picked up a fallen rose petal that had fallen from one of the baskets of flowers that was placed by her grave during the committal service. I held it in my work-calloused hands. *For a paper-pushing prof, you're sporting some pretty respectable callouses! Not bad, preppy!*

The fragile rose petal against the rugged callous of my hand. Such a contrast of surfaces—battle-hardened skin, delicately soft flower! Like Cory's life: so out of place in this sin-sick, tainted world where people hate, rocks fall, frost kills, serpents bite, and beautiful dreamers die young.

All right, that's enough, as this is starting to hurt again, really bad, so more journal writing for the time being. I guess that means it's time for another walk. Cairenes, the guy you see sobbing into his handkerchief or slouched motionless against a banyan tree by the Cairo Borg or staring blankly at the sky or babbling to himself like an idiot on Kasr el Nile Bridge, or staring into the Nile River by the hour, or peering into the nighttime sky by the sphinx in front of the Cairo Museum, well, 'tis I—alone, forlorn, broken, and utterly cast down. Try as I might, I'll never be able to turn off the faucet of these tear-red eyes.

Chapter 35

Jude's Journal (Continued):

Words, words, words! Is there no end to them? Will I never be finished? On the other hand, what will I do when I've completed these entries? What will fill the Pacific Ocean of those empty, worthless hours? Ay, there's the rub! Well, that dismal end will come, but first I'll agonize to scrawl a few more impressions.

Months later in Pastor Gabriel's office:

Pastor coordinated my brief visit with one of his psychiatrist friends, Dr. Greenbaum. Because Gabe knew that I wanted to talk about a couple matters of a psychological nature, he brought the good doctor in to join our conversation, though at the time I didn't know he had made this arrangement. The following reconstructs that momentous conversation.

"So how are you, Jude?" Pastor Gabe gently began. Gabe always had a way of putting people at ease more completely than anyone I've ever met.

"The same. Cory's on my mind constantly, and I'm so depressed that I even stopped working on my recent poems." I stopped when I said this much, wanting to get Gabe's reaction and probably hoping to elicit some pity. "You'll find that hard to believe, but it's true." *If I pause for a moment, maybe I can recover a modicum of decorum and decency. Last thing I want to do is become a babbling idiot who spews an endless wake of wild and whirling words!* During those days, I wavered between profuse verbiage, the norm most of the time, or its opposite, stony silence, when I'd lapse into my incommunicado mode for hours at a stretch.

"Go on, my son."

"The strangest thing, Gabe, is that I keep hearing Cory's voice. This is what I wanted to talk about to you…and Dr. Greenbaum. She cries out to me whether I'm asleep or awake, and it's always the same. 'Jude, Jude!' It's as though she's actually present." After a pause: "Sometimes it's so real that I feel her body against me or even smell the sweet scent of her breath. As I'm doing right now in this room. I've even felt her actually shaking me."

Dr. Greenbaum calmly responded. "We understand."

I turned to the psychiatrist. "Doctor, is that crazy? I lack the words to describe the intense reality of her voice and screams in my ear. Is it natural to hear voices that are so tangibly alive?" He didn't offer an immediate response, so I gushed on. "Sometimes I also sense Zoe directly beside me licking my face." Dr. Greenbaum looked at me quizzically. "Zoe was our dog who was incessantly with us and the Mohney family. Though a dog, his presence among us was, well, almost angelic." *I feel stupid using that word, but what other word describes our inimitable Zoe?*

"Perfectly natural, Jude," Dr. Greenbaum finally responded. "Because the imagined reality is more desirable than your current painful reality, you often escape to that world. Why not?"

"No truer words were ever spoken!"

"After the death of a loved one, people crave the imagined reality so much that they often personify the departed individual and give him or her flesh-and-blood characteristics—like speech, touch, and even scent. It's not uncommon for people to experience such tangible reminders."

He paused, the wise professional's intentional suspension of words which gave me time to absorb his heady precepts. I remember looking at him and thinking, *What a kind and gentle person!* A tall gentleman, he wore the most peaceful look of calm. *Just being in their presence makes me feel better!* "Maybe then I'm not as crazy as I thought!" *But like Hamlet, I fear my wit's diseased!*

Dr. Greenbaum continued. "I wouldn't be surprised if you'd start to see her too. Has that happened yet? You think she's in the room with you or doing something with you?" I nodded. "You'd be surprised at the number of people who hear, talk to, see, and even interact with their departed loved ones, usually doing common, day-to-day things."

"Yes, I experience some of that too," I finally replied, "but it's her voice that's so hauntingly real to me." I then looked over to Pastor Gabe. "Gabe, there's something I'd like to discuss that's of a personal nature."

"Now is a good time."

"The question lies more in the spiritual domain than the psychological. As the doctor in *Macbeth* says, 'More needs she [Lady Macbeth] the divine than the physician.' That's the same with me since my question is more for a clergyman than a psychiatrist." I forced a laugh. "Perhaps I should return some other time since I don't want to intrude on your visit with Dr. Greenbaum. But first, if you don't mind, I'd like to take a book or two from the library for reading."

"Whatever you wish."

I walked over to the library shelves on the other end of the room to reach for a book. *These priceless volumes contain nuggets of truth which I desperately need!* I randomly selected a volume of Charles Hadden Spurgeon's sermons from the shelf. *Speak to this soul, wise man of God!* Wouldn't you know it, the book I chose was one which Cory had gifted to the library in memory of her mother! There I was, reading Cory's touching inscription on the front page! Seeing her handwriting and being in that place suddenly filled me with nausea. *I better postpone part two of our discussion, since I fear the onset of an anxiety attack!* I bowed my head and, my back to the two men, inconspicuously raised the book to my lips, kissed her name, and turned to exit the room.

But I wasn't fast enough. "Jude, you don't have to leave," Pastor Gabe said.

As I continued walking, I remembered something Hamlet said—*"O come away! My soul is full of discord and dismay."* *Mine too, Hamlet—all is discord and dismay!* "I don't want to interrupt your conversation with Dr. Greenbaum."

"Maybe you ought to work through this, Jude." Chastened by his words, I stopped at the door. "The good doctor is on his way to the hospital and, at my request, merely stopped by for a few minutes. You and I can speak now, unless it's too difficult. I know every nook and cranny of this hallowed church is saturated with memories of Cory." *Did he see me kiss the book?* "Believe me, I feel her presence too."

I deliberated for a brief moment before answering. "Thanks, Gabe. I'll stay if you're sure I'm not intruding. Thank you, Dr. Greenbaum. I really appreciate your comforting counsel. You gentlemen give me hope that I might eventually regain my sanity!" I forced a second laugh, but my heart wasn't in it, and the noise that issued forth—gravelly, guttural, ghastly—embarrassed me.

After the psychiatrist departed moments later, I dove straight into the problem. "Morley Spencer, the security supervisor at the mine, had located footage of the ambulance exiting the mine on the day of the accident. The film clip he produced was lifted from that security camera footage."

"That's a unique thing to preserve."

"It shows Cory in the back of the ambulance while we were stopped at the mine entrance door." I looked at Gabe with unnecessary severity, hoping, I guess, that my deliberate body language would alert him to the profundity of the words I was on the verge of uttering. "That footage captures her final moments of life." Again, I hesitated. "The very last words she ever spoke." *Are you hearing me, Gabe?* I bowed my head and ran my fingers through my hair. "Morley reformatted the sequence, especially of Cory's head, so it's in slow-mo, blowup format. What Cory's saying is plain as day." I stopped abruptly. *I can't say anymore!*

"I know you have more to say, so I think it's better for you to soldier on since you've started into this most difficult of subjects."

Yes, much to say, but how killing to say it! I decided to blurt it out. "I know what those words are, pastor, and they've shattered my life!"

"I see that but don't understand."

"I told Morley that I didn't remember what she said, but that was an awful, black lie." I paused and drummed my fingers on the Spurgeon volume which I had laid on Gabe's desk. "Though she was dying, she regained consciousness for those brief moments in the ambulance when we waited for the large entry door to rise. That seemed to take forever, but during those moments, she temporarily came out of her coma."

"I'm surprised to hear that given the extent of her injury."

"When she came to, she lifted her head toward me, actually lifted her head, and looked directly into my eyes, even though to this point she hadn't moved a muscle. In fact, her heartbeat was so weak that the paramedics could barely get a pulse, but here she was with her one eye open—the other was a mere slit—lifting her head to talk!" Again overwhelmed, I stopped babbling.

"Continue when you're able, my son."

"What she said has robbed me of sleep for weeks." I started sobbing at this point and wiped my tears with a handkerchief. "'Promise me...you'll write...Jude. Promise...' Then her head collapsed back onto the pillow. Not gently, it snapped down with a jerk, and she lapsed into a coma again."

"How difficult this is for you!"

"I think she started slipping away right then, though the medics and doctors never said so. They were probably trying to spare me massive guilt! Well, that expenditure of energy to raise her head and speak took her life." Crying so hard by this point, I couldn't even see Gabe through my tears. "If so, she laid down her life to utter those final words. 'Promise me you'll write.' Those words haunt me, Gabe—positively haunt me!"

"Of course, they would."

"That's the last thing she ever said—'Promise me you'll write.'"

By this time, I was sobbing so hard I was sounding inhuman. I again dabbed my eyes with my tear-drenched handkerchief, walked over to the church window to calm myself, and started to gaze out the window but caught myself in the nick of time. *That was a close call. The last thing I want to do is look across the cemetery at Cory's grave! That will come later if ever!* I sat down beside his desk. "Can you imagine what's on my mind every waking moment of every horrid day? *Might as well say it!* Cory destroyed her chances of survival by speaking those last words! She laid down her life to make me promise to write!"

Trying to absorb the impact of this verbal shock wave, Gabe was quiet for some time but at last spoke. "If that's the case, then her last act was utterly selfless, but that was our Cory. *I need to redirect Jude's guilt.* But from a medical point of view, we can't be certain that this gesture took her life."

I didn't reply but, diverting my eyes from the graves in the cemetery, walked over and sat in Old Mary's chair so I could slouch against the wall and regain my composure. "Gabe, can you see how this matter weighs on me?" I swiveled my head round and round to ease the tension in my shoulders.

"Yes, of course."

"Here's the other thing that's killing me. Her struggle to utter those few dying words flashes me back to Grandpa's last words. He did the same thing, exactly the same: lifted his head, spoke a few disjointed syllables about the whereabouts of his novel, and was sucked instantly into the swirling vortex of ugly death. I can't take it! Now I'm reliving Grandpa's death as well as Cory's. I caused Cory's death, just as I did Grandpa's!"

"Jude, you know that's overstated."

"It isn't! Just get me close to something I love with all my heart and watch me kill it." I stopped my rant and slammed my fist so hard on the Spurgeon book that I feared a broken hand! "Might as well call me the destroyer!" I've never seen Gabe without words, but this time he just sat in shocked silence, a tear running down his cheek.

He reached across the desk, picked up the volume of Spurgeon sermons, and held it closely to his breast. Deep in thought, he furrowed his brow, bowed his head, and closed his eyes for a moment, and then at last spoke. "Now I remember." He hurriedly turned to a sermon in the Spurgeon book. "I think it was a March 1855 sermon."

"What are you looking for?" I said, massaging my hurting hand.

"One of Spurgeon's brilliant sermons on suffering. Here it is—March 11, 1855, Consolation Proportionate to Spiritual Sufferings." He continued to skim-read as he leafed through the pages. "This is the passage I was looking for. 'Great hearts can only be made by great troubles.' That simple statement is such a powerful truth." He buried his head in the book and continued to read. "'The spade of trouble digs the reservoir of comfort deeper, and makes more room for consolation.' Watch where Spurgeon takes this metaphor. 'God comes into our heart; he finds it full; he begins to break our comforts and to make it empty. Then there is more room for grace.'"

"That's a brilliant image," I interrupted.

"It is that." Gabe continued to browse the page. "'God always gives us comfort when we are most fit for it. That is one reason why consolations increase in the same ratio as trials.'"

"I must admit that's a profound thought, but the digging in the foundation of my heart has toppled the entire building!" I thought my self-lacerating image was pretty clever, but Gabe made no reply and merely buried his head in the book.

"No wonder we love Spurgeon's sermons," he at last replied, locating the sentence for which he searched. "As a professor of English, you'll appreciate this next metaphor. 'Wherever you find great fogs of trouble and mists of sorrow, you always find emerald green hearts, full of the beautiful verdure of the comfort and love of God.'"

"'Emerald green hearts.' That is sheer poetry."

Gabe paraphrased one of Spurgeon's points. "God gives the heart comfort but only when it's fit to receive it. Think about that, Jude."

"I needed to hear that, Gabe, because for months I've been feeling that my highest calling in life, my ultimate destiny, was to destroy my beautiful dreamer!" I bowed my head and wept burning hot tears.

Chapter 36

Jude's Journal (Continued):

My time with Gabriel was, in the end, profoundly useful. After a while, my torrent of self-pitying words ceased, and I actually began to absorb his scriptural gems which stabilized me greatly. His reading of Psalm 91 as we walked up the cemetery lane was especially helpful.

"'For He will command his angels concerning you to guard you in all your ways.' Listen to this part. 'In their hands they will bear you up, lest you strike your foot against a stone.'"

"That's beautiful." *Now if I just believed it!*

Although Gabe had stopped talking as we strolled in the cemetery, I knew he was preparing to expound on those magnificent verses, so I waited. "The angels will bear you up, Jude, but not while you're sitting in your armchair. You must position yourself in such a way that you receive angelic provision and protection. Remember Spurgeon's words—hearts are made great by great troubles. To witness the miraculous blessings at the Red Sea, Moses and the Israelites first had to endure enormous troubles, which included a trek through the howling desert wasteland and standing helplessly by the perilous waters of the Red Sea. They had to leave the known world of the tantalizing flesh pots of Egypt in the past."

"Yes, I understand, but I'm here in the Center Hill graveyard, not by the Nile River." I didn't intend harshness, but my words were nevertheless stridently assertive, even a tad angry.

"We need to apply this to your situation." He looked at me gravely. "You must take the risk of going on without your beloved Cory, just as the ancient Israelites ventured into the unknown. It means entrusting to God the post-Cory life, which our loving sovereign God has in mind for you. Spurgeon said it—make room in your heart for God's grace." He put his comforting hand on my shoulder.

"Sorry to be so negative, but I truly think that's impossible."

"It will be very difficult, but your task… No, it's more than a task. It's your God-ordained obligation to move into the future and not luxuriate in the golden past with Cory. The present also has a song to sing, though you doubt that in every ounce of your being during these post-death months."

As always, Gabe's words were comforting and brilliant. During our conversation, he even addressed a second aspect of my guilt. "When Grandpa died," I explained as Gabe and I stood by his grave, "Grandma was so devastated that she even teetered on the brink of incoherence at times."

"Many have told me that those were difficult days for her."

"I think that's because she linked Grandpa's death to writing. 'If Jeremiah had not been a writer,' she often said in those days, 'he would not have died. My dear husband would still be with me. Sometimes I want to curse that book he was writing!' The two subjects, writers and their premature deaths, were inextricably bound together in her distraught mind."

"I see. No one ever made that point before."

"She'd say over and over again, 'Writers meet bad ends and die very tragic deaths. Look at Poe and Marlowe, Virginia Woolf, Shelley, Keats, Emily Dickinson, Chatterton, and the list is endless. Now my dear Jeremiah, though not a famous writer, joins their ranks.' I was very impressed that she could refer to so many great writers, but of course she had learned of them through Grandpa. Yes, Grandpa, that literary giant who quoted the great writers every chance he could!"

"For a man of humble roots and no education, Jeremiah was extremely learned. In that regard, he reminds me of the great George Washington—little formal education but exceptionally intelligent."

"I completely agree. Hamlet says 'A knavish speech sleeps in a foolish ear,' but precious little slept in Grandpa's quick ear!" I reached down and grasped the top of the headstone at Grandpa's grave. "Well, in that black period after he died, Grandma was completely convinced that Satan tempts writers who, as a consequence of that temptation, bring suffering and even death upon themselves and others. I can hear her say it, 'Little Jude, don't forget that it was Satan who killed my dear Jeremiah. The Bible calls him Abbadon, the destroyer, and he killed my Jeremiah. Don't you write, little Jude. Promise me because I don't want anything happening to you! Grandpa lives on in you, but you see where writers end. So please don't become a writer, since you're my last remaining link to Grandpa. We can't allow evil Abaddon to destroy you too!'"

My session with Gabe was helpful, but it didn't alter my block about writing. I had made this childhood promise and was, at some deep, subconscious level, tied to it—the proverbial Monarch Butterfly, longing to romp through lush meadows but currently imprisoned in a suffocating cocoon. I managed some poetry, especially mandatory college assignments, but I could never scale the steep cliff of my own rigid conscience, since every time I picked up a pen, I felt I was defiantly violating a covenant I had made to God never to write.

As a child, I remember thinking that if I wrote, I sinned, and I couldn't escape the stranglehold of that errant thinking. That's probably why I rarely wrote in my college years and why of late I've written so little of these exciting international lecturing tours. In the murky recesses of my unconscious, I still feel I'm somehow doomed if I do. Talk about sacrificing yourself on the altar of rigid legalism! My only reprieve came during the brief Cory months when, in her presence, I wrote and wrote—both poetry and these tedious, pathetic journal entries.

Thank goodness Pastor Gabe was able to share with me the difference between legitimate guilt—the kind people experience when they've deliberately transgressed God's inviolable precepts—and false guilt, which occurs when people elevate subjective emotions over objective Scriptural truth. Relentlessly bound to an emotional roller coaster, these latter victims believe they're guilty just because they *feel* guilty, thereby using emotion, instead of God's immutable Word, as the yardstick to gauge righteous merit.

After bidding farewell to Pastor Gabriel in his office, I remember walking out of the church and standing on the porch. *Right here, by this railing, Cory and I had first talked after that Bible study on the night of our reconciliation.* I touched the railing. *Her hand rested on this exact spot!* Then I wandered aimlessly into the cemetery again, this time alone, and meandered in the direction of Cory's grave, passing the final resting place of many of those friends of bygone years. *I think I can get up the courage to sit by her grave.* I stopped and looked at Mrs. Mohney's headstone. *Ruby, you too were a beautiful woman!*

It was a lovely autumn day. Field corn ringed the domed knoll of Center Hill, and newly-mown hay covered its crest. Reminders of autumn were everywhere. *How right you were, Robert Browning: "Days decrease, And autumn grows, autumn in everything." The end draws apace, and autumn is everywhere— especially in me, especially in me.* A dog barked in the distance, cars darted by on Route 28, and the wind rustled through the trees. I gazed at the graves and, to escape, lifted eyes to the McKelvey homestead, and thought of the evening basketball games there under the spotlight all those years ago. I looked at everything but Cory's grave. *Not it, not yet!*

Finally, I got up the nerve and sat down on the grass beside her grave. Leaning against her headstone, I remembered a scene from the film *Doctor Zhivago* when the doctor, as a little boy, imagines seeing his deceased mother in the coffin. He pictures her in that dark and silent underground world, still radiant in her beauty. I used to think what an amazing thing that Director David Lean had shown the deceased inside the casket way underground. As I reclined on Cory's grave, I fell into a reverie, or did I actually fall asleep and dream? I'm not sure, nor have I ever been able to explain what happened next, except that this experience had a distinctly visionary quality to it.

While picturing Cory in her casket, I fell into a surreal dream and imagined that I had bored into her grave. I heard the sound of the drill penetrating through the dirt and rocks and the cement vault. The whining, screeching sound as it struggled to pierce its way through the thick metal casket unnerved me. Once the hole was completed, I threaded a remote-controlled camera, equipped with night-vision lens, though the opening and lowered it into the casket.

First, I saw nothing through the camera lens and thought I had faulty equipment or had done something wrong. *I knew this crazy idea was too good to be true!* Then I realized I was seeing nothing because the camera was pointed away from Cory toward the dark side of the casket. When I slowly rotated it, I picked up the edge of Cory's dress—"the fleecy folds of her dress," as I wrote in an earlier journal entry. *It's so vividly colorful! That's my Cory—right there!* My finger shook so much that I could barely operate the remote control! Slowly, very slowly, I calmed down and moved the camera along the length of her body.

I'm getting close! Then I saw strands of her long hair, and all of a sudden, I beheld Cory in all of her beauty! She lay as she had in the morgue—exquisitely beautiful and untouched by the ravages of death. *"Death lies on her like an untimely frost Upon the sweetest flower of all the field." My sweet flower, my beautiful dreamer, how exquisite you are, even in death! You lovely Crimson Glory Rose!*

When I guided the camera by the remote mechanism, the propeller generated a slight current of wind which blew a flower petal from her cheek and a few stray wisps of hair across her forehead. *That created the exact same effect as in the photo on my desk! How hauntingly still, but how lifelike she is! "Death, that hath sucked the honey of thy breath, Hath no power yet upon thy beauty." No power at all, Shakespeare, and how beautiful she is even in death!*

I stopped the camera at the side of her head and marveled at her profile. *People boast that Elizabeth Taylor has the most perfect facial features of any woman. Not so—it's my beloved Cory! This is the regal face of beautified perfection! You can have your Helen of Troy. Petrarch, you can have your Laura; Dante, your Beatrice; Antony, your Cleopatra; Romeo, your Juliet. You, Corinna Adelena, are, as the psalmist David says, the crowning pinnacle, the matchless pillar sculpted in palace style* [Psalm 144:12].

Deeper into my trance, I somehow penetrated her head—even, strangely, her very thoughts—and saw where she was, what she did, how she looked. I didn't try to identify her location, since I just wanted to feast my eyes on her and marvel at her beautiful white linen gown and magnificent crown.

As she joyfully danced, she directly faced me for a moment, her partner looking in the opposite direction. *I can't tell with whom she's dancing, but, my dearest beloved, how beautiful you are!* She slowly pivoted in a circle, exactly as she had pirouetted around the pillar in the mine. *I'm seeing my pirouetting Spanish ballerina again, but now she's radiantly diaphanous and angelically beautiful. My beautiful dreamer has indeed awakened to me!*

As they turned 180 degrees in a slow-motion spin, Cory now faced away from me, her partner toward me. I finally realized that she was in heaven, and it was He. *She's dancing with Jesus!* I could not believe it. In my dream, I shouted, "Cory, you're in heaven! Is that where you are, and are you dancing with Jesus? You are! I'm absolutely certain!"

She looked at me with the same smile she had in my desk photo, though now it was fuller, more radiant, more ecstatic. *Sounds of the rude world, heard in the day, have truly passed away for you, Cory.* I was ecstatically happy for her, yet another part of me simultaneously, and selfishly, was unspeakably sad that the cares of life's busy throng were not gone from me too. *I'm still here and so very alone—without you, Cory, without you, beautiful dreamer!*

Then I came to, roused myself out of my stupor, dream, reverie, trance—whatever it was—and reached out to clutch the cold gravestone. *Alas, I was only dreaming!* Like Caliban in Shakespeare's *The Tempest*, "when I waked, I cried to dream again." *I want to be in that dream again!*

I cried because I could not stay in that lovely dream and was ejected, instead, into the harsh world with no drill or camera beside me. Just a grave, a giant hole in my heart, and no hint of emerald green. *Just rolling banks of murky fog and billowing mists of sorrow black!*

But through it all, her perpetual cry, "Jude, Jude!"

Chapter 37

Jude's journal (Continued):

Because my non-existence was taking a heavy toll, I knew I had to do something to shake off my paralyzing lethargy. A year had rolled by and then another. Empty, numb years, of which I remember little, accomplished less, and, like Keats, limped along like a graceless frog in the fog. "Sleepwalking my way through life," my IUP student/friend Eric once described it. What an apt description!

I was the literal embodiment of the narrator in Keats's "Ode to a Nightingale: "My heart aches, and a drowsy numbness pains My sense, as though of hemlock I had drunk." But in my case, it wasn't hemlock I had drunk but my soulmate I had lost. How I grieved my way through those long winter months, those interminably cold, fiercely dark months! May I never again experience such a death-in-life period! How did I get through it? I remember virtually nothing and even stopped journaling for a time.

After a major expenditure of psychic energy, I steeled myself to attempt a lecture tour through the Mid-East. I accepted invitations and keynote addresses to several internationally renowned Egyptian universities, including Ain Shams University near Heliopolis, where I had formerly taught for a while, Cairo University, and Al Azhar University—that prestigious bastion for Islamic Studies in the Muslim world. This particular lecture tour had also taken me to both Mansoura and Zagazeeq Universities in Lower Egypt, then over to the University of

Damascus in Syria, and finally to the University of Jordan in Amman, where I concluded my whirlwind lecture circuit.

The trip was beneficial for the way it prompted me to start journaling again. That wasn't much, but at least it offered a modest reentry into the world of writing. Up to this point, I couldn't even sit to type or hand-write my journal because writing reminded me so intensely of Cory. She had been by my side in Little Gidding during the emerald green months when I wrote in my journal by the hour.

Now that she was gone, each act of writing evoked such vivid memories of my beautiful dreamer that I collapsed, every single time, in a quivering mass of shattered nerves. When I wrote during the months of our love, I'd often stop to massage my hand or rest my eyes, look up at Cory, and watch her paint away and hear her hum or sing. Now, when I look up, I see walls that jeer and halls that leer, and how they mocked me!

Why do I bring this up in my account of Cory's passing? Three different former students, Dr. Enas and Dr. Anwar in Egypt and Dr. Hussein in Jordan, asked a variation of the same question during this lecture tour. "Doctor, why don't you go back and visit the mine again?"

Nearly spilling my tea when Dr. Hussein first asked the question, I tried to remain calm. "I couldn't do that."

"Think about it, professor. Many years have gone by since your beloved Cory died. A visit to the spot where you lived and loved might inspire you."

"Our Jordanian friend is right," Anwar prodded. "It might help you work your way out of your malaise."

Seated there by the Nile, I tried to appear calm, but I was literally dumbfounded. The very idea of returning to the mine filled me with such horror that it nearly induced an anxiety attack of the sort I experienced the day Cory enacted Grandpa's death on the Pittsburgh stage.

The travel-abroad experience came to a climax when another former student, Dr. Manal Saad, escorted me to various places in Egypt where the Holy Family had stayed when they fled from King Herod. She had taken me to a number of holy sites—Al Hammam and Anba Ibram Monasteries in Fayoum, the Al-Muharraq Monastery in Assuit in the Southern Nile Valley, Matariyah in Cairo, and Deir Al Adra, Monastery of the Virgin, on Gabal Al Tayr, the latter constructed by Empress Helena in AD 328. According to well-documented historical research, these were the holy places where Mary and Joseph had sojourned with the infant Jesus when they escaped to Egypt.

The trek through the desert afforded us hours of animated conversation, during which Dr. Manal again brought up the matter. "You seem to be giving my idea of visiting the mushroom mine some thought, doctor. Am I correct?" Her sensitivity to my emotional state was welcome and astute. "I understand that it would be difficult for you, but maybe seeing these Holy Family places may inspire you to attempt it."

"I don't think anything I've ever seen has touched me like these sacred places."

"Perhaps a return to writing would compensate for the pain you'd feel in revisiting those old haunts which are saturated with memories of Cory?"

That question prompted a serious discussion on the previously forbidden subject. During our desert visit, I was so deeply touched that the Holy family, the infant Jesus Himself, had been in these very places that instead of deflecting the topic of writing, as had become my entrenched pattern over many long months, I faced it head on as surely as beautiful dreamer had faced her tortured past on a stage in Pittsburgh.

The details of that experience are imprinted on my mind. Dr. Manal and I were seated at the monastery dining hall for dinner one evening. During tea afterward, she cited the prophet Elijah's question to the nation of Israel. The emboldened prophet's query, as he made the Israelites consider who they would worship, Jehovah or Baal, was characteristically pointed: "How long will you halt between two opinions" [1 Kings 18:21]?

Her follow-up question, though gentle, detonated my resolute stand never to visit the mushroom mine again. "Doctor, forgive my forthrightness, which I don't intend, but might you be doing this very thing, faltering between two opinions—to visit or not visit the mine?"

That's pretty much all it took. Though my rational mind didn't realize it at the time, the seismic shift in my life's destiny occurred right there in the desert monastery. My brain would ascertain later that its decision-making ability had been completely trumped at that very moment, for in that hallowed monastery Dr. Manal had played the ace of spades. But I didn't tell her that, nor did she realize the far-reaching impact of her forthright question.

On a later evening, prior to my departure from Cairo, I was seated with several students and professors by the Nile River at my favorite waterside café for our farewell party. We were sipping tea under the beautiful Cairene sky and gazing at the stars. In those years, I was a big fan of identifying various constellations.

"There's the constellation Orphiucus in the house of Scorpio." I waited till all lifted their gaze upward. "Do you know what's happening in this constellation?" I had asked to initiate the discussion. I pointed to the stars, quite visible even in the well-lit sky above the Cairene cityscape. "While touring the Temple of Danderah in Upper Egypt, I learned that the contemporary interpretations of the Zodiac, evident in modern Horoscopes, differ completely from the ancient meaning. This constellation right there," by now I was pointing at a group of prominent stars, "is a good example. In this constellation, Scorpio pictures Satan who is poised to sting Orphiucus on the heel. But look at Orphiucus's foot, the lower, bigger star of those two."

The folks in our party helped each other identify the correct stars.

"I see it there."

"Yes, now I see it."

"Yes, those stars there," I assured them.

"What about it?"

"Orphiucus is going to trample on Scorpio, but consider the larger, intended meaning. Satan, pictured as Scorpio in this constellation, is preparing to sting Orphiucus on the heel, but Orphiucus is a picture of Christ [I used the Arabic word for Christ, 'Isa al-Masih' so as not to offend my Muslim friends]. Scorpio merely wounds Orphiucus, whereas Orphiucus kills Scorpio. In other words, this constellation shows Isa al-Masih defeating the deadly Serpent, Satan."

"That's amazing!" Anwar exclaimed. "Who would ever think that these constellations bear a religious message?" All of us marveled at the bright stars overhead. "You'd never know that when reading today's horoscope!"

"Look how clear these stars are in this eastern sky," I commented. "I agree with you, Anwar. The constellations are spiritually laden."

We continued to look at the sky between sips of tea. "Look over there," I resumed. "Do you see that bright star? There, above the right corner of The Ramses Hilton. That's the clearest I've ever seen the star in the forehead of Hercules. It's called Ras-Al-Gethi and means, 'the head of him who bruises.' The star's name refers back to Genesis 3:15, which says Satan bruises Jesus's heel, but Jesus bruises his head, meaning He inflicts the devastating, mortal blow. That star is rarely so bright in Pennsylvania."

The waiter came and gave us more hot water for our pitcher of tea leaves. Down river, our group could see Twenty-Sixth July Bridge crossing into Zamalek on the Nile. Hussein changed the subject. He knew I had been in Paris lately and made a clever connection. "Is it true that Eiffel had constructed this bridge after he completed the Eiffel Tower in Paris? A friend recently told me that Eiffel had designed it as a drawbridge which could be raised during times of riot or revolution. He said that the drawbridge never operated properly. Anyone know if that's true or false?" He was looking at the Egyptians in our party—Dr. Maghraby, Dr. Mary, Dr. Manal, Dr. Laila, and Dr. Anwar.

"No," Dr. Maghraby said speaking for the group. "I also once heard this but never verified it."

The river traffic was particularly robust this evening. Many of the Cairenes, enjoying a boat ride on the Nile River during the Eid-ul-Fitr, the three-day, post-Ramadan holiday, were joyously singing and laughing. Merriment was in the air, hearts were light, and people were dressed in their bayramlik, their holiday finery.

As I looked at the people floating down the Nile River, I thought of Cory. That was funny thing to write—*when don't I think of Cory?* She had always wanted to ride a boat down to the famous confluence of the three rivers, called The Point in Pittsburgh, where the Allegheny merged with the Monongahela to form the Ohio River. Why had we not done it when we had the chance? *How stupid of me!*

I took a hearty sip of Earl Grey tea to calm my nerves and tried to listen, but my mind had totally diverted to beautiful dreamer. A woman in a nearby boat on the Nile, seated by her man, wore a shawl the exact same shade of blue as the dress in which Cory was buried, the one I saw so clearly in my casket dream—yes, the fleecy folds of her favorite dress. "I love this shade of blue," she had once said while painting in Little Gidding and I worked on a poem. "If Vermeer can use that color so successfully in his skies, so can I! What do you think, Professor Jude? I've just thrown down the gauntlet, and this is one joust I can win!"

"I was saying, doctor, why don't you visit the mine again?" Manal startled me to attention and looked at me a moment without speaking further. I knew what was going through her mind: how far, in the presence of her distinguished colleagues, could she tactfully push the subject of revisiting the mine? "You say the pain has lessened over the years. Visiting that important place might stir you to creativity." Though the others in our party were oblivious, I knew she was continuing the discussion the two of us had initiated in the faraway desert when we visited the Holy Family sights. "What do you think, doctor?"

"I've thought of doing that, many times in fact, but the mine is closed since the whole operation was shut down shortly after the disaster." I ate a bite of biscuit and watched the feluccas glide along the Nile.

Blue-shawl woman has drifted downstream. I saw you by the river for those floating, magical moments, and now we drift apart. Forever. Goodbye, beautiful dreamer look-alike, on your way to Alexandria to a whirlwind of vivacious life…while my love sleeps in her cold, dark tomb. Enjoy your life, lovely woman, and touch others warmly and deeply and beautifully as beautiful dreamer touched me. And love that lucky man beside you; and, sir, love her with all your heart, and don't take one second for granted, because she too might be snatched away and cruelly flung into the black cave of eternal night.

I was embarrassing myself by pausing too long between responses but couldn't help it. "The cave-in that killed Cory started a chain reaction of cave-ins throughout the mine. When I inquired about going back to the mine several months later, the plant geologist told me that multiple cave-ins had prompted a slight shift in the tectonic plates or maybe it was the opposite. I don't remember. But whatever, the region experienced an unprecedented earthquake which was felt in even distant parts of the county.

"Is it safe now?" Dr. Mary inquired. "Do you think the mine has stabilized over the years? If so, maybe you can get special permission to visit the mine. Surely they wouldn't deny your request." I added another sprig of mint to my tea and said nothing for the moment. *Much as I hate to admit it, Dr. Mary makes a very good point.*

Stalling for time—deflecting the topic is actually what I was doing—I bought a couple jasmine petal necklaces from a strolling vendor for the females in the group. "Here," I said to the women. "You can be like Cory. She loved flower necklaces, and jasmine was her very favorite. Forgive me, friends! I'm not much of a conversationalist this evening. You can tell I've been day-dreaming about a certain person!"

Fortunately, the topic turned to jasmine necklaces which evolved into a discussion of jasmine teas among my friends. I participated in the conversation briefly. "The bouquet in the tea is so refreshing to me."

That was my last comment, and I was back in the mine with Cory riding our cart up and down the corridors like giggling college kids. *"Preppy, can you stop talking about Shakespeare for three consecutive minutes?"*

"Here's the deal. I'll stop talking about Shakespeare if you stop talking, at least for thirty seconds, about Rembrandt, Monet, Bernini, or Caravaggio!"

After a moment, I noticed that my guests were again watching me and awaited my response. *Whoa—I think they asked if I had the courage to go back to the mine if it ever opened again. I hope that was the question!* "It was a complicated decision, but that battle against nature, along with ongoing problems with the union, finally won the day. The difficult decision was made to end the decades-long mushroom farm operation. The mine is barred shut and sealed as tightly as…well, as an underground vault."

The people in our group seemed to think my answer made sense even if the vault metaphor was unnecessarily morbid. *Pathetic really! Perhaps they didn't know how disengaged I was during those last moments.* "Now the mine is in ruins, an underground ghost town like those in movies of the Old West."

And like the much nearer one in my heart!

Chapter 38

Jude's Journal (Continued):

When my professor friends began to converse about the football team's recent victory—they were referring to Zamalek's famous soccer team—I for the first time gave serious thought to visiting the mine, though I kept the idea to myself. *Such a visit would constitute that drastic, last-ditch step. Has enough healing occurred for me to actually do it? Ah, yet another rub. But there's another real concern too: would I be granted permission to enter the condemned property?*

In the final analysis, my trip to the Middle East was very successful and with every stop kept getting better. The students responded to my lectures on Shakespeare and Milton—for that a speaker is always relieved and grateful—but the thing they wanted me to talk about the most during Q&A sessions was not the content of my lectures but Cory. Having read and enjoyed my earlier novels, the students couldn't get enough of hearing about Cory and our love.

"How close to the actual Cory is the Deirdre of the novels?"

"Is the place where the lovers' stroll on the ridge at Reesedale a real place, and, if it is, did you and Cory often walk there?"

"Is the underground mushroom mine a real place? Were you and Cory actually employed there?"

"Did you and Cory work the same kinds of jobs as Deidre and Lucas?"

I had gone to the Middle East to make the break with the past complete, or at least to stuff it safely into my unconscious again, but my constant talking about Cory made her as alive as those magical days when we lived for love.

In the end that trip, nevertheless, was my salvation. I had not written for months and was so emotionally battered by that stage in my life that I thought I would never write again. The places I visited and the things I did, however, stirred me greatly. At first my writing was timid, tentative, ridiculously self-conscious, and just plain bad. I was so psychically dead in those months and my emotions so numb that I had become like the persona in Keats's "Ode to a Nightingale"—a dead clump of earth in the presence of the bird's ecstatic anthem: "To thy high requiem I am become a sod." Abe may be the clod, but I'm definitely the sod!

Experiences like climbing the pyramids of Egypt, which breathed enchanting pharaonic encrustations from every molecule, began to rouse me from my lethargy. Agog at the ancient temples of Edfu, Danderah, Abydos, Luxor, Kom Ombo, and Aswan, I slowly began to awake from my death-like trance. I went abroad in large measure to see if I was capable of response. I had been so dead to external stimuli that the things that used to energize me did so no more. It was an immense relief to me to feel at least some of the old excitement when exploring that ancient pharaonic world.

One morning, I relaxed in the palatial gardens at the Marriott Hotel in Zamalek, Cairo, sipping tea in front of the opulent edifice which had once been King Farouk's palace. Basking in those resplendent gardens, I remembered a song from the seventies musical, *Chorus Line,* which I had once seen in London. I can't remember much about it, but in this particular song one of the chorus line members, possibly her name is Morales, laments that, when on stage, she acts poorly simply because she can't feel anything. Because she can't get her heart into it, her acting, thus, is pathetically lack-luster. Then she learns that Mr. Karp, her acting teacher, died. The lyrics which I had committed to memory flitted in my brain as I surveyed the statuary-lined walks of the Marriott's luxurious gardens:

Six months later I learned that Karp had
    died.
And I dug right down to the bottom of my
    soul...
And cried 'cause I felt nothing.

How like Morales I had become, feeling nothing ever! Nothing excited me, nothing roused me; but fortunately, that death-in-life season seemed to be passing the longer I stayed in Egypt. In that regard, Egypt was my salvation.

The private garden parties and receptions with renowned dignitaries further fueled my desire to get my life back on track. These soirees were set amid the lush villas in Zamalek, that exotic island in the Nile River at Cairo which housed countless embassies and aristocratic villas. At one of the garden parties, Dr. Mary Massoud introduced me to the Irish ambassador to Egypt who was a personal friend to the brilliant English film director David Lean.

We talked endlessly of Lean's films—*The Bridge over the River Kwai, Doctor Zhivago, Ryan's Daughter, A Passage to India*, and others—as we imbibed the aromatic splendor of the luxuriant villa garden. "Zhivago is tragic," the ambassador expounded, "for the way he is so conflicted, torn between duty—devotion to the ever-faithful and beloved wife Tonia—and dream—love of the ineffably beautiful Lara. Torn, I guess we could say, between what is and what isn't, between what he has and what he wants."

Torn between death and life, I wanted to say. *Like not having Cory vs. having her!*

Those were heady days for me, and much of it now is a phantasmagoria of images that whirl in my mind with such ferocity that they still overheat my synapses. I especially recall during one reception at the villa of the American ambassador to Egypt when several prominent people—the Minister of Culture, the Minister of Higher Education, one of Egypt's ranking Egyptologists, President Sadat's top advisor, and countless others—persisted in their effort, like the students in my lectures, to get me to talk about Cory.

It was an utterly strange affair. I was trying to escape the past and talk of Egypt. After all, these were important people, and I knew my place: a lowly professor—a "peon," as I always jokingly referred to myself among my IUP undergraduates—who had developed a very modest following from my novels and who had absolutely nothing in common with these important dignitaries. My little domain amounted to a cubicle classroom, theirs the sweeping international arena of power-play politics. But the more I tried to get them to talk about themselves, their heady careers and the tense political situation in the Middle East, the more they shifted the conversation to Cory.

"How autobiographical is Deirdre?"

"Is she patterned, professor, on your beautiful Cory?"

"Which novel happenings adapt actual events from your lives?"

The questions were endless. But despite the alluring glitz and glamor of the garden parties with the rich and famous, the places in Egypt where the Holy Family lived stirred me the most. Those sacred moments transcended all the other grand experiences—tramping the ruins in the ancient city of Petra, walking on Mount Nebo in Jordan where Moses lies buried, or emoting my way through the private dinners in the homes of my wonderfully warm Egyptian and Jordanian students.

All of these experiences touched me profoundly and helped me slough off layers of accumulated ennui. In that regard, they made me feel like Milton's blinded Samson coming out of his depression in the Gaza mill—"one past hope, abandoned, And by himself given over." That was I: a walking dungeon, past hope and intensely despairing. *But now, at last, I've regained the will to return to life.*

A peak experience occurred to me on a Sunday morning when I sat in a service at All Saints Cathedral in Cairo, right before my return to Pennsylvania. I was so stirred by the rector's sermon that I spontaneously started jotting down some notes.

When I saw how excellent his homily was, I requested a typed copy of the sermon which, fortunately, was made available. The pastor spoke of the prophet Elijah's depression after Jezebel had threatened to kill him:

Good people, it's essential that we keep this important fact in perspective. Elijah had just been the agent of one of the most dramatic miracles in the entire Old Testament. At his hand, some 450 false prophets were slain. At his hand, the fire of God burned up the sacrifice on the water-drenched altar. And at his hand, the three-and-a-half-year drought started and stopped.

But because Jezebel did not capitulate in the face of the disastrous defeat of Baal worship, Elijah became very despondent. Let me read 1 Kings 19:4 again. "And he [Elijah] prayed that he might die, and said, "It is enough. Now, Lord, take my life." Can you imagine this level of depression in the wake of such a string of matchless victories? How could he turn inward so completely that he forgot this cluster of miraculous interventions?

We too see evidence of God's handiwork around us, and while obviously not so dramatic as these examples, we still witness God's participatory presence in our daily lives. That being the case, why do we fixate on the bad circumstances instead of the power of the indwelling Lord in our lives? Why do we focus on external phenomena, negative as it often is in today's crazy world, instead of the infilling power of the Holy Spirit? This was Paul's point to the church at Ephesus when he said that God does "exceedingly abundantly above all that that we ask or think, according to the power that works in us" [Ephesians 3:20].

If you tap into that power, you will be able to shake loose the debilitating thoughts and patterns that restrain you. The key is the power of God, not your own feeble strength. Humble yourself under the mighty hand of God. Humble yourself so that you rely on that indwelling power and, thus positioned, complete the glorious work which God has specifically designed for *you*. Amen.

It wasn't much, but for the first time in many months I started writing there in the All Saints Cathedral Guest House. That sermon, which helped me slough off my sloth, put me in direct contact with the fountainhead of my own being. I can say with absolute certainty that those cryptic scribbles about my novel represented my return to writing and, simultaneously, solidified my resolve to visit the mine. *I'm going to do it. I will visit it at last!* It would be a monumental step, but at last I had acquired sufficient courage to take it.

Why am I talking about a lecture trip to the Mid-East? Have I lost my focus just a bit? Is this a story about our love or an elaboration of my post-death coping mechanisms? Well, I'm doing what Cory always said I masterfully did. When dealing with the unpleasant realities that overwhelm, I conveniently divert my focus. What better way to handle the pain of dealing with Cory's death than to avoid writing about it altogether through deflection? The longer I dealt with my grief over her passing, the more I realized that it had created a vicious vortex in my heart which sucks in the opportunities and challenges of reality, grinds it to shards, and then flushes it, like incinerated trash, out the back into galactic oblivion.

With the decision firmly in place that I would start living again, I came across a verse in my devotions which perfectly suited my freshly-minted resolution. "For, lo, the winter is past, the rain is over and past." *Maybe now that's the case for me too.* "The flowers appear on the earth." *To belabor the obvious, the flowers appear...minus a certain red rose!* "The time of singing has come." *What a deathly silence it's been!* [Song of Solomon 2:11–12].

But would I be able to lure the flowery summer season into the frozen tundra of my soul? I wanted that more than anything, for Cory's sake as much as mine, and a visit to the mine was the first major step in realizing the dream. But would the smoldering wick of this new, wispy resolution be able to illuminate that cold and lonely prison cell—my head—and leverage it to glorious action?

Chapter 39

Jude's Journal (Continued):

A short time later—this was years after the mine had closed and a short time after my recent lecture trip to the Mid-East—I decided to contact, of all people, Duke Manningham. We were friends of a sort by now, though I had had little contact with him the last year or so. He had acted on his promise, married Tina, and dutifully helped her raise Tony whom, as most everyone suspected, he had indeed fathered, subsequently proved by DNA tests. In the intervening years, Tina bore a second child, a lovely baby girl named Marilyn, and they were as happily married as any couple I've ever known.

Duke told me that his son Tony had asked him to talk about his and his mom's reformation in large measure because Tony, experiencing the predictable rebellion of youth, wanted his father to speak of the big change that had occurred in their lives a number of years previously. Duke and Tina spoke forthrightly about their wayward past and even became advisors of the Center Hill youth group in an effort to encourage young people to refrain from the dissolute living that had wrecked their lives.

When Tony pushed his dad about this, Duke decided, at Tina's urging, to compose an account of his turnaround. Though not a writer, Duke thought it a good idea since such an honest account may help the struggling youth of the church. He recently mailed me a copy which I like so much that I brought it along to Egypt.

Duke's Account of His Conversion (excerpt):

The Center Hill Church of the Brethren held annual revival services. I'll begin by talking about that, though I'm not a writer. You'll see that in a second. Heck's fire Ma Henry flunked me in eleventh grade English, and that, folks, is a fact. I still get mad when I think of that F because she accused me of cheating on the final exam but I didn't. Well, I won't get into that except to say I was set up.

I want to talk about what happened at the church that evening of the revival service even if I can't write for crap. I'm doing this because it might help the teens in our church. They sure need it because I know what they face in the future. This world is as messed up as I was!

In the old days, churches held revival meetings, and they were part of a long-standing tradition. These meetings emphasized renewal and rededication and things like that. That tradition was very much alive for Pastor Gabe Wyant. He was not what Jude and Cory called a "hell, fire, and brimstone" pastor like some ministers must be. I mean he never tried to frighten people through scare tactics. He spoke with passion, but he never tinkered with people's emotions to entice them to salvation.

He accepted people just as they was. I liked that. He never put me down though I had a rough past. People who know me would vouch for that. But he let his people know that their souls waged a life-and-death fight against evil. He made it so simple that even I got it. I wrote down what he said during one of his sermons. Here it is word for word. "Sin is the enemy, and Satan is the predator while the Word of God is the life-giving

Truth, which perishing people need. Christ is the sole antidote for the killing poison of sin." Those are true words, and I like them a lot.

I never used such words, but I know what he meant. We all did. There was a bad poison in me which made me sick and caused me to do crazy things. Like the time I was with Cory at Beatty's Mill and acted really bad. The booze in me made me do crazy and evil things like that. That particular memory is so bad in my mind that to this day when I think of it, I shudder all over and want to cry. Cory's being gone makes that even worse. Somehow it makes it even harder. I thought the world of that woman.

Pastor Gabe said a verse in Ecclesiastes describes me and other unsaved people. "The hearts of the sons of men are full of evil. Madness is in their hearts while they live, and after that they go to the dead" [9:3]. I couldn't find a verse that described me better. Evil heart, mad as the dickens, and headed for hell after death. That's me all the way!

I'm not going to say how bad those days were. I'd shock the daylight out of you kids! I included some examples but erased them because the Official Board would censure them anyhow!

Pastor Gabe gave me other verses that describes exactly what I was in those days. One of them is Proverbs 25:28. "Whoever has no rule over his own spirit is like a city broken down, without walls." That also describes me perfectly, broken down like a city without walls. Back in the old days I couldn't control my spirit no matter how hard I tried. I don't want you guys to be like me.

Pastor Gabe believed that man has fallen, and all people are cursed. The effects of that curse have to be reversed. Jesus is the only One to do it. It worked for me, so I know it's true. I wish the guys at the mine heard this message since a few of them really need it. I can name several.

This was the theme of the revival series which Tina and I went to. The sermons were about Nicodemus in John 3. On the night of the cave-in, we was sitting in the Center Hill church listening to Pastor Gabe preach. He said all people need salvation and a new beginning in Christ.

"What is the recurring word in these opening verses of John 3?" Pastor Gabe paused during his sermon to give us time to think. He said it was the word "born." Gabe said that eight times in these six verses Jesus says that people must be "born again." Pastor Gabe quoted from the Bible as he always did. "That which is born of the flesh is flesh, and that which is born of the Spirit is spirit."

The Holy Spirit don't live inside of us until we are born again. We have to be born a second time. One's first birth gives life to our flesh, whereas the second birth gives life to our Spirit. If we don't have the Spirit of God living in us, we are like walking dead zombies. This was a big point in the sermon.

Gabe asked us if we remembered the sixties thriller of several decades ago, called *Night of the Living Dead*. I always liked that spooky film because some of my friends were extras in it. The movie was filmed here in western Pennsylvania. Blassey is in that movie. I kid you not. You guys don't know Blassie, but I work with him at the mushroom mine. He's a good egg.

He's in the opening scene in the Evans City Cemetery. He took me to that town one day and we visited the cemetery. He showed me exactly where that film was shot. It was a big deal to him. He told me all about his part and showed me that freaky walk they use in the movie. I used to walk like that all the time just to mock him. Mocking others always came easy to me, so I did it all the time. But now I see that mockery and sarcasm are the tools of weak and insecure people. Gabe told me that.

Gabe told us that people without a quickened inner spirit are walking zombies. Until Christ inhabits our bodies, we are walking dead dudes. Gabe was right. I was as dead as a doornail and dumber than an ox.

Gabe then said that this Bible passage forces us to ask a tough question. Are you a walking dead person? Meaning, are you like one of those zombies in *Night of the Living Dead*? Of course you don't feel like it just as I didn't at the time. I was a brute of a guy back then. In fact, I was really strong. Gabe said we boast about our strength and our busy schedules.

As I sat in that revival meeting, I thought of all the bad stuff I did, and there was so much of it. I held Tina's hand as he spoke and felt rotten inside. Such shame for what I did to her and lots of people. Too many women. Especially the beautiful woman I told you about, Cory. Some of you might remember her. She's the one who died, and she attended services in this very church. If the church doors were open, she was here!

I wrote this down later. Jude said that Pastor Gabe's line, that we "lead lives of quiet desperation," is very famous. He told me who said it but I don't remember. He said it was a famous American writer. [Jude later told me it was Thoreau in *Walden Pond*, but I won't tell the kids that. They could care less!]. Gabe said that all that busyness reflects the quietly desperate life of the flesh.

What of the new man? That's what the Apostle Paul calls the new nature after a person is born again. Is the new man alive in us? This is the irony of life. It's possible for your body to be very alive but your spirit to be as dead as the beautiful GTO Spike smashed up a couple years ago. I hated seeing him get rid of it. Me and Spike and the guys had good times in that car. We used to cruise around the Cadet restaurant by the hour on Friday and Saturday evenings. That was the big show in town, and everybody thought we were so cool.

The entire congregation easily followed the Pastor's sermon that night because of Gabe's special gift of preaching. Not over people's heads but right on our level. I asked Jude to describe Pastor Gabe a bit, and he wrote this. "Though a learned man who once delighted in the philosophic discourse of the academy, Pastor Gabe had come to love the country people. His sole intent was to emulate Christ by preaching profound Scriptural truth in easily-understandable language." Jude said that he used "an expository approach that centered on biblical analysis and real-life application."

I'd never say it that way because Jude is sometimes like Abe and over my head! But one thing is certain. Gabe made us see Jesus better and understand Him more. To me, He was somewhat like the Lord. When I think of what

Jesus must be like, I think of Pastor Gabe. That's the highest compliment a person can be paid. At least that's what I mean.

In the tradition of our church, Pastor Gabe gave us a chance to walk forward to the altar after the sermon to confess our sins and to make Jesus the Lord of our lives. People went forward for other reasons too. Some wanted special prayer, and some wanted to rededicate their lives to Jesus. A couple went up to be anointed because they was going through a rough patch. Some like Tina and me went forward to be saved.

Each of the pastor's words was a soothing drop to my parched soul. "He's talking to us," Tina whispered to me toward the end of his sermon. "Every word convicts me." I saw Tina look down at her feet. She whispered to me, "All I have to do is take the first freaking step, and the rest will easily follow. Move, feet. I want to do this! I have to go forward and join the people at the altar." She was whispering softly, but I heard every word.

Pastor invited us to come forward to "drink the life-giving water." Gabe said that when people cross a huge desert wasteland, they need to keep themselves hydrated. "That's exactly what's happening to us in this life. We're marching through the Sahara Desert, and our sun-parched souls need a lot of water if we're going to make it through the desert."

I'll never forget Gabe's words. "I invite you to come to the Fountainhead. Come and drink liberally of Christ's life-giving water. That's the only river that gives eternal life." I loved those beautiful words because I could picture Buffalo Creek and West Glad Run on the opening day of trout. They're beautiful streams flowing through God's creation, and the first day of trout season is one of my favorite times of the year.

Well, from all over the sanctuary people started walking forward to the altar. Pastor and some deacons and elders prayed with them. "We have to do this!" Tina said. She slid her feet several inches and tried to stand but told me later that she felt a weight holding her down.

"What's going on?" After the service she told me about the conflict in her heart. "Lord, you know that I want to confess and repent because no one in this building is half the sinner as me. They are godly people, and I don't fit in with them at all. Hell, I don't even belong in the same room, so give me strength to come to you."

She tried again and then Pastor Gabe quoted a verse. I didn't remember it, but I talked to him so I'd get it right for this story because I want it to be accurate. He said, "For God satisfies the longing soul and fills the hungry soul with goodness" [Psalm 107:9]. It was that verse that helped Tina get the courage to go forward. She struggled to her feet. Inch by inch she put one foot in front of the other and slid by me and the other people in our pew. Soon she was in the center aisle walking toward her goal, gliding right along.

I was amazed at her strength. I was such a coward compared to her. I was a horrible sinner and didn't want to go forward in front of these holy people. I felt so out of place and conspicuous you might say. Tina always spoke of her sins and need to reform her ways, but deep down in my heart, I knew I was the lost prodigal son if there ever was one. If you guys ever read the prodigal son story, think of me. But instead of prodigal son, read Duke. That parable is about me. Period.

How did Tina have the strength to do what she did? I watched with envy as she walked the aisle. She went slow at first and then walked fast. Tears were streaking down her face, but her eyes gleamed with a hope she never had before.

I looked down at my feet. I was fighting the same struggle. Why can't I be as strong as her? Then the congregation started to sing "Just as I Am." I looked up the song to get the words right. Every one hit me with the power of my 30-30 Winchester.

Just as I am, and waiting not
To rid my soul of one dark blot,
To Thee whose blood can cleanse each spot.
O Lamb of God, I come.

That's what I am, a walking dark blot of horrible sin! I thought of the night at Beatty's Mill when I tried to do a very bad thing to the lovely princess. Jude always called her "beautiful dreamer." I remembered how I walked out on Tina in the past. How many women and how many marriages had I ruined? I even abandoned my wonderful son Tony. I thought of my fits of anger when I'd get drunk and smash people's faces and rip places to bits. What a wretch of a human being I was! No wonder I loathe my disgusting self!

Just as I am, though tossed about
With many a conflict, many a doubt,
Fightings and fears within, without
O Lamb of God, I come! I come!

That's me. Fightings and fears within. How can I ever escape my past? How can I stop giving into the flesh when I love it so much? The devil has his hooks in me so deep I'll never get free.

Sitting there, I recalled my past feats of bravery. I beat everybody in the mine in arm-wrestling, even Huddy Weaver. I took on three men at one time in a brawl at The Inn when they were hassling Tina. That was the night some dude at the bar said I was as strong and tough as Jack Lambert. That's the biggest compliment I was ever paid. Once I picked up a five-foot rattlesnake bare-handed just because one of the guys with Ken Bowser dared me. We was up north in Elks County near Benezette campground. How could I be so strong all those times and yet so weak now? I have to do this. I kept saying that to myself.

I saw Tina there at the altar. Pastor Gabe was standing beside her and put a comforting hand on her shoulder. They prayed together. What a picture of love and forgiveness! That was the final straw. I struggled to my feet. I was done putting it off. I walked to the front, slow steps at first—like Tina's. Then a fast walk, but I was almost running as I neared the altar.

After the service was over and people were departing for home, Tina and I talked to Pastor Gabe. Tina spoke first. "It was as though I couldn't move. Almost as if I was held down by one of those giant mushroom trays. I wanted to go forward during the altar call but couldn't. I had worked my way through all the nervousness but still felt glued to my seat. By that time, it had nothing to do with my will or desire. I tried to move but couldn't. I was paralyzed and just couldn't make my freaking—sorry—couldn't move my feet."

"Same with me," I said.

Gabe then explained. "We pastors would say you were in demonic warfare." I don't remember his exact words, but he said that the demons were trying to keep us "incarcerated in bondage"—that phrase I do remember. The evil forces of this world hate it when they lose souls to the "kingdom of Light." He said that's why we couldn't move our feet and why it was hard to take those first steps.

Well, that's pretty much how it happened. I wrote this story for you young people. I hope it will make you think twice when you're being tempted. I don't want my Tony doing the nonsense I did. Giving my life to God is the best thing I ever did. I'm sorry for my past and for all the people I hurt. I hope they forgive me. I apologize to all of them and honestly beg for their forgiveness.

But at least I know I'm now forgiven, and that's the best feeling in the world. I know that because Pastor Gabe constantly reminds us that if we confess our sins, Jesus is faithful and just to forgive us our sins and to cleanse us from all unrighteousness. For a goofball sinner like me, that is the best thing you can ever hear.

Oh, I remember one more thing. Gabe once used an image we liked. He said each sin we commit is like a large rock we put in our backpack and that through life we're climbing up a tall mountain. He said to imagine the weight of that backpack as we accumulate our sins. The ever-increasing weight kills us as we climb, climb, climb; and that's why we have to lay down that burden of sin at the cross. Ever since I did that, I feel light as a feather and good all over.

End of Duke's Account

Chapter 40

Jude's Journal (Continued):

By this time, my desire to see the mushroom mine had intensified so much that I asked Duke about the possibility of going there. "I'd like to see it again," I said to him one evening on the phone.

"Are you sure? It's been boarded up for years and is very dangerous."

"I have nothing to lose. If I perish, I perish. Cory said that once, and things worked out for her. At least for a time. Maybe it will for me too." *Without Cory, nothing works out!*

I could tell he was dragging his feet. "I don't know, Jude."

"You shouldn't have any trouble getting permission. Can't you help out an old friend?"

I called Duke because I knew he had maintained contact with the people who owned the mine. If anyone could get clearance, it would be Duke. Permission was granted, though reluctantly, and I merely had to sign waivers. To this day, I remain grateful to those folks for giving me the opportunity to visit the mine again.

Duke leveled with me. "You're crazy but go ahead if you want to do it that much. It's just that you have to assume responsibility for what might happen in that death trap, and that's what it is, a vicious death trap."

A week or so later, I was driving on 422 between Indiana and Kittanning, that route I used to travel between the university and the farms in Armstrong County. On impulse, I stopped the car where I had all those years ago when driving to Kittanning to see Cory for the first time. How beautiful our love had been for those brief, golden hours!

Again, I walked to the top of that knoll, lifted eyes across the verdant fields, and, upon looking at the stretching fields below, remembered something she had said once about meadows. She had been painting in Little Gidding, and I had run out to the car to get some new oil paint she had forgotten. Upon reentering our hideaway, I asked her, "So how are you doing?" She said, "Well, the larks are still singing sweetly in the meadows of my mind." Looking on the lush panorama below, I thought of the beautiful dreamer who had made the larks sing in the meadows of my mind during our summer of love. "Jude, Jude!"

After a short visit with Grandma—she was still very much alive and doing well, though getting around with more difficulty and a little more bent over than in the past—I was on my way to the mine. My hands trembling on the wheel, I played the fifties-era songs, to which Cory and I listened incessantly. Neither one of us were quite sure why we did it, but because those songs were Grandma and Grandpa's favorites, we listened to them most of that summer and came to really like them.

As I drove along the roads to the mine, I played song after song which I had purposely selected—Connie Francis's "Among My Souvenirs," the Everly Brothers' "Walk Right Back," Nat King Cole's "Pretend," Patsy Cline's "Just out of Reach," Don McLean's "And I Love Her So," Pat Boone's "Sugar Moon," Patty Page's "Allegheny Moon," and numerous others. Some of these songs, like "Green Fields," we had never heard before, but they became favorites across those summer months. Today they created the right frame of mind for this momentous experience.

I met Duke near the top of the hill at the turnoff to the mine. *What a handsome man he is: responsible, well groomed, and confident!* Finishing up his bachelor's degree, he was gainfully employed at Penn United. Though dressed casually, he looked very sharp. His exercise and weightlifting regimen having paid good dividends, he was in better shape now than during the time we worked in the mines. I had heard he was a trustee at Center Hill church, taught a Sunday school class, and was co-youth advisor too.

"Look at these pictures of Tina and my two kids. See why I say I'm one happy dude!"

What a joyful family! "That's a lovely family, Duke. You're one fortunate man. Tina is absolutely beautiful." And she was. Now off the booze and away from the wild living, she had become a "virtual model of rectitude," as Charles once quipped. I could tell from the picture that she was a very changed woman. *They are happy and in love—exactly what Cory and I always wanted but were denied!* Despite the pig pen he lived in for years, Duke's dream came true, but mine died right down there in that horrible place. Wormwood, wormwood!

"You'll be shocked, Jude. I came down here last spring just to look around and was astounded to see the mine. Everything's rusted and dingy. You know the place has been shut down for years and is as dilapidated as can be. But it's the inside you want to see, and that will be much the same." He stopped and looked at me. "Are you sure you have the courage to do this? Sorry to be so frank, but you look a mess."

"I know."

He peered at me as though I had something to say. I didn't. *Not a syllable!* "You don't need to feel embarrassed if you back out. I don't mind coming down here even if it was for nothing. You need to think twice about going into that death trap."

"No, I want to see it. I've thought of doing this for years but didn't have the nerve. It's something I have to do even though I'm scared to death."

"If you say so."

"It's important that I beat my fear."

"I brought my golf cart here on my flat-bed truck. You can use it to drive around. And be sure to wear this helmet. You don't need to be told that, right? I see you still sport a scar there near the temple." Duke came closer to get a better look at the side of my head. "You almost died with her that day. You do know that? I talked to the doctors who took care of you. They couldn't believe you survived the accident. They thought you'd need brain injury, and you lost so much blood. You were a lucky guy."

"Well, maybe." *If you say so!* That's all I said, but Duke got my point. I always knew he was an intelligent guy.

He looked down the hill toward the gate at the main entrance. "One more thing—be careful, Jude. Like I said, you're nuts for wanting to drive through the mine. Rocks and debris are everywhere on the floors, and you don't want to plow into one of those big chunks of limestone. I'd like my golf cart back in one piece!"

When he laughed hard, I was struck by his handsome smile. Duke never used to smile much, but now that he had his teeth work done, he had the smile of a Hollywood actor. *He looks like Bruce Willis in* Die Hard! "You're aware that there were other major cave-ins after the one that killed Cory?"

"Yes, I heard."

"I know you're doing this to satisfy your emotions…or conscience, but reality is reality."

"I know. I'll take it easy and bring back your golf cart in one piece!" I laughed when I said that, and it struck me at the time that that was one of the first times I had genuinely laughed in ages. *I don't laugh anymore. I have of late lost all my mirth. If I perish, I perish, but no better place to die than here. At least that's one way of ending this pain in my heart, and what a consummation devoutly to be wished!*

Moments later we arrived at the mine entrance. I couldn't believe the change. The parking lot was full of weeds which had grown through the cracks in the asphalt, and so much runoff had accumulated around the door that we had to shovel dirt away just to open it. Windows were broken, graffiti marred the walls, and rusted machinery was strewn about like junk yard wreckage. "This place is a fright," I said.

"I warned you."

I was nervously talking just to calm down. Gabe once quoted Proverbs 17:27 to me: "He who has knowledge spares his words, and a man of understanding is of a calm spirit." *I speak a lot because I don't have knowledge, at least anymore, and I definitely don't have a calm spirit!*

Duke unloaded the golf cart for me and drove it toward the door. "Take your time. I'm in no hurry. They just stocked Buffalo Creek with rainbow trout, so I can fish for hours, and Tina's shopping with the boys, so no need to rush." Duke looked in the direction of the stream. "See that open spot to the right of the big Oak tree? That's where I'll be. Just give a shout when you're ready to leave. Oh, and here. Take this walkie-talkie. Buzz me if you need me for anything."

What a good man! People can change, and you, Duke, are living proof. From animal man to angel. He's on the ascent while I'm on the descent. The truth hurts, but it's an unalterable fact that he found his world while I lost mine. I took my place in the golf cart. *Would I find it in these corridors?*

Once inside, I immediately shed a tear. Much was exactly the same. A couple of the vending machines were still there, the time clock with the cards hung on the wall, and the same decrepit furniture sat in the lounge. Donning my helmet, I drove down the long corridor to the main entrance door which was still operational. Duke had given me instructions on how to lift it manually if the electric control didn't work. So far so good.

While the door was rising, I paused to look up at the security camera—the one that photographed the ambulance as it waited here that fateful day, the camera that showed the close-up of the dying Cory, Cory who had said with her dying breath, "Promise me you'll write. Promise, Jude." And the rest is silence. *So like Prince Hamlet!*

We had wanted to watch a Hamlet production in Pittsburgh, not live it. We wanted to witness an on-stage tragedy, not be cast as its center-stage protagonists! She desired to impersonate Ophelia, not die like her! Too much of water hast thou, poor Ophelia, but too much of rocks hast thou, poor Corinna! Well, if all things are brought to their destined end, why am I driving around in this mine? To stitch up the hole in my heart or luxuriate in the pain? Did I come to be healed or inflict, at last, the final deathblow?

Onward into the dark I drove. I had forgotten how well illuminated the mine was when a bustling operation. Big lights had hung at regular intervals so that, though far underground, the corridors and rooms were always fairly well lit. Now, as I motored along in total pitch black, I was in the underworld and felt, around the bend ahead, I'd see Charon at the River Styx waiting to escort me to eternity. Or should I say across the Jordan River? "There is a river whose streams make glad the city of God." That was the verse Cory had framed which sat on my IUP desk. Cory and I never found that river of life, glistening like gold.

Actually, that's not true. We found it for those few glorious moments, but it couldn't last. Nothing gold can stay, yet another Frost poem. You had that one right too, Mr. Frost. Nothing gold ever lasts. Since I can't have the river of glistening gold, I might as well cross this murky river of death just around the bend. Let's be honest: I've been dabbling my toe in its waters for years, lured by its enchanting siren song. One good thing: crossing it will put me in the New Jerusalem and with my beloved at last!

What lay ahead around the next corner? The opening lines of Dante's *The Inferno* flashed in my mind: "Midway on our life's journey I found myself In dark woods, the right road lost. To tell About those woods is hard." That was one of the poetic passages I quoted to Cory the first night we were reconciled in the Center Hill church cemetery. To tell about those woods is hard. "Is hard?" I call that understatement of the first order. Try totally impossible, and now that right road is lost forever!

I had told her once that the right road was lost because she wasn't on it. Yet since she was among the living at that time, there was hope, and we did indeed find the road and strolled it together. At least for those sublime, Elysian hours. But now the right road is forever gone; and midway on my life's journey I find myself in dark woods, the right road lost forever.

The two lights on the cart and my miner's hat—that triad of bouncing wisps of illumination—impotently flashed their thin rays of light into the inky dark as I drove along. Once the cart passed by, the corridors instantly darkened again, that abiding blackness of eternal death. The phenomenon—here for a second and then gone forever—reminded me of those times when Cory and I used to skip stones across the gliding rivers of the Allegheny River. "Look, Jude, at those momentary splashes—a barely noticeable succession of ripples—and then the water seals over them forever, just as though they'd never been disturbed."

Cory was that skipping stone in my life, joyously shooting across the top of the water, defying gravity for those moments of unspeakable rapture, divine bliss, ecstasy untold; and then she was sucked into the dark abyss forever. I motored on, swallowed up by grief as surely as the skipping pebbles in the Allegheny. What did I now have? Memories that wouldn't die. "Jude, Jude!"

Patsy Cline's "Just out of Reach" played on my cassette player as I drove along:

> Love that runs away from me,
> Dreams that just won't let me be,
> Blues that keep on bothering me,
> Chains that just won't set me free—
> Too far away from you and all your charms,
> Just out of reach of my two open arms.

The first place I sought out was the room with the Romanesque arches. We had a name for it back then, but I don't remember it—another intentionally suppressed detail? It was the place where we used to play cart tag. Once there, I stopped and pointed the lights on the stretching arches, looking in the dark like the Roman aqueduct I had seen outside of Caesarea in ancient Israel. In my mind, I saw us playing cart tag here as we so often did, Cory in the lead and I following or vice versa—all in slow motion.

A tear fell as I glanced at the arches. It all happened right here when we wove the cart through these arches. I walked over to the central one where we once had stopped and madly embraced. I ran my hand along the hard limestone. How cold and jagged it was! How hot and smooth as ivory was her hip the day when I allowed my fingers to gently glide along it at Beatty's Mill! I had never seen anything so beautiful in my life as that forbidden white flesh. She had pressed that loveliness against this arch. *Right here!* I ground my midsection into it and wept.

When I drove the cart to the opposite end of the room, I dismounted and looked back at the stretch of arches. It was from this angle that I had obtained one of my favorite photos of Cory, the one that had appeared in various books and magazines. Her head was thrown back, and her bright eyes sparkled with the reflected rays of the overhead light. She had just said, "Catch me if you can."

Cory, I would catch you if I could, but you're just out of reach of my two open arms! You had played that song by the hour because you said it embodied so perfectly your feeling during the silent years of our agonizing separation. Now it's my turn to reach, to sing, to wish, but now you lie beyond my desperate reach.

As I departed the Roman room, I had a temporary resurgence of fear, so I delayed visiting the spots I wanted to see the most—the growing rooms where Cory usually worked and, the big one, Little Gidding. I longed to visit it again, but how could I muster the courage? I delayed the agony, and the ecstasy, and motored toward the packhouse instead.

On the way to it, a phrase from the famous Eliot poem, *Little Gidding*, hammered in my brain. "In windless cold that is the heart's heat." I thought of the cold in my lifeless heart. In this poem, Eliot describes the "Pentecostal fire In the dark time of the year." Pentecostal fire? Seriously? There's barely a glow in this cold heart let alone blazing Pentecostal fire!

Eliot had asked in the poem, "Where is the summer, the unimaginable Zero summer?" I ask the same. Where is the summer? How do we get back to the good, summery days? The words of Eliot's poem cut deep into me: "You are not here to verify, Instruct yourself, or inform curiosity Or carry report. You are here to kneel Where prayer has been valid."

Oh, yes, Eliot! To kneel in that sacred hiding place where we oft, so very oft, knelt in heartfelt prayer! I will go to Little Gidding not to verify, or be instructed, or be curious. I will cease all intellectual analysis and will go simply to rediscover, to be near my beautiful dreamer, and somehow, if possible, resuscitate my code-blue spirituality. In Eliot's words, I will go there to pray.

That is, when I have the courage. But not just yet.

Pulling into the packhouse, I experienced another vivid flashback when I remembered something that happened right before the Fourth of July, that festive, midsummer holiday when a joyous mood was palpably felt in the mines. Everyone was extra joyful this particular day not only because of the impending holiday but also because the employees had been given special permission to clock out two hours early. Several of the men and women had congregated here at the packhouse to await the final ticks of the time clock.

Assembled with the others, Cory decided to fill the minutes with an improvised game. I was not part of the fun at the beginning because I had arrived late but watched the proceedings from the doorway. Cory had lined up a group of men on one side—I think there were five altogether—and a matching number of women on the other, probably some twenty-five feet between the two lines. She drew a big bull's-eye on poster board, which she fastened to the back of the center woman. The women had their backs turned to the men.

The game was to see who could score the most bull's-eyes out of ten throws. Discarded, oversized mushrooms were the designated projectiles, the women throwing at the bull's-eye at the back of the center man, and the men doing the same for the center woman. The team that won was given the honor of clocking out first, the other team idly waiting in "ignominious defeat," the phrase Cory had jokingly used when she laid down the rules for her makeshift game. I remember leaning against the doorpost and musing, "This will be fun!"

The men won the coin toss and threw first, each man taking turns throwing at the target. When Moser threw, he hit the center woman square on the buttocks. The place howled with laughter. Then it was time for the women to throw at the men.

"Mose," the man who had hit the woman in the derrière, was given a severe "penalty" and had to stand in the center and face the women instead of standing with his back toward them. When it came time for the women to throw, they formed a little huddle and planned their strategy—a conspiracy, as it turned out—to try to hit him on the helmet instead of the chest. Moser was allowed to keep his face down so he wouldn't be hit in the face with a wild pitch.

When it came Cory's time to throw, she picked up a gigantic mushroom the size of a baseball, wound up, and delivered a perfect strike to the groin. When Moser collapsed to the floor in a heap, the place broke up with gales of laughter. Elaine, one of the contending women, said to Cory, "Thanks, hon, for giving me a break tonight. Husband will definitely be out of commission!"

She then offered Cory a whole basket of mushrooms, commenting, "Goodness knows, I need a break from animal man!" A couple of the men and women who faced Moser held up their pointed index finger and curled it downward, indicating loss of an erection. The laughter could have been heard up the hill at the main office.

As I entered the packhouse, I was instantly transported to that amusing moment all those years ago. Every vivid detail came back to me. *Cory stood here, right here, the picture of effulgent laughter, the nerve center of the cheering, raucous crowd!* The men, bent over in side-splitting laughter, were relentless in harassing Moser for getting nailed in the crotch. The ribald comments were endless, all of course at Mose's expense. July 4 weekend—the peak of summer fun, and my beloved beautiful dreamer, radiant with life.

Today in the same place, it's the pit of winter despair. Shakespeare once said, "Now is the winter of our discontent made glorious summer," but now the glorious summer of our paradise is made discontented winter.

Before exiting the packhouse, I paused for a moment and allowed myself to reflect on that group of holiday celebrants, seeing the scene as a scrapbook photo. As I slowly scanned the picture, I thought of their joy in the packhouse that summer day and contrasted it to their fate in the ensuing years.

Buzz ended up in the Union Baptist Church graveyard, killed in a car crash at the 422 intersection in Worthington. Alex, the tall hulking chap in the center of the picture, died in the Armstrong County Memorial Hospital after a year-long struggle with leukemia, a gnarled little ball of frailty half the size of his massive bulk. Harold, far right, married into money and operated a thousand-acre ranch in Texas. Once the Marcellus wells were drilled on his property, he and his progeny were set for life. As I zeroed in on their employee name badges, I saw them morph into other forms—one on a hospital death bed in the Armstrong County Memorial Hospital, or a cemetery tombstone, or on a fancy mailbox in front of a sprawling mansion at Plainfield, Texas.

I'm talking too much again, just as I did when I ran at the mouth about lecturing in the Mid-East. Why am I stalling? Shakespeare's Duke of Mowbray in *Richard II* says, "Truth hath a quiet breast." Alas, no quiet breast here. Why not just get on with the story? The answer is obvious: I cannot bring myself to face the pain of talking about my time in Little Gidding, just as I had delayed my trip to that hallowed spot on the day when I visited the mine. But I have to do it because it's the main reason why I went back to the mine.

I had thought for years about retrieving a number of items in Little Gidding: some books, Cory's sketches and paintings, her art supplies, photograph albums, and a scrapbook which contained precious mementoes of our summer love—ticket stubs to places like a Pirates game at Three Rivers, the productions of *Les Miz* and *A Chorus Line* at The Benedum, and the Three Rivers Art Show. I wept when I thought of the ticket stubs and playbills to The Three Rivers Shakespeare production of *Hamlet*, neatly pasted into the album and inhabiting their silent world on a table near her easel. I longed to enter that inner sanctum but was deathly afraid to do it. Agony and ecstasy.

As I drove away from the packhouse, I reflexively started to pray. "Lord, give me the strength to do this. 'The fervent effectual prayer of the righteous man avails much.' I am righteous only because You live in me, because Your righteousness and not my own has cleansed me and given me eternal life. Give me the strength, I pray, to face this sacred place, this priceless centerpiece of our love, so that I can benefit from it, so that I can be inspired to write the books which You have put on my heart, and so that I can maximize the gifts You have undeservedly bestowed on me, Your humble servant. Breathe into me the Pentecostal fire which Eliot speaks of in his poem, *Little Gidding*, for without that animating fire I am a lifeless shell of a man. Without it, I'm done, washed up. You know it, I know it. Amen."

I drove off into the eerie dark toward Little Gidding.

Chapter 41

Jude's journal (Continued):

As I pulled into the corridor leading to Little Gidding, still cordoned off, I flung the barrel aside. How often we had carefully positioned this barrel to preserve our secret! Today I gave it a reckless toss and heard the echo of the clanging barrel throughout the corridor. *No need to worry about discovery. Little Gidding's secrecy is eternally safe!*

I approached the fancy paneled door, pressed down on the latch, and slowly opened the creaking door. The brilliant lines from Eliot's "Little Gidding" darted in my mind like summer fireflies.

> We shall not cease from exploration
> And the end of all our exploring
> Will be to arrive where we started
> And know the place for the first time.

Is that how it would be for me? Would I arrive where Cory and I had started, in this hallowed room, and know the place for the first time? I mean really know it at last? Know what it meant to us, know why we were privileged to experience it, why I was allowed to enjoy it with my beautiful dreamer?

The kerosene lights that Cory and I had brought to Little Gidding in case of a power outage were still on the table. I took the matches from my shirt pocket, which I, fortunately, had remembered to bring, and lit the two lamps. A soft, warm light infused the room—a feather-brushed, golden halo of fairy dust.

I slumped onto the couch, coiled my knees up to my chest, and sobbed like a father who has just received the devastating news that his son was killed in action. Slouched on the sofa, I reached for the copies of the Bible and Shakespeare's plays, which lay on the coffee table, and placed them on my chest. *What verses or what Shakespeare quotation can I turn to that will quiet this throbbing heart?* Eliot had described faith as "A condition of complete simplicity (Costing not less than everything)," and certainly Cory and I had given everything for our love. Many times over, we had given all, but in the end that sacrifice took her life.

I glanced down at the volume of Shakespeare's plays and thought of the line from *Richard II*: "Truth hath a quiet heart." *Lord, grant me that quiet heart, I pray.* When with shaking hand I reached for the Lincoln bust on the coffee table, the stirring conclusion of his *Second Inaugural Address* came into my head: "So still let it be said, that the judgments of the Lord are true and righteous altogether."

Were the judgments against Cory righteous altogether? How was her early death right? The spinning wheel of my brain haphazardly stopped on James 1:4—"Let patience have its perfect work in you so that you may be perfect and entire, lacking nothing." I knew that patience did not abide in me and that I lacked, well, everything. *How in this fallen world does one learn such patience?*

The refrains of tunes which we listened to here by the hour pounded in my mind: Ray Charles's "I Can't Stop Loving You"; Connie Francis's "Among My Souvenirs"; Patsy Cline's "Sweet Dreams"; and Elvis Presley's "My Wish Came True." I thought of the line from the Elvis tune, "When you stood there before my eyes," as she had that first day when I saw my statuesque beauty exit the lunchroom. Crouched behind the cart in stupefied amazement, I beheld the classic beauty who stood there before my eyes!

As I sat on the edge of the couch, the waves of nauseous pain slowly faded, and a numbing calm spread over me like a rolling bank of murky fog. I managed to lift my eyes to the end of the room, where Cory spent most of her time and where her precious possessions were: her easel, the sketch of me, not quite finished ("Just a few final touches and it's yours, boss!"), the scrapbook, the photo albums, two large red roses, the picture of the Allegheny River at Reesedale, and the photo of beautiful dreamer and me standing on the Kittanning Bridge getting ready to drop our roses into the river.

I couldn't walk to her easel, not just yet, and instead slowly trudged over to the large executive desk inlaid with sandal, mahogany and walnut woods. *"You look like a CEO sitting there, Jude. You really do."* Several of our treasured photos sat in their places on the coffee table: the two of us making apple butter in the age-old copper kettle, posing by the large rocks at Buttermilk, and another at Indian Head Rock with the velvety-soft, lichened rocks back-dropped behind us like a flood-lit, emerald theater curtain. In a third photo we were sitting on the rock ledge by the stream at Heath Station near Clear Creek State Park. I picked up each photo, stared at Cory's features, and kissed her face in each one. "Jude, Jude!" *Beautiful dreamer, I'm calling to you as often as you call to me!*

Along with the photos, we had kept a framed quotation on the desk which the plant manager had put there—"Love never allows failure to be final." *Well, sir, it did this time. Love failed completely and failed fast! And the rocks came tumbling down, and all the king's horses and all the king's men couldn't put my beautiful Cory together again.*

I slowly rose out of the office chair and walked toward Cory's easel. My heart was pounding so hard at this point that I almost fainted. The nausea that flooded over me felt like the intense rush of heat that had swept across my body when the doctor had injected the dye during my recent heart catheterization.

Closing my eyes, I stepped right to the place where Cory had stood by the hour. *Right here she stood!* I opened my eyes to peer at the canvas. "Another couple strokes of the brush, and this one's in the can. In French, peinture est termine!" Or something close to that. I stood there and bowed my head. Never has she been more real to me. I could even feel her body pressing against mine. *I'm going to drive myself mad!*

I quickly loaded the irreplaceable objects—pictures, books, photos, the sketch of me, her drawings, scrapbooks and mementoes—into a box and carried them out to the golf cart. I returned to Little Gidding, turned off one of the kerosene lamps and dimmed the other to a faint glow. Cory was so close to me in those moments that it was as though I could reach out and touch her.

Then I heard her talk. "Preppie, when are you going to start that novel? Will I be the heroine? You'll be dead meat if there's another female in the novel beside me, and if there is, she better not be half as beautiful as me. She can be a hick or a hag who makes you gag, but she can't be a thing of indescribable beauty—well, like me!" Then that full-throated laugh that morphed into her inimitable child-like lilt.

I felt her presence in the dark—her breath on my face, moisture on my cheek, the warmth of her body pushing firmly against me. Tears oozed down my face, and the stabbing pain in my heart was never more intense. The sound of "Jude, Jude!" screamed in my ear. *Beautiful dreamer, wake unto me!*

I surveyed Little Gidding from side to side one last time, turned off the kerosene lamp, and then it was sealed in eternal darkness, never to be disturbed again, forever quiet. I thought of Keats's line from "Ode to a Grecian Urn"—"Thou still ravished bride of quietness." My mission complete, I took the last step to the door.

Keats says in his Grecian Urn ode, "Heard melodies are sweet, but those unheard are sweeter; therefore, ye soft pipes play on." *Well, if that's true, then the unheard sounds of this room will be rapturously sweet. In fact, they'll be completely quiet so, soft pipes, play on to your heart's content, because nobody will ever hear you again as I seal this coffin lid forever!*

At the door, I finished my final left-to-right pan of the room with my miner's lamp, deliberately ending on Cory's easel. As I did so, the flood-light beam of my miner's lamp picked up a bit of paper, protruding from the lower corner, which the dim, fairy-dusted light of the kerosene lamp had not illuminated. *What in the world is that?* I rushed back into the room to check, stumbling on the couch as I did so. *What could that be?*

Only the slightest edge of the paper protruded—slight, very slight, like the slightest edge of a metal plate, atop a leaning pole, which had supported a huge limestone slab. In that case, it wasn't enough. Not near enough, for one slight touch of the pole, and the rocks came tumbling down. But in this case, the slight edge enabled me to see that some piece of paper had been stuffed behind the sketch. *What could it be?*

I hurriedly pulled out the paper, nearly knocking the easel over as I did so. It was a note which Cory had composed immediately before we had departed Little Gidding! If I thought my tears were coming to an end, I was dead wrong. I was holding Cory's letter! I threw myself onto the couch to read.

My true love, Jude,

You think I'm sitting here at the desk just to take a break from your portrait. I finished it except for a few last touches, but I put it aside to write these few words. Why? I have no idea. I fully intended to sit beside you for a moment before we go "cave-exploring," as you call it, but I decided to write this note instead.

You know what I've been doing here for the last couple minutes? Looking at you. I'm not kidding! As I started to get up and come to the couch, I looked at you, sitting there engrossed in deep thought, reading Milton's *Paradise Lost*, pausing to stretch, and rubbing your eyes. You just lifted your eyes to look at the framed quotation on the wall. How we both love it and have read it a hundred times: "If it's of man it's forced. If it's of God it flows." We've found that to be so true. How the river of our love wonderfully flows because it's of God!

Jude, I love you. You have no idea how my every waking minute is consumed with you. I constantly think of you. I picture you in the mine driving the shop mule, or in your Papa's library at home, or helping Joey in the backyard or the fields. You're always on my mind. It's not possible to love another more than I love you. I can't imagine the joy of not separating, of being with you constantly, of giving myself completely to you. I await that rapture, our wedding day, in a way I can't describe.

Thank you, Jude, for loving me so much. You brought me back from the very brink. I was in bad shape when you came into my life last spring. We call each other Lazarus come back from the dead. In my case, I really was. I love you, Judah, my angel, my darling, my forever love. You've called me "Beautiful Dreamer" a lot in recent weeks. Well, sorry it's hopelessly trite, but you're my handsome castle knight!

Guess what: I told Dad that we were going to get married soon, very soon. He instantly smiled and said, "Don't wait! How about tomorrow?" He loves you almost as much as I do.

With all my love ever,
Cory, your beautiful dreamer

I lay back down on the couch after reading Cory's letter and held it to my face. *Her hand had been right here—writing these words, resting here on the paper.* Even now I felt her hand resting on me, pushing down on me, gently caressing my head as she so often did. Then I cried. So many tears ran down my face that my collar and shoulder were drenched.

I tried to say, "Cory, Cory!" to match her incessant cries of "Jude, Jude!" but the words were vaulted deep in my breast. Those untold words and lyrics of love which I would never be able to say to her ever again and the love poems I would never write for her—all of it was another bride in my heart, another bride of quietness like the urn in Keats's Ode, which would never walk the flower-strewn aisle of speech.

I lay in the dark and emitted a guttural groan, the only sound I could produce. How I wanted, in the gloom, to reach out and touch that face, so near that I could feel her arm around me, her hands upon me. I carefully folded the letter, the last thing she ever wrote, kissed it, and put it in my shirt pocket. Heard melodies are sweet but those unheard are sweeter, but neither are as sweet as these penned words!

I mounted the cart and drove out of the mine.

Rejoining Duke after a couple hours of separation was difficult since I was in no mood to talk. He understood this and gave me space for which I was grateful. At the top of the hill, I heartily thanked him and again commended his turn-around. He had become a happily contented man surrounded by a loving wife, great kids, and unspeakable joy.

I was the malcontent, trapped in a never-ending nightmare of lost love and lifeless as the limestone caverns below me. I bade him goodbye and drove away from the mine forever.

Chapter 42

Jude's Journal (Continued):

Before going to sit by Cory's grave for the evening, I had one more difficult task to complete—visiting the Mohney farm. Pete had sold the farm some time ago and was living in a small house on the Slate Lick-Cadogan Road. Joey and Laura married and happily settled on Thirteenth Street in Pittsburgh's South Side after Joey got a job in the city. Laura was currently finishing her degree at Duquesne University. The Mohney farm had been purchased by a Mrs. Dampe, her son, and his wife a couple years back. Life for them had seemingly started out well in their new agricultural setting, but that was the result of effective appearance management. Misfortune had been their lot from the start.

Joey told me that the son and wife soon divorced, his alcoholism taking its toll both on his health and their marriage. The wife, Joey explained, was tired of being battered and got out. "She flat walked out. 'That's it. I can't take this loser anymore!' And off she went. The mother doesn't even know where she ended up. Maybe over in Ohio." The son, Joey learned, died shortly thereafter. "The woman didn't say, but it might have been lung cancer. The mother said, 'You think I smoke a lot. I'm in the little league compared to him!'" She was an embittered mother who stayed on but, completely overwhelmed, no longer made an attempt to run the farm.

Eking out a life of drudgery that grew harder by the week, she made a series of catastrophic choices. Joey continued the saga. "First, she had sold off the tractor and farm equipment to make ends meet instead of hiring one of the many competent farmers in the area to operate the farm. Then she got rid of our prized cows. Those were some of the best Holsteins and angus cows around. Dad was so proud of them. Last to go were the beautiful horses, including Bullet. Bullet ended up on that big horse farm on the Boggsville Road. I hated to learn he was gone, Jude. Sorry if that makes me sound like a sentimentalist, but I loved that horse. Maybe I should try to see him one day." I can still hear Joey's lament.

Now the woman inhabited a run-down farmhouse. She ceased mowing the yard, the flower beds had gone to seed, the paint was peeling badly, and the shutters were falling from the house. Joey had driven by rather recently and was shocked beyond words. Fortunately, he had forewarned me about the deterioration of the farm and the sad condition of the woman's heart, the latter more devastated than the former, as I learned full well.

My purpose in visiting the house was not just nostalgic. Yes, I wanted to see the farm again, even in its forlorn state, especially the kitchen which I knew would fill me with a mix of emotions, since in many ways it had been one of the nerve centers of our love—the place where the Mohney family had spent so much time together, that hallowed cloister where Cory and I had whiled away many of the sweet hours of our summer love.

My main purpose in returning to the farm, however, was to try to get my hands on two boxes, the contents of which were priceless—Cory's paintings, her other journals, her poetry volume (she had written quite a few poems that summer), my collection of poems which I had composed and given to her, and the other big one, the engagement ring which I had planned to give Cory after our tour of the newly refurbished mine room.

After the funeral I had shown the ring to Pete. Somehow it comforted him so much that I let him have it. It was such a painful reminder to me that having it out of my sight was actually a welcome relief, much like the photo Morley had given me of Cory in the back of the ambulance. Joey told me that the engagement ring was packed with "Cory's other things." "It's on the very top of the bigger box. What a beautiful ring! Laura really liked it."

What happened at the time of the move was unusual but understandable. Pete had gone downhill precipitously after Cory's death and Joey's marriage. Once Joey and Laura decided that they did not want to move into the farm, much as they had wanted, Pete made up his mind to sell it. When the contents were moved into his smaller house, he forgot that he had placed the two boxes of "Cory's things" in the upstairs attic. Because the attic had been previously cleaned out and vacated, Pete, in his highly distraught state, forgot to make the final check on the day of the move.

Only recently, on a day of exceptional, and increasingly infrequent, mental clarity, Pete remembered the forgotten boxes. He instantly called Joey. "Joey, you won't believe this, but there are two boxes of Cory's precious things up in the attic. I had put them off by themselves so they'd be protected, but I was so shaken on the day of the move that I forget to get them. I'd really like to have them. Jude would desperately want them too. Speaking of Jude, I wonder how he is these days."

"He's struggling. It's been really tough for him. I hear little, but what I've heard isn't the best."

"I thought he was going to die of a broken heart. The last time I talked to him he completely broke down. He cried so hard he didn't even say goodbye."

"I can imagine."

"There was silence for such a long time, and then he just hung up. I really worry about him, Joey, 'cause I think he's in bad shape."

Joey called the woman on the phone and told me about his conversation with "an angry woman called Dee Hampe." Joey told me that she was "nobody's dummy" and gave me a sample of what "Mrs. Granite Heart" said on the phone. "Yea, I remember the damn stuff. I came across it and some other junk that was left behind. It made me mad as hell 'cause your old man told me the place was 'broom-clean.' Hell, there were two giant boxes up there I could barely budge. You call that broom-clean! The old geezer pissed me bad!"

Joey said he was going to try to arrange his very busy schedule and make a visit to Kittanning the following weekend to retrieve the boxes, but overwhelmed by his hectic schedule, he didn't make it. That's when I offered to go instead. "Joey, if you want, I could get the boxes. I'm going back to Armstrong County anyway."

Joey jumped at the chance. "Dad and I would be grateful if you'd take care of this last remaining detail. There are precious belongings in those boxes, Jude—treasured keepsakes I'm sure you'd like to have." He had paused for a long moment. Knowing something else was coming, I remained silent. Finally, he worked up the courage. "You know Cory's engagement ring is there too—on the very top."

I think I said, "Yes, I know," but can't be certain. It was as though that statement short-circuited my brain in the same way that one's heart has an instantaneous change when going into atrial fibrillation or ventricular tachycardia—an instant reconfiguration of the mental apparatus when everything goes haywire.

Having been warned about the woman's cynical personality, I approached my task with real trepidation. Because Joey had put me on guard ("Jude, she's not the overly sentimental type if you get my meaning"), I figured that the emotional-plea approach ("Cory was my sweetheart, and I'd really appreciate having these keepsakes of our love") was not the way to win over Mrs. Granite Heart. Then too, because she would recognize me as the guy in the photos, it was time to play the deceit card.

I ended up with a pretty convincing disguise that I had obtained from the IUP Theater Department. Jennifer Dougherty, a former student, was only too happy to come to my aid. "You look like a middle-aged man, Professor Jude. Very convincing. She'll never know, but just don't play around with your mustache or your hat. Our drama coach told us that a lot of actors give themselves away by fiddling around with facial hair, hats, and things they're not used to wearing. You'll do fine, but remember that you've worn your cool mustache for decades. It's a natural part of you, so don't toy with it!"

Decked out in my broad-brimmed hat, thick-rimmed glasses, and mustache, I hobbled up the porch stairs of the Mohney farmhouse, leaning on a cane. With trembling hand, I knocked on the door since the doorbell had stopped working long ago. A large woman came to the door, her red stringy hair matted and uncombed, top buttons of her food-stained dress unbuttoned, false teeth out, and a cigarette dangling from her mouth.

"What you want? I ain't buyin' nothin'! Just get the hell out if that's your deal!"

That was my warm greeting. I stole a peek into the kitchen. *That hallowed place where we had spent all those happy hours is such a wreck!* The sink and counter were full of dirty dishes, boxes were stacked throughout the room, dirty clothes hung on the chairs, and multiple cats ran everywhere including the countertops. The smell was unbearable.

"Hello, ma'am. My name is Jed Johns. I'm a friend of the Mohneys." Those first words filled me with panic. *Ah, oh, I spoke in my natural voice, but my youthful voice is a mismatch for this elderly disguise!* I tried to modulate my voice by making it raspy. "I learned from Mr. Mohney's son Joey that you had come across two boxes in the attic, which they forgot to take when they moved. Joey told me he talked to you."

The woman gave no reply.

I shifted my weight to my other leg as one with knee problems does, a bit of acting on my heart but a diversion too. *I'm more nervous than I thought I'd be!* "They apologize for the error and told me that I could pick up the boxes since I was passing this way. That's why I've come. I'll be happy to take the boxes off your hands."

She took a long, deep drag on her cigarette, flicked the ashes, some of which fell on my shoe. "Yea, there was two boxes of junk up 'ere." She paused and took another drag on her cigarette, looking me over as she did so. Wincing in pain, she massaged her hip. "Damn hip. A while back, I watched this special on TV. The guy said to keep a sharp lookout for mildew and mold in unused places. Like basements and closets and such places. I remembered them boxes up in the attic and thought about the cancer that moldy junk would give me. If it's one thing my family don't need, it's more cancer. It killed that damn son of mine." She took another drag on her cigarette. "Don't get me going on that sorry loser!"

She paused long enough to take another drag on her cigarette. When a fleeting image of her disgusting black lungs came to my mind, I felt obliged to cover the silence. "I'm sorry about your son."

"I swear the SOB is better off. Well, about the boxes, good riddance to them. I burned that worthless crap on the trash pile a few days ago."

I don't believe it! I fell backward a step and caught myself on the porch railing.

Chapter 43

Jude's Journal (Continued):

Nauseous by now and breathing hard—"palpitating" is the more accurate term—I tried to cover my shock and nervously stroked my mustache. *I'm afraid I'll throw up right here on the porch!* Fighting for control, I overcompensated by trying to look like a man of unrattled poise, another huge lie. I stood with unnatural stiffness.

She stopped talking and gave me another of those piercing looks. *Is she seeing through my disguise?* I was relieved when Madame Pleasant resumed speaking. "I damn near killed myself lugging that crap to the burn pile. It was just a bunch of papers—an old scrapbook and a couple photo albums—but it weighed a ton. Nothing of value, just junk. I know 'cause I looked through it."

When she stopped talking and looked at her cigarette, I managed to say, "I see," or something similarly innocuous. She studied how to articulate her next thought, but her eyes were back on me. I thought to myself, *Oh boy, here it comes. She's going to say that I'm wearing a disguise!*

"I'll tell you one thing if you want my opinion. That woman's boyfriend was one strange bird. And she, why, she had to be a loon, a real nutcase. The woman painted every damn thing she looked at. Who has frigging time to laze around and paint when there's things to do?" Another hefty drag. "I'll give you my honest opinion. Some people got it made in life while others of us have to work for a living. Yea, I'd like to cruise my way through life too. Just waltz along, easy-like." She flipped a piece of stringy gray hair from her eye. "You all right, Mister? You have the wateriest eyes I ever seed in my life!"

"Yes, I'm fine. Thank you," I said, leaning on my cane. *I intended the cane to be a prop only, but now I definitely need the support! I didn't expect my acting debut to be this tough. What Cory did on a Pittsburgh stage was ridiculously difficult, but this is every bit as challenging!*

"All this poetry and stuff, and books on Shakespeare, and more junk like that. Bet Gorgeous, her silly-ass boyfriend, never worked a day in his life. I heard he had a cakey-ass professor job. Probably just laid around all day and read books and farted his way through life just like queenie. Believe me, I know that lazy-arse kind."

How this woman offends me! "I suppose everyone isn't cut out for the life of an intellectual."

"'Life of an intellectual'!—ha! If you want my opinion, here it is. It was probably some a-hole like him who flunked my kid in college English." *When she pursed her lips and squinted in agitation, I knew she had hit on a sore point. I need to get out of here. I can't endure her ridiculous invective, but her beady eyes are on me yet again. Heart, get ready. The philosopher is about to share more of her Delphic words of priceless wisdom.*

"What a loser that kid always was. The red-haired punk had a .8 grade-point average at the end of his first semester of college. Can you imagine anyone being that damn dumb? He really got his act together the second semester. I came down hard on the party animal and told him what side his bread was buttered on. Lot of good that did! He finished his freshman year with a sizzling 1.6!"

Thankfully, she's taking another drag on her cigarette. Good! Maybe she's moving on. "Can you imagine anyone being that dumb?" *How wrong I was! She has more to unload.* "He must have had his Dad's brains because he sure as hell didn't have mine." I took a step toward the porch stairs as if leaving, but my conspicuous body language meant nothing to Mrs. Aristotle. "Hell,

I was headed somewhere in life before his old man knocked me up. My advice to young girls? Stay out of car back seats and keep your clothes on." *I had no idea it would be this bad!* "What an embarrassment those men were to me! Both of them but especially junior, the red-haired genius!"

She paused long enough to catch her breath and look at her yellow-stained fingers with their dirty fingernails. "Well, all the stuff in the boxes—I threw it the hell out because it pissed me real bad. Mohney said he'd have the place cleaned out. What a damn liar!"

She's looking at my mustache again. Does it look that phony? The woman is not stupid. I'm afraid she's going to reach over and rip it off. I took a step backward. *I don't much care about being found out—who cares since I'll never see her again—but I desperately want those boxes.* I was weeping inside and could barely stand and maintain the ridiculous charade.

She began to speak again. "Here's what I think if you want my honest opinion. Those two lovebirds must have doted on each other like idiots. In every picture, they're hanging all over each other. Bet it was just a freaking lie. If you want my opinion, here it is. I bet he was making out with half the women in the county. Just like my man. Hey, I started out in love too. She'll find out!

I got up the nerve and looked in the kitchen and could imagine Cory standing at the sink, smiling radiantly. *That joyful soul, that indescribably beautiful woman!* "But true love is beautiful. For a rare handful of people, it flows like a river of glistening gold."

"'A river of glistening gold!' Holy shit, what the hell planet are you from? They'll find out where the love road leads. I'll tell you what. I did Mohney a favor by getting rid of that junk. I ought to send that old geezer a bill for trash removal!" She gave me another of those piercing looks. "You doin' all right? How's come you keep dabbing your eyes every other second? You are one suspicious bird, and sumpin' don't seem right about you!"

"I'm doing fine, but my allergies explode this time of year."
I have to get out of here, but how do I terminate this madness?

"You better get you some eye drops. You need to sit yourself down? You seem like you're an emotional wreck if you want my opinion, and you keep shifting back and forth on your feet. Nervous-like. Speaking of feet, I gotta get off mine."

"I'll let you get back to your day. I'll go now."

Wincing in pain, she shifted her weight to her other foot. It was as though I said nothing, as if I hadn't interrupted. "I hurt my bad hip carrying out that frigging junk. Like I said, I burned it all. What a bon fire it made! I felt the heat here on the porch when it went up in flames. You can tell the old man there was nothing of value in the boxes. He won't care. The mental one has a foot in the grave already." She buttoned one of her dress buttons. "I'll let you in on something. You don't know the guy, but I actually had to endure talking to him. Here's my opinion. That guy is one pitiful wretch, and life has beat the hell out of him. What a bitter soul! Wait till you see him. Hope I never get as down and out as that disgusting loser."

So ended my interview with Madame Pleasant. She turned and shut the door. Not in my face, but there was no goodbye, no word of parting. I turned and limped my way down the stairs. The limp in my walk was a fake, but the one in my spirit nearly dropped me flat. As I hobbled toward the car, I heard the door open, so I turned to look and saw Happy Face Aristotle standing in the doorway. Her bellow was so loud that the ground nearly shook. "Hey, Mister, I just thought of something."

She finished lighting her cigarette, slowly raised it to her mouth, and took the longest drag I've ever seen in my life. *I wonder how much smoke she inhaled in that single drag!* As I limped a few steps back toward the porch, she spoke. "A strong wind came up the day I burned that trash, and junk was blowing everywhere. That happens all the time. I wait for a calm day to burn and no sooner get the fire lit and, wouldn't you know it, a freaking cyclone blows through. Hey, that's my lot in life. Try to do your best, and life dumps crap on you. Well, maybe some of the unburned stuff blew up against the fence. That happens a lot. You can look there if you want. Maybe you'll find one of queenie's sonnets or a picture of Gorgeous, her hot-to-trot lover!"

She wiped some fallen cigarette ash from her stained dress and then looked over at the barn. "If you want my opinion, I wish some sparks would blow the whole way to the barn and catch that rat trap on fire. Then I'd collect on the insurance. Did you ever see such a rickety barn as that eyesore?"

"It's in pretty bad shape." *How pristine it was the glorious summer of our love!*

She took a step toward the door but turned to speak one last time. "Well, you seemed to care a hell of a lot about those boxes. Are you sure those aren't tears, or do you just git runny eyes like me?"

"I'm fine.

"Like I said, I can't imagine anyone would care about that junk. If you want my opinion, it was just poetry, pictures and crap like that. Those lovebirds were idiots with their heads in the stars. I'm positive about that. Well, you can rummage through the burn pile if you want. I gotta get off my damn feet! Like I said, I ought a file a law suit against that damn Mohney, or at least send him a trash-removal bill!"

She turned and started walking away. *Good. At last that joyful experience is now over.* But then, darn my luck, she turned to face me again. *Oh, no, here she comes again to offer yet another priceless pearl of wisdom!*

"Hey, don't be tripping on that busted sidewalk. I don't need some wise arse filing a lawsuit." She said this while looking at the barn, but then those ever-friendly eyes settled on me one last time. "How's come you keep fiddling with your mustache? *My worst fear!* Seems like you hain't very used to it." *Jennifer told me not to fiddle with my mustache, but in my nervousness, I can't stop!* She turned and went back inside, slamming the door so hard I feared it would break the hinges.

I could barely disguise my excitement and actually took a normal step or two, forgetting to limp. My hobble to the burn pile was faster than it should have been, but there was a limit to what I could endure, Madame Pleasant having exhausted my patience a long time ago.

As I neared the burn pile, I walked past the milk house and remembered the day Joey and I had replaced some shingles on the roof. *Joey had nearly fallen when he stepped down to the ladder which had shifted. As if to warn him, Zoe—dear, dear Zoe—had barked like crazy and averted a broken leg.*

The happy past dances in my brain like an Argentinian tango dancer. Look at the shed! How immaculate it had been—fresh paint, grass neatly edged to the walk! The whole farm was in tip-top shape. Now everything is in horrible disrepair. The shingles on the shed roof have blown off, the door hangs loose on its hinges, many of the windows are broken. What a mess! Cory, I'm glad you're not seeing this wreck!

I found a stick near the burn pile, and like a madman I used it to rummage through the ashes. *Dust to dust and ashes to ashes.* Because I was out of sight of Happy Face in case she was looking, I worked feverishly, no bum-leg disguise necessary. Furiously stirring through the ashes, I finally unearthed the remnants of two metal binders, the one a photo album, the other a scrapbook. The entire contents had burned, but I nevertheless recognized them as Cory's albums. *Ashes to ashes!*

I found nothing else and then went over to the fence. As she said might be the case, some papers had wedged against the bottom rail. My hands shook as I leaned over to pick them up. A few of the scraps of paper had remnants of Cory's hand-writing, mere scraps of papers with burned edges and marred words! Half of one photo—of Zoe looking directly at me—had survived the conflagration! Dear Zoe, how Cory loved you!

Seeing the photo reminded me of how he had always licked my cheek. Even at that moment, I felt his moist tongue on my cheek and heard his breathing in my ear. I put these precious artifacts in my pocket next my heart and, in disgust, angrily speared the stick into the burn pile.

When I did so, the stick hit with a thud. Out of curiosity I poked the stick around in that area of the burn pile. *There's something solid under the ashes.* I kept jabbing into it, hearing the same thud with each hit. Scraping the ashes away, I pried up a thick scrap of asbestos which had not burned. I hastily rummaged through the contents which, safely preserved underneath, were completely intact! I was amazed since the temperature of the fire above the asbestos was a minimum 1100 degrees Fahrenheit.

Under the protective asbestos cover, I saw Cory's small photo album, the album which I had given her on her June 10 birthday! I had never saw the photos which she placed in it but knew it was a project she had worked on for some time. "It's a surprise, professor. You'll see it soon enough." I was holding Cory's album!

Having been protected by its asbestos shield, the album was not damaged at all. I carefully lifted it, opened the pages, and found a couple photos and a Super-8 film cartridge. *What is this?* After more rummaging, I satisfied myself that no other treasures had been protected by the asbestos.

I ran to the car. Yes, I ran, as there was no need to continue the chicanery. Once in the car, I sped over to Grandma's house, where I intended to put the Super-8 film in Grandpa's old film projector. As far as I knew, there weren't many of those around anymore. I ran into the kitchen and pulled out the film. As I did so, an attached note fell to the floor. What could this be? It was an envelope with "To Jude" written on the front in Cory's handwriting! I was holding Cory's letter!

I dashed up to my bedroom, the envelope next to my heart!

Chapter 44

Jude's Journal (Continued):

　　Up in my bedroom I hurriedly tore open the envelope and read Cory's letter.

Dear Jude,

Happy birthday! Here's my birthday gift to you. These are the pictures I've been madly working on at Little Gidding in the evenings, the "other things" besides your portrait. This explains what the secret trips and errands were all about. Joey and I were going to all those places so I could get some photos! Kid brother helped me with the camera work. As you'll see, he's a whiz at photography and did a good job. And here you thought I was working on your portrait the whole time! Got you that time, professor! So you see that you're not the only master of surprises!

　　What do you think? I hope you'll like our project. I'll explain what we did before you look at the film. It starts with the camera on my paintings and then dissolves to those actual places. The paintings and video are exactly the same, meaning I maintain the same angles and perspectives. Pretty cool, don't you think?

By the way, thanks for your part. What is that? Remember the night I showed you these eight photographs and asked you to select the fifties and sixties songs from your Grandpa's oldies collection which, just based on appearance, seemed to match the photos? Irony of ironies—*you* selected some of these songs! We randomly chose a couple we never heard simply by their title. Don't worry if the songs don't match the paintings. The sound track part for the project is the last remaining detail which we can finish later. I'm rushing this so I get it to you by your birthday.

Happy birthday, Jude!

All my love ever,
Cory, your beautiful dreamer

I knew she had been working on a series of water colors in Little Gidding, but she would never allow me to see them and glibly said she was working on a surprise for my August 3 birthday. She had lined up the eight watercolors of our favorite haunts, each a replica of the photos she and Joey had taken. The camera started on her paintings and then dissolved to live footage of the exact places where they stood when taking the photos. The camera framed each setting with a wide-angle establishing shot, and then Joey and she continued filming as they moved deeper into the scene—along the stream, across the field, into the woods, and so on.

After each sequence, the movie smoothly dissolved to the next. The music matched the setting either by lyrical content or past association, though as Cory's letter indicates, a couple of the songs were randomly selected—"a complete shot in the dark," as I had said a few times when she asked me to help select the tunes.

The first shot was of Vinlindeer, that wonderful panorama we loved so much. The camera started on her water color and dissolved to the actual scene. Cory and Joey visited the exact spots on Vinlindeer where Cory and I spent all those hours. The song playing in the background to this marvelous footage was "Green Fields" by The Brothers Four. By summer's end, both of us had come to like this 1960 hit which, prior to the summer of our love, we had never heard. For us, it suited the painting perfectly:

> Once there were green fields kissed by the
>   sun;
> Once there were valleys where rivers used
>   to run;
> Once there were blue skies with white
>   clouds high above,
> Once they were part of an everlasting love.
> We were the lovers who strolled through
>   green fields.

As the song played, I opened a nearby album and looked at other panoramic pictures from atop Vinlindeer. The lyrics of the song were driving me crazy, but I could not tear myself away. Some of the photos were of the ridge itself, while others, taken from atop the ridge, detailed sections of the panorama below. "Green Fields" continued to play as I leafed through the album.

> Green fields are gone now, parched by the
>   sun,
> Gone from the valleys where rivers used to
>   run,
> Gone with the cold wind that crept into my
>   heart,

Gone with the lovers who let their dreams
    depart.
Where are the green fields that we used to
    roam?

Yes, parched by the sun and gone forever—just like my beautiful dreamer. *Cory, you couldn't know the joy and pain this gives me. Ecstasy, because the memories of our love are so well preserved—that is priceless—but agony, because the green fields of our love are now parched, the rivers dry. You once wondered if the river of our life journeyed into the future. It didn't, baby. There is no river because it terminated back there in the valley of death amid the shoals and crushing rocks of life.*

The second painting featured the full moon as seen over the Kittanning Bridge and Riverfront Park from the Tarrtown Road. The large full moon is visible over the bridge, the flanking hills backdropping the scene. Patty Page's "Allegheny Moon" accompanied the picture.

Allegheny Moon I need your light
To help me find romance tonight
So shine, shine, shine
Allegheny Moon your silver beams
Can lead the way to golden dreams
So shine, shine, shine

Silver beams of what? Golden dreams of what? Dead beautiful dreamers and glistening rivers of gold, which dry up and terminate in death and destroy time-hallowed dreams? After we had come out of Heinz Chapel in Oakland, Cory had dejectedly lamented, "Instead of a river of glistening gold, I see only corridors of ghastly gloom!"

Beautiful dreamer, if you only knew how prophetic you were. "Corridors of ghastly gloom." No silver beams, no golden dreams! Nada! How right you were! Many corridors of ghastly gloom. Like my life since you're gone. Now I know why I've lost all my mirth!

The third watercolor was of "Jude and Cory's Trail" above the Allegheny River at Reesedale. Cory and I loved this trail which we often strolled. In the spring when we first reconciled, back in early May, the trail was lined on both sides with the blossoming mountain laurel, a sea of pinkish white blossoms that saturated the air with sweet springtime aroma. As I looked at the winding lane which meanders atop the high ridge, Connie Francis's song, "Together," played in the background:

> We strolled the lane together
> Laughed at the rain together,
> Sang love's refrain together,
> And we won't pretend it will never end.

Foolishly, we did pretend it would never end, because we had no way of knowing of its instant termination. Why would we? How could we? We knew this path well and had seen its many faces. In the spring ("Jude, this place is as beautiful and fragrant as the flower exhibits at Phipps Conservatory!"), at evening sunset ("Look how the river catches the glint of the setting sun, as red as the Nile River when Moses turned it to blood."), during the hot afternoon ("It's so cool up here in the shade trees when the cool breeze gently rises from the valley floor below."), and in the early morning sunrise ("The thick fog is like a deflated cloud which fluttered downward and cuddled the hills in its fleecy, gray blanket.")

> But one day we cried together,
> Cast love aside together.
> You're gone from me but in my memory
> We always will be together.

We always will be together, Cory. No truer words were ever spoken. Always and always. This particular sequence, the photo and the video, was really hard for me to watch since we had ambled along this lane and looked down at the Allegheny River valley so often.

"But one day we cried together." Technically, that's not true. You died, I cried. "Cast love aside together." Also, not exactly accurate. We cast our sick past aside and fought through the jungle of life to get to our river of love, gliding gently along like the Allegheny below us. Stoically fighting the current, we rejoined each other midstream but couldn't stay there. We did not "cast love aside"—never! We'd never allow that to happen after our five-year separation. No, the casting aside was done for us. Gratis.

I fast-forwarded through the eight paintings, weeping and ecstatically emoting the whole time. Aristotle—the real one, not Mrs. Happy Face now living at the Mohney farm—says art should make one experience catharsis, a relief of tension and anxiety. Now there's one truthful statement, wise Athenian philosopher! Talk about catharsis! Well, I was having the biggest one of my life right there in Grandma's farmhouse.

I bade Grandma goodbye and hopped into my car.

Chapter 45

Jude's Journal (Continued):

After viewing the video, I first went to the Younkins farm on Dutch Hollow Road. One of the paintings was of this vista—"near the highest point in Armstrong County," we had often been told. When I stopped at the farmhouse to get permission to visit the hill, what a flood of memories came back to me. At this farm Cory and I had enjoyed the church picnic, except for the abortive feedsack-climbing contest in the barn when my climbing fear was exposed.

I got out of my car and walked over to the barn. The door was open so, impulsively, I peered inside. *All I had to do was climb that barn beam and fling a feedsack up there in the loft, but I couldn't do it. Backed out like a coward!* Cory had stood by me over there in the far corner. *"Don't worry about it, Jude. Many of the strong men don't compete in this particular contest. I'll still stand by my man!"* But what a compensation! Zoe had mysteriously come into our lives that evening.

I drove up the long lane, parked my car at the top of the knoll, and walked to the area from which the photo had been taken. Entering the world of the movie, I trod the path Joey and Cory walked when they shot it, the same path Cory and I strolled when we lived and loved. Elvis Presley's "I'm Yours," the song Cory had selected for this watercolor scene, played in my mind as I walked the knoll.

My heart I offer you now
My heart and all it can give
For just as long as I live I'm yours
No arms but yours dear will do
My lips will always be true
My eyes can only see you, I'm yours

"Don't you just love the organ in that tune?" Cory remarked. "That's so lovely!" I completely agreed. It was exquisite, but today it was the lyrics that fascinated me because of their perfect description of my feelings. "I offer you my heart and all it can give." *I really did, Cory. I gave you everything.* "For as long as you live I'm yours." *And you were, my love—completely. But like John Keats, you died young, your art, like his, violently ended.*

I picked up a rock and angrily tossed it to the ground. By happenstance, it hit the midsection of a wild Oxeye Daisy stem which, now broken, dangled helplessly from the stock—cruelly and untimely struck by that savage blow. *"Death lies on her like an untimely frost Upon the sweetest flower of all the field." The sweetest flower of all the field—like this one that forlornly sways on its gallows in the wind.*

I looked across the field at the sea of colorful wild flowers. *Swaying and dancing in the breeze, they're beautiful and cover the entire hillside.* "Consider the lilies of the field, how they grow: they neither toil nor spin, and yet I say to you that even Solomon in all his glory was not arrayed like one of these" [Matthew 6:28–29]. I picked the dangling daisy from its broken stock and carefully looked at it. *So true, Jesus! Look how finely arrayed it is. Just one of the exquisite flowers has been destroyed prematurely. Only one, the sweetest flower of all the field, was mercilessly cut down in its youth. Out of thousands, why this one?* I again examined the disc florets at its center—intricately small, tubular, and bright yellow. *What intricacy, what dazzling artistry in these simple flowers of the field!*

I went back to my car and drove up on the field opposite the domed hill in Center Hill, another of our favorite places. Once when Cory and I were meandering on this field, she commented about the center hill that lay before us. "It's full and rounded like a perfect circle. Let's pretend that all of life is neatly round and orderly, just like it is."

At that very moment, Nat King Cole's song "Pretend" started playing on the handheld cassette which we sometimes carried with us when we were taking a walk or sitting on a blanket to watch life pass by. "Wasn't that amazing?" Cory exclaimed. "Just as I said 'Let's pretend,' the first line of the song, 'Pretend you're happy When you're blue,' started playing at the exact same time!" We laughed at the coincidence and, as a result, always associated "Pretend" with the domed Center Hill knoll.

As I looked across the vale to the center hill and the vista beyond—Franklin Village Mall, the Kittanning Country Club, and the faraway fields—I listened to Nat King Cole's "Pretend":

> Pretend you're happy when you're blue;
> It isn't very hard to do.
> And you'll find happiness without end
> Whenever you pretend.
> Remember anyone can dream,
> And nothing's bad as it may seem.
> The little things you haven't got
> Could be a lot if you pretend.

If it were that easy! "Happiness without end." *In this life?* "You'll find happiness without end whenever you pretend." *How false that is! Yes, I have a vivid imagination. Would anyone who knows me doubt that? But this fertile imagination can pretend only so long, and then reality encroaches.* "Nothing's bad as it may seem." *Sorry, Mr. Cole. I absolutely love your song, and Cory thought your voice was "positively enchanting," but these lyrics are not true, for my life is every bit as bad as it seems.*

On to Boggsville. The road along the stream there—I don't even know its name: maybe South Scenic Drive?—was another favorite haunt. We used to sit by this quiet stream and watch the water lazily meander along under the low-hanging canopy.

Often, we'd come here in the evening to star-gaze and walk along it in the moonlight, but we'd usually kiss like crazy before we strolled along the stream.

I wonder if people know how much fun kissing is. Yes, just plain kissing. I read the other day that couples get away from kissing the longer they're together. Because they kiss so much less, it loses its joy, but that was not true for us! We were pro-kissers. I mean deep kissing when I could feel her tongue slide along and wrap around mine or, best of all, when she'd fondle my curled tongue with her flower-soft lips. *Oh, how we kissed when parked by this stream! The chirping of the crickets and tree frogs and the reflection of the moon on the water plop me smack dab in the middle of that enchanted world of yesteryear.*

Strains of Pat Boone's fifties song "Sugar Moon" wafted along the breeze as I gazed down the tree-flung stream.

> O, sugar moon, come out tonight;
> Bring me your glow of angel light.
> Here in my arms our love will bloom,
> If you will shine, O sugar moon.

And it did bloom, as we ambled by this stream under the tree-scored halo of the moon, her hand clutching mine.

> While you shine down from up above,
> I'll hold her close and talk sweet love,
> And in your glow we'll hear love's tune,
> Then she'll be mine, O sugar moon.

I'll hold her close. Oh, beautiful dreamer, that I could! That I could!

I drove to the other spots, for the most part in the immediate vicinity, but because one was located further up the Allegheny River, I contacted my friend Casey and asked him if he was game for a boat ride. Assuring me that he had absolutely nothing else to do, we were soon navigating the Allegheny River near Templeton and took the familiar cut up Mahoning Creek.

"This is your creek, Cory."

"What are you talking about, ever crazy one? Why is this creek mine?"

"It's supposed to be Mohney Creek, but the early settlers misspelled it, so we're left with 'Mahoning' instead of 'Mohney,' just because dummy couldn't spell! But you and I know this cozy little creek is named after you. Welcome to Mohney Creek, your world!"

"You are one crazy Jude dude!"

Casey and I glided up that stream a short distance until we came to the rock where Cory and I used to sit and dream and talk. Patsy Cline's "Just out of Reach," again by design, played on the cassette player. Once we were blissfully reconciled and back in each other's arms, she'd say to me when this song played, "You're not out of reach of these arms, Buddy Boy. It won't happen again—ever!" Then she'd squeeze me tightly. I sensed her squeezing me even now and felt her caressing hands on my face. "Jude! Jude!"

Over the next two days, I visited these eight spots so often that soon I had every detail of her movie memorized. The more intensely I immersed myself into the world of her watercolors and the corresponding locations, the more real she became, because the paintings and music comprised the figurative womb that birthed the memory of the real woman. From the moment she died, I could always feel Cory near me. That had been the case from the start—immediately present and tangibly real.

But now at times I actually felt her rousing me or cradling me or bending over me. I'd even feel her shaking my body, and I tried to come out of my stupor but couldn't, nor did I want to. I looked at her watercolors on the seat beside me. *How grateful I am for this movie, recovered from the ashes of a burn pile. How close I had come to losing this most tangible link to Cory! Well, most tangible except for the constant cry in my ear—"Jude, Jude!"—that screaming voice which has been so very real from the start.*

297

After visiting these locations, I'd often end up at Cory's grave and sit beside her headstone and caress it as though it were Cory herself. On the last night when I visited "the hallowed spots of the watercolors," as I came to call them, I conceived the idea of the Little Gidding poems. I add this passing footnote so I remember to tell a couple of my friends who asked me what inspired that volume of poetry. That was it, guys. I conceived the idea the last night I sat by her grave.

The paths of glory lead but to the grave. Your life, my dearest Cory, was one beautiful life of glory, but it tragically ended here!

Chapter 46

Jude's Journal (Continued):

I said goodbye to Cory yet again, sprinkled rose petals on her grave, and lifted eyes to the surrounding tombstones and then to the old McKelvey farm, heaving its mass out of the surrounding farmland like one of the huge glacier-deposited boulders along the northern Allegheny. I shed a tear as I surveyed the surrounding autumn fields and thought again of Tennyson's great poem:

> Tears, idle tears, I know not what they
>   mean,
> Tears from the depth of some divine despair
> Rise in the heart, and gather to the eyes,
> In looking on the happy autumn-fields,
> And thinking of the days that are no more.

The happy autumn fields, the days that are no more! Oh, Cory, my beautiful dreamer! Tears, idle tears, but these aren't so idle. They are, rather, lava-scalding and Old Faithful-gushing.

One last thing remained for me to do. Back at Grandma's farm, I dusted off the old motorbike, still in running condition because I had maintained it over the years. I ran my hand over the gash on the front fender and thought again of the bike wreck at Beatty's Mill and Cory's near-rape. *How close that was! Duke, you were such an animal that night! Pastor Gabe, you could use Duke as a fitting example of what happens to a potentially good*

person when under the influence of alcohol. Come to think of it, I'm
sure you already have, possibly multiple times.

She had escaped the near-rape disaster but not the one in the
mine—not the catastrophic cave-in!

I took off in the direction of Beatty's Mill, the images of
the past assaulting my brain as quickly as the familiar roadside
scenes which I passed en route. I often relived the night when
I took the shortcut down the dirt trail, which I hadn't ridden
since that dreaded evening. I motored along the Worthington-
Slate Lick Road and cut off onto the old dirt bike trail which
connected it to the lower Beatty's Mill road. Little remained of
the trail, since area boys no longer biked on it.

When I started down the rugged path, the horrible recol-
lections shook my mind as completely as the bike had shaken
my body: the wild shimmy, the flying wheel, the hurtling crash
at the bottom, and the mad sprint to Duke's car. *A minute later*
and the tragedy would have occurred—one fleeting minute, beau-
tiful dreamer!

Although I slowed considerably as I proceeded along the
downhill trail, the shaking of my bike became more and more
intense. My whole body began to quiver so violently that I felt
I was about to crash a second time, as though I was actually
careening wildly down the path as I did before. The cry of
"Jude, Jude!" in my ear mounted to such a loud crescendo that
I couldn't concentrate on driving. *This shaking is going to make*
me wreck again!

Besides the incessant cry of my name, I heard other inex-
plicable sounds but couldn't make them out, raucous noises
which I eventually recognized as jumbled syllables and even
whole words. Then more sounds of yelling and screaming, followed by a voice of panic and a barrage of hysterical noises.
But the cacophonous din in my head was unintelligible—just
fragments, incoherent noises, snippets of words, and then later
snatches of phrases: "Get up..." "We have to..." The words
crashed into my brain like a tidal wave. "Jude, Jude!"

Soon the sounds started to make sense. Someone was speaking words—real, intelligible words. *Is someone behind one of these trees on the hillside above Beatty's Mill? My brain is being assaulted by this din of sounds, by the shaking, by the images of the forest trail and the rocks and logs on the path as I jounce along, by the memories of my reckless flight down this trail—all of it a kaleidoscopic jumble of maddening sense stimuli that relentlessly hammers my poor, poor brain. What is happening?*

"Please wake up. Jude, why can't…you hear me? Are you all right?"

The shaking was so violent that I couldn't keep my hands on the wheel. *Oh, no, I'm going to wreck! Watch that tree, that branch across the path! What are these words? Where do they come from? Are the trees talking to me?*

Then more words sledge-hammered my ears. "We have to get out of here. This whole place might cave in! You have to come to." The voice was hysterical. "We're going to die down here!"

I felt a stabbing pain in my head and then a hand. *A hand is softly dabbing and caressing my forehead. Am I dreaming?*

Desperately, I tried to open my eyes. Slowly, one eye opened to a slit, and then the other. Though I knew I was in a very dark and scary place, I couldn't force my eyes to focus. *Why can't I see the mountain trail and the Beatty's Mill stream down at the bottom? Is this the darkness of reality or a gaping black hole in my brain?*

I closed my eyes and then a moment later opened them again but could only see shadows and light, but slowly an imperceptible outline took shape. *Is that diaphanous shape a body? What happened to the trail? The trees? Why can't I see the stream?* The form began to take shape. *It seems to be a person! Is it?* "Jude, Jude!"

My mind played more tricks on me. *I think I'm seeing Cory! This is ridiculous. It can't be Cory! I'm seeing a ghost just as Hamlet did. Holy heck, I'm reliving Hamlet, but this time I really am Hamlet and am confronting a real live ghost like the one he saw on the castle ramparts! Angels and ministers of grace, defend me!*

Chapter 47

Jude's Journal (Continued):

"Is that you Cory?" I still could not focus my eyes. *Am I seeing Cory or a ghost? Am I Jude or Hamlet? Where is the mountain trail? Why can't I find my bike?* The shaking of my shoulders grew more intense.

I'm going to talk to the shape. "Cory!" I struggled to say. "Is that…you? Am I…talking to…your ghost?" Words tried to form and surface from the deep canyon in my head, but the ghostly shape didn't respond. "Is that you? You died years ago!" *Why won't she answer? Something isn't right. It's because I'm talking to a ghost!*

I thought I was speaking, but the words died within. Again, I tried; again, I failed. Words stuck, a clogged cacophony of gurgling groans. Then, instead of beautiful dreamer in front of me, I saw falling rocks and trees and a rugged mountain trail. I was trapped between the whirling images in my mind and this hovering, screaming shape in front of me. *What's going on? Why won't my brain work? Why can't I talk?*

Finally, I managed to get beyond groans and grunts, and a word issued from my mouth, or I thought it did. "What…?" That was it. That's all I could say, but at last I had articulated a real word. My eyes began to focus, and then I mumbled more words. "Cory, is that…you? Is that you, Cory, or am I…seeing a ghost?" *Did I say these words or just imagine doing so? I can't be certain.* I tried to touch the shape to be certain.

"Cory, what's… Co—ry!" As coherent words slowly tumbled forth from the depths of my being, the ghostly shape in front of me kept yelling hysterically. *Why do I keep hearing this scream? Why are you screaming?*

"Jude, you're coming too! Praise God!"

I got to my knees and tried to stagger to my feet but fell backward to my knees. *Blood is seeping from my throbbing head, and my collar and shoulder are soaked in blood!* I gingerly raised a hand to my head. *My head has been wrapped with a cloth.*

"Cory, is that you?" Real words came forth. *I can talk!* "I thought…you were dead. Cory, is that…you, or am…I dreaming?"

Cory struggled to her knees, and we hugged each other madly. She was crying hysterically but joyfully managed to shout, "You're alive! Praise God, my Jude, my love, my darling has come to at last!"

Cory struggled to lean over, held my head in her hands, and kissed me passionately.

"Cory, I dreamed…you died…were killed. In the cave-in. Many…years ago." I paused, again trying to make sense of what was happening, trying to get my brain to focus and to speak rationally. *What happened to the mountain trail? Why is everything so dark? Where are we?* I held her tightly, as much to prove I was holding a live body as to express my passionate love. "Cory, you're alive! I'm not dreaming! You're here!" I squeezed her hard.

"You're back with the living at last! I love you!"

My mind started thinking rationally, and I was, at last, able to speak in semi-intelligible sentences. "I imagined everything— your funeral, my sad life after you died…everything imaginable. I thought you were dead!" I looked at her again to make certain Cory was here in real life. "You can't imagine how real it all was." I pulled her near me to look in her face. *I'm looking at Cory. She's alive!* "I had this unbelievable dream…of how I desperately struggled to survive…after you were gone. It was so life-like… that I could write a book about it!"

I squeezed against her living body and couldn't stop touching her. "Cory, you're alive! Is this you? *Was I dreaming in the past or am I dreaming now?* Cory, squeeze me again so I know I'm no longer dreaming. Your death was so real. I thought for sure you died…while I was in my coma."

"You were unconscious all that time. I've been frantically trying to rouse you."

In my hysteria, I started gushing. "You had died, and I dreamed of the funeral, your grave, what happened after you died, how I couldn't manage, and how I grieved my way through a sick life! Oh, Cory, say you're alive again so I know this isn't a dream!"

Cory sobbed and sobbed for joy that I was alive. Though her hysteria soon subsided, she kept saying, "You are not dead. You're here, and this body is real! Hold me to see how alive I am! Praise God that I have my Jude back!"

"And I have my Cory. My beautiful dreamer lives!"

Chapter 48

Jude's Journal (Continued):

As we slowly calmed ourselves, we assessed the gravity of our situation. We were both injured, and I was thinking poorly, the blow to the head, and serious loss of blood, having greatly diminished my mental function. Cory cradled my head, stroked my face, and then swabbed the blood flow on my shoulder and arm. She looked again at the ceiling and the perilously hanging slabs of limestone. "I hate to be the harbinger of bad news, but our happy reunion is going to have an end as bad as Van Gogh's if we don't get out of here immediately!"

I craned my head around as best I could and looked at the enormous crevasse that had opened up in the ceiling. "You aren't kidding!"

She sat beside me on her knees and again hugged me. "Shut your eyes." She shined her flashlight on my head wound. "This is one very nasty gash, and you've lost a lot of blood. Sorry to be so blunt upon your reentry to reality." She gingerly dabbed my wound. "But we have no time to mince words since we have to get out of this death trap right now!"

I struggled to stay focused and actually nodded off for a second but came to right away. "What happened? I'm so caught between reality and illusion that I don't even know what's going on!"

Though in a desperate place, Cory proceeded slowly, sensing perhaps for the first that my powers of cognition were radically compromised. Her simple sentences were for my benefit.

"Like an idiot, I circled around the support brace. Remember the support post over there? When I swung around it upon entering the room, the limestone above jiggled loose. You saw those enormous slabs above my head. I didn't, so you gave a loud yell."

"I remember all that very clearly. I just knew you'd be killed."

"When the rocks started to fall, you ran toward me like crazy. As you neared me—you were only some twenty feet away by then—you were conked on the head." She looked around. "By that monster piece of limestone." She pointed to a large slab of limestone. "That one with blood on it. Your blood!"

"No wonder I have a crusher headache!"

"It knocked you out cold. You've been lying here unconscious for the longest time. At first, I thought the boulder killed you! How relieved I was when I heard you groaning and saw you move your leg. Zoe went over to you instantly and has been licking your face and trying to rouse you ever since the cave-in."

She paused in her narration to wipe the tears with the back of her shirt sleeve. "I eventually managed to crawl to you despite my hurt leg, but you wouldn't respond to anything, even my shaking and yelling 'Jude, Jude' hundreds of times. You didn't respond to Zoe's bark or even his nuzzling you with his snout and licking you." She paused again to see if my headwound was bleeding.

"Talk about lights out!"

"You didn't even come to when I wrapped your head in my scarf. It's a good thing that I had worn one around my shoulders because it worked perfectly to wrap your head. Your bleeding to death was my biggest fear. Look at the blood on your shirt."

I had trouble comprehending all that she was saying, but slowly rationality returned, though at the time I didn't realize the severity of my head injury. I was totally disoriented in those first minutes after I came to. "I thought years had gone by. I was living in the next decade of my life without you, and it was one never-ending, botched tragedy!

"I hope so!" Cory joked, trying to lighten the atmosphere.

"It was all so incredibly life-like to me. I thought you were killed years ago! In my trance, I kept calling you beautiful dreamer! You wouldn't believe how real every detail was to me. That life without you was one big, bleeding, hurting gash!"

Still incredulous that she was live, I looked into her beautiful eyes. Tears streamed down my face amid the spattered blood and the coal and limestone dust that had covered my face. It was my turn to lighten the atmosphere. "You can just call me Lazarus, and by the way if you ever want to know what your grave headstone will one day look like, just ask me. I've memorized every minute detail!"

As I slowly regained my wits, I tried to assess where we were, what had happened, and how critical our plight was. I attempted to suppress my alarm about our situation and Cory's injuries which I was taking stock of for the first time. "You're holding your ankle. What happened?"

"The limestone hit the top of my foot pretty hard. I don't think it's broken, just a very bad bruise, but it hurts a lot. The good news is that I can move it, but the bad news is that I can't put my weight on it. I found that out when I tried to walk and collapsed instantly!"

"How'd you get here?"

"I kept screaming from over there after you went down like a rifle shot, but you wouldn't respond. I had no choice but to crawl on my hands and knees like one of our soldiers in Vietnam. Then I bandaged your head and tried to rouse you."

"I never felt a thing."

"I was afraid that you'd bleed to death since blood was everywhere. Look at your shoulder. It's soaked in blood. I kept yelling like a maniac, and my knees are even scraped raw from sitting here shaking you and trying to get you to wake."

"Cory, I can't believe it. I thought *you* were dead."

"Zoe protected me. He hovered over me when I was lying over there. Then he came here to you and pulled at your shirt. He licked your face numerous times and even barked. Your whole face has been bathed, but nothing worked. You were out cold the whole time." A fresh flow of tears formed in her eyes. "Praise God, you're alive. You thought I was dead! Well, I was certain you were *brain* dead!"

"Maybe I am!"

"I was really frightened that there would be an even worse cave-in." When Cory looked back at where she was lying, she peered again at the newly-formed fissure in the roof. "We have to get out of here." She shined her flashlight toward the roof. "Look at that ceiling. The widened fissure looks very dangerous."

"I agree." I flashed my light too. "See those two large boulders wedged against each other in the mouth of the crevasse?"

"Yes. What's holding them?"

"Very little." I paused for a moment and looked again at the crevasse. "What's that?" I was looking at a small, unidentifiable object, wedged between the limestone slabs, which was visible in the crevasse. At this distance, I could not determine what it was, but it looked very suspicious.

"What's what? What do you see?"

"I'm not sure." Some kind of foreign object has been planted there." I was sure of that but didn't want to tell Cory. Yet the more I thought of it, the more I feared a planted explosive. I remember my thought process in those agonizing moments. *I have to suppress my fear, since Cory has been through enough already and doesn't need another crisis to worry about! Time to resort to my well-honed diversion game! I thought of how Cory often buoyed her spirits by thinking of Scriptural verses.* "Any relevant verses in your head that could lift our spirits as we concoct our escape plan?"

Taking my question seriously, she thought for a moment. "I recall something Pastor Gabe said when President Reagan was shot back in March of 1981. He quoted Psalm 74. It went something like this: 'The dark places of the earth are full of the haunts of cruelty' [vs. 20]. I call that pretty relevant!"

"It's perfect because we're trapped in the haunts of cruelty—right here, right now. No truer words were ever spoken!"

At last with Zoe's help I tried to get to my feet. He tugged at me, and when I started to rise, he came to my side to act as a brace so I could push down on him while struggling to get up. With his black body, white boots, and border collar ancestry, he reminded me of the intelligent shepherd dogs that had historically herded livestock. That made an image flash in my mind. *Zoe is the shepherd who has come to the aid of his helpless little lamb!* I patted him on the head. "If you're the shepherd, I guess that makes me the lost little lamb! That's a pretty major role reversal!"

"Your little lamb buddy is right beside you!" Cory was also quick to see the inversion.

Knowing our need to get out of our predicament right away, I tried to assess the extent of Cory's injury. "Did you say you can move your leg a little? How bad is your injury?"

"It hurts, but I wouldn't be able to move it this way if it was broken. If you can support me, I can hop on one leg to the cart. We need to get out of here before that seams lets go, or before your head wound starts bleeding again."

I know we have well over a hundred feet to get to the cart out in the corridor, but come on, Jude, be tough. We can do this but not by dwelling on the negative. "This will be a bit of an effort to get to the cart, but after one bumpy ride—I promise to drive slowly—we're home free. We can do this, beautiful dreamer, we can do this! And supporting you, my love, won't be a problem!"

"Of course, we can make it." She lovingly put her hand on my forearm. "Oh, Jude, can you believe we survived the cave-in! How our good God protected us!"

"As for our story, the rest will not be like Hamlet's—silence—but rather music divine and the ecstasy of a good life together."

"How wonderful to get this behind us!"

"Yes, we will make it, beautiful dreamer."

Chapter 49

Jude's Journal (Continued):

As we assessed the severity of our situation, Zoe, in the stance of a pointing birddog, intently looked in the opposite direction. At first, I thought he was focused on the roof crevasse. We had experienced his sixth sense countless times, and this appeared to be another instance in a long line when he embodied human concern and cognition. We used to joke about it. "It's not so much a canine sixth sense since it's more protective and angelic than that!" Zoe again began to bark. First, he peered at the roof, apparently sensing the danger, then stole a quick at Cory and me; but most of the time he gazed into the dark. I flashed my light in that direction. "There's nothing over there. Settle down, Zoebud!"

By now, I had donned my backpack and helped Cory to her feet. We slowly limped our way toward the cart. Huge chunks of limestone hung perilously above our heads, the support beam having caromed across the floor like a toothpick. It had been deeply gouged by a falling boulder and lay uselessly on the mine floor, a battered tree post, splattered in blood. I staggered over to where the beam was and tried to reposition it to prevent another cave-in, but, too long, it could no longer be vertically wedged under the hanging slabs. It impotently leaned at an awkward seventy-degree angle. *Still, it might keep us safe till we're out of this trap!*

Having taken a few steps toward the cart, we were a minute from driving away to safety. That's when Zoe's barking became most intense, even ferocious. He had moved toward the dark corner. "Zoe, what are you barking about?" *What's making him act this way? I've learned through hard experience never to dismiss him!* I flashed my light in the direction he was looking. "Darkness, Zoe, pitch black darkness. Now get back here!"

We limped along at a faster pace, Cory keeping her hurt foot up and hopping on the other as she leaned into me for support. I was encouraged that we had walked some twenty paces and neared the center of the room. "We're going to make it, sweetheart. The cart is just out there in the corridor. We'll get ourselves patched up in the ER and be good as new in no time. Vinlindeer, here we come!"

"You're such an encouragement. Thank you!"

"Just keep the faith and your powder dry. We'll soon have this little episode behind us and say goodbye to our death trap forever."

All of a sudden, when Zoe growled viciously, I experienced one of the greatest shocks of my life.

Abe Badoane waltzed around the corner!

Chapter 50

Jude's Journal (Continued):

"Hello, my darlings," Abe smugly began. "How are you this fine evening? Going somewhere?" He looked at our wounds and scanned the rock debris. "I see you've had a bit of bad luck there." He was holding a bag in one hand and a piece of rope and a package of some sort in the other. *I don't know what it is, but it seems to be the focus of Zoe's fierce barking.*

"Abe, what's going on?" I asked, more than a hint of anger in my voice. "I thought this room was safe since all the signs are down and the light's green."

"I see that."

"We have to get out of this hellhole. What are you doing here?" I pointed to the crevasse in the ceiling. "We could all be killed, including you!"

"Somehow the warning signs, ropes, and safety cones wandered over here around the corner and ended up in a neat little pile." He held up the rope and one of the signs. "Wonder how they got there. Strange, very strange indeed." Deliberately and slowly, he then took a home-fabricated stick of dynamite from the bag and waved it in the air. "'These violent delights have violent ends.' You'll recognize the line from Shakespeare. *Romeo and Juliet*, I believe. Did I guess properly? Yes, I believe so. Well done, Abe. You still remember your Shakespeare."

"Be serious! This is no time to be quoting Shakespeare!"

He held up the stick and looked at it. "Or maybe you prefer a line from Eliot's *The Hollow Men*: 'This is the way the world ends[.] Not with a bang but a whimper.' But not in your case. Eliot's line will be reversed as your world ends with a bang and not a whimper." He looked at the explosives in his hand. "A very big bang. Whimpering is past tense, banging present tense."

He took another stick of dynamite from his bag and waved it in the air. Zoe snarled ferociously and, ears flattened on his head, slowly commenced slinking toward him. Instinctively, Abe peddled backward in fear. "This dynamite *will* detonate. It's fail-proof, unlike the handmade explosives there in the crevasse in the ceiling. I see it's still there, a failed experiment. Guess I'll have to take that little experiment in explosives back to the drawing board."

He again waved the dynamite in the air. "Abe, what are you doing?" I screamed. "Are you crazy? That dynamite is highly explosive. You're out of your mind!"

The events of the next moments happened so quickly that they're almost impossible to narrate. I remember that Zoe continued his attack-mode stalk toward Abe, his back hair straight up, his growl savage. Intensely frightened by his ferocity, Abe panicked and hurriedly reached for the matches in his pocket to light the dynamite.

"Abe, don't do that!" I screamed. "What are you doing? We'll all be killed!" I held my arms tightly around Cory as we stumbled our way toward the cart. "I have something I have to tell you," I screamed. Limping along, I looked over my shoulder. "Something really important to tell you! Listen to me! Put those matches away!" Screaming in sheer panic, I stopped and faced Abe. "Please listen to me! Put that down!"

"I'm sure you have lots of things you'd like to say, and if I'm not badly mistaken, most of them deal with your imminent desire for immediate safety. Or possibly the most expeditious exit strategy? Is that a correct assumption, professor? Of course, it is!" Never taking his eye off Zoe, he said, "Let me explain the plan." Holding up the dynamite, he waved it back and forth. "When I arc this in your direction, I'll have enough time to run to my cart and make a getaway before the explosion. A major cave-in over there won't affect my cozy little neck of the woods here around the corner."

"Abe, you're crazy! Don't do that!" My scream of panic was inhuman.

"You look very agitated, a state of extreme duress and mental perturbation, obviously because you comprehend my plan very well. Have I made all of this abundantly clear, my son?"

"Don't throw it. I have something to tell you—something about us, about you and me." Seeing I was getting nowhere, I screamed, "I am your son! Abe, I *am* your son! You are my father!"

"Of course, you are! As I'm the prophet Jeremiah or Isaiah or maybe Ezekiel."

When I said this, Zoe broke into a run toward Abe who, in a state of sheer panic, lit the fuse of the dynamite and wildly threw it. For those few slow-motion seconds, I watched it arc through the air—a sparkling fuse spinning in free-wheeling circles like a Fourth of July fire cracker.

"No!" I screamed. "Run!" Peripherally, I saw Abe dash out of sight around the corner.

Because he had thrown the dynamite between us and the cart, we had no choice but to divert our path and hobble in the opposite direction. Instinctively, we scrambled to a niche in the wall, where we huddled against each other in survival mode. As Cory and I squeezed ourselves into a tight, small ball, Zoe shielded us by standing on his back feet and spreading his body over us. I could distinctly feel his paws pushing into my back. Then all of a sudden, he seemed to disappear, and I stopped feeling his paws against me. A sweet-scented warmth encompassed us as we crouched for those horrifying seconds in the shadow of death.

All of this happened in an instant, and then we waited. *A very long fuse?* The lyrics of "Beautiful Dreamer" darted into my mind. *What's the line? "Gone are the cares of life's busy throng." The cares will be gone all right but with a bang, not a whimper!*

Then, in a nanosecond, another line from "Beautiful Dreamer": "Waiting to fade at the bright coming morn." *I knew life would one day fade, but I had hoped for gradually fading light after a long full life, not the blinding light of an explosion!* Of course, I voiced none of this to Cory in that fleeting instant.

The meteor thoughts kept flashing in my fevered brain, even as I, helplessly, waited for the explosion. *Now I'm sure about the meaning of the phrase, "tattoo cross explodes the game!" Abe, you are indeed the tattoo man with the cross, and an actual explosion ends the game!*

Soft as a whisper, a Stephen Foster line escaped my lips. "Now is the moment when all clouds of sorrow depart." I wrapped my arms across Cory's breasts, daring the slightest cupping with my hands. *How beautifully soft. Indescribable sweetness! Was this it? Is this all I'm allowed—a caress of her bare hip at Beatty's Mill after a near-rape and this momentary, divine touch?*

How cruel life can be! How unjust this destined end! I intend no blasphemy, no judgment against Almighty God's righteous judgments, but how I understand Job: there are things we mortals can't comprehend in this life!

I cradled her head against me, as she had cradled mine earlier, and kissed her hair. "Goodbye, beautiful dreamer. 'Starlight and dewdrops are waiting for thee!'"

Like the volcano at Mount Vesuvius, the dynamite exploded—that awful, deafening blast.

The End

About the Author

Dr. Ronald G. Shafer was a professor for over forty years at Indiana University of Pennsylvania where he holds a lifetime distinguished University Chair. His accolades include a Senior Fulbright Visiting Professorship to Egypt; Silver Medalist Professor-of-the-Year Award in the Carnegie Foundation/CASE's national top-professor search; citation by CHANGE magazine for outstanding professorial leadership; Exemplary Teaching Excellence Award from the American Association of Higher Education, IUP's President's Medal of Distinction, and a flagship grant by the National Endowment for the Humanities. He has traveled to some fifty countries for teaching-abroad stints and invited guest lectures. Shafer has authored numerous scholarly articles, edited two volumes of essays, and presided over The Pennsylvania College English Association. Founder of The Friends of Milton's Cottage, he was executive head of this organization, which (1) helped to restore the home where John Milton completed *Paradise Lost* and which (2) initiated the first two International Milton Symposia. At Milton's Cottage, Chalfont St. Giles, United Kingdom, Shafer enjoyed audience with Her Majesty, Queen Elizabeth. The three film documentaries he has co-produced and co-directed on Poets Laureate Robert Pinsky and Donald Hall and renowned author John Updike have garnered national and international acclaim. He has written a series of six novels, the first of which, *The Rose and the Serpent,* was published by WestBow Press. *The Pittsburgh Hamlet,* the second installment in this compelling saga, was published by Christian Faith Publishing. Now in retirement, he continues to enjoy extensive world travel, novel-writing, and the love of his life—his five granddaughters.

CPSIA information can be obtained
at www.ICGtesting.com
Printed in the USA
BVHW070404091220
594980BV00002B/6

9 781098 055332